"Kiss me," she urged in a whisper.

"I have to go," he said shortly, and pulled back while he was still able.

But Garrett moved with him, her hands reaching up to grip his head on either side, the way he'd taught her. The strength of her fingers electrified him.

"Kiss me," she commanded, "or I'll break your nose."

The threat startled a ragged laugh from him. He shook his head as he looked at her, this fearsomely capable woman who loved geese and was afraid of spaghetti, and could either wield a scalpel in a complex surgical procedure or use it as a throwing-knife.

There had always been a cold streak in him, but he couldn't seem to find it now, when he needed it most. He was breaking apart inside. He would never be the same after this.

"Christ, you've ruined me."

By Lisa Kleypas

LISA KLEYPAS

Hello Stranger

The Ravenels, Book 4

AVONBOOKS

An Imprint of HarperCollinsPublishers

Excerpt from *Devil's Daughter* copyright © by Lisa Kleypas.

HELLO STRANGER. Copyright © 2018 by Lisa Kleypas. All rights reserved. Printed in the United States of America. No part of this book may be used or reproduced in any manner whatsoever without written permission except in the case of brief quotations embodied in critical articles and reviews. For information, address HarperCollins Publishers, 195 Broadway, New York, NY 10007.

First Avon Books mass market printing: March 2018
First Avon Books hardcover printing: February 2018

Print Edition ISBN: 978-0-06-237191-1
Digital Edition ISBN: 978-0-06-237189-8

Cover illustration by Alan Ayers

Avon, Avon & logo, and Avon Books & logo are registered trademarks of HarperCollins Publishers in the United States of America and other countries.
HarperCollins is a registered trademark of HarperCollins Publishers in the United States of America and other countries.

FIRST EDITION

18 19 20 21 22   QGM   10 9 8 7 6 5 4 3 2 1

To Greg,
the pulse of my heart

Chapter 1

London
Summer, 1876

SOMEONE WAS FOLLOWING HER.

The uneasy awareness crept along the nape of Garrett's neck until the fine hairs stood on end. Lately she had the feeling of being watched whenever she went on her weekly visit to the workhouse infirmary. So far there had been no evidence to justify her unease—no glimpse of a person behind her, no sound of footsteps—but she could *feel* him somewhere close.

Carrying her leather doctor's bag in her right hand and a hickory cane with the other, Garrett continued to walk at a brisk pace. Her gaze took in every detail of the environment. The East London parish of Clerkenwell was not a place to be careless. Fortunately, she was only two blocks away from the new main road, where there would be a hansom cab for hire.

As she passed the grates that covered Fleet Ditch, noxious fumes wafted upward and made her eyes water. She would have liked to cover her mouth and nose with a scented handkerchief, but that wasn't something a resident of the parish would do, and she wanted to blend in.

The soot-blackened tenements, built as close as a row of teeth, were eerily quiet. Most of the dilapidated buildings had been condemned and closed in preparation for a new development site. The glow from the lamps on either end of the street strained through the fog that had settled in the recent summer calms, nearly obscuring the bloodshot moon. Soon the usual assortment of hucksters, pickpockets, drunkards, and prostitutes would emerge to crowd the area. Garrett intended to be long gone by then.

But her pace faltered as a few figures emerged from the reek and gloom. It was a trio of soldiers dressed in off-duty uniforms, laughing raucously as they advanced in her direction. Garrett crossed to the other side of the street, keeping to the shadows. Too late: one of them had caught sight of her and was swerving in her direction.

"Here's luck," he exclaimed to his companions. "A handy lightskirt for our evening sport."

Garrett surveyed them coolly, while her grip tightened on the crook handle of her cane. The men were obviously the worse for drink. No doubt they'd been loitering at a tavern all day. There were few amusements to occupy common soldiers during their off-duty hours.

As they approached, Garrett's heartbeat escalated. "Allow me to pass, gentlemen," she said crisply, crossing the street once again.

They moved to block her, chortling and weaving. "Talks like a lady," observed the youngest of the trio. He was bareheaded, his hair springing up in rusty coils.

"She b'aint a lady," remarked another, a hulking, hatchet-faced man whose patrol jacket was missing.

"Not if she's out walking at night, all of 'er lone." He regarded Garrett with a yellow-toothed leer. "Go stand next to the wall and lift your skirts, fancy piece. I'm in the mood for a three-penny upright."

"You're mistaken," Garrett said shortly, attempting to walk around them. They barred her way again. "I'm not a prostitute. However, there are brothels nearby where you can pay for such services."

"But I don't want to pay for it," the large man said nastily. "I want it free. *Now.*"

This was hardly the first occasion when Garrett had been insulted or threatened while visiting impoverished areas of London. She had trained with a fencing master to defend against this kind of situation. But she was exhausted after attending to at least two dozen patients in the workhouse infirmary, and infuriated to be confronted by a trio of bullies when she wanted to go home.

"As soldiers in Her Majesty's service," she said acidly, "has it occurred to you that your sacred duty is to *protect* a woman's honor instead of violating it?"

To her disgust, the question elicited hearty chuckles instead of shame.

"Needs to be taken down a peg," commented the third man, a stout and coarse-looking fellow with a pockmarked face and heavy-lidded eyes.

"She can ride on my peg," offered the young one, rubbing his crotch and pulling the fabric of his trousers tight to display the shape of his endowment.

The hatchet-faced man grinned at Garrett with easy menace. "Over to the wall, my fine lady. Whore or no, we're going to make use of 'ee."

The stout soldier pulled a bayonet knife from the

leather frog sheath on his belt, and held it up to display the wickedly serrated edge on the spine. "Do as he says, or I'll carve ye like bacon for larding."

Garrett's stomach flipped unpleasantly. "Drawing a weapon while you're off duty is illegal," she observed coldly, her pulse thundering. "That, added to the offenses of public drunkenness and rape, will earn you a flogging and at least ten years in prison."

"Then behap I'll cut out yer tongue, so ye won't tell anyone," he sneered.

Garrett didn't doubt that he would. As the daughter of a former constable, she knew that pulling out a knife meant it was likely he would use it on her. More than once in the past, she had stitched up the slashed cheek or forehead of a woman whose rapist had wanted to give her "something to remember me by."

"Keech," the younger man said to him, "there's no need to terrify the poor girl." Turning to Garrett, he added, "Let us do what we want." He paused. "It'll go easier on you if you don't fight."

Taking strength from a surge of anger, Garrett recalled her father's advice about handling confrontation. _Maintain your distance. Avoid being flanked. Talk and distract while you choose your moment._

"Why force an unwilling woman?" she asked, carefully setting down her doctor's bag. "If it's for lack of coin, I'll give you shillings enough to visit a brothel." Surreptitiously her hand dipped into the outer pocket of the bag, where she kept a leather roll of surgical knives. Her fingers closed around a slim silver handle of a scalpel, and she deftly concealed it from view as she stood. The familiar delicate weight of the instrument comforted her.

In the periphery of her vision, Garrett saw the stout soldier with the bayonet knife circling around her.

At the same time, the hatchet-faced man began to close the distance between them. "We'll take those shillings," he assured her. "But first we'll make use of ye."

Garrett adjusted her grip on the scalpel, resting her thumb on the flat side of the handle. Gently she applied the tip of her index finger along the blade's spine. *Make use of this*, she thought. After drawing her hand back, she released the scalpel in a slinging motion, snapping her wrist straight to ensure no spin. The wickedly sharp little blade sank into his cheek. He roared with astonished fury, stopping in his tracks. Without pausing, Garrett pivoted around to the soldier with the bayonet knife. Whipping her cane in a horizontal forehand strike, she smashed it against his right wrist. Taken by surprise, he cried out in pain and dropped the knife. Garrett followed the blow with a backhand strike against his left side and heard a rib crack. She jabbed the tip of the cane at his groin to make him double over, and finished him off with an upward vertical strike of the handle against his chin.

He sank to the ground like an undercooked soufflé.

Garrett snatched up the bayonet knife and spun to face the other two soldiers.

In the next moment she froze in surprise, her chest rising and falling rapidly.

The street was silent.

Both men were sprawled on the ground.

Was this a trick? Were they pretending to be unconscious, to lure her closer?

She was filled with quivery, nerve-jangling energy,

her body slow to recognize that the emergency was over. Slowly she ventured forward to have a closer look at the fallen men, taking care to stay out of arm's reach. Although her scalpel had left a bloody wound in the larger one's cheek, that wouldn't have been enough to render him unconscious. There was a red mark on his temple that appeared to have been caused by blunt force.

Her attention went to the younger soldier, whose nose was streaming blood and had almost certainly been broken.

"What the devil . . . ?" Garrett murmured, looking up and down the silent street. She had that feeling again, the prickly awareness that someone was there. There *had* to be. Obviously these two soldiers hadn't knocked themselves to the ground. "Come out and show yourself," she said aloud to the unseen presence, although she felt a bit foolish. "There's no need to lurk like a rat at the back of the cupboard. I know you've been following me for weeks."

A masculine voice came from a direction she couldn't detect, nearly causing her to jump out of her sensible shoes.

"Only on Tuesdays."

Garrett turned a quick circle, her gaze chasing over the scene. Seeing a flicker of movement at one of the tenement doorways, she gripped the bayonet knife handle more firmly.

A stranger emerged from the shadows, cool darkness spun into the form of a man. He was tall and well-proportioned, his athletic form clad in a plain shirt, gray trousers, and an open vest. His head was covered by a flat cap with a slight brim at the front, the kind worn by longshoremen. Stopping a few feet away, the stranger removed his cap, revealing straight dark hair cut in efficiently short layers.

Garrett's jaw slackened as she recognized him. "You again," she exclaimed.

"Dr. Gibson," he said with a brief nod, resettling his cap with a tug. He kept his fingertips on the brim for an extra second or two, a deliberate gesture of respect.

The man was Detective Ethan Ransom, of Scotland Yard. Garrett had met him on two previous occasions, the first nearly two years ago, when she'd accompanied Lady Helen Winterborne on an errand in a dangerous area of London. Much to Garrett's annoyance, Ransom had been hired by Lady Helen's husband to follow them.

Last month she'd encountered Ransom again, when he had visited her medical clinic after Lady Helen's younger sister, Pandora, had been injured in a street attack. Ransom's presence had been so quiet and unobtrusive that one might have taken little notice of him, except that his dark good looks were too striking to ignore. His face was lean, the mouth firm and distinctly edged, the nose strong with a slightly thickened bridge, as if it had once been broken. His eyes were piercing and heavy lashed, deeply set under straight thick brows. She couldn't recall the color. Hazel, perhaps?

She would have thought him handsome, if not for the air of toughness that robbed him of gentlemanly refinement. No matter how polished the surface, the impression of a ruffian would always lurk beneath.

"Who hired you to follow me this time?" Garrett demanded, executing a deft spin with her cane before resting the tip on the ground in the "ready" position. It was a bit of a show-off move, admittedly, but she felt the need to display her skill.

Subtle amusement flickered across Ransom's face, but his tone was grave. "No one."

"Then why are you here?"

"You're the only female physician in all of England. It would be a shame for anything to happen to you."

"I need no protection," she informed him. "Furthermore, if I did, you're not the one I would hire to provide it."

Ransom gave her an inscrutable glance before going to the soldier she had bashed with her cane. The unconscious man was sprawled on his side. After using a booted foot to roll him onto his front, Ransom pulled a length of cord from his vest and bound the man's hands behind his back.

"As you just saw," Garrett continued, "I had no difficulty in trouncing that fellow, and I would have defeated the other two on my own."

"No, you wouldn't," he said flatly.

Garrett felt a simmer of irritation. "I've been trained in the art of cane fighting by one of the finest *maître d'armes* in London. I know how to take down multiple opponents."

"You made a mistake," Ransom said.

"What mistake?"

As Ransom held out his hand for the bayonet knife, Garrett gave it to him reluctantly. He slid it into the leather sheath and hooked it onto his own belt as he replied. "After you knocked the knife from his hand, you should have kicked it away. Instead you bent to pick it up, and turned your back on the others. They would have reached you if I hadn't intervened." Glancing at the bloodied pair of soldiers, who had begun to groan and stir, he remarked to them almost pleasantly, "If either of you moves, I'll castrate you like a capon and throw your balls into Fleet Ditch." His tone was all the more chilling for its casualness.

They both went still.

Ransom returned his attention to Garrett. "Fighting in a fencing master's studio isn't the same as fighting in the street. Men like those"—he flicked a contemptuous glance at the soldiers on the pavement—"don't wait politely for you to fight them in turn. They rush simultaneously. As soon as one of them came within reach, your cane would have been useless."

"Not at all," Garrett informed him smartly. "I would have jabbed him with the point, and felled him with a hard strike."

Ransom moved closer to her, stopping within an arm's length. His shrewd gaze slid over her. Although Garrett held her ground, she felt her nerves spark with instinctive warning. She wasn't quite sure what to make of Ethan Ransom, who seemed both a little bit more, and less, than human. A man designed like a weapon, long in the bone and muscular, with a fluid, limber way of moving. Even standing still, he conveyed a sense of explosive power.

"Try it with me," he invited softly, his gaze locked on hers.

Garrett blinked in momentary surprise. "You want me to hit you with my cane? Now?"

Ransom gave a slight nod.

"I wouldn't want to hurt you," she said, prolonging her hesitation.

"You won't—" he began to reply, just as she surprised him with an aggressive thrust of the cane.

As fast as she was, however, Ransom's reaction was lightning swift. He dodged the cane, turning sideways so the tip barely grazed his ribs. Grasping the cane mid-shaft, he leveraged Garrett's forward momentum with a strong tug, pulling her off her feet. She was stunned to feel one of his arms close around her, while he twisted the cane from her grip with his free hand. So easily, as if divesting people of weapons was child's play.

Gasping and infuriated, Garrett found herself held firmly against his body, the knit of muscle and bone as unyielding as cordwood. She was utterly helpless.

Perhaps it was the reckless velocity of her pulse that accounted for the strange feeling that came over her, a velvety quietness that routed her thoughts and smothered every awareness of the scene around them. The world disappeared, and there was only the man at her back, his brutally hard arms around her. She closed her eyes, conscious only of the faint scent of citrus on his breath, and the measured rise and fall of his chest, and the wild tumult of her heart.

The spell was broken by his soft chuckle, the sound rippling gently along her spine. She tried to wrench free of him.

"Don't laugh at me," she said fiercely.

Carefully Ransom released her, assuring himself of her balance before handing the cane back to her. "I wasn't laughing at you. I only liked it that you caught me off guard." He held up his hands in a gesture of surrender, a dance of amusement in his eyes.

Slowly Garrett lowered the cane, while her cheeks

burned as red as poppies. She could still feel his arms enclosing her, as if the sensation of him had sunk into her skin.

Reaching into his vest, Ransom pulled out a small silver whistle shaped like a tube. He blew three shrill blasts.

Garrett gathered he was summoning a constable on patrol. "You don't use a police rattle?" she asked. Her father, who'd had a beat in King's Cross, had always carried one of the official weighted wooden rattles. To raise an alarm, a constable swung the rattle by its handle until the blades made a loud clapping sound.

Ransom shook his head. "The rattle's too cumbersome. And I had to give it back when I left the force."

"You're no longer with the Metropolitan Police?" she asked. "Who employs you now?"

"I'm not officially employed."

"You do some kind of work for the government, however?"

"Yes."

"As a detective?"

Ransom hesitated for a long moment before replying. "Sometimes."

Garrett's eyes narrowed as she wondered what he did for the government that couldn't be handled by the regular police. "Are your activities legal?"

His grin was a brief dazzle in the gathering darkness. "Not always," he admitted.

They both turned as a constable dressed in a blue tunic and trousers came hurrying along the street with a bull's-eye lantern in hand. "Hallo," the approaching man called out, "Constable Hubble here. Did you raise the alarm?"

"I did," Ransom said.

The constable, a portly man whose blunt nose and florid cheeks were perspiring from exertion, regarded him intently from beneath the brim of his helmet. "Your name?"

"Ransom," came the quiet reply, "formerly of K division."

The constable's eyes widened. "I've heard of you, sir. Good evening." His tone was instantly textured with deference. In fact, his posture became positively submissive, his head lowering a degree or two.

Ransom gestured to the men on the ground. "I found these three drunken sods in the process of physically assaulting and robbing a lady, after threatening her with this." He handed the sheathed bayonet knife to the constable.

"By George," Hubble exclaimed, glancing down at the men on the ground with disgust. "And soldiers too, more's the shame. May I ask if the lady was harmed?"

"No," Ransom said. "In fact, Dr. Gibson had the presence of mind to drive one of them off with her cane, after knocking the knife from his hand."

"Doctor?" The constable regarded Garrett with open amazement. "You're the lady doctor? The one in the papers?"

Garrett nodded, bracing inwardly. People rarely reacted well to the idea of a woman in the medical profession.

Continuing to stare at her, the constable shook his head in apparent wonder. "Didn't expect she'd be so young," he said as an aside to Ransom, before addressing Garrett again. "Beg pardon, miss . . . but why are you a doctor? It's not as if you was a horse-face. Why, I know least two blokes in my division who'd be willing to tie the knot with you." He paused. "If you could do some cooking and mending, that is."

Garrett was inwardly annoyed to observe that Ransom was struggling to hold back a grin. "I'm afraid the only mending I do pertains to wounds and fractures," she said.

The large soldier on the ground, who had risen up on his elbows, spoke in a thick, scornful voice. "Female doctor. Unnatural, I say. I'll wager she's got a tallywag under those skirts."

Ransom's eyes narrowed, his amusement vanishing instantly. "How would you like a boot to the head?" he asked, striding to the soldier.

"Mr. Ransom," Garrett said sharply, "it's unsporting to attack a man who's already on the ground."

The detective stopped in his tracks, throwing a baleful glance over his shoulder. "Considering what he intended to do to you, it's lucky he is to be breathing."

Garrett found it vastly interesting that the hint of an Irish brogue had stolen into his last few words.

"Hallo!" came a call as another constable approached. "I 'eard the whistle."

While Ransom went to confer with the new arrival, Garrett went to retrieve her doctor's bag. "The wound in the soldier's cheek may require stitches," she said to Constable Hubble.

"Don't come near me, y' she-devil," the soldier exclaimed.

Constable Hubble glared at him. "Shut your bonebox, or I'll put a hole through your other cheek."

Recalling that her scalpel hadn't yet been recov-

ered, Garrett asked, "Constable, would you mind holding your lamp a bit higher to illuminate the street? I
would like to search for the knife I threw at this man
earlier." She paused as an alarming thought occurred
to her. "He may still have it."

"He doesn't," Ransom said over his shoulder, pausing temporarily in his conversation with the other
constable. "I do."

Two thoughts occurred to Garrett simultaneously.
First, how could the man be listening to her while simultaneously carrying on a conversation a few yards
away? And second . . .

"You picked up the knife while fighting him?" she
asked indignantly. "But you told me never to do that."

"I don't follow the rules," Ransom said simply, and
turned back to the constable.

Garrett's eyes widened at the calm arrogance of
the statement. Scowling, she drew Constable Hubble
a few feet farther away and whispered, "What do you
know about that man? Who is he?"

"You're asking about Mr. Ransom?" The constable
kept his voice very low. "He was raised right here in
Clerkenwell. Knows every inch of the city, and has
the run of it. A few years ago, he applied to the police force and was assigned to a beat in K division. A
bruising fighter. Fearless. He volunteered to patrol in
the slum districts where other officers wouldn't dare
set foot. They say he was drawn to detective work
from the start. He had a sharp mind, with an eye for
the odd detail. After walking the beat at night, he
would go to the division office files and sort through
unsolved cases. He cracked a murder that had baffled
the division's sergeant-detectives for years, cleared the

name of a servant falsely accused of jewel theft, and recovered a stolen painting."

"In other words," Garrett murmured, "he was working outside his rank."

Hubble nodded. "The division superintendent considered charging him with misconduct. But instead he recommended promoting Ransom from fourth-class constable to inspector."

Garrett's eyes went wide. "You're saying Mr. Ransom moved up *five levels* of advancement in his first year?" she whispered.

"No, in his first six months. But before the promotion examination could be administered, Ransom left the force. He was recruited by Sir Jasper Jenkyn."

"Who is that?"

"A higher-up in the Home Office." Hubble paused, looking uneasy. "Well, that's all I know."

Garrett turned to glance at Ransom's broad-shouldered form, silhouetted in the glow of lamplight. His stance was relaxed, hands shoved negligently in his pockets. But she didn't miss the quick turn of his head as he monitored the environment while talking with the other constable. Nothing escaped him, not even the scuttling rat near the end of the street.

"Mr. Ransom," Garrett said.

Breaking off the discussion, he swiveled to face her. "Yes, Doctor?"

"Will I be required to give a statement about the events of this evening?"

"No." Ransom's gaze moved from her face to Constable Hubble's. "It's best for all concerned if we protect your privacy—and mine—by giving Constable Hubble the credit for apprehending these men."

Hubble began to protest. "Sir, I couldn't take the credit for your bravery."

"It was my bravery as well," Garrett couldn't resist pointing out tartly. "I defeated the one with the knife."

Ransom came to her. "Let him have the credit," he said in a gently coaxing undertone. "They'll give him a commendation and reward money. It's not easy to live on a constable's salary."

Being all too familiar with the limitations of a constable's salary, Garrett muttered, "Of course."

One corner of his mouth tugged upward. "Then we'll let these men handle the matter, while I walk with you to the main road."

"Thank you, but I have no need of an escort."

"As you wish," Ransom said readily, as if he'd fully expected her to refuse.

Garrett looked up at him suspiciously. "You're going to follow me anyway, aren't you? Like a lion stalking a stray goat."

A smile deepened the outer corners of his eyes. As one of the constables moved by them with a lantern, a stray shaft of light caught in the long sweep of his lashes, and struck hints of brilliant, jarring blue in the darkness of his pupils. "Just until you're safely in a hansom," he said.

"Then I'd prefer you to walk beside me in a civilized fashion." She extended her hand. "My scalpel, please."

Ransom reached for the inside shank of his boot, withdrawing the small gleaming knife. It had been wiped clean, more or less. "A beautiful instrument," he commented, regarding the lancet-shaped blade admiringly before handing it to her with care. "Sharp as the devil. You strop it with oil?"

"Diamond paste." After replacing the scalpel in her bag, Garrett hefted the bulky weight with one hand, and picked up her cane with the other. She was nonplussed when Ransom tried to take the bag from her.

"Allow me," he murmured.

Garrett moved back, gripping the leather handles more tightly. "I can carry it myself."

"Obviously. But I'm offering as a courtesy to a lady, not questioning your ability."

"Would you make the same offer to a male physician?"

"No."

"I would rather you consider me as a physician, not a lady."

"Why must you be one or the other?" Ransom asked reasonably. "You're both. I have no difficulty carrying a lady's bag while at the same time respecting her professional competence."

His tone was matter-of-fact, but something in his gaze unnerved her, an intensity that went beyond the regard of strangers. At her hesitation, he held out his hand and urged quietly, "Please."

"Thank you, but I can manage on my own." She began to walk toward the main thoroughfare.

Ransom fell into step beside her, sliding his hands into his pockets. "Where did you learn to throw a knife like that?"

"While I was at the Sorbonne. A group of medical students made a game of it to amuse themselves after college hours. They constructed a target behind one of the laboratory buildings." Garrett paused before admitting, "I never mastered the underhand technique."

"A good overhand throw is all you need. How long did you live in France?"

"Four and a half years."

"A young woman attending the best medical school in the world," Ransom mused aloud, "far from home, taking classes in a foreign language. You're a determined woman, doctor."

"No medical school here would admit a female," Garrett said pragmatically. "I had no choice."

"You could have given up."

"That is never an option," she assured him, and he smiled.

They passed a stunted building with a closed shop front, its broken windows plastered with paper. Ransom reached out to guide Garrett around a pile of empty oyster shells and broken pottery, and what appeared to be a set of rotting bellows. Reflexively she shrank from the slight pressure of his hand on her arm.

"You've no need to fear my touch," Ransom said. "I was only going to help you across the path."

"It's not fear." Garrett hesitated before adding a touch sheepishly, "I suppose my habit of independence is too firmly fixed." They continued along the pavement, but not before Garrett caught his brief, longing glance at her doctor's bag. A brief chuckle escaped her. "I will let you carry this," she offered, "if you'll speak to me in your real accent."

Ransom stopped and looked at her with a flash of surprise, a notch appearing between his dark brows. "What was the slip?"

"I heard the hint of a brogue when you threatened one of the soldiers. And the way you touched your hat . . . it was slower than the way Englishmen usually do it."

"I was born to Irish parents and raised here in Clerkenwell," Ransom said matter-of-factly. "I'm not ashamed of it. But at times the accent is a disadvantage." Extending his hand, he waited until Garrett handed the bag to him. A smile crossed his face, and his voice changed, turning resonant and deep as he spoke in a brogue that seemed to have been warmed slowly over a low flame. "Now then, lass, what would you have me say?"

Taken aback by his effect on her, the pang of nerves at the pit of her stomach, Garrett was slow to reply. "You're too familiar, Mr. Ransom."

His smile lingered. "Ah, but that's the price of it, if you want to hear an Irish brogue. You'll have to put up with a bit o' sweetheartin'."

"Sweethearting?" Disconcerted, Garrett resumed walking.

"Compliments to your charm and beauty."

"I believe that's called blarney," she said crisply, "and I beg you to spare me."

"'Tis a clever, stirring woman you are," he continued as if he hadn't heard her, "and to be sure I have a weakness for green eyes—"

"I have a cane," Garrett reminded him, profoundly irritated by his mockery.

"You couldn't hurt me with that."

"Perhaps not," she conceded, her hand tightening on the cane's handle. In the next moment, she whipped the length of hickory around in a horizontal strike, not hard enough to inflict serious damage, but sufficient to deliver an uncomfortable lesson.

Instead, to Garrett's outrage, *she* was the one who received the lesson. The blow was blocked smartly by her own leather bag, and once again the cane was twisted from her grasp. The bag thudded to the ground, its contents rattling. Before Garrett had time to react, she found herself hauled back against Ransom's chest and trapped by the cane across her throat.

The beguiling whiskey-warm voice fell against her ear. "You signal your moves in advance, darlin'. 'Tis a bad habit."

"Let go," she gasped, writhing in helpless outrage.

Ransom's grip didn't ease. "Turn your head."

"What?"

"Turn your head to ease the pressure against your windpipe, and grasp the cane with your right hand."

Garrett went still as she realized he was telling her how to break the hold. Slowly she obeyed.

"Use an inside grip to protect your throat," Ransom said, and waited until she had complied. "Aye, just so. Now, tug down on the end of the cane, and use your left elbow to jab me in the ribs. Lightly, if you please." After she'd made the motion, he bent forward as if doubling over. "Good. Grab the cane with both hands now—wider—and give it a hard twist as you duck under my arm."

Garrett followed his instructions, and then . . . almost miraculously . . . she was free. She turned to stare at him with baffled fascination. She couldn't decide whether to thank him or bash him over the head.

Ransom bent to pick up the doctor's bag with a bland smile. He had the nerve to proffer his arm, as if they were a sedate couple going on a stroll through Hyde Park. Ignoring the gesture, Garrett began walking again.

"Being choked from the front is the most common way women are attacked," Ransom said. "The second is to hold her from the back, with an arm across her throat. The third is to grab her from behind and carry her off. Hasn't your fencing master taught you to defend yourself without a cane?"

"No," Garrett was forced to admit. "He doesn't instruct in hand-to-hand combat."

"Why hasn't Winterborne provided a driver and carriage for your outings? He's not a miserly man, and he usually takes care of his own."

Garrett frowned at the mention of Winterborne, who owned the clinic where she practiced. The clinic had been established for the benefit of the nearly thousand employees of his department store. Rhys Winterborne had hired her when almost no one else had been willing to give her a chance, and for that he would always have her loyalty.

"Mr. Winterborne has offered the use of a private carriage," she admitted. "However, I don't wish to impose on him any more than I already do, and I've been trained in the art of self-defense."

"You're overconfident, Doctor. You know just enough to be a danger to yourself. There are a few simple tactics that could help you escape an assailant. I could teach them to you, of an afternoon."

They turned a corner and came to the main road, where knots of raggedly dressed people stood at doorways and steps, while pedestrians in all manner of dress threaded along the pavement. Horses, carts, and carriages passed to and fro along the tramway pavers that had been laid out along the road. Stopping at the curbstone, Garrett looked down the street and waited for a glimpse of a hansom.

As they waited, Garrett considered Ransom's words. Clearly the man knew far more about street fighting than her fencing master. His maneuvers with her cane had been impressive. While half of her was inclined to tell him to go to the devil, the other half was more than a little intrigued.

Despite his previous nonsense about "sweethearting," Garrett was certain he had no romantic designs on her, which suited her perfectly. She had never wanted a relationship that might have interfered with her career. Oh, there had been a minor dalliance here or there . . . a stolen kiss with a handsome medical student at the Sorbonne . . . a harmless flirtation with a gentleman at a dance . . . but she had deliberately avoided anyone who might have posed a real temptation. And any involvement with this insolent stranger could lead to trouble.

However, she did want to learn a few of his street-fighting maneuvers.

"If I agree to let you teach me," she asked, "would you promise to stop following me on my Tuesday rounds?"

"Aye," Ransom said easily.

Too easily.

Garrett gave him a skeptical glance. "Are you a truthful man, Mr. Ransom?"

He laughed quietly. "With my job?" Looking past her shoulder, he saw an approaching hansom, and signaled it. His gaze returned to her face and held intently.

"I swear on my mother's grave, you have nothing to fear from me."

The hansom rolled to a jangling, rattling halt beside them.

Abruptly Garrett made a decision. "Very well. Meet me tomorrow at four o'clock, at Baujart's fencing club."

Ransom's eyes flashed with satisfaction. He watched as Garrett ascended to the footboard of the two-wheeled vehicle. With the ease of vast experience, she ducked beneath the overhanging reins and climbed up to the passenger seat.

As Ransom handed the doctor's bag to Garrett, he called up to the driver. "Mind you take care not to jostle the lady." Before Garrett could object, he stepped onto the footboard and gave the driver a few coins.

"I can pay my own fare," Garrett protested.

Ransom's midnight-blue eyes stared steadily into hers. Reaching out, he pressed something into her hand. "A gift," he murmured. Easily he descended to the ground. "Tomorrow, Doctor." He touched the brim of his hat, letting his fingers linger in that way he had, until the vehicle pulled away.

Feeling slightly dazed, Garrett looked down at the object he'd given her. The silver whistle, slightly warm from the heat of his body.

What nerve, she thought . . . but her fingers closed gently around it.

Chapter 2

BEFORE GOING TO HIS flat on Half Moon Street, Ethan had one more appointment to keep. He took a hansom to Cork Street, which was almost entirely occupied by Winterborne's, the famous department store.

A few times in the past, Ethan had done private work for the store's owner, Rhys Winterborne. The jobs had been easy and quick, hardly worth his time, but only a fool would turn down a request from such a powerful man. One of them had involved shadowing Winterborne's then fiancée, Lady Helen Ravenel, when she and a friend had visited an orphanage in a hazardous area near the docklands.

That had been two years ago, when Ethan had first met Dr. Garrett Gibson.

The slim chestnut-haired woman had been battering an assailant twice her size with precisely aimed strikes of her cane. Ethan had loved the way she'd done it, as if attending to some necessary task, like carrying a household bin out to the rubbish carter.

Her face had been unexpectedly young, her complexion clean-scrubbed and as smooth as a tablet of white soap. All cheekbones and cool green eyes, with a sharp little rampart of a chin. But amidst the elegant angles and edges of her features, there was a valentine of a mouth, tender and vulnerable, the upper lip nearly as full as the lower. A mouth with such pretty curves that it did something to Ethan's knees every time he saw it.

After that first encounter, Ethan had taken care to avoid Garrett Gibson, knowing she would be trouble for him, possibly even worse than he would be for her. But last month he'd gone to visit her at the medical clinic where she worked, for information concerning one of her patients, and his fascination had ignited all over again.

Everything about Garrett Gibson was . . . delicious. The dissecting gaze, the voice as crisp as the icing on a lemon cake. The compassion that drove her to treat the undeserving poor as well as the deserving. The purposeful walk, the relentless energy, the self-satisfaction of a woman who neither concealed nor apologized for her own intelligence. She was sunlight and steel, spun into a substance he'd never encountered before.

The mere thought of her left him like a stray coal on the hearth.

He had already sworn to himself that he would take nothing from her. All he intended to do was keep her safe on her visits to the Clerkenwell workhouse, or the Bishopsgate orphanage, or wherever she chose to go on her Tuesday rounds. That much he would allow himself.

It had been a mistake, arranging to meet her tomorrow. Ethan still wasn't sure how that had happened—he'd heard the words leaving his lips as if they were being spoken by someone else. Once he'd made the offer, however, he couldn't retract it, and then he'd found himself longing for her to accept.

One hour in Garrett Gibson's company, and then he would never approach her again. But he wanted, needed, craved those minutes alone with her. He would hoard the memory for the rest of his days.

Winterborne's department store appeared as an unbroken row of grand marble-faced buildings, fronted with massive display windows. The famed central stained-glass rotunda towered over four stories of columned arcades. It was a palatial structure, built by an ambitious man who'd wanted the world to know that a Welsh grocer's son had made himself into someone of consequence.

Ethan walked to the street behind the department store, where the mews, delivery yard, and loading docks were located. Winterborne's private house was at the far end of the street, connected to the store through private passageways and stairwells. It was Ethan's habit to enter at the back, through the door used by servants and deliverymen.

A footman admitted him inside. "Mr. Ransom. This way, if you please."

Ethan followed him, hat in hand, as they proceeded to the central staircase of the five-story house. The hallways were lit with crystal sconces and lined with paintings with views of mountains, oceans, and sunny pastoral scenes. A long pier table set against a wall had been laden with blue and white chinoiserie vases filled with ferns and lavish sprays of orchids.

As they passed a trio of potted palms, Ethan noticed a few black grains of dirt on the floor beside one of them. He paused and ducked low enough to look beneath the feathery fronds. A little parade of carved wooden animals, the kind that might belong to a Noah's ark set, had been set up in the soil around a tiny hut made of matchboxes. It looked like a child's secret hiding place. Amusement tugged at the corners of Ethan's lips as he recalled that Lady Helen's young half sister, approximately five years old, was being raised by the Winterbornes. Seeing that one of the toy elephants had fallen onto its side, he surreptitiously set it back on its feet.

"Sir." The footman had stopped to look back at him, frowning at the guest's untoward interest in a houseplant.

Ethan stood, giving him an innocent glance. "Just admiring the palm." He continued to follow the footman after bending to whisk the telltale flecks of soil away from the pot with a quick swipe of his hat.

They proceeded to the gentlemen's room where Ethan had met with Winterborne on previous occasions. The masculine parlor was seasoned with pleasant hints of oiled leather, cigar tobacco, expensive liquor, and a dry whiff of billiard chalk.

After entering the room, Ethan paused near the doorway, his gaze sharpening.

Winterborne stood beside a massive terrestrial globe set in a walnut floor stand, spinning it idly, while another man browsed among a nearby wall rack of billiard cues. The two were laughing quietly together in the manner of long-standing friends.

Noticing his presence, Winterborne said easily, "Ransom, come in."

Ethan didn't move, his nerves crawling with the awareness that he had been manipulated. Winterborne, the bastard, had led him to expect that he would be alone.

At six feet, Ethan was hardly a small man, but Winterborne eclipsed him by at least four inches in height. Winterborne approached in a relaxed manner. He was large and powerfully built, with the shoulders and sturdy neck of a prizefighter. Big fists. A punishing reach. From instinct and habit, Ethan's brain rapidly calculated the most efficient sequence of moves to defeat him. *Start with a dodge to the side—grab the shoulder of his jacket—hammer him with a few left hooks to the solar plexus and lower ribs—finish him with a knee to the gut—*

"Ethan Ransom, allow me to introduce Mr. Weston Ravenel," Winterborne said, gesturing to his companion. "One of my wife's relations. He asked if I would arrange a meeting with you."

Ethan's gaze shot to the stranger, a man in his mid to late twenties with brown-black hair, polished good looks, and an easy smile. He was lean and exceptionally fit, his clothes impeccably tailored. Curiously, his complexion was sun bronzed, and his hands were work roughened, like someone in a manual trade.

To London society, the Ravenel name connoted aristocratic privilege and power. But the Ravenels had never settled into staid respectability like the Cavendishes or Grosvenors. They were a hot-blooded lot, intemperate and reckless in nearly everything they did. The Ravenel lineage had nearly come to an end with the last earl's death, but they'd managed to find a distant cousin to assume the title.

"Please forgive the subterfuge," Weston Ravenel said pleasantly, coming forward. "I have a bit of business to discuss with you, and I didn't know how else to reach you."

"Not interested," Ethan said coldly, turning to leave.

"Wait. It's in your interest to hear me out. I'll pay for your time if necessary. God, I hope you're not expensive."

"He is," Winterborne assured him.

"I suppose I should have—" Ravenel began, but stopped as he drew close enough to have a more thorough look at Ethan in the light. "Damn," he said quietly, looking into his eyes.

Ethan drew in a measured breath and released it slowly. Focusing at a blank space on the wall, he considered his options. There wasn't much point in dodging the bastard now; he might as well find out what he wanted. "I'll stay for ten minutes," he said curtly.

"Would you make it twenty," Ravenel asked, "if Winterborne opened a decent bottle of cognac?" He glanced at Winterborne. "By 'decent,' I'm referring to the Gautier '64."

"Do you know how much that costs?" the Welshman asked him in dawning outrage.

"I've come all the way up from Hampshire. How often do you have the pleasure of my company?"

"Pleasure is not what I usually call it," Winterborne grumbled, and went to ring for a servant.

Ravenel grinned after him before leveling an assessing glance at Ethan. The mask of easy charm settled back into place. "Shall we?" he asked, gesturing to the grouping of deep leather chairs.

Stone-faced, Ethan went to occupy one of the chairs. He leaned back with his fingers laced lightly across his midriff. As the silence stretched out, he deliberately focused on the rosewood-and-brass mantel clock.

"Counting the minutes, are we?" Ravenel asked. "Very well, I'll go to the point as quickly as possible. Three years ago, my older brother unexpectedly inherited an earldom. Since he knew nothing about estate management, or God help us, farming, I agreed to move to Hampshire to help him make a go of it." Ravenel paused at a knock on the door.

The conversation paused while a butler brought in a silver tray bearing a set of egg-shaped glasses and the bottle of Gautier. Ceremoniously the cognac was poured and served. After the butler had departed, Winterborne sat on the arm of a heavy leather chair. He held a glass of cognac in one hand, while using the other to lazily turn the globe as if contemplating which parts of the world he wanted to own next.

"Why would you change your life like that?" Ethan couldn't resist asking. Leaving London for a quiet rural existence was his idea of hell on earth. "What were you trying to escape?"

Ravenel smiled. "Myself, I suppose. Even a life of debauchery can become tiresome. And I discovered that estate farming suits me. The tenants have to pay attention to me, and I'm easily amused by cows."

Ethan was in no mood for light banter. Weston Ravenel reminded him of things he'd spent most of his twenty-eight years trying not to think about. The elation he'd felt after meeting with Garrett Gibson had drained away, leaving him surly and annoyed. After taking a swallow of the fine cognac and barely tasting it, he said curtly, "You have eighteen minutes left."

Ravenel lifted his brows. "By all means, Chatty

Cheerful, I'll get to the point. The reason I'm here is that my brother and I have decided to sell some family property in Norfolk. It's a large house in good condition, set on approximately two thousand acres. However, I just found out that we can't do anything with it. Because of you."

Ethan gave him a questioning glance.

"Yesterday," Ravenel said, "I met with our former estate manager and family solicitor, respectively Totthill and Fogg. They explained that selling the Norfolk property is impossible because Edmund—the old earl—left it to someone in his will by means of a secret trust."

"What is that?" Ethan asked warily, having never heard of such a legal device.

"A declaration, usually verbal, concerning a bequest of property or money." Ravenel lifted his brows in a mocking expression of astonishment. "Naturally, we were all rather curious as to why the earl would have left such a generous gift to a man we'd never heard of." After a long pause, he continued in a more serious tone, "If you wouldn't mind talking to me about it, I think I know why—"

"*No*," Ethan said stonily. "If the trust wasn't written down, ignore it."

"I'm afraid it doesn't work that way. According to English law, a verbal trust is absolute. It's illegal to ignore it. There were three witnesses to the trust: Totthill, Fogg, and the earl's longtime valet, Quincy, who has confirmed the story." Pausing, Ravenel swirled the remaining cognac in his glass. His steady gaze met Ethan's. "Totthill and Fogg tried to notify you about the trust upon the earl's death, but you were nowhere to be found at the time. Now it falls to me to relay the happy news: Congratulations, you're now the proud owner of a Norfolk estate."

With great care, Ethan leaned to set his glass on a nearby table. "I don't want it." All the tricks he knew to control his emotions, the regulation of his breathing, the deliberate refocusing of his thoughts, weren't working. He was appalled to feel a bloom of sweat on his face. Standing, he rounded the grouping of chairs and headed for the door.

Ravenel followed him. "Damn it, *wait*," came his exasperated voice. "If we don't finish this conversation now, I'll have to go to the trouble of finding you again."

Ethan stopped in his tracks, facing away from him.

"Whether or not you want the property," Ravenel continued, "you have to take it. Because even though the Ravenels can't do anything with the godforsaken place, we're paying annual taxes on it."

Ethan reached into a trouser pocket, pulled out a wad of pound notes, and flung it at Ravenel's feet. "Let me know the balance of what I owe," he snapped.

To Ravenel's credit, if he were rattled by the gesture, he didn't show it. Turning to Winterborne, he remarked casually, "No one's ever showered me with cash before. I must say, it inspires feelings of instant affection." Ignoring the scattered pound notes at his feet, he went to lean back against the billiards table. He folded his arms across his chest, leveling an appraising stare at Ethan. "Obviously you had no great liking for Edmund Ravenel. May I ask why?"

"He hurt someone I loved. I'll not dishonor her memory by taking anything from a Ravenel."

The brittleness in the air seemed to ease. Ravenel uncrossed his arms and reached back to rub the nape of his neck, a rueful smile pulling at the corner of his mouth. "Are we being sincere now? Then I beg your pardon for being a flippant ass."

If the man were anyone other than a Ravenel, Ethan might have liked him.

Winterborne stood and crossed the room to the sideboard where the butler had left the silver tray. "You might consider selling the property to him," he said to Ethan, refreshing his glass from the cognac decanter.

It was the perfect solution. Ethan would be able to dispose of the unwanted land and cut any possible ties to the Ravenel family. "I'll sell it to you for one pound," he told Ravenel promptly. "Have the papers drawn up, and I'll sign them."

Ravenel frowned. "Not for a pound. I'll buy it at a reasonable price."

After giving him a baleful glance, Ethan went to the window and stared out at the vast mosaic of smoke-blistered rooftops. London was readying for the night, adorning itself with strands of lights, humming in anticipation of sin and pleasure.

He had been born to this city, nursed on it, until its violent rhythms were woven through him as surely as the network of his own veins. His blood coursed with its sounds and sensations. He could go anywhere, into the vilest rookeries or most dangerous criminal dens, an infinity of dark and secret places, fearing nothing.

"I'll be staying in London for the next month," West Ravenel said. "Before I return to Hampshire, I'll have a proposal drawn up for sale of the Norfolk property. If you like the terms, I'll be happy to take it off your hands." He pulled out a white calling card from a waistcoat pocket. "Let's exchange cards: I'll call on you when I've come up with some figures."

"Winterborne can tell you how to send a message to me," Ethan replied. "I don't have a calling card."

"Naturally," Ravenel said darkly, still holding out the card. "Take mine anyway." At Ethan's silent refusal, he exclaimed, "Good God, are you always like this? Your company is remarkably tedious, and that's coming from someone who spends most of his time around farm animals. Civilized men exchange cards after they meet. *Take it.*"

Deciding to humor him, Ethan tucked the white card, engraved with glossy black lettering, into the folding wallet he kept in an interior vest pocket. "I'll see myself out," he said. After retrieving his hat from a table, he settled it on his head and let his fingers graze the brim in a deferential gesture. It was his version of good-bye; he had the Irishman's reluctance to say the word aloud.

Chapter 3

EMERGING FROM THE LADIES' dressing room at Baujart's with her cane in hand, Garrett passed a series of private exercise and instruction rooms. She had changed into the standard lady's fencing costume, a close-fitting jacket with a high neck, a white skirt hemmed just below the knees, thick white hose, and soft flat leather shoes.

Familiar sounds seeped through the closed doors: the clashing of foils, sabers, and canes, the bursts of footwork on oak flooring, the familiar commands of instructors. "Disengage! Straighten the arm. *En guarde . . . longe . . .* disengage . . ."

Monsieur Jean Baujart, the son of a famous fencing master, had taught the science of defense at French and Italian academies before opening his own fencing club and school in London. Over the past two decades, Baujart's had acquired an unmatched reputation for excellence. His public exhibitions were always heavily attended, and his instruction rooms were constantly filled with students of all ages. Unlike most of his contemporaries, Monsieur Baujart not only allowed but also encouraged female students to attend his school.

For four years, Garrett had attended group classes

and taken private lessons from Baujart and his two assistant *prévôts* in the use of both foil and cane. Baujart insisted on a classic style of combat. Irregular movements and infringements of the rules were forbidden. If a fencer ducked, twisted, or ran back a few paces, he was gently mocked and corrected. One did not "hop about like a monkey" or "twist like an eel" at Baujart's. Form was everything. The result was a finished, polished style that was greatly admired by other fencing schools.

As Garrett reached the instruction room, she hesitated with a slight frown as she heard sounds coming from within. Had the previous lesson run overtime? Carefully she inched the door open and peeked inside.

Her eyes widened as she saw the familiar form of Monsieur Baujart attacking an opponent in a sustained series of *phrases d'armes*.

Baujart, like the instructors at the school, dressed in an all-black fencing uniform, whereas club members and students wore the classic attire of unbroken white. Both men's faces were concealed by French wire masks, their hands gloved, their chests protected by leather plastrons. The foils, capped with *boutons* for safety, flashed and scissored in a rapid exchange.

Even if Baujart hadn't worn the black instructor's costume, his flawless form would have made him immediately recognizable. Baujart was a superbly fit man of forty, an artist who had perfected his craft. Every thrust, parry, and riposte was precise.

His opponent, however, was fencing in a style unlike anything Garrett had seen before. Instead of allowing the match to settle into familiar rhythms, he attacked unexpectedly and retreated before Baujart could touch him. There was something catlike about his movements, a vicious grace that raised every hair on Garrett's body.

Fascinated, she let herself inside and closed the door.

"Good afternoon, Doctor," the man in white said without even looking at her. For some reason, a few of her heartbeats collided as she recognized Ethan Ransom's voice. After parrying a lunge, he dropped low and attacked beneath Baujart's blade.

"*Arrêt*," Baujart said sharply. "That wasn't a sanctioned hit."

The two men disengaged.

"Good afternoon," Garrett said cordially. "Have I arrived early for our session, Mr. Ransom?"

"No. Monsieur Baujart had reservations about allowing me to teach you until he judged my abilities for himself."

"It's worse than I feared," Baujart said darkly, his masked face turning toward Garrett. "This man is unqualified, Dr. Gibson. I cannot condone your association with him—he will ruin every method you have learned here."

"I hope so," Ransom muttered.

Garrett pressed her lips together, struggling to hold back a grin. No one ever dared speak to Baujart with such insolence.

The sword master returned his attention to Ransom. "*Allons*," he snapped. Another duel commenced, so lightning fast that the blades blurred.

Ransom twisted, parried an attack, and deliberately

shoved his shoulder against Baujart to knock him off balance. After making a strike, he dropped to the floor in a roll, sprung to his feet, and jabbed Baujart a second time.

"*Arrête!*" Baujart shouted in fury. "Colliding with an opponent? Rolling across the floor? This is not a tavern brawl, you madman! *What do you think you're doing*?"

Turning to face him with the foil lowered, Ransom said calmly, "Trying to win. Isn't that the object?"

"The object is to *fence,* according to the Amateur League's official code of rules!"

"And that's how you've taught Dr. Gibson to fight," Ransom said.

"*Oui!*"

"For what?" Ransom asked with blistering sarcasm. "To take part in a spontaneous fencing match that's going to break out in some East End slum? She didn't come here to learn how to fight *gentlemen*, Baujart. She needs to know how to defend herself against men like me." Removing his mask, Ransom cleared away the locks of hair that hung in front of his eyes with a quick shake of his head, the short dark layers seeming to come alive before settling into place. He skewered the *maître d'armes* with a hard stare. "Dr. Gibson has no idea what to do if someone disarms her in the middle of those pretty *moulinette* cane twirls you've taught her. You've lived in Paris—you must know some *savate*. Or at least *chausson*. Why haven't you shown her any of that?"

"Because it's not correct," Baujart retorted, ripping off his own mask to reveal a narrow, flushed face and black eyes slitted with fury.

"Correct for what?" For a moment, Ransom looked genuinely bewildered.

Monsieur Baujart gave him a scornful glance. "Only a peasant thinks the purpose of fencing is to stick someone with the pointy end of a sword. It's a discipline. It's visual poetry *with rules.*"

"God help me," Ransom said, staring at him incredulously.

Garrett decided it was time for diplomacy. "Mr. Ransom, there's no need to berate Monsieur Baujart. He's instructed me to the best of his ability."

"Have you?" Ransom asked the *maître d'armes,* his voice soft and savage. "Or have you given her lessons suited for a lady's parlor exercise? Teach your other students how to be picturesque. But teach this one how to fight for her life. Because one day she might be doing just that, armed only with the skills she's learned from you." He gave the other man a withering glance. "I suppose when she's lying on the street with her throat slit, at least she'll be able to console herself that she didn't score any illegal points."

A long, long silence passed while Baujart's vehement breathing slowed. His rage faded into an expression that Garrett had never seen from him before. "I understand," he eventually said with difficulty. "I will make the necessary adjustments to her training."

"You'll include some *savate*?" Ransom pressed.

"I'll bring in a special tutor if necessary."

The men exchanged bows, and Garrett curtsied to her fencing master. It troubled her that Monsieur Baujart wasn't quite able to meet her gaze. He departed with great dignity, closing the door behind him.

Left alone with Ethan Ransom, Garrett watched as

he went to set the fencing foil and his other gear in the corner. "You were rather hard on poor Monsieur Baujart," she said gently.

"Not hard enough," Ransom said, switching to his Irish accent. "I should've spent fifteen minutes paintin' hell to him." He unstrapped the plastron and dropped it to the floor. "You've more of a practical need for self-defense than any student here. His arrogance—or laziness—has put you at risk."

"I don't know if I should feel more insulted for Monsieur Baujart's sake or my own," Garrett said dryly.

"I didn't insult you." Ransom stripped off his gloves and tossed them aside.

"You implied that I'm incompetent."

Ransom turned to face her. "No. I've seen you fight. You're an opponent to be reckoned with."

"Thank you," Garrett said, somewhat mollified. "For that, I'll overlook your remark about my *moulinet* twirls."

She saw the flash of an elusive grin. "A waste of motion, they are," he murmured. "But very pleasing to the eye."

Garrett realized this was the first time she'd ever seen him in good lighting. The stunning brightness of his eyes—blue from across the room—sparked an unfamiliar but pleasant tingling high up under her ribs, like delicately tightening knots. His features were ruggedly masculine, with that strong nose and geometric jaw . . . but the long sweeps of black lashes were a luxurious touch of softness . . . and when he'd smiled, she could have sworn there was the hint of a dimple in one cheek.

Ransom began to meander along a wall of framed

illustrations of fencing positions, viewing them with feigned interest. Garrett was more than a little charmed by the hint of boyishness, as if he weren't quite certain how to approach her.

He cut a splendid figure in the fencing uniform, a head-to-toe scheme of all white that usually did the male form no favors. The canvas jacket—buttoned on one side and closely fitted down to the high hip—tended to make the average man's shoulders appear narrow and the waist look thick. The snug, flat-fronted trousers would highlight even the slightest tummy bulge. But on Ransom, the severely tailored garments only served to emphasize a physique of remarkable proportions. His body was lean, lithe, powerful, with no trace of softness anywhere.

Garrett's gaze traveled from the broad shoulders down to the slim hips, and then even lower to his thickly muscled thighs. As it occurred to her that she was staring, she glanced upward, and blushed like a schoolgirl as she met his questioning gaze.

"I was just noting the unusual development of your quadriceps extensors," she said in her professional voice.

His lips twitched. "Are you paying me a compliment, doctor?"

"Certainly not. It was merely an observation. Your physical build might lead one to assume you were a sailor, or a blacksmith."

"I've done a bit of forging and pressing," Ransom said. "But only light metalwork. Nothing so difficult as what a blacksmith does."

"What kind of metalwork?"

He straightened one of the frames on the wall.

"Locks and keys, mostly. I apprenticed for a prison locksmith as a boy." Without looking at her, he added, "My father was a turnkey at Clerkenwell."

Most prisons, including Clerkenwell, were unsanitary, hazardous, and crowded, as it was believed they should have a deterrent atmosphere. In her opinion, no boy should have been allowed to work under such conditions.

"A dangerous place for a child," she commented.

His shoulders hitched in a shrug. "It was safe enough, as long as I heeded the rules."

"Did you have brothers or sisters?" she asked.

"No. I was an only child."

"So was I." Although Garrett rarely volunteered personal information, she found herself continuing, "I always wanted a sister. My mother died when I was born, and my father never remarried."

"He was a constable in E division, aye?"

Garrett looked up at him quickly. "Yes. How did you know that?"

"I read it in the newspaper."

"Oh. Of course." She made a little face. "Reporters insist on portraying me as a curiosity. Rather like a talking horse."

"You're an unusual woman."

"Not really. Many thousands of women have the minds and temperaments to practice medicine. However, no medical school here will admit a female, which is why I had to study and train in France. I was fortunate to become certified before the British Medical Association closed the loopholes to prevent other women from doing the same."

"What did your father say about it?"

"At first he was against the idea. He thought it indecent for a woman to have such an occupation. Viewing unclothed people, and so forth. However, as I pointed out to him, if we're made in God's image, there can be nothing wrong with the study of the human body."

"And that changed his mind?"

"Not entirely. But when he saw the opposition I faced from friends and relations, it put him on his mettle. He can't bear anyone telling me what I can't do, and so he decided to support me."

Amusement tugged at Ransom's lips as he came to stand beside her. A shadow of whisker grain was visible beneath the close-shaven skin. His complexion was clear and fair, a striking contrast to his rich dark hair.

Slowly he reached out to take the cane from her. "We won't need this for now."

Garrett nodded, while a pulse tapped in her wrists, throat, the backs of her knees. "Shall I remove my gloves?" she asked, trying to sound businesslike.

"If you like." Ransom set the cane on the floor, along the wall, and turned toward her. "This will be easy for you," he said gently. "You might even enjoy it. In a few minutes, I'll let you throw me to the floor."

That startled a laugh from her. "You're twice my size. How could I do that?"

"I'll show you. But first we'll start with something simple." He waited until she tossed her gloves aside. "Do you remember what I said about the most common way women are attacked?"

"They're choked from the front."

"Aye. Usually against a wall." Carefully he took Garrett's shoulders and guided her backward until she felt her shoulder blades touch the hard surface. His big hands lifted to her throat, the fingers strong enough to bend copper coins. A frisson of alarm chased down her spine, and she stiffened.

Ransom let go instantly, his brows drawing together with concern.

"No," Garrett assured him hastily, "I . . . I'm perfectly all right. It's just that I've never had someone take me by the throat before."

His voice was soft. "You've nothing to fear from me. Ever."

"Of course." She paused before adding wryly, "Although when I mentioned you to my father, he warned that you were dangerous."

"I can be."

Garrett gave him a superior glance. "Every man likes to think there's a part of his nature that remains untamed and unsubdued."

"You know all about men, do you?" he asked with an edge of mockery.

"Mr. Ransom, the male sex has ceased to be a mystery ever since my first course in practical anatomy, which included the dissection of a cadaver."

That should have set him in his place, but instead he laughed quietly. "I've no doubt you can carve up a man like a jugged hare, Doctor, but that doesn't mean you understand the first thing about him."

Garrett regarded him coolly. "You think me naïve?"

Ransom shook his head. "I see no fault in you," he said, with a quiet sincerity that threw her off guard.

His fingers, dry and warm, returned to her neck with the lightest possible pressure. She felt the texture of a callus on his forefinger, like the rasp of a kitten's tongue. The contrast between the brutal strength of his hands and the incredible gentleness of his touch caused gooseflesh to rise everywhere.

"Now then," Ransom murmured, his thick lashes lowering as he focused on the tender front of her throat where his thumbs rested. "In this situation, you have only a few seconds to react after he takes hold."

"Yes," Garrett said, aware that he could feel her breath and pulse, and the movements of her swallowing. "The pressure on the trachea and carotid arteries would cause unconsciousness very quickly." Tentatively her hands came up to grip his elbows. "If I pulled down on his arms like this . . . ?"

"Not if he was my size. You couldn't budge him. Tuck your chin down to protect your throat, and put your palms together, as if you're praying. Push them up through the circle of my arms . . . good, higher . . . until it forces my elbows to bend. Can you feel how that loosens my grip?"

"Yes," she said in pleased discovery.

"Now grab my head."

Disconcerted, Garrett gave him a blank look.

"Go on," he encouraged.

To her embarrassed annoyance, a nervous giggle escaped her. She *never* giggled. Clearing her throat, she made herself reach out and shape her fingers over his skull, until the heels of her hands rested against the neat outer curves of his ears. The short-cropped locks of his hair were like coarse silk.

"Take hold closer to my face," Ransom said, "so you can push your thumbs into the eye sockets."

Garrett winced. "You want me to gouge a man's eyes out?"

"Aye, show the bastard no mercy, as he'll show none to you."

She adjusted her grip tentatively, resting the pads of her thumbs not directly on his eyes, but at the outer corners where the skin was fine and hot. It was difficult to meet his gaze. The color of his eyes was so intense that she had the sensation of being pulled into blueness, almost drowning in it. "As you apply pressure to the eyes," he continued, "you'll be able to push the head back easily. Then jerk it down until the nose hits your forehead." Before she moved, he cautioned, "Slowly. I've had my nose broken before, and it's not an experience I'm after repeating."

"How did it happen?" she asked, envisioning some life-threatening situation. "Were you quelling a riot? Stopping a robbery?"

"I tripped over a bucket," he said wryly. "In front of two constables and a reception cell filled with a half dozen prisoners on remand, a deserter from the army, and a man in default of bail."

"Poor lad," Garrett said sympathetically, although she was unable to hold back a chuckle.

"It was worth it," he said. "A fight was brewing among the prisoners, but they all started laughing so hard, they forgot about it." Abruptly he turned businesslike. "In a real situation, pull your opponent's head toward you with as much force as you can. Bash him as many times as it takes to make him let go."

"Won't I knock myself unconscious?"

"No, this is too hard for that." Ransom paused to tap a knuckle gently against her forehead, as if knocking on a door panel. "It will hurt him far worse than you."

His hand returned to her neck, fingers curving almost tenderly around the sides.

Carefully Garrett pulled his head down until she felt his nose and mouth on her forehead. The contact lasted only an instant, but it was electrifying. The smooth touch of his lips and the warm rush of his breath drew up another rush of feeling, a warmth that seemed to radiate from her quick. She breathed in the scent of him, the scrubbed-leather pungency of a clean and healthy male.

Ransom drew back slowly. "You could follow that with a knee to the groin," he said, "if your skirts aren't too heavy or narrow."

"Do you mean I should use my leg to . . ." Her gaze flickered to his crotch.

"Like this." He demonstrated with a subtle motion of his knee.

"I think walking skirts would allow for that."

"Then do it," Ransom said. "It's the most devastating target on a man. The pain shoots all through your innards."

"I've no doubt it would," Garrett mused. "There's a nerve in the scrotum called the spermatic plexus that extends into the abdomen." Noticing the way he averted his face, she said apologetically, "Have I made you uncomfortable? I beg your pardon."

Ransom lifted his head to reveal eyes glinting with laughter. "Not at all. It's just that I've never heard a lady talk as you do."

"As I told you . . . I'm not a lady."

Chapter 4

THE LESSON THAT FOLLOWED could not have been more different from Garrett's sessions with Monsieur Baujart or his *prévôts*, who emphasized discipline, silence, and perfect form. This, by contrast, seemed like a rough-and-tumble form of play. In fact, every minute of twisting, grappling, and shoving was so absorbing that Garrett lost all awareness of time passing. Although she wasn't used to having a man's hands on her, Ransom's touch was so careful and gentle that she quickly came to trust him.

Patiently he demonstrated various moves and encouraged her to repeat them until he was satisfied that she'd learned them properly. He praised her efforts, calling her a warrior, an Amazon, and more than once he chuckled at her enthusiasm. As promised, he taught her how to throw a man to the floor by hooking a foot around his leg and using it as leverage to push him off balance. Every time he hit the ground, he rolled in a fluid motion and came to his feet again.

"Where did you learn to do that?" Garrett asked.

"After I left K division, I was sent away for special training."

"Away to where?"

For some reason Ransom seemed reluctant to answer. "India."

"India? Good heavens. For how long?"

"A year and a half." Seeing her interest, Ransom explained cautiously, "I was instructed by an eighty-year-old guru, who was as limber as a lad of sixteen. He taught a fighting system based on animal movements, like the tiger, or the snake."

"How perfectly fascinating." Garrett would have liked to ask more, but he motioned for her to face away from him.

"This is what to do if someone seizes you in a bear hug." He hesitated. "I'll have to put my arms around you."

Garrett nodded and held trustingly still as his arms enclosed her. His grip was firm but not crushing, taking enough of her weight that her heels nearly began to lift from the floor. His body was hot, almost steaming inside the fencing jacket. She was surrounded by the strength of him, breathing in the salt and heat of male exertion, while the motion of his breathing pressed against her rhythmically.

"Do bears actually hug like this?" she asked breathlessly.

"I don't know," Ransom said, his amused voice close to her ear. "I've never been close enough to one to find out. Now then, you'll want to keep me from picking you up and carrying you off. Shove your hips back, and use all your weight to plant your feet hard on the ground." He waited until she had complied. The movement had obliged him to lean over her, altering his center of gravity. "Good. Take a sidestep, and that will give you a clear path to deliver a hammer-blow to the groin." He watched as she knotted her fingers into a ball. "Not like that. Has no one ever taught you to make a fist?"

"Never. Show me."

Releasing her, Ransom turned her to face him. He took her hand in both of his, molding it into the proper shape. "Curl your fingers and cross your thumb over them. Don't tuck it inside, or you'll break it when you hit someone. And don't clench so tight that your little finger starts to collapse inward." He tested the tension of her closed hand, running the pad of his thumb across her knuckles. The dark fans of his lashes lowered. She thought he would let go then . . . but instead . . . his fingertips slowly began to explore the miniature valleys between her fingers, the buffed surface of her nails, the soft flesh at the base of her thumb. Garrett's breath caught as he touched the tender inside of her wrist, where a pulse beat light and fast.

"Why were you named Garrett?" she heard him ask.

"My mother was convinced that I was going to be a boy. She wanted to name me after one of her brothers, who died while he was still young. But she didn't survive my birth. Above the objections of friends and relations, my father insisted on calling me Garrett anyway."

"I like it," Ransom murmured.

"It suits me," Garrett said, "although I'm not certain my mother would have approved of giving a masculine name to a daughter." After a reflective pause, she surprised herself by saying impulsively, "Sometimes I imagine going back in time, to stop the hemorrhage that killed her."

"Is that why you became a doctor?"

Garrett pondered the question with a slight frown. "I've never thought about it that way before. I suppose helping people could be my way of saving her, over and over. But I would have found the study of medicine fascinating regardless. The human body is a remarkable machine."

His fingers stroked over the back of her hand as if he were smoothing out a tiny silk handkerchief.

"Why did you enter into law enforcement?" she asked him.

"When I was a boy, I always liked watching the constables when they brought the prisoner van every morning. Big, strong chaps, in their blue uniforms and shiny black shoes. I liked the way they brought order to things."

"What made you want to be one of them?"

Ransom drew the tip of his forefinger gently over each of her knuckles, a bit furtively, as if it were something he knew he shouldn't be doing. "My father earned five pounds a week. It was good pay, especially as we were allowed to live in a watch-house on the prison grounds. But even so, there were times when we couldn't make the money stretch. When Mam worried that I'd had naught but potatoes and milk for weeks, or too many bills had gone unpaid, she would slip away to visit a married gentleman she had an arrangement with. Later Da would see the new soles on my shoes, or a fresh stock of candles and coal in the house . . . and he would beat her without a word. Then he beat me for trying to stop him, and he wept while he did it. The next day, all three of us would carry on as usual. But I couldn't forget about it. I kept telling myself that someday I'd have the power to stop Da, or any man, from hurting Mam. To this day, when I see a woman being threatened or harmed, it's like setting flame to gunpowder."

Seeming to realize he was still holding Garrett's hand, Ransom abruptly let go. "I was too young to understand what Mam had done with her gentleman friend, or why Da—who fair worshipped her—should have beaten her for it. Or why Mam wouldn't let me speak against him. Any husband might be moved to thrash his wife, she said. It was the nature of men. But she hoped I would be better than that." He gave her a troubled, worn-around-the-edges look. "I told her I would never strike a woman, and I never have. I'd cut off my arm first."

"I believe you," Garrett said gently. "Your mother was mistaken. It is not men's nature to commit violence against women, it's a corruption of their nature."

"I'd like to think so," he muttered. "But I've seen too much evil to be sure."

"So have I," Garrett said simply. "Nevertheless, I know I'm right."

"I envy your certainty." What a smile he had, like something that had just been unleashed.

She'd never talked like this with a man in her life. The conversation was easy on the surface, but beneath . . . it reminded her a little of the feeling she'd had the day of her first classes at the Sorbonne. She'd been terrified and exhilarated by the world of mysteries about to be revealed.

"We'll have to end the lesson soon," Ransom said reluctantly. "We've gone overtime."

"Have we?" she asked, bemused.

"It's been almost two hours. We'll practice the last move once more, and that will be the end of it."

"I'm sure there's much more for me to learn," Garrett said, facing away from him. "When shall we plan to meet next?"

Ransom's arms slid around her from behind. "I'm afraid I have obligations that will keep me busy for a while." After a long pause, he said, "After today, you won't see me again."

"For how long?"

"Ever."

Garrett blinked in surprise. She turned in the circle of his arms to face him. "But . . ." She was mortified to hear the plaintive note in her voice as she asked, "What about Tuesdays?"

"I can't follow you on Tuesdays any longer. Soon I'll have to go to ground for a while. Maybe for good."

"Why? Are you planning to save England? Defeat an evil mastermind?"

"I can't tell you."

"Oh, twaddle. Anything you say will be shielded by doctor-patient confidentiality."

Ransom smiled slightly. "I'm not your patient."

"You could be someday," Garrett said darkly, "considering your occupation."

His only response was to turn her around to face away from him.

A bleak feeling crept through her as she complied. How could it be that she might never see him again? Did it really have something to do with his job? Perhaps that was a convenient excuse, and the truth was that he had no interest in her. Perhaps the attraction was only on her side. Garrett was appalled to feel a knot of disappointment forming in her throat.

"Remember to push against—" Ransom began, when the door opened unceremoniously.

They both looked at the doorway, where Monsieur Baujart stood glowering. "I need to use this room for a scheduled lesson," the fencing master announced. His eyes narrowed at the sight of them locked together. "Is this the way you're teaching Dr. Gibson to fight for her life?" he asked sarcastically.

Garrett replied in a matter-of-fact tone. "This is a defensive maneuver, monsieur. I'm about to deliver an incapacitating strike to the groin."

The fencing master regarded them both with a stony gaze. "Good," he grunted, and the door closed smartly behind him.

Before Garrett could continue, she felt Ransom press his face against the back of her shoulder, chuckling like a mischievous boy in church. "Now you've done it," he said. "Baujart won't be satisfied unless I limp out of here in agony."

A reluctant grin crossed her lips. "For the sake of England, I'll have mercy on you." As he had taught her before, she pushed her hips back and leaned forward. The fit between them was close and compact, their bodies aligning like puzzle pieces. Her mind went blank as she felt the pure visceral pleasure of his weight and warmth over her.

His arms tightened, and there was a quiet catch in his throat, as if he weren't certain whether to breathe in or out.

In the next moment, he had released her and collapsed to a seated position in an uncharacteristically clumsy movement. His long arms curled around his bent legs, and he rested his forehead on his knees.

Alarmed, Garrett lowered to her knees beside him. "What's wrong?"

"Strained muscle," he said in a muffled voice.

But it appeared more serious than that. His color was high, and he seemed on the verge of hyperventilating.

"Do you feel dizzy?" Garrett asked in worry. "Lightheaded?" She laid her palm against the side of his face, testing his temperature, and he jerked away from her touch. "Let me check your pulse," she said, reaching for him again.

Ransom snatched her wrist, his gaze meeting hers in a blaze of unearthly blue. "Don't touch me, or I'll—" Breaking off, he rolled away and rose to his feet in a single easy motion. He went to the opposite wall and braced his hands against it, his head lowered.

Garrett stared after him, her jaw sagging.

Before he'd turned his back, she'd caught a glimpse of something that was most definitely *not* a strained muscle. It was a different kind of problem altogether.

As the fencing trousers displayed so flagrantly, he was aroused. Prodigiously, impressively so.

Color invaded Garrett's face until her cheeks felt scorched. At a complete loss for what to do, she remained kneeling on the floor. All her skin felt tight and seared, and she was filled with a sense of . . . well, she didn't quite know what it was . . . not embarrassment, although her complexion had turned beetroot red. Not pleasure, exactly, although her nerves thrummed with giddiness.

She had never been a woman whose presence excited the male ardor. Partly because she'd never cultivated the skills of flirtation and feminine charm. Also because when she first met a man, she was usually jabbing him with suture needles or injection syringes.

"Would . . . would it help if I fetch a glass of cold water?" she dared to ask, in a timid voice that didn't even sound like hers.

Ransom replied with his forehead leaning against the wall. "Not unless you pour it down my trousers."

A strangled laugh was wrenched from her throat.

He turned to give her a sideways glance then, a flash of hot, infinite blue, conveying the force of a desire as immolating as a lightning bolt. Even with Garrett's reams of knowledge about the workings of the human body, she could only begin to comprehend all that was contained in that blistering look.

His voice was dry and fractured with self-mockery. "As you said, Doctor . . . there's a part of every man that's untamed and unsubdued."

Chapter 5

"WHAT DID HE SAY after that?" Lady Helen Winterborne whispered across the tea table, her blue-gray eyes as round as silver florins. "What did *you* say?"

"I can't remember," Garrett confessed, amazed to feel her face heating up even now, three days later. "My mind turned to mush. It was so unexpected."

"Had you never seen a man . . . in that state?" Helen asked delicately.

Garrett gave her a sardonic glance. "I'm a former nurse as well as a physician. I darcsay I've seen as many erections as a brothel madam." She frowned. "But never one that had anything to do with me."

Helen hastily crammed a linen napkin against her lips, muffling a laugh.

As was their weekly habit, they had met for lunch at the renowned tea room of Winterborne's department store. The tea room was a serene refuge from the heat and bustle of the day, a tall-ceiled, airy room decorated with frothy green potted palms, the walls lined with mosaics of blue, white, and gold tiles. The main floor was crowded with ladies and gentlemen clustered at the round tables. Each corner of the tea room featured an inset alcove where the table was set back enough to allow for private conversation.

As Winterborne's wife, of course, Helen was always seated at one of the alcove tables.

Garrett had been friends with Helen ever since she'd been hired as one of Winterborne's staff physicians. She had quickly discovered that not only was Helen kind, sensible, and loyal, she could also be trusted to keep her mouth shut. They had a great deal in common, including a commitment to helping those less fortunate. In the past year, Helen had become the patroness of several charities benefitting women and children, and worked actively for reform causes.

Recently Helen had insisted that Garrett start attending some of the fundraising dinners and private concerts she and Winterborne hosted. "You can't work *all* the time," Helen had told her in a gentle but resolute tone. "Now and then you must spend an evening in the society of others."

"I'm in the company of people every day," Garrett had protested.

"At the clinic, yes. But I'm referring to a social evening, when you put on a nice dress, and make small talk, and perhaps even dance."

"You're not going to try matchmaking for me, are you?" Garrett had asked suspiciously.

Helen had given her a chiding smile. "There's no harm in making the acquaintance of a few unmarried gentlemen. You're not *opposed* to the idea of marriage, are you?"

"Not exactly. But I've never been able to see how my life could accommodate a husband. He couldn't be the sort of man who insisted that the household revolve around his needs, nor could he expect me to be a traditional wife. He would have to be as uncon-

ventional as I am. I'm not sure such a man exists."
Garrett had shrugged and smiled wryly. "I don't mind
being 'on the shelf,' as they say. It happens to be a very
interesting shelf."

"If he's out there," Helen had told her, "you certainly won't find him by staying at home. You're coming to our next dinner, and that means we must have a
new evening dress made up for you."

"I have an evening dress," Garrett had said, thinking of her sapphire brocade, which was a few years old
but had worn like iron.

"I've seen it, and it's very . . . nice," Helen said,
damning the garment with faint praise. "However,
you need something more festive. And lower cut. No
women our age wear high-necked evening gowns—
those are only for young girls or dowagers."

Acknowledging that fashion was not necessarily
her forte, Garrett had agreed to visit the store's in-
house dressmaker, Mrs. Allenby, after tea with Helen
today.

Her thoughts were drawn back to the present as
Helen regained her composure and murmured, "Poor
Mr. Ransom. It must be dreadfully embarrassing for a
man to be caught in that state."

"No doubt it was," Garrett said, nibbling at a miniature sandwich made of a nasturtium leaf and cream
cheese pressed between two thin slices of French roll.
But Ransom hadn't seemed embarrassed. A ticklish
sensation wove through her as she recalled the look
he'd given her. A starving-tiger look, all desire and
instinct. As if it had taken every last flicker of his will
to hold himself back from her.

"How did the lesson end?" Helen asked.

"After we had changed into our street clothes, Ransom met me outside, and hailed a hansom cab for me. Before I climbed into the seat, he thanked me for the time we'd spent together, and said he regretted very much that we couldn't meet again. I can't remember what I said, only that I extended my hand for him to shake, and he . . ."

"He what?"

Fractious color rose in her face. "He . . . kissed it," Garrett managed to say, remembering the sight of his dark head bent over her gloved hand. "It was the last thing I expected. That big, blue-eyed ruffian doing something so gentlemanly . . . especially after we'd spent the past two hours grappling and slamming each other all around the fencing room." A gesture so tender, it had left her stunned and speechless. Even now, the thought of it sent flutters of pleasure and heat through her. It was madness. With all the patients she had examined and operated on, all the people she had held and comforted, nothing had ever felt so intimate as the pressure of his lips on her glove.

"I haven't been able to stop thinking about it," Garrett continued. "I can't keep from wondering what it would be like if . . ." She couldn't say the rest of it aloud. She began to fiddle with a tiny sorbet spoon. "I want to see him again," she confessed.

"Oh, dear," she heard Helen murmur.

"I don't know how to reach him." Garrett slid her a guarded glance. "But your husband does."

Helen looked uncomfortable. "If Mr. Ransom says he can't meet with you, I think you should respect his decision."

"He could visit me on the sly, if he wished," Garrett

pointed out irritably. "The man skulks around London like a stray cat."

"If he did meet you in secret, where would it lead? Or rather, where would you want it to lead?"

"I'm not sure." Garrett set aside the sorbet spoon, picked up a fork, and stabbed a strawberry. She used a knife to mince it into miniscule bits. "Obviously Ransom is not an appropriate companion for me. I should put him—and his private parts—completely out of my mind."

"That might be for the best," Helen said cautiously.

"Except that I can't." Setting down the utensils, Garrett muttered, "I've never been ruled by unwanted thoughts or feelings. I've always been able to put them away as if they were folded linens in a drawer. What's the matter with me?"

Helen slid a cool, pale hand over her clenched fist and gave it a comforting squeeze. "You've been all work and no play for much too long. And then one night a mysterious and handsome man appears out of the shadows, fending off attackers on your behalf—"

"That part was annoying," Garrett interrupted. "I was doing quite well at being my own hero until he jumped in."

Helen's lips curved. "Still . . . it must have been a little flattering."

"It was," Garrett grumbled, taking refuge in examining the plate of tea sandwiches. She selected one filled with a translucent slice of pickled artichoke heart and a sliver of boiled egg. "In fact, it was ridiculous, how dashing he was, all brass and brawn. Only to you would I admit that when I heard his Irish brogue, I nearly began batting my eyelashes and simpering like the ingénue from some second-rate playhouse."

Helen laughed gently. "There's something charming about a man with an accent, isn't there? I know it's considered a defect—even more so if the accent is Welsh—but to me there's poetry in it."

"Nowadays having an Irish brogue is the surest way to have a door slammed in one's face," Garrett said darkly. "Which is no doubt why Mr. Ransom conceals it."

During the past ten years, the political unrest of those who believed in Ireland's right to govern itself had fueled an atmosphere of growing intolerance. Rumors of conspiracies were everywhere, and the people found it difficult to separate prejudice from reason. Especially, now, after a recent spate of terrorist activities, including a recently foiled attempt on the Prince of Wales's life.

"The man is neither respectable nor gainfully employed," Garrett continued. "He's also sneaky, violent, and apparently as randy as a stoat. I can't possibly be attracted to him."

"Attraction isn't something one chooses," Helen mused. "It's a kind of magnetism. An irresistible force."

"I will not be held hostage by invisible forces."

Helen regarded her with a sympathetic smile. "This reminds me a bit of what you told me after Pandora was injured in the street attack. You said she'd received a shock to her entire nervous system. I think Mr. Ransom has been a shock to your system. Among other things, I think he's made you realize that you might be a bit lonely."

Garrett, who had always taken pride in her self-sufficiency, shot her an indignant glance. "Impossible. How could I be lonely when I have you and my other friends, my father, Dr. Havelock, my patients—"

"I meant a different kind of loneliness."

Garrett scowled. "I'm not some dewy-eyed girl with a head full of spun sugar. I should hope I'm more high-minded than that."

"Even a high-minded woman can appreciate a fine pair of . . . what did you call them? Quadriceps?"

One could hardly miss the sly teasing in Helen's demure tone. Taking refuge in dignified silence, Garrett drained another cup of tea while a waitress came to the table with little glass cups of lemon sorbet.

Helen waited until after the waitress had departed before saying, "Hear me out before you refuse: I want very much to introduce you to my cousin West. He'll be in town for a fortnight. You didn't meet him the last time he was here to see Pandora. We'll all have dinner at Ravenel House one evening."

"*No.* I beg you, Helen, do not put me— or your cousin—through such pointless torture."

"West is very handsome," Helen persisted. "Dark-haired, blue-eyed, and charming. I'm positive you'll like each other. After a few minutes in his company, you'll forget all about Mr. Ransom."

"Even in the unlikely event that Mr. Ravenel and I formed an attachment, it would never work. I can't live in the country." Garrett tried a spoonful of sorbet, letting the tart, sugary frost dissolve into a cold flood on her tongue. "Among other things, I'm afraid of cows."

"Because of their size?" Helen asked sympathetically.

"No, it's the way they stare. As if they're plotting something."

Helen chuckled. "I promise, when you come to visit Eversby Priory someday, all scheming cows will be kept out of sight. And as far as living in the country is concerned, West may be willing to move back to London. He's a man of many interests and talents. Oh, do say you'll at least meet him!"

"I'll consider it," Garrett said reluctantly.

"Thank you, that sets my mind at ease." A new, serious note entered Helen's voice. "Because I fear there's a very good reason Mr. Ransom has decided to stay away from you."

Garrett looked at her alertly. "What is it?"

Helen frowned, seeming to debate something within her mind before continuing. "I know some information about Mr. Ransom. I'm not at liberty to relay all of it, but there's something you should be made aware of."

Garrett waited with forced patience while Helen glanced around to make certain no one was approaching the alcove.

"It has to do with that incident at the Guildhall last month," Helen said softly. "You'll recall that Pandora and Lord St. Vincent attended the reception."

Garrett nodded, having heard from Pandora herself about how a loose plank had led to the discovery that bombs had been laid beneath the floor. Within a few minutes, the panicked crowd had rapidly fled the building. Fortunately, the explosive devices had been dismantled before they could be detonated. No arrests had been made in connection to the plot, but it had been blamed on a small group of radical Irish nationalists.

"One of the reception guests passed away that night," Helen continued. "An undersecretary from the Home Office, Mr. Nash Prescott."

Garrett nodded. "As I recall from the account in the *Times*, he had a weak heart. In the midst of all the alarm and confusion, he experienced a fatal cardiac seizure."

"That's the official story," Helen said. "But Lord St. Vincent told Mr. Winterborne privately that Mr. Prescott had known about the bomb plot in advance. And it was none other than Mr. Ransom who found Mr. Prescott's body, not far from the Guildhall grounds." She paused. "After having given chase to him."

"Ransom chased him from the reception?" Garrett looked at her sharply. "Believe me, no one in the middle of a cardiac event would be running *anywhere*."

"Exactly." Helen hesitated. "No one knows for certain what caused Mr. Prescott's death. However, it's possible that Mr. Ransom . . ." Her voice trailed away, the suspicion too terrible to be uttered out loud.

"Why would he do that?" Garrett asked after a long moment. "Do you think he may be on the side of the conspirators?"

"No one knows what side he's on. But he's not a man you should have anything to do with." Helen gave her a worried, affectionate look. "My husband has a saying about risk taking: 'God is good—but never dance in a small boat.'"

THE CLOUD OF gloom that Helen's information had cast over Garrett was not helped the following day when her father waved the latest copy of the *Police*

Gazette beneath her nose, asking pointedly, "What do you make of this, daughter?"

Frowning, Garrett took the newspaper from him, her gaze skimming rapidly over the page.

On Wednesday night, the King's Cross Court holding jail was broken and entered by an unseen intruder, who proceeded to attack a cell of three prisoners. The victims are soldiers in Her Majesty's 9th Regiment of Foot, confined on charges of assault against a lady whose person has not been publicly identified. The intruder escaped before he could be apprehended. All three soldiers will remain in custody without chance of bail until their future appearance at the assizes. Any person giving information to W. Cross, Chief Constable, leading to the apprehension of the unknown offender shall, on his conviction, receive ten pounds reward.

Struggling to conceal the signs of inner chaos, Garrett handed the paper back. Dear God, how could Ransom have attacked three men in custody?

"There's no proof that Mr. Ransom did it," she said crisply.

"Only Jenkyn's men would be capable of going in and out of a heavily guarded court jail without being caught."

Garrett brought herself to meet her father's gaze with difficulty. After recent weight loss, the skin of his formerly full-cheeked face now hung slightly loose, and there were deep pockets under his eyes, and he looked so kind and tired that it made her throat tighten.

"Mr. Ransom can't tolerate any manner of violence against women," she said. "That's no excuse, of course."

"You made light of what happened that night," her father said soberly. "You said those soldiers only insulted you, but it was worse than that, wasn't it?"

"Yes, Papa."

"Then those jackals deserved whatever Ransom did to them. He may be a cold-blooded cutthroat whose soul is bound for hell, but he has my thanks. I'd thrash the bastards myself, if I could."

"I wouldn't approve of you doing that any more than I would him," Garrett informed him, folding her arms. "A vigilante is no better than a thug."

"Is that what you're going to tell him?"

A wry smile edged her lips. "Are you trying to trick me into some kind of admission, Papa? I have no intention of seeing Mr. Ransom again."

Her father snorted and lifted the gazette to continue reading. His voice floated out from behind the rustling pages. "Just because you can look a man in the eyes when you lie doesn't mean you've fooled him."

THE NEXT FEW days were nothing but annoyance and drudgery. Garrett delivered the baby of a department manager's wife, set a broken collarbone, and performed minor surgery to remove a benign tumor, and all of it felt perfunctory. Not even an interesting case of rheumatic effusions of the knee joints could cheer her up. For the first time in Garrett's life, her enthusiasm for work, the thing that had always filled her with purpose and satisfaction, had inexplicably disappeared.

So far, she had managed to avoid dinner with the Ravenels, pleading exhaustion after having stayed up twenty-four hours with the patient in labor, but she knew another invitation would soon be forthcoming, and she would have to accept.

On Tuesday afternoon, as Garrett loaded her bag with supplies for her Tuesday visit to the workhouse, her partner at the clinic approached her.

Although Dr. William Havelock had made no secret of his objections when Winterborne had hired a female physician, he had soon become a mentor and a trusted friend. The middle-aged man, with his distinctive shock of white hair and large, leonine head, was everyone's idea of what a doctor *should* look like. He was a man of remarkable skills and judgment, and Garrett had learned a great deal from him. To his credit, Havelock, despite his gruff manner, was a fair and open-minded man. After some initial resistance, he came to regard Garrett's surgical training at the Sorbonne with interest rather than suspicion, and had soon adopted the antiseptic methods she had learned from Sir Joseph Lister. As a result, the patients at the Cork Street clinic experienced a substantially higher and faster rate of postoperative healing than average.

Garrett looked up as Dr. Havelock came to the doorway of the supply room with two small glass laboratory beakers containing pale gold liquid.

"I've brought you a restorative tonic," he said, coming forward to hand her one of the beakers.

Lifting her brows, Garrett took the beaker and sniffed the contents cautiously. A reluctant smile crossed her lips. "Whiskey?"

"Dewar's whiskey." Regarding her with a shrewd

but kindly gaze, he raised his beaker in a toast. "Happy Birthday."

Garrett's eyes turned round with amazement. Her father hadn't remembered, and she'd never told the date to anyone. "How did you know?"

"The date was on your employment application. Since my wife keeps the files, she knows everyone's birthday, and never forgets a one."

They clinked glasses and drank. The whiskey was strong but very smooth, flavors of malt, honey, and cut hay lingering on Garrett's tongue. Closing her eyes briefly, she felt the soft fire travel down her esophagus. "Excellent," she pronounced, and smiled at him. "And much appreciated. Thank you, Dr. Havelock."

"One more toast: *Neque semper arcum tendit Apollo.*"

They drank again.

"What does that mean?" Garrett asked.

"'Not even Apollo keeps his bow drawn all the time.'" Havelock regarded her kindly. "You've been in a sour mood of late. I don't know the specifics of your problem, but I have an idea as to the general cause. You're a dedicated physician who has shouldered many responsibilities in such a capable manner that all of us, including you, tend to forget something: You're still a young woman."

"At eight and twenty?" Garrett asked bleakly, and took another swallow. Still holding the beaker, she reached for a box of adhesive plasters and dropped it into her bag.

"A mere babe in the woods," he said. "And like all young people, you tend to rebel against a harsh taskmaster."

"I've never thought of you that way," Garrett protested.

Havelock's mouth twisted. "I'm not the harsh taskmaster, Doctor, *you* are. The fact is, recreation is a
natural necessity. Your work habits have turned you
into a wet blanket, and you will continue being a wet
blanket until you find some leisure activity outside of
this clinic."

Garrett frowned. "I have no outside interests."

"If you were a man, I'd advise you to spend a night
at the best bawdy house you could afford. However, I
have no idea what to recommend to a woman in your
position. Look at a list of hobbies and pick one. Have
an affair. Go on holiday to a place you've never been
before."

Garrett coughed on a sip of whiskey, and regarded
him with wide, watering eyes. "Did you just advise me
to have an affair?" she asked hoarsely.

Havelock let out a rusty chuckle. "I've surprised
you, haven't I? Not as stodgy as you thought. There's
no need to stare at me like a dyspeptic nun. As a physician, you're well aware that the sexual act can be
separated from procreation without descending to pros-
titution. You work like a man, you're paid like one,
and you might as well take your pleasures like one, so
long as you're discreet about it."

Garrett had to drain the last of her whiskey before
she could reply. "Moral considerations aside, the risk
isn't worth it. Being caught in an affair wouldn't ruin
a man's career, but it would ruin mine."

"Then find someone to marry. Love is not something to be missed, Dr. Gibson. Why do you think I,
a comfortable widower, made a fool of myself over

Mrs. Fernsby until she finally consented to be my wife?"

"Convenience?" she guessed.

"Good God, no. There's nothing convenient about joining your life to another person's. Marriage is a sack race: you may find a way to hop together toward the finish line, but you would still reach it more easily without the sack."

"Then why do it at all?"

"Our existence, even our intellect, hangs upon love—without it, we would be no more than stock and stones."

Inwardly astonished by such a sentimental speech coming from Havelock, of all men, Garrett protested, "It's no simple task to find someone to love. You make it sound as easy as shopping for a good melon."

"Obviously you've done neither of those things. Finding someone to love is considerably easier than finding a good melon."

Garrett smiled wryly. "I'm sure your advice is well-intentioned, but I have no use for melons or grand love affairs." She handed the empty beaker to him. "However, I'll try to come up with a hobby."

"That's a start." Havelock went to the doorway and paused to glance over his shoulder. "You're very good at listening to other people, my young friend. But you're not nearly as good at listening to yourself."

NIGHT WAS FALLING by the time Garrett had finished her rounds at the Clerkenwell workhouse infirmary. Fatigued and hungry, she removed her white apron and donned her dark brown walking jacket, trimmed with silk braid and cinched with a thin leather belt around the waist. After gathering up her cane and doctor's bag, she left the workhouse and stopped just beyond the iron gate, on a front walkway mottled with light and shadow.

In the weary hush of the summer evening, she started on the walk back to the main road. The wail of a distant train rode on the dull thunder of churning rods, hissing boilers, and metal wheels. Her steps faltered as she realized that she was reluctant to return home. There was no compelling reason to be there: Her father was playing his weekly game of draw poker with his friends and wouldn't miss her. But she couldn't think of where else to go. The clinic and the department store were closed, and it certainly would *not* do to appear uninvited at someone else's home. Her stomach growled beneath the confines of her light corset. She realized she'd forgotten to eat lunch.

One of the cardinal rules of navigating through the dangerous areas of the city was to appear confident. And here she was, pausing at a street corner, her feet as heavy as lead. What was she doing? What was this terrible feeling inside? Sadness, wrapped around yearning. A hollow feeling that no blasted hobby or holiday was ever going to fix.

Perhaps she should go visit Helen unannounced, manners be damned. Helen would listen to her worries, and know what to say. But no . . . that would only lead to more urging to meet Weston Ravenel, a substitute for the man she truly wanted to see . . . an amoral, oversexed government assassin with a dimple in one cheek.

Garrett's mind sifted through remnants of conversations she'd had during the past week.

"No one knows what side he's on. But he's not a man you should have anything to do with."

"Ransom is a cold-blooded cutthroat whose soul is bound for hell . . ."

"If he did meet you in secret, where would it lead?"

And Ransom's low voice . . . *"I see no fault in you."*

As Garrett stood there, trapped in that mysterious ache of a mood, she could hear a couple quarreling on a nearby street, the bray of a donkey, the cries of a watercress seller as he rolled his handcart along the pavement. The accumulated hum of city noise filled each passing second as London eased from the tumult of the day to the seething excitement of a warm summer night. It was a mean, big-bellied, prosperous city, shod in brick and iron, wearing a thick overcoat of factory smoke, carrying a million secrets in its pockets. Garrett loved it, all of it, from the dome of St. Paul's down to the lowest sewer rat. London, her friends, and her work, had always been enough for her. Until now.

"I wish . . ." she whispered, and bit her lip.

Where was Ransom at this moment?

Maybe loving the sewer rat was taking it a bit far.

I wish . . . a phrase she never used.

If she closed her eyes—which she was *not* idiotic enough to do in a parish containing three prisons—she felt as if she might actually be able to see him, like an image trapped in a fortune-teller's crystal ball.

Garrett was bemused to discover the silver police whistle was in her hand. Without even being aware of it, she had fished the whistle from her jacket pocket. The pad of her thumb rubbed across the gleaming surface.

Obeying a lunatic impulse, she raised the whistle

to her lips and gave an abbreviated blow. Not enough to produce a shrill alarm that would alert a constable, just a little chirp. She closed her eyes and counted to three, waiting and listening for an approaching footstep.

Oh, I wish, I wish . . .

Nothing.

Her lashes lifted. No one was there.

It was time to go home. Morosely she tucked the whistle back into her pocket, unhooked the cane from her left arm, and turned to leave.

A smothered exclamation was torn from her as she walked into a wall, the leather bag dropping from her hand. "Suffering savior!"

Not a wall. A man. Her face was mashed against the center of a broad chest.

Before her mind fully comprehended what had happened, her body had already recognized the feel of tough, heavy muscle, the big hands gripping her securely, the clean masculine scent that was nicer than anything in the world. Dark blue eyes took swift and thorough inventory of her, assuring himself of her well-being.

Ransom.

He'd been following her after all. A shaken breath of laughter escaped her. As she looked up into his hard face, exhilaration flooded her as if it had been injected directly into an artery. She was shocked at how good it felt to be with him. Her soul was leaping.

"That whistle is only for when you need help," Ransom said in a low voice. A scowl darkened his face, but his fingertips flexed slightly as if he longed to fondle and caress the shape of her.

Garrett couldn't help smiling up at him. "I do need help," she replied, striving for a normal tone. "I'm hungry."

A hint of raw emotion stirred beneath his controlled surface. "*Acushla*," he said in a rough whisper, "don't do this."

"It's my birthday," she told him.

His hot gaze turned her inside out. "Is it?"

She nodded, trying to look forlorn. "I'm alone and hungry, and it's my birthday."

Ransom uttered a curse as soft as a vesper prayer, and lifted his hand to her face, gently cupping her jaw. The touch of his fingers was so pleasant that she felt a change come over all her skin. After surveying her for a burning moment, he shook his head grimly, as if marveling at a particularly unfortunate turn of fate. He bent to pick up her bag.

"Come," he said.

And she went with him, neither asking nor caring where they were going.

Chapter 6

GARRETT TOOK RANSOM'S ARM as they walked. He was dressed in workingman's clothes, with a vest made of leather as thin and soft as glove material. The muscled surface of his arm was hard beneath her palm. He guided her through streets lined with rows of serried buildings. They passed beer shops, a public house, a chandler's shop, and a store selling second-hand clothes. The street became increasingly populated with sailors and jolly tars, men in greatcoats, shop girls, costers, and well-dressed tradesmen's wives. Garrett relaxed her usual vigilance, knowing that not a soul would dare approach her in the company of a big, healthy bruiser who was so obviously at home in the streets. In fact, *he* was the one who made other people fearful.

Which reminded her about the jail break-in.

"I needn't ask what you've been doing since we last met," she said, "since I read an account of your latest exploit in the *Police Gazette*."

"What exploit?"

"Breaking into the holding jail," she chided. "At-tacking those three soldiers. It was very wrong of you, and quite unnecessary."

"I didn't attack them. There was a bit of a scuffle

at first, but that was only to get their attention while I spent a few minutes blistering their ears."

"You broke in to *scold* them?" she asked skeptically.

"I made it clear that any man who tries to harm you will have me beating hell's torment on him. And if I ever found out they attacked another woman, I told them I'd—" He broke off, apparently thinking better of what he'd been about to say. "Well, I made them afraid to do it again."

"And that's why you were described as an unknown offender? Because they were too terrified to identify you?"

"I'm good at scaring people," he said.

"Apparently, you've appointed yourself judge, jury, and executioner. But all of that should be left in the hands of the British system of justice."

"The law doesn't always work when it comes to men like that. All they understand is fear and retaliation." Ransom paused. "If I had a conscience, it wouldn't be troubled over those bastards. Now, tell me about your visit to the workhouse."

As they walked, Garrett told him about the patients she'd seen in the infirmary, and her worries about the poor conditions of the place. The improper diet of mostly porridge and bread was especially harmful for children, for without sufficient nourishment, their growth would be permanently stunted and they would be vulnerable to disease. And yet her appeals to the workhouse officials had fallen on deaf ears.

"They said if workhouse food were improved, too many people would be pushing their way in to obtain it."

"They say the same about prison food," Ransom said, darkly amused. "Make it too good, the argument goes, and people will commit crimes just to have it. But no one who's ever found himself on the wrong side of a prison door would ever say that. And the only crime someone commits to end up in a workhouse is to be poor."

"Obviously some common sense is needed," Garrett said, "which is why I've decided to go over their heads. I'm compiling a report for the Home Secretary's Office and the Local Government Board, to explain in detail why workhouse administrators should adopt a minimum set of standards. It's a matter of public health."

A faint smile touched his lips. "As busy as a stocking full of fleas," he murmured. "Do you ever make time to enjoy yourself, Doctor?"

"I enjoy my work."

"I meant kicking up your heels now and then."

"I had a similar conversation with Dr. Havelock earlier today," Garrett said with a rueful laugh. "He called me a wet blanket. I suppose you'd agree with him."

Ransom let out a soft breath of amusement. "Do you, now?" he asked. "A wet blanket smothers fire. You're what starts the fire."

That threw her off guard. "Of course, I'm an infamous temptress," she said sardonically. "Anyone could see that."

"You think I'm mocking you?"

"Mr. Ransom, it's one thing for you to pay me a reasonable compliment, but it's quite another to carry on as if I were Cleopatra."

Instead of looking chastened or abashed, Ransom regarded her with a touch of perplexed annoyance. "Come with me," he muttered, taking her arm and urging her toward a narrow lane, where a row of costermongers' wagons and carts had been turned on their ends and chained together, with their shafts aimed upward. A strong aroma of toasted herring and burnt chestnuts wafted from a lodging house nearby.

"Into a dark alley? I think not."

"I'd rather not discuss this on the street."

"There's no need to discuss it. I've made my point."

"And now I'm after making one." Ransom's grip on her arm was very firm. The only reason she didn't twist away was that she was curious about what he would say.

Guiding her into the shadows of an empty doorstep, Ransom set down her bag and cane, and turned toward her. "Whatever else you may think about me," he said gruffly, "I would never play that kind of game with you. The devil knows how you could doubt my attraction to you after our lesson at Baujart's. Or didn't you notice that being near you made me as randy as a prize bull?"

"I noticed," Garrett whispered sharply. "However, the male erection isn't always caused by sexual desire."

His face went blank. "What are you talking about?"

"Spontaneous priapism can be caused by scrotal chafing, traumatic injury to the perineum, a flare-up of gout, an inflamed prostatic duct—" Her list was interrupted as Ransom hauled her against him, front to front.

She was alarmed to feel his entire body shaking. It

wasn't until she heard a ragged chuckle near her ear that she realized he was struggling not to laugh.

"Why is that funny?" she asked, her voice muffled against his chest. He didn't reply, couldn't, only shook his head vehemently and continued to wheeze. Nettled, she said, "As a physician, I can assure you there's nothing humorous about involuntary erections."

That nearly sent him into hysterics.

"Holy God," he begged, "no more doctor-talk. *Please.*"

Garrett held her tongue, waiting while he fought for a measure of control.

"It wasn't from scrotal chafing," Ransom eventually said, a last tremor of laughter running through his voice. Letting out an unsteady sigh, he nuzzled against the side of her head. "Since we don't seem to be mincing words, I'll tell you what caused it: holding a woman I'd already dreamed about more than I should. Being near you is all it takes to put me in high blood. But I've no business wanting you. I shouldn't have come to you tonight."

At first Garrett was too stunned to reply. He wielded honesty like a weapon, she thought dazedly. Now he'd left them nowhere to hide. Coming from a man as secretive as he was, it was astonishing.

"You had no choice," she eventually said. "I summoned you." Her cheek curved against his shoulder as she added, "My genie of the whistle."

"I don't grant wishes," he said.

"A second-rate genie. I should have known I'd get one of those."

A last whisk of amusement sank into her hair, and his fingertip charted the soft rim of her ear.

Garrett's head lifted. As she saw how close his mouth was, and felt the clean, warm rush of his breath, her stomach did an odd little flip.

She'd been kissed before, once by a charming doctor while working as a nurse at St. Thomas's Hospital, and another time by a fellow medical student at the Sorbonne. Both occasions had been something of a disappointment. The sensation of a man's mouth against hers had not been unpleasant, but she certainly hadn't understood how anyone could describe kissing as a rapturous experience.

With Ethan Ransom, though . . . she thought it might be different.

He was still, his gaze locked on hers with an intensity that sent a jolt through her. He was going to kiss her, she thought, and she went weak with anticipation, her heart thudding and pumping.

But he let go of her abruptly, his lips twisting with self-mocking amusement. "I promised you something to eat. We have to keep you in fighting trim."

They went back to the main street and proceeded toward a steady thrum of noise. As they turned a corner, Garrett saw Clerkenwell Green ahead of them, bustling with a massive crowd. All the shop fronts were lit, and at least a hundred temporary market stalls had been set up and trestled in double rows. Originally a village green with walks, trees, and mown lawn, the space was now a paved public gathering place bordered by houses, shops, inns, factories, public houses, and coffee rooms. Near the center of the green, a space had been cleared for dancing jigs, hornpipes, and polkas to the music of fiddles and cornopeans. Street singers wandered through the milling throng, stopping here and there to perform comic songs or sentimental ballads.

Garrett regarded the scene with amazement. "It looks like a Saturday-night market."

"It's to celebrate the new underground London Ironstone line. The railway owner, Tom Severin, is paying out of his own pocket for fairs and concerts across the city."

"Mr. Severin may be taking credit for the celebrations," Garrett said wryly, "but I can assure you, not a shilling of it has come from his own pocket."

Ransom's gaze flashed to her. "You know Severin?"

"I'm acquainted with him," she said. "He's a friend of Mr. Winterborne's."

"But not yours?"

"I would call him a friendly acquaintance." A ripple of delight ran through her as she saw the notch between his brows. Was it possible he was jealous? "Mr. Severin is a schemer," she said. "An opportunist. He contrives everything for his own advantage, even at the expense of his friends."

"A businessman, then," Ransom said flatly.

Garrett laughed. "He certainly is that."

They skirted the crowd and headed to a row of stalls, each independently lit with self-generating gas lamps, grease lamps, or candle flames covered with rush light shades. Food was kept hot in large cans resting on iron firepots, or in tin and brass machines with fragrant steam issuing from little funnels at the top.

"What kind of food would you—" Ransom began, but broke off as his attention was caught by a minor disturbance near a cluster of stands. A plump, rosy-faced young woman wearing a felt hat festooned with colored silk ribbons was clutching a long, flat market basket while a red-haired constable tried to tug it away from her. People were gathering to watch the spectacle, some laughing, others lobbing insults at the constable.

"'Tis Maggie Friel," Ransom said in a rueful tone. "I know the family well—I was friends with her brother. Would you mind if I take care of this?"

"By all means," Garrett said readily.

Ransom strode to the arguing pair, while Garrett followed close behind. "What's this, McSheehy?" he asked the constable.

"I'm confiscatin' her ribbon spool for givin' me sass, is what it is," the officer snapped, wresting the basket from the woman's grasp. It contained threads, scraps of fabric, and a long dowel holding rolls of laces and ribbons.

The sobbing woman turned to Ransom. "He can't take me ribbands just cos I cheeked him, can he?"

"I can, and I will," the constable told her. With his face flushed from outrage and exertion, and his ruddy brows and hair, he was as red as a live coal.

"You great bully," the woman cried. "May the cat eat ye, and the devil eat the cat!"

"Hush now, and hold your clack, Maggie," Ransom interrupted quietly. "*Colleen*, would it harm you to speak more kindly to a man who's charged with keeping the peace?" As she made to reply, he raised his hand in a staying gesture and turned to the constable, his voice lowering. "Bill, you know selling those ribbons is her livelihood. Taking them from her is the same as taking bread from her mouth. Have a heart, man."

"She called me a dispargin' name one time too many."

"Bandy-Shanks?" Maggie taunted. "Ye mean that one?"

The constable's eyes narrowed.

"Maggie," Ransom warned softly, sending the woman a meaningful glance. "Stop cheekin' the poor man. If I were you, I'd make peace and offer him a length of ribbon for his sweetheart."

"I have no sweetheart," the constable muttered.

"'Tis shocked I am," Maggie said acidly.

Ransom chucked her beneath the chin with a gentle forefinger.

Heaving a sigh, Maggie turned to the constable. "Oh, fie, I'll give ye a ribband, then."

"What would I do with it?" McSheehy asked with a frown.

"Are ye daft?" she demanded. "D'ye know nothing about sweetheartin'? Give it to a girl ye fancy, and say it flatters her eyes."

Grudgingly the policeman handed the basket back to her.

"*Slán*, Éatán," Maggie said as she began measuring out a length from the spool.

As Ransom drew Garrett away with him, she asked, "What did she say to you?"

"The Irish are superstitious about using the word *good-bye*. Instead we say *slán,* which means 'go in safety.'"

"And the other word? . . . *Ay-ah-tahn*. What does that mean?"

"Éatán is how the Irish say my name."

Garrett thought the three syllables were lovely, with

a musical lilt. "I like that," she said gently. "But your last name . . . Ransom . . . that's English, isn't it?"

"There have been Ransoms in Westmeath for over three hundred years. Don't make me prove I'm Irish in public, lass—it would prove embarrassing to us both."

"No need," she assured him, a grin crossing her face.

His free hand slid to the small of her back as they walked. "Have you been to Clerkenwell Green before?"

"Not for a long time." Garrett nodded toward a tidy church with a single tower and spire, set on a hilly rise above the green. "That's St. James, isn't it?"

"Aye, and over there stands Canonbury House, where the Lord Mayor lived with his daughter Elizabeth long ago." Ransom pointed toward a manor in the distance. "When he found out Elizabeth had fallen in love with young Lord Compton, he forbade her to marry, and shut her in the tower. But Compton managed to sneak her out of the house and carry her off in a baker's basket, and they wed soon after."

"How could she fit inside?" Garrett asked skeptically.

"A baker's basket used to be large enough for a man to carry on his back."

"I still can't picture it."

"'Twould be an easy matter if she were like you." His glinting gaze slid over her slim form as he added, "Pocket size."

Unaccustomed to being teased, Garrett laughed and turned pink.

As they made their way past stalls and carts, Garrett heard a variety of accents: Irish, Welsh, Italian, and French. Ransom knew many of the hawkers and peddlers, and bantered back and forth with them, exchanging friendly insults. More than once, Garrett was slyly warned about keeping company with "yon soople-tongued rascal," or "that pretty-faced vagabone," and was offered no end of advice about how to bring such a troublesome young man to heel.

The variety of wares was staggering: stacks of brown haddock fried in batter, pea soup crowded with chunks of salt pork, smoking-hot potatoes split and doused with butter, oysters roasted in the shell, pickled whelks, and egg-sized suet dumplings heaped in wide shallow bowls. Meat pasties had been made in half-circle shapes convenient for hand carrying. Dried red saveloy and polony sausages, cured tongue, and cuts of ham seamed with white fat were made into sandwiches called trotters.

Farther along the rows, there was an abundance of sweets: puddings, pastries, buns crossed with fat white lines of sugar, citron cakes, chewy gingerbread nuts dabbed with crackled icing, and tarts made with currants, gooseberries, rhubarb, or cherries.

Ransom guided Garrett from one stand to the next, buying whatever caught her interest: a paper cone filled with hot green peas and bacon, and a nugget of plum dough. He coaxed her to taste a spicy Italian veal stew called *stuffata*, which was so delicious that she ate an entire cup of it. Nothing, however, could induce her to try a bite of *spaghetti*, a plate of long white squiggly things, swimming in cream.

"No, thank you," she said, eyeing it uneasily.

"It's like macaroni," Ransom insisted, "only cut into cords instead of tubes."

Garrett shrank from the sight of the unfamiliar food. "It looks like worms."

"It's not worms. It's made of flour and eggs. Have a taste."

"No, I can't. I truly can't." Garrett blanched as she watched him twirl a long strand around the fork tines. "Dear God, please don't eat it in front of me."

Ransom was laughing. "Are you so squeamish? And you a doctor?"

"Take it away," she begged.

He shook his head with a rueful grin. "Wait here." After handing the tin plate to a pair of boys standing near the stall, he paused to purchase something else. He returned and gave her a beverage in a brown glass bottle.

"Ginger beer?" she guessed.

"*Brachetto rosso.*"

Garrett took a tentative swallow and gave a little hum of appreciation at the taste of sweet red wine. She continued to drink from the bottle as they walked along the edge of the crowd that had gathered in the center of the green. "What is everyone waiting for?" she asked.

"You'll find out soon." Ransom led her to the west side, where the imposing sessions house loomed, its classical pediment supported by gigantic columns.

"My former headmistress, Miss Primrose, would be appalled if she could see me," Garrett commented with a grin. "She always said that eating in the street was evidence of low breeding."

"Where did you go to school?"

"In Highgate. My Aunt Maria paid for my tuition at an experimental boarding school. They taught girls the same subjects taught to boys: mathematics, Latin, and science."

"So that's how the trouble started," Ransom said. "No one told you that girls can't learn science."

Garrett laughed. "As a matter of fact, my father's entire family said that. They were outraged by the idea of sending me to such a place. My grandmother said education would strain the female mind so severely, I would be left mentally and physically enfeebled for the rest of my life. Not only that, my future children would be debilitated as well! But Aunt Maria persisted, bless her. My father eventually went along with the plan, mostly because I'd reached the age of ten and he didn't know what to do with me."

They came to the sessions house, and Ransom drew her into a sheltered space between a gigantic column and the grand flight of stone stairs. It was cool and dark, and slightly dank with the scents of stone and rust.

After setting down the doctor's bag and cane, Ransom turned to face her, his gaze steady and interested. "Did you like boarding school?"

"I did. I was grateful to be given a real education. It changed my life." Garrett set her back against the staircase wall and took another swallow of wine before continuing pensively. "Of course, living at boarding school wasn't the same as having a family. The students were discouraged from forming attachments to the teachers. If we were distressed or sad, we kept it to ourselves and tried to stay busy. Miss Primrose wanted us to learn endurance and self-reliance." She paused, her teeth catching lightly at her lower lip. "Sometimes I think . . . perhaps . . . I may have taken those lessons too much to heart."

"Why do you say that?" Ransom leaned a shoulder against the wall as he looked down at her, his big, sheltering form very close.

Garrett was chagrined to realize how much she'd been talking. "I'm being tiresome, babbling on and on about my childhood. Let's change the subject. How do you—"

"I like the subject," Ransom interrupted, his voice lowering to a velvety pitch. "Tell me what you were going to say."

Garrett drank again to bolster her nerve before replying. "It's only that I . . . tend to keep others at a distance. Even with a good friend like Lady Helen, I hold back things that I know would shock or distress her. My work . . . the way it's shaped me . . . and perhaps having lost a mother . . . I can't seem to be close to people."

"'Tis a habit, is all." The glow of a streetlamp found sapphire gleams in the depths of his eyes. "Someday you'll trust someone enough to let down your guard. And then there'll be no holding back."

They were interrupted as a young girl walked along the pavement in front of the sessions house, calling, "Flowers! Fresh-cut flowers!" She stopped in front of them. "Posy for the lady, sir?"

Ransom turned to the girl, who wore a colorful scarf over her long dark hair and a patchwork apron over her black dress. She carried a flat basket filled with posyes, their stems wrapped with bits of colored ribbon.

"There's no need—" Garrett began, but Ransom ignored her, browsing over the tiny bouquets of roses, narcissus, violets, forget-me-nots, and dianthus.

"How much?" he asked the flower girl.

"A farthing, sir."

He glanced at Garrett over his shoulder. "Do you like violets?"

"I do," she said hesitantly.

Ransom gave the flower-girl a sixpence and picked out one of the posyes.

"Thank you, sir!" The girl scurried away as if fearing he might change his mind.

Ransom turned to Garrett with the cluster of purple blossoms. Reaching for the lapel of her walking jacket, he deftly tucked the ribbon-wrapped stem of the posy into a buttonhole.

"Violets make an excellent blood-purifying tonic," Garrett said awkwardly, feeling the need to fill the silence. "And they're good for treating cough or fever."

The elusive dimple appeared in his cheek. "They're also becoming to green-eyed women."

Self-consciously she glanced down at the posy and touched one of the velvety petals. "Thank you," she murmured. "This is the first time a man's ever given me flowers."

"Ah, darlin' . . ." His perceptive gaze searched her face. "Do you intimidate men so badly, then?"

"I do, I'm horrid," Garrett confessed, and a mischievous laugh broke out. "I'm independent and opinionated, and I love telling people what to do. I have no feminine delicacy. My occupation either offends or frightens men, or sometimes both." She shrugged and smiled. "So I've never been given so much as a single dandelion. But it's been worth it to live as I choose."

Ransom stared at her as if spellbound. "A queen, you are," he said softly. "I could travel the world the rest of my life, and not find another woman with half your ways."

Garrett's knees seemed to have turned into isinglass. Somewhere in her dissolving brain, it occurred to her that there was a reason she felt so warm and chatty and comfortable. Frowning, she held out the wine bottle and regarded it suspiciously.

"I've had enough of this," she said, handing it to him. "I don't want to become tipsy."

His brows lifted. "You've scarce had enough to make a field mouse tipsy."

"It's not just the wine. Dr. Havelock poured a glass of birthday whiskey for me earlier. And I must keep my wits about me."

"For what?"

She floundered for a reason but fell silent.

Ransom drew her deeper into the shadows. His hand pressed her head to his shoulder, against the soft, supple leather of his vest. She felt him stroke her cheek gently, as if he were smoothing the wing of a small bird or the easily torn petals of a poppy. The sweet scent of violets clung to his fingers. For the rest of her life, she thought hazily, that smell would bring her back to this moment.

"You're used to being in charge," he murmured, "every second of the day. With no one to catch you if you set a foot wrong." His voice curled around her ear, making her shiver. "But I'm giving you the night off. You'll have my arms to hold you steady. Drink more wine, if you like. There'll be music and dancing later. I'll buy a ribbon for your hair, and waltz you across the green at midnight. What do you say to that?"

"I say we'd look a fine pair of fools," Garrett said.

But she let herself relax into the power and heat of him, conforming bonelessly to the hard framework of his body.

A brush of silky warmth against her temple raised the little hairs on her arms and the back of her neck. The movements of her breathing pressed into the rise and fall of his chest until the rhythms blended. She was distantly aware of other couples nearby, indulging in bits of amorous fondling and a stolen kiss or two. Before tonight, Garrett had never understood why people indulged in such shameless behavior in public. Now she did. Shadows didn't always harbor fearful things. Sometimes shadows were the only place for a little magic to hide.

People were dimming streetlamps. The lights in shop windows and public houses were vanishing. A woman was singing somewhere nearby—one of the street entertainers, performing a ballad in Gaelic. Her voice was supple and airy, weaving an intricate melody that fell on the ear like an audible heartbreak.

"What is that song?" Garrett asked.

"Donal Og. One of my mam's favorites."

"What do the lyrics mean?"

Ransom seemed reluctant to answer. After a long moment, he began to translate quietly near her ear. "Black as coal is the grief all around me. You've stolen the future and past from me, you took the East and West from me. The sun, moon, and stars from my sky you've taken—and God as well, if I'm not mistaken."

Garrett was too moved to speak.

Ethan Ransom could never fit in with the pattern of her life as it was now, nor in any of its possible future shapes. He was an anomaly, dazzling and temporary.

A shooting star, burning up from the friction of its own velocity.

But she wanted this man. She wanted him with an intensity that was beginning to make a number of deranged ideas seem like sensible plans of action.

The crowd occupying the green was stirring in anticipation. Carefully Ransom began to turn Garrett to face away from him, ignoring her muffled protests.

"Turn around," he insisted, "so you'll be able to see."

"See what?" she asked, wanting to stay against him just as she was. Ransom pulled her back firmly against his chest and crossed an arm around her waist. Before another minute had passed, a long, ear-splitting whistle cut through the air, punctuated by a crackling burst of blue sparks in the upper vault of darkness. Garrett started reflexively, and Ransom clamped his arm more securely around her, his chuckle tickling her ear.

The sky over central London exploded with a simultaneous release of approximately three dozen aerial maroon rockets. Exhilarated cries and cheers erupted from the crowd as pyrotechnic volleys pierced the air: fiery tourbillion spirals, plumes, shells, and rains of colored stars. Elfin light danced over the crowd on the green.

Garrett leaned against Ransom, her head tilted back on his shoulder. She was suffused with a feeling that slid back and forth between happiness and wonder, like one of the shot silk fabrics that appeared to change colors when viewed from different angles. Was this really happening? Instead of being safe at home in bed, she was in the middle of the city at night, breathing in air perfumed with violets and the faint char of phosphorous, watching fireworks with a man's arms around her.

Even through the layers of their clothing, she could feel the resilient toughness of his flesh, his muscles flexing subtly to accommodate her slightest movement. His head dipped lower, until she felt a soft, hot pressure at the side of her neck.

A shiver went through her, as fine and distinct as the vibration of a harp string. His mouth found an unbearably sensitive place and lingered in an erotic caress that made her toes curl inside her sensible walking boots. When she made no objection, his lips slid lower, his night beard a prickle of velvet as it brushed the tender skin. Another kiss, careful and slow, as if to soothe the wild velocity of her pulse. Hot darts of feeling went down her spine and radiated through every soft place in her body. The palms of her hands and the backs of her knees grew damp, and an unexpected, mortifying twitch awakened between her thighs.

All awareness sank down to the kisses he strung along the side of her throat. Every throb of her heart sent fire through her veins. Her legs wobbled with the alarming inclination to buckle, but his arms anchored her firmly. She tensed, quivered, bit back a gasp. Eventually his head lifted and one of his hands went to the front of her throat. His fingertips explored lightly, weaving hot and cold chills across her skin.

She became dimly aware that the last celestial glints were floating downward. The crowd broke apart, some returning to swarm the food stalls, while others gathered near the center of the green, where a band had begun to play. Ransom continued to hold Garrett, the two of them concealed in the shadowy nook at the front of the sessions house. They watched people clap and dance. Fathers and mothers hoisted children onto their shoulders, groups of elderly women sang well-remembered songs, old men puffed on their pipes, and boys ran about in search of mischief.

Ransom spoke absently, his cheek pressed against her hair. "To the politicians and bluebloods, we're all alike. They think the working man is a beast of burden with no wit or soul. The pain of loss must not cut him as deep, they think, because he's so used to hardship. But there's as much tender feeling and honor in any of these people as there is in a duke and his kin. They're not pawns. None of them deserves to be sacrificed."

"Sacrificed by whom?" Garrett asked.

"Selfish bastards who only give a damn about their own power and profit."

She was silent for a moment, wondering if the "selfish bastards" were men he worked for. Perhaps he was referring to members of Parliament who were against Irish independence. Which side of the "Irish question" was he on? Did he have sympathy for secret societies such as the one that plotted the Guildhall bombing? It was difficult to believe he would conspire to harm innocent people, especially after what he'd just said. But she couldn't deny that she was too blinded by her own attraction to have any objectivity about who or what he really was.

Garrett turned to face him, wondering whether or not she wanted to know the truth about him. *Don't be a coward,* she told herself, and looked directly into his eyes. "Éatán . . ." She felt the subtle tightening of his grip. "I've heard rumors about you and your work. I don't know what to believe. But—"

"Don't ask." Ransom's hands dropped away from her. "You'd be a fool to trust any answer I gave you."

"You would lie to me?"

"I lie to everyone."

"Still, I must ask about the night of the Guildhall reception . . . the man who died . . . did you have anything to do with that?"

His fingertips touched her lips to silence her.

"Would the truth make me think better or worse of you?" she persisted.

"It doesn't matter. Tomorrow we'll be strangers again. As if tonight never happened."

There was no mistaking the finality in his voice.

In the past, whenever there had been a conflict between Garrett's head and her heart, her head always won. This time, however, her heart was putting up a ripping fight. She couldn't fathom how she was going to make herself accept such an abrupt end to the promise of a relationship unlike anything she'd ever experienced.

"I don't see how that's possible," she said.

"We both know I'm not for the likes of you," Ransom said quietly. "Someday you'll have a good, decent husband of the ould stock, who'll give you a fireside of children, and take you to church of a Sunday. A man with some softness to him."

"I'll thank you to let me choose my own companion," Garrett said. "If I took a husband, I certainly wouldn't choose some milksop."

"Don't mistake softness for weakness. Only a strong man can be soft with a woman."

Garrett responded with a distracted flick of her hand, having no patience for aphorisms when so many thoughts were colliding in her head. "Also, I don't plan to have children. I have a career. Not every woman's destiny is to go from maidenhood to motherhood."

Ransom tilted his head, studying her. "The men of your profession can have a family. Why can't you?"

"Because—no, I won't be drawn into a diversionary argument. I want to talk with you."

"We are talking."

A mixture of impatience and desire had made her reckless. "Not here. Somewhere private. Do you have a rented room? A flat?"

"I can't take you where I live."

"Why not? Is it dangerous there?"

Ransom took an unaccountably long time to reply. "For you, it is."

Every inch of Garrett's skin heated in the darkness. She could still feel the places on her neck where he'd kissed, as if his lips had left invisible scorch marks. "That doesn't worry me."

"It should."

Garrett was silent. The air felt tight and thin, as if the oxygen had been pressed out of it. Tonight had turned out to be one of the happiest nights of her life, a gift that had somehow fallen into her hands. She had never bothered much over the question of her own happiness, having been far too busy working toward her goals.

She had just become a cliché, a lovelorn woman of spinsterish age falling for a handsome and mysterious stranger. But in time, Ethan Ransom's dark and dangerous allure would probably vanish, and he would seem entirely ordinary to her. A man no different from any other man.

As she looked up into his shadowed face, however, she thought, *He would never seem ordinary to me, even if he were ordinary.*

And she heard herself asking, "Would you escort me home, please?"

Chapter 7

No MATTER THE TIME of day or night, a ride in a hansom cab was a breakneck dash that made conversation impossible. The vehicles typically careened and swayed with violent disregard for the laws of traffic or physics, rounding corners so recklessly one could feel the wheels lifting from the street.

However, Garrett Gibson, well versed in the hazards of hansom cabs, was unperturbed. She sat braced in the corner of the seat, stoically observing the passing scenery.

Ethan stole covert glances at her, unable to interpret her mood. She'd turned quiet after he'd refused to answer her question about the night of the Guildhall reception. He guessed that she was beginning to grasp how unsavory a character he was, and had come to her senses. *Good.* From now on, she would want him to stay away from her.

If there was one thing this night had made clear, it was exactly how great a danger Garrett posed for him. He wasn't himself around her . . . or perhaps the problem was that he *was* himself. Either way, she was making him unfit for his job at the time he most needed to be dispassionate.

"The secret to staying alive," another of Jenkyn's

men, William Gamble, had once said to him, "is not giving a damn."

It was true. If you started to care, it changed the reactive choices you made, even about small things such as dodging to the left or the right. In his line of work, a man's desire to preserve his own life was usually the thing that doomed him. So far, it had never been a problem for Ethan to remain more or less philosophical about his future: when your number was up, it was up.

But lately that necessary dispassion had begun to unravel. He'd caught himself wanting things he knew better than to want. Tonight he'd behaved like a besotted lunatic, flirting and lusting after Garrett Gibson. Running to her like a well-trained sheepdog as soon as she'd whistled. Accompanying her out in public, and watching pyrotechnics with his hands wandering all over her. He'd lost his bloody mind, taking such chances.

But how could any man keep his wits around such a woman? Garrett had bewitched him like a love charm on a May-morning. She was at once respectable and subversive, worldly and innocent. Hearing her say "involuntary erection" in that crisp, ladylike voice had been the high point of his year.

He wanted her so badly, it had put the heart crossways in him. This woman, in his bed, spread beneath him . . . he actually trembled at the thought of it. She would try so hard not to lose her dignity even as he teased it away from her, little by little, kissing the spaces between her toes, the soft creases behind her knees—

Enough, he told himself grimly. She wasn't his. She would never be his.

They approached a row of identical Georgian-style terrace houses. It was an orderly middle-class street with a paved walk and a few weatherbeaten trees. The vehicle came to a rattling, jingling halt in front of a crimson-bricked house with a separate railed basement entrance for servants and deliverymen. One of the upper floors was brilliantly lit, the sound of men's voices drifting through an open window. Three men . . . no, four.

Ethan descended from the hansom with the doctor's bag and cane. He reached up to Garrett. Although she didn't need assistance, she took his hand and alighted from the vehicle with an agility that even a corset couldn't constrain.

"Wait here," Ethan told the driver, "while I escort the lady to her door."

"Cost extra for the waitin'," the driver warned, and Ethan responded with a short nod.

Garrett looked up at him with the clear-eyed seriousness that captivated him a thousand times more than any come-hitherish pout or seductive glance. She had the most direct stare of any woman he'd ever met. "Will you come inside with me, Mr. Ransom?"

The momentum of fate ground to a halt. Ethan knew he should walk away from her. No, he should break into a full-bore run. Instead, he hesitated.

"You have guests," he said reluctantly, his gaze flickering to the upper windows.

"It's only my father's weekly draw poker game. He and his friends usually stay upstairs until midnight. My surgery takes up most of the ground floor—we can talk privately there."

Ethan hesitated. He'd begun the evening intending

to follow this woman at a safe distance, and now he was considering going into her house, with her father and his friends there. How the hell had it come to this?

"*Acushla*," he began gruffly, "I can't—"

"I have an operating room, and a small laboratory," Garrett continued in an offhand tone.

His curiosity was sparked by the mention of the laboratory. "What do you keep in there?" he couldn't keep from asking. "Rats and rabbits? Dishes of bacteria?"

"I'm afraid not." Her lips quirked. "I use the laboratory for mixing medicines and sterilizing equipment. And viewing microscopic slides."

"You have a microscope?"

"The most advanced medical microscope available," she said, seeing his interest. "With two eyepieces, German lenses, and an achromatic condenser to correct distortion." She grinned at his expression. "I'll show it to you. Have you ever seen a butterfly's wing magnified a hundred times?"

The cabbie had been following the conversation attentively. "Lad, are you daft a'thegither?" he asked from his perch. "Don't stand there like stuffed beef—go inside with the lady!"

Giving him a narrow-eyed glance, Ethan handed up a few coins and sent the hansom away. He found himself following Garrett to the front of the house. "I won't stay for long," he muttered. "And devil take you if you try to introduce me to anyone."

"I won't. Although we won't be able to avoid my cookmaid."

As Garrett fished a key from the pocket of her

walking jacket, Ethan ran an assessing glance over the front door. A brass plate emblazoned with the name *Dr. G. Gibson* had been affixed to one of the upper panels. His gaze slid lower, and he was almost startled by the sight of an iron rim-mounted box lock beside the door handle. He hadn't seen a design that ancient since he'd apprenticed for the prison locksmith.

"Wait," he said before Garrett unlocked the door. Frowning, he handed her the bag and cane, and lowered to his haunches to have a better look. The primitive lock was laughably inadequate for a street door, and had probably been installed when the house had first been built. "This is an old-fashioned warded lock," he said incredulously.

"Yes, a good, stout one," Garrett said, sounding pleased.

"*No*, there's nothing good about it! It doesn't even have tumblers. You might as well not have a lock." Appalled, Ethan continued to examine the ancient contraption. "Why hasn't your father done anything about this? He should know better."

"We've had no problem with it."

"Only by the grace of God." Ethan became more agitated by the second as he realized she went to sleep every night with nothing but a crude rattletrap lock between her and the entire criminal population of London. His heart began to beat fast with anxiety. He'd seen what could happen to women who didn't have sufficient protection from the predators of the world. And Garrett was a public figure who attracted both admiration and controversy. Someone could enter the house so damned easily, and do whatever they wished with her. He couldn't bear to think about it.

Garrett stood there with a skeptical smile, seeming to think he was overreacting.

In his agony of worry, Ethan couldn't find the words to make her understand. Still crouching in front of the door, he gestured toward Garrett's tiny hat, which was little more than a flattened velvet circle decorated with a twist of ribbon and a knot of small feathers. "Give me that."

Her eyebrows lifted. "My hat?"

"Your hatpin." He waited with his hand extended upward.

Looking mystified, Garrett extracted the long pin that attached the hat to her coiffure. It was topped with a small brass medallion.

Taking the pin, Ethan bent the blunted needle tip into a forty-five-degree angle. He inserted it into the lock and twisted deftly. Five seconds later, the warded lock clicked open. After withdrawing the makeshift pick, he rose to his feet and gave it back to her.

"I believe you unlocked that door more quickly with a hatpin than I could with my key," Garrett exclaimed, regarding the bent hatpin with a slight frown. "How skilled you are."

"That's not the point. Any clumsy halfwit of a burglar could do what I just did."

"Oh." Her lips pursed thoughtfully. "Perhaps I should invest in a new lock?"

"*Aye*. One that was made this century!"

To his exasperation, Garrett didn't appear alarmed in the least. Her eyes crinkled at the corners. "You're very kind to be concerned for my safety. But my father is a former constable."

"He's too old to leap a gate," Ethan said indignantly. "And I can defend myself quite—"

"*Don't*," he warned in an ominous tone, certain he would explode if she gave him another of her confident little speeches about how well she could look after herself and how indestructible she was, and how she had nothing to fear from anyone because she knew how to twirl a cane. "You need to change the lock right away, and take down that brass plate on the door."

"Why?"

"Your name is on it."

"But all doctors have these," she protested. "If I removed it, my patients couldn't find me."

"Why don't you just paste an advertisement on your door saying 'Defenseless Woman with Free Pharmaceutical Supplies'?" Before she could reply, he continued, "Why aren't there iron window guards on the basement and ground-floor levels?"

"Because I'm trying to attract patients," she said, "not scare them away."

Ethan rubbed the lower part of his jaw, brooding. "Strangers coming and going," he muttered, "with nothing to stop them from doing as they please. What if you let a lunatic in here?"

"Lunatics need health care too," Garrett said reasonably.

He gave her a speaking glance. "Do the windows have sash locks, at least?"

"I think some of them do . . ." she said vaguely. At his quiet curse, she said in a soothing tone, "You really mustn't worry: it's not as if we're keeping the crown jewels in here."

"You're the jewel," he said gruffly.

Garrett stared at him with wide, unblinking eyes, while the moment turned awkwardly intimate.

No one in Ethan's adult life had ever truly known him, not even Jenkyn. But as he stood there on Garrett Gibson's doorstep, caught in her searching gaze, he realized he could hide nothing from her. Everything he felt was there for her to read.

Hell and damnation.

"Come inside," Garrett said gently.

Ethan followed her, worried about what else he might do or say. After closing the door, he stood in the entranceway with his cap in hand and watched, fascinated, as she removed her gloves with little tugs at the fingertips. Her beautiful hands emerged from the dyed kid leather, her fingers slender and elegantly precise, like a watchmaker's tools.

The sound of footsteps heralded the approach of someone from the basement level. A mob-capped and white-aproned woman appeared, plump and buxom, with ruddy cheeks and lively brown eyes. "Evenin', Dr. Gibson," she said, taking Garrett's gloves and hat. "You're home late tonight." She glanced in Ethan's direction, and her eyes widened. "Sir," she said breathlessly, and bobbed a curtsy. "May I take your cap?"

Ethan responded with a shake of his head. "I'll be leaving soon."

"This man is a patient," Garrett told the cookmaid, removing the posy of violets from the buttonhole of her walking jacket before handing the garment to her. "I've brought him here for a consultation—please see that we're not disturbed."

"Consultation for what?" the maid asked slyly, her

gaze traveling from Ethan's head to his toes, and back up again. "'E don't look all that peaked to me."

Garrett's brows lowered. "You know better than to comment on a patient's appearance."

Leaning toward her, the cookmaid said in a stage whisper, "I meant to say I 'opes you can do something for this poor, sickly wreck of a man."

"That will be all, Eliza," Garrett said firmly. "You may go."

Amused by the cookmaid's impudence, Ethan studied the floor and fought to suppress a smile.

After Eliza had gone back downstairs, Garrett said with chagrin, "She's not usually so impertinent. No, never mind: she is." She led him to the open room at the right of the entranceway. "This is the waiting area for patients and their families."

As she busied herself with closing the raised-panel shutters, Ethan wandered through the spacious room, which was furnished with a long, low settee, a pair of deep upholstered armchairs, and a pair of small tables. There was a fireplace with a white painted mantel, an escritoire desk, and a cheerful painting of a country scene. Everything was immaculate, the woodwork polished and gleaming, the glass windows sparkling. To Ethan, most houses were stifling and uncomfortable, the floors crowded with furniture, the walls lined with fussy wallpaper. But this place was serene and soothing. He went to look closely at the painting, which portrayed a parade of fat white geese strolling past the doorway of a cottage.

"Someday I'll be able to afford real art," Garrett said, coming to stand beside him. "In the meantime, we'll have to make do with this."

Ethan's attention was drawn to the tiny initials in the corner of the work: *G.G.* A slow smile broke over his face. "You painted it?"

"Art class, at boarding school," she admitted. "I wasn't bad at sketching, but the only subject I could manage to paint adequately was geese. At one point I tried to expand my repertoire to ducks, but those earned lower marks, so it was back to geese after that."

Ethan smiled, imagining her as a studious school-girl with long braids. The light of a glass-globe parlor lamp slid across the tidy pinned-up weight of her hair, bringing out gleams of red and gold. He'd never seen anything like her skin, fine and poreless, with a faint glow like a blush-colored garden rose.

"What gave you the idea to paint geese in the first place?" he asked.

"There was a goose pond across from the school," Garrett said, staring absently at the picture. "Sometimes I saw Miss Primrose at the front windows, watching with binoculars. One day I dared to ask her what she found so interesting about geese, and she told me they had a capacity for attachment and grief that rivaled humans. They mated for life, she said. If a goose was injured, the gander would stay with her even if the rest of the flock was flying south. When one of a mated pair died, the other would lose its appetite and go off to mourn in solitude." Her slim shoulders hitched in a shrug. "I've liked geese ever since then."

"So do I," Ethan said. "Especially roasted with chestnut stuffing."

Garrett laughed. "In this household," she warned, "poultry is not a subject to be treated lightly." Her eyes crinkled as she crooked her finger at him. "I'll show you the surgery."

They went to the operating room at the back of the house. Astringent smells laced the air: carbolic acid, alcohol, benzene, and other chemicals he couldn't identify. Garrett lit a series of oxyhydrogen lamps, until a brilliant glow chased shadows from the tiled floors and glass-paneled walls, and bounced from reflectors overhead. An operating table built on a cabinet base occupied the center of the room. In the corner, a metal stand sprouted arms with reflective mirrors affixed to rack movements and ball pivots, the whole of it resembling a mechanical octopus.

"I use the methods developed by Sir Joseph Lister," Garrett said, glancing around the room with pride. "I attended a class he taught at the Sorbonne, and assisted in some of his operations. His work is based on Pasteur's theory that wounds suppurate because of germs that enter the body and multiply. My surgical equipment and supplies are always sterilized, and I dress wounds with antiseptic fluids and gauze. All of it gives my patients a far greater chance of survival."

Ethan wondered at her willingness to take on the responsibility of life or death, even knowing the outcome would sometimes be tragic. "How do you manage the pressure?" he asked quietly.

"One becomes used to it. And there are times when the risk and the nerves help me to perform at a level I didn't know I could reach."

"I understand," he murmured.

"Yes . . . I'm sure you do."

Their gazes met, and a flush of warmth swept over him. She was so beautiful, with those upward-slanting cheekbones balancing the strength of her jawline. And the softly erotic curves of her mouth. "Doctor," he said with difficulty, "I should probably—"

"The laboratory is over here," Garrett interrupted, walking to another part of the room to push back a folding partition. She lit another of those scientific lamps, illuminating a space that included a stoneware sink with a hot- and cold-water supply, a heavy copper drying oven with burner plates, metal tables, and marble surfaces, and meticulously organized shelves containing bins, dishes, flasks, and intricate appliances.

Busying herself at the sink, Garrett started a flow of water. Ethan went to her side, almost dragging his feet in his reluctance. She had stuck the violet posy he'd given her into a test tube filled with water. After fitting the glass cylinder into one of the holes of a wooden rack, she removed a microscope from a rosewood case and set it beside the lamp. "Have you used one of these before?" she asked.

"Once. It belonged to a chemist on Fleet Street."

"For what purpose?"

"I needed help to examine evidence." Ethan watched as she adjusted tiny mirrors and lenses. "Back when I was still with K division, I was looking into an unsolved murder case. A man was said to have committed suicide with his own folding razor, which was found on the floor next to his body. But the razor was almost fully closed. It made no sense that he would have tried to fold the blade after slitting his own throat."

Ethan regretted the words instantly. It was not at

all appropriate conversation, given the company and the circumstances.

"How deep was the cut?" she surprised him by asking.

"Both carotids and jugulars were severed."

"Instantly fatal, then," Garrett said. "If it had been suicide, he wouldn't have lived long enough to close the razor."

Ethan began to enjoy the novelty of having such a discussion with a woman. "The main suspect was a brother-in-law," he told her, "who had both motive and opportunity. Within a few hours after the crime had been committed, he was found with a bloodstain on the sleeve of his coat. He claimed he'd visited a butcher's shop that afternoon, and had gotten the stain when his sleeve had dragged the counter. There was no way to prove whether the blood was animal or human. The case was set aside, and the evidence was stored in the division office's property room. After I read the file, I took the razor and a sample of the bloodstained fabric to a chemist, who examined them with a microscope. He found two kinds of fiber caught in the sawtooth edge on the back of the razor. One of them was a perfect match for the blue wool coat."

"And the other?"

"A strand of hair from a white poodle. It turned out that the brother-in-law owned just such a dog, and the hair had transferred from his coat to the murder weapon. He broke down and confessed under questioning."

"It was clever of you to approach the case in a scientific manner."

Ethan shrugged, trying to conceal his pleasure at Garrett's admiring gaze.

"You may be interested to learn that now there *is* a way to distinguish animal blood from human," she said. "In birds, fish, and reptiles, the blood corpuscles are oval-shaped, whereas in mammals, including humans, the corpuscles are circular. Furthermore, human ones are larger in diameter than most other creatures."

"How do you know so much about blood cells?"

"I'm trying to learn all I can." A shadow spread across her expression. "My father has a disorder of the blood."

"Is it serious?" Ethan asked gently.

She responded with the tiniest possible nod.

Understanding the grief that awaited her, knowing she must always be aware of it looming in the not-too-distant future, Ethan wanted to reach for her. He wanted to hold her and promise he would be there to help her through it. The fact that he couldn't struck a note of anger—always the most easily accessible of his emotions—and he felt all his muscles tighten.

They both glanced toward the closed surgery door as they heard the creaks and thumps of heavy feet descending the stairs. Multiple voices filled the entranceway. From the sound of it, the men who'd been playing cards with Garrett's father were departing.

"Eliza," one of them asked, "why didn't Dr. Gibson come up to visit as usual?"

"The doctor came in late tonight, sir," came the maid's reply.

"Where is she? I should like to bid her good evening, at least."

The maid's voice ratcheted to a higher pitch. "Oh, you can't, Mr. Gleig, she's with a patient."

"At this hour?" another man asked, sounding disgruntled.

"Indeed, Mr. Oxley." In a moment of inspiration, Eliza added, "Poor lad broke 'is tiblin bone."

Upon hearing the unfamiliar word, Ethan gave Garrett a questioning glance.

"Tibia," she said, dropping her forehead to his shoulder in a defeated gesture.

Ethan smiled and curved a loose arm around her. She smelled like freshly laundered things, with a faint salty coolness beneath. He wanted to follow the fragrance along the tender warmth of her throat and down beneath her bodice.

Outside the door, Eliza proceeded to explain the dangerous nature of "tiblin" injuries, which, if not treated properly, could lead to "knee gimps," "ankular hitchments," and even "limputations." Garrett fidgeted in annoyance at the maid's authoritative lecture.

"She's giving us cover," Ethan whispered, amused.

"But they'll go out and repeat her gibberish," she whispered back, "and before long I'll have a waiting room full of patients with tiblin complaints."

"It's a new field of medicine. You'll be a pioneer."

He heard her muffled chuckle. She continued to lean against him while the trio of constables expressed sympathy for the unfortunate patient. Eventually the men departed with a chorus of hearty farewells. Ethan discovered that his other arm had stolen around Garrett. Making himself let go of her was like trying to uncoil a steel spring.

"You should go up to your father now," he said with difficulty.

"Eliza will look after him while I take a few minutes to show you some slides. I have insect wings . . . pollen grains . . . flower petals . . . What would you like to see?"

"The inside of a hansom cab," he said softly. "I can't be alone with you, darlin'."

Garrett touched the edges of his vest, fingers clamping on the thin leather. "Ethan." A blush rose in her face, like light glowing through pink frosted glass. "I don't want to end this. We . . . we could meet in secret, now and then. No one would have to know. We would make no claims on each other. We'll just . . . do as we please."

The way she fumbled with the words, so unlike her usual precise way of speaking, devastated Ethan. He could only guess what it cost her to lay open her pride like this. He wasn't certain what she was offering, or even if she knew. Not that it mattered. He wanted, craved, needed anything she was willing to give. But he had to make her understand that it was impossible. And even if it were, the idea was beneath her.

"Have you had that kind of arrangement with a man before?" he brought himself to ask.

Her eyes were the green of deep summer and lush growing things. "I'm a woman who makes her own decisions and handles the consequences."

"That means no," Ethan said softly. At her silence, he continued, "You'd be risking your reputation. Your career."

"Believe me, I understand that better than you."

"Have you ever shared a bed with a man? Even once?"

"Why is that relevant?"

Her evasive response sent a pleasure-pang down to the pit of his stomach. "That means no," he said again, his voice even softer than before. He took a slow breath, trying to steady himself, while his blood sang with the knowledge that she'd been waiting for him. She was meant to be his. God, he wanted her beyond any reckoning of earth or heaven. But her well-being mattered a thousand times more than his own desires.

"Garrett . . . I'm a man full o' trouble. When I vowed to let nothing harm you, I included myself on that list."

A frown crimped her forehead. She closed her grip on his vest until her fists were tight as pine knots. "I'm not afraid of you, or your trouble." Her green eyes were narrowed and intent as she tugged him closer. "Kiss me," she urged in a whisper.

"I have to go," he said shortly, and pulled back while he was still able.

But Garrett moved with him, her hands reaching up to grip his head on either side, the way he'd taught her at Baujart's. The strength of her fingers electrified him.

"Kiss me," she commanded, "or I'll break your nose."

The threat startled a ragged laugh from him. He shook his head as he looked at her, this fearsomely capable woman who loved geese and was afraid of spaghetti, and could either wield a scalpel in a complex surgical procedure or use it as a throwing-knife.

There had always been a cold streak in him, but he

couldn't seem to find it now, when he needed it most. He was breaking apart inside. He would never be the same after this.

"Christ, you've ruined me," he whispered.

His arms went around her, one hand gripping the heavy silken mass of her braided chignon. She guided his head down, and he lost the battle, all his will vanquished as he began to kiss her as if the world were about to end.

For him, it was.

Chapter 8

*I*N TRUTH, THE KISS started a bit awkwardly. Garrett puckered her lips into an innocently round shape, as if she were pressing them against someone's cheek. Had Ethan not been so inflamed, he would have smiled. He brushed his mouth over the gathered circle of her lips, playing softly, coaxing without words . . . *Like this* . . . nudging at her lips until she parted them hesitantly.

All the hungering minutes of his life, the years of bitter struggle, had led to this moment. The scars his soul had worn like armor were dissolving at her touch. She allowed the gentle intrusion of his tongue, made a little sound of pleasure, and to his eternal delight, she tried to pull him deeper. The graceful hands he so admired lifted to his head, slender fingers wandering behind his ears and into his hair, and the feel of it was so exquisite, he all but purred.

The kiss turned into something dark and dreaming, an unspoken language of heat and silk, tenderness and greed. He was so famished for her, had worshipped and wanted her for so long, but he'd never expected to have her in his arms. He'd never imagined she would yield to him like this, her response natural and searing. Nothing had ever devastated him the way she did. He pulled her closer, as if he were trying to protect her with his entire body, and she moaned softly, clinging to him as her knees began to give out like slip-joint hinges.

Lifting her easily, Ethan sat her on the edge of a metal table and collected her against him, one of his hands guiding her head to his shoulder. She conformed to him bonelessly, her legs forced to part beneath her skirts. Her breath came in flutters, like the bursts of a sparrow's wing beats.

Take her right now, came the lust-drenched thought. He could make her want it. He could have her begging for it, right there on the table. It would feel so damn good, better than anything either of them had ever experienced. It would be worth anything.

"Don't trust me," he managed to warn unsteadily.

Garrett's breath struck his neck in a little puff of amusement. "Why?" she whispered. "Are you going to seduce me in my own laboratory?"

Clearly she had no idea how close he was to doing just that.

Ethan crushed his mouth against her smoothed-back hair, his gaze wandering over shelves filled with vaguely menacing instruments and flasks of mysterious fluids. "What man wouldn't be carried away in a setting like this?" he asked dryly. Although there actually was something provocative about it, this scientific room of cold, hard surfaces, and the pretty green-eyed creature in his arms. She was the only soft thing in here.

"Science is romantic," Garrett agreed dreamily, missing the sarcasm. "There are secrets and wonders waiting to be discovered in this laboratory."

Ethan's lips twitched as he charted the length of her

spine with his palm. "The only wonder I see is you, *acushla.*"

Garrett drew back enough to look at him, the tip of her nose brushing his. "What does that word mean?"

"*Acushla?* It's . . . a word for female friend."

After a moment of consideration, a skeptical grin crossed her face. "No, it isn't."

It was pure reflex to kiss her again, a response to an impulse before it had even reached his brain. Her mouth shaped to his with a willingness that drew a primitive grunt of satisfaction from his throat. He felt the innocent tightening of her thighs against his hips, and his groin pumped with heat.

Ethan damned himself as his fingers went to the buttons of her basque. Just a few minutes more, and he would live on it to the end of his days. The front of her bodice fell open to reveal a chemise fastened with a tiny silk bow, and a simple white corset with elastic panels, the kind women wore for riding or exercise. With great care, he untied the little bow and ran his forefinger inside the loosened chemise. As the back of his knuckle brushed her breast, a rush of intense excitement made it difficult to breathe. He eased the fine white cotton down to reveal a soft pink nipple peeking over the molded corset edge.

He bent over her, compelling her to lean back on his arm, and slipped his fingers beneath the boned fabric to lift the firm, silky weight of her breast. His head lowered. Taking the rosy tip into his mouth, he tugged it into a stiff bud. She gasped and trembled, her hand gripping his shoulder repeatedly, like a cat kneading her paws.

For Ethan, the sexual act had always been a transaction or a weapon. He'd been trained in the arts of seducing anyone, man or woman, into yielding their most closely guarded secrets. He knew endless ways to stimulate, torment, and satisfy, how to make someone mindless with desire. He'd done things, and had things done to him, that most people would consider beyond decency. But he'd never experienced anything like the intimacy of this moment.

He spread a path of slow kisses to her other breast, taking his time, savoring the unbelievable smoothness of her skin. As his lips reached the edge of her chemise, Garrett fumbled to pull the garment down. Even as aroused as Ethan was, he grinned briefly at her impatience. Cupping beneath her breast, he kissed the pale curve, deliberately avoiding the pink center. Her fingers slid into his hair as she tried to guide his mouth to where she wanted it. He resisted, blowing gently against the contracted point. Garrett quivered in frustration as he hovered over the nipple for a torturously long moment, making them both wait. Finally relenting, he caught the firm bud, pulled it deep, teased it with his tongue.

That was all he could stand before he had to pull his mouth away. She strained upward to kiss him, but he shook his head and held her off. He'd never been so aroused, his flesh so hard that every throb of his pulse hurt.

"I have to stop," he said hoarsely. Now, while he still could.

Her arms crept around his neck. "Stay with me tonight."

Filled with lust and yearning, Ethan nuzzled her

flushed cheek. "Ah, darlin'," he whispered, "you don't want that. I wouldn't be nice. I'd bring you to the edge of wanting, and keep you there 'til you were cursing and screaming your pleasure for all the neighbors to hear. And after I'd brought you to a long, hard come, I might turn you over my knee for being such a noisy lass. Is that what you want? To spend all night in bed with a big, mean bastard?"

Her voice was muffled against his shoulder. "*Yes.*"

A laugh stirred in his throat.

Her legs dangled from her seated position on the table. White cotton stockings, sensible walking boots. The way she sat with her thighs parted should have made her appear wanton, but instead the posture reminded him of a young tomboy. He couldn't believe she would make herself so vulnerable to him.

He leaned forward, his mouth finding hers. She quivered and opened for him, letting him taste her. The finely wrought muscles of her leg tensed as she realized his hand had stolen beneath her skirts and was working up her thigh.

Even the most demurely styled ladies' drawers were constructed with a long slit at the crotch. While the garments were perfectly modest when a woman was in a standing position, they opened completely when she was seated. Reaching the seamed edge of the gap, he let his thumb rest gently against the delicate skin of her inner thigh.

Garrett pulled her mouth from his and buried her face in his throat.

Ethan tightened his arm around her back, while his thumb slid higher, circling into the edge of a silky-rough patch of hair. He skimmed the tops of the curls, stirring the hairs with teasing strokes that awakened vague echoes of sensation at the roots.

Gently he murmured in the hollow space just behind her earlobe, guessing at what might excite or intrigue her. "In India, before a man marries, he's taught how to please his wife according to ancient texts on the erotic arts. He learns about the embraces, kisses, strokes, and bites that bring fulfillment."

"Bites?" she asked dazedly.

"Love bites, darlin'. Nothing that would hurt you." To demonstrate, he bent to her neck and nibbled softly. She made an agitated sound and arched toward him. "'Tis said the joining of two who are well-matched is a high union," he whispered. "And if they become so intoxicated by love as to leave faint marks on the skin, their passion for each other will not be lessened even in one hundred years."

Garrett's voice was wobbly. "Did you learn any of those erotic arts?"

His lips curved against her skin. "Aye, but I'm still a novice. I only know one hundred and twenty positions."

"A hundred and . . ." She broke off as he let two fingers slide gently between the soft lips of her sex, teasing back and forth. After a convulsive swallow, she managed to say, "I doubt that's anatomically possible."

His lips grazed the edge of her jaw. "You're the medical expert," he mocked gently. "Who am I to argue?"

She squirmed as one of his fingertips wriggled through soft curls and came to rest on an acutely sensitive place. "Who taught you?" she managed to ask.

"A woman in Calcutta. I'd never met her before. For the first two nights, there was no physical contact at all. We sat on bamboo mats on the floor and talked."

"About what?" She stared at him with dilated eyes, her flush deepening as he continued to fondle the silky, intricate shape of her.

"The first night she explained about *Kama* . . . a word for desire and longing. But it also refers to the well-being of the soul and senses . . . the appreciation of beauty, art, nature. The second night we talked about pleasures of the body. She said if a man was a true male, he would use the rule of his will to cherish the woman, and fulfill her so thoroughly she would have no desire left for another."

On the third night, she had undressed him and pulled his hand to her body, whispering, *"Women, being of a tender nature, want tender beginnings."*

That had been the most difficult part for Ethan, showing tenderness to her. To anyone. He'd always feared any kind of weakness in himself. But there had been no choice—he had been committed to doing whatever was necessary to become what Jenkyn had intended him to be.

This was different. This woman owned the sum of him, his tenderness and violence, everything good or bad.

His head lowered over hers, and he kissed her for long, luxurious minutes, learning what made her tremble and her breath come fast. All the while, he let his fingers tickle and play between her thighs. With his thumb and forefinger, he rubbed each fragile inner lip as if releasing perfume from flower petals. She whimpered, her sex nudging upward into his palm. He traced around the swollen bud, close but not touching, and massaged the plump hood just above it.

"Oh please," Garrett gasped, writhing at the slow torture.

He made the circles smaller, his touch spiraling inward until he reached her clitoris and feathered it with a few light strokes. She moaned, her legs closing on his hips. As her pelvis lifted and froze at the brink of release, he withdrew his touch. She clutched his neck almost angrily, trying to haul him closer.

"Easy, now, darlin'," Ethan said with an uneven laugh, even though he was sweating and aching with his own vicious need. "It won't help you to strangle me."

Her brows lowered, and her fists slid down to grip his vest. "Why did you stop?"

Ethan lowered his forehead to hers. "I was taught that satisfying a woman properly should take at least as long as making dough for bread."

Garrett writhed helplessly. "How long is that?"

"You don't know?" he asked, amused.

"No, I can't cook. How long does it take?"

He let his smiling lips brush her cheek. "If I told you, you'd probably time me."

Reaching down to part the tender furrow, he caressed her until he felt a touch of wetness. The feel of that silky feminine elixir, coolness and heat, sent a charge of lust through him. He stroked the entrance to her body and insinuated a fingertip. Feeling the tiny muscles clenching to keep him out, he murmured soft words and crooning sounds—soothering, was the Irishman's word for it—and worked carefully deeper. She went motionless at the feeling of being entered. Invaded.

"Relax," he whispered, "and I'll be able to reach places that will give you pleasure."

Garrett looked up at him with hazy confusion. "What places? I've studied reproductive physiology, and there are no—" She broke off with a little yelp as he reached up to her breast and gave the nipple a quick double pinch. Her body tightened around his finger in surprised response. As soon as the inner muscles loosened, he searched more deeply, and covered her mouth with his. Her legs spread wider beneath the skirts, her body straining toward him.

The depths of her body were fluid and snug, working frantically to pull him in. Drawing his thumb through the gloss of feminine moisture, he caressed the intricate shape of her, teasing and swirling, while his finger began a gentle nudging, mimicking the way he wanted to thrust inside her.

His cock was excruciatingly full, as hard as stone as it pressed against the metal edge of the table. Delving his other hand beneath her skirts, he played with her, fingertips tapping and pattering softly like raindrops. After tracing the slightly distended folds, he tickled between them, grazing the swollen center again and again. No matter how she tried to hurry him, he was relentless and deliberate, stroking slowly, building her pleasure, torturing himself as well as her. Whimpers climbed in her throat. Opening her mouth with his, he licked at the sounds, relishing the way her body shivered and danced at his touch.

She was too far gone now to resist the feeling he was giving her, struggling a little, wanting everything faster, harder, closer, but he went even slower, ruthlessly patient and steady, drawing out the tension. The strong pulses began, her flesh wringing out an intense release, her thighs cinching hard on either side of him. Taking her sharp cry into his mouth, he caressed her, worked her, while her head dropped to his shoulder as if she were too weak to hold it up any longer. She breathed in soft little coos of pleasure and relief, the most delectable sounds he'd ever heard.

Eventually Ethan drew his hands away and wrapped his arms around her. "I'd love you night and day, if I could," he whispered. "There'd be no limits for us. No shame. You and me, in the dark . . . that's all I've ever wanted." Carefully he slid a hand between them to cup her breast, and kissed it before settling it gently back into the confines of her corset. He did the same with the other side, and began to fasten her bodice.

Garrett sat in front of him quietly. When Ethan had finished the last of her buttons, she settled a palm over his heartbeat. "Come back to me," she whispered. "Find a way to see me."

Ethan held the slim relaxed weight of her against his chest, and lowered his cheek to her hair. "I can't."

"You could if you wanted."

"No." It would have been better to let her think the worst of him, especially after all his reckless indulgence tonight. But he couldn't stand the idea of deceiving her in any way. She was the one person he didn't want to lie to. "Garrett . . . I'm about to become a marked man. I've betrayed someone who's been a mentor to me. After he finds out, my life won't be worth a farthing."

Garrett was silent for a moment, toying with a button on his shirt placket. "You mean Sir Jasper."

"Aye."

"Does it have anything to do with the night of the Guildhall reception? And the man who died? Mr. Prescott?"

It was such a good guess that Ethan smiled darkly. Given the chance, he thought, she could pry him open like a tin of sweets.

Taking his silence for affirmation, Garrett asked in a neutral tone, "Did you kill him?"

"If I tell you, I'd be putting my life in your hands."

"I'm used to that."

It was true, he reflected with a touch of surprise. In all likelihood, she dealt with matters of life and death more often than he did. Staring down into her expectant face, he said slowly, "I helped to fake his death, and smuggled him out of the country in exchange for information."

"About what?"

Ethan hesitated. "A conspiracy involving government officials. If I succeed in exposing them, God willing, it's worth the cost."

"Not if the cost is your life."

"One man's life isn't important when weighed against many."

"No." Garrett sounded urgent now, her hand closing on a fold of his shirt. "Every life is worth fighting for."

"It's your job to believe that. It's my job to believe the opposite. Trust me, I'm expendable."

"Don't say that. Tell me what you're planning to—"

"Garrett," he interrupted gently, taking her head in his hands, "it's not my way to say good-bye. I'll take a kiss instead."

"But—"

Ethan covered her mouth with his. He felt as if he'd been running for thousands of nights through violence and shadows, and had stumbled upon some serene place on a cool spring morning. She had brought him closer to joy than he'd ever been before. But like all moments of surpassing pleasure, it was tempered with the bittersweet awareness of its transience.

"Forget me," he whispered after their lips parted.

And he left swiftly, without looking back.

THE NEXT MORNING, Garrett emerged from a troubled sleep, and began the day as usual. She woke her father and administered his medicine, and had a breakfast of bread, butter, and tea while reading the newspaper. As soon as she arrived at the clinic on Cork Street, she checked on the overnight patients, made notes in their charts, gave instructions to the nurses, and began to receive patients with scheduled appointments.

On the surface, everything was routine. But underneath, she was miserable, giddy, and shamed, all at once. The effort to regulate herself was exhausting.

Would she ever see Ethan Ransom again? How in God's name was she supposed to forget him after the things he'd done to her? Every time she thought of those knowing masculine hands, the slow kisses and soft whispers, she wanted to melt to the floor. *"You and me, in the dark . . . that's all I've ever wanted."*

Thinking about him could drive her mad, if she let it.

Nothing went right. The way the nurses trilled "Good morning" set her teeth on edge. The medical supply cabinets and closets were disorganized. The staff talked too loudly in the hallways and common rooms. At lunchtime, she ate at the staff commissary, and the cheerful bustle she usually enjoyed was profoundly irritating. Oblivious to the conversation around her, she picked morosely at an artful arrangement of cold sliced chicken, watercress-and-cucumber salad, and a tiny dish of cherry tapioca.

There were more patient appointments in the afternoon, some correspondence and bill paying, and then it was time to return home. Glum and weary, Garrett descended from the hansom, walked up to her front door . . . and paused to look at it with a bewildered frown.

The familiar name plate was still there, but a heavy bronze mortise lock had replaced the old outdated one. There was a new cast-bronze doorknob, and a lion's-head knocker, its jaws clamped on a heavy ring. Unlike the standard snarling, squinty-eyed design, this lion looked rather friendly and sociable. The door's casing had been repaired and reinforced. Old hinges had been replaced with sturdy new ones. A draft-proof weather strip had been added to the bottom edge of the door.

Hesitantly Garrett reached for the door knocker. The ring hit the handsome engraved bronze backplate with a satisfying clack. Before she could continue knocking, the door opened smoothly, and a beaming Eliza took her bag and cane.

"Evenin', Dr. Gibson. Look at this door! It's the finest one in King's Cross, I'll warrant."

"Who did it?" Garrett managed to ask, following her into the house.

Eliza looked puzzled. "Didn't you hire a locksmith?"

"I most certainly did not." Garrett removed her

gloves and hat, and gave them to her. "What name did he give? When did he come?"

"This morning, after you left. I took your father out for a constitutional in the park. We were gone no more than an hour, but when we came back, there was a man working on the door. I didn't ask his name. He and Mr. Gibson exchanged a few pleasantries while he was finishing up, then gave us a set of steel keys and left."

"Was it the man from last night? My patient?"

"No, this one was old. Gray-haired and stoop shouldered."

"A strange man let himself into the house and changed the lock, and neither you nor my father asked for his name?" Garrett asked with an incredulous scowl. "Good God, Eliza, he could have robbed us blind."

"I thought you knew about it," the cookmaid protested, following her into the surgery.

Anxiously Garrett went to see if any of her supplies or equipment were missing. Nothing appeared to have been disturbed. Folding back the partition to her laboratory, she checked to make certain the microscope was safely in its case. Turning, she ran her gaze over the shelves of supplies, and froze.

The dozen glass test tubes in the wooden rack had been filled with violets. The blue petals were as vivid as jewels in the utilitarian environment. An intoxicating scent drifted from the row of tiny bouquets.

"Where did those come from?" Eliza asked, standing beside her.

"Our mysterious locksmith must have left them as a prank." Garrett removed one of the blossoms and touched it to her cheek and lips. Her fingers were trembling. "Now my test tubes are all contaminated," she said, trying to sound cross.

"Dr. Gibson, are you . . . are you about to cry?"

"Of course not," Garrett said indignantly. "You know I never do that."

"Your face is all red. Your eyes are watery."

"An inflammatory reaction. I'm hypersensitive to violets."

Eliza looked alarmed. "Shall I toss 'em for you?"

"*No.*" She cleared her throat and spoke more softly. "No, I want to keep them."

"Is everything all right, Doctor?"

Garrett let out a slow breath and tried to reply in a normal tone. "I'm just tired, Eliza. Nothing to worry about."

There was no one she could confide in. For Ethan's sake, she had to stay silent. She would do as he'd asked, and forget him. He was only a man.

The world was full of men. She would find another one.

"*A good, decent husband of the ould stock, who'll give you a fireside of children . . .*" Would Ethan ever want children? Would she? There was no logical reason for her to have children, or marry at all, but she was astonished to realize it was something she might consider.

A humbling thought occurred to her. *When you meet the right man, the list of things you would never do suddenly becomes much shorter.*

Chapter 9

THE DOOR TO JENKYN'S office had been left slightly ajar. Ethan paused to knock on the jamb, trying to remain outwardly relaxed despite the weight of foreboding at the pit of his stomach. His ability to shut away his emotions—one of his most useful assets—had disappeared. He was all exposed nerves and raw appetite. He felt as transparent as glass, and there were too many lies he had to keep straight.

He'd been like this for the past week, ever since the night he'd spent with Garrett Gibson. The thought of her was deep inside him, at the center of every thought and sensation, as if he existed only as a vessel to contain her.

Life had been a damned sight easier when he'd had nothing to lose. It was killing him not to go to her. The only thing that stopped him was the need to keep her safe.

"Enter," came Jenkyn's relaxed voice.

Ethan let himself inside. He'd come into the new government building by way of the back entrance used by servants and junior clerks. Even without the need for discretion, he would have preferred that to going through the brazenly elaborate main entrance and reception rooms, with their plasterwork thickly coated in gilt and the stands of marble columns rising from lapis floors. Ethan found it suffocating. The ostentatious interiors were intended to proclaim the power and grandeur of an empire that ruled almost one quarter of the earth's surface and refused to yield even an inch of its territory.

It had been at Jenkyn's insistence that the collection of contiguous offices under the roof of the newest building at Whitehall had all been shut off from each other. The Home Office kept all connecting doors perpetually locked, so no one could walk from there directly to the Foreign Office, India Office, or Colonial Office. Instead, visitors had to go down into the street, walk the outside length of the building, and ascend another staircase. Free communication between offices would have made Jenkyn's scheming and plotting more difficult.

The corner office provided a view of a nearby building that had originally contained a cockfighting pit. Ethan suspected Jenkyn would have preferred it if the cockpit still existed: he was the kind of man who enjoyed blood sports.

The air was hot enough to braise a plucked capon. Jenkyn always kept a fire lit, even in summer. The spymaster cut an elegant figure, his build long and stiletto thin as he occupied one of two heavy leather smoking chairs positioned in front of the fireplace. Orange flickers played over his thinning blond hair and austere features as he regarded Ethan through distal spirals of cigar smoke. His eyes were a shade of cinnamon brown that should have appeared warm, but somehow never did.

"Ransom," he said pleasantly, nudging a table-top

cigar stand toward him. "We have much to discuss this evening."

Ethan hated the taste of tobacco, but a cigar from Jenkyn was a mark of favor that no one refused. As he sat, he took a cigar from the carved ebony stand. Conscious of the older man's attentive regard, he performed the ritual with care. Jenkyn had always emphasized the importance of details: A gentleman knew how to light a cigar, how to sit a horse, how to make introductions properly.

"You'll never pass for a born gentleman," Jenkyn had once told him, "but you'll at least be able to mix with your betters without calling attention to yourself."

After clipping the end of the cigar with an engraved silver cutter, Ethan lit a long match and toasted the outer binding. He put it to his lips, rotating it slowly while igniting the filler, and released the draw expertly.

Jenkyn smiled, something he rarely did, perhaps out of the awareness that his smiles gave the impression of a feeding predator. "Let's attend to business. Did you meet with Felbrigg?"

"Yes, sir."

"What's got his back up this time?" Jenkyn asked disdainfully.

There was a vicious rivalry between Jenkyn and Fred Felbrigg, the commissioner of the Metropolitan Police. Jenkyn and his eight secret service men had become direct competition for Felbrigg and his team of a half dozen plainclothes "active officers." Jenkyn treated Scotland Yard with open contempt, refusing to collaborate or share intelligence. He had said publicly that London police were incompetent, a pack of fools.

Instead of using them for extra manpower, Jenkyn had sent for Royal Irish constables from Dublin.

To add insult to injury, Jenkyn's position at the Home Office wasn't even legal: he and the secret service force had never been approved by Parliament. One could hardly blame Scotland Yard and Fred Felbrigg for being livid.

However, Jenkyn acquired power as easily as breathing. His influence extended everywhere, even to distant foreign ports and consulates. He had created an international web of spies, agents, and informers, all answerable to no one but him.

"Felbrigg complains that he hasn't seen any embassy intelligence in a year," Ethan said. "He says the information goes directly from the consulates to you, and you haven't shared a word of it."

Jenkyn looked smug. "When the national security is at stake, I have the authority to do as I see fit."

"Felbrigg is going to meet with the commissioner and the Home Secretary, to take up the matter with them."

"The idiot. Does he think it will do any good to whine in front of them like a schoolboy?"

"He'll do more than whine," Ethan said. "He says he has intelligence that proves you're endangering British citizens by withholding crucial information."

Jenkyn gave him a look that could have peeled a turnip. "What intelligence?"

"A report that a schooner bound from Le Havre to London sailed two days ago, carrying eight tons of dynamite and twenty cases of fuse. Felbrigg is going to tell the commissioner and the Home Secretary that you were aware of it but kept it to yourself." Ethan paused, taking a gentle pull on the cigar and exhaling a stream of smoke before continuing tonelessly. "The London Port Police weren't even warned. And now the cargo has mysteriously disappeared."

"My own men are handling it. The Port Police don't need to know, they would bungle what's been set in motion." A short pause. "Who sent the information to Felbrigg?"

"A port official from Le Havre."

"I want his name."

"Yes, sir."

In the silence that followed, Ethan was grateful for the cigar, a prop that gave him something to do, something to look at and fiddle with. Jenkyn had always been able to read him so accurately that it was well-nigh impossible to hide anything from him. It was all Ethan could do to keep from confronting him about the missing dynamite. The bastard was planning to do something evil with it, and the knowledge sickened and enraged him.

But there was another part of Ethan's heart that grieved. He and Jenkyn had formed a bond over the past six years. A young man who'd needed a mentor, and an older one who'd wanted someone to mold in his image.

Deliberately Ethan focused his thoughts on the early years when he'd worshipped Jenkyn, who had seemed to be the fount of all knowledge and wisdom. There had been endless training from various instructors . . . intelligence gathering, combat and firearms, burglary, sabotage, survival skills, wireless telegraphy, codes and ciphers. But there had also been days Jenkyn had spent with him personally, instructing him about things like wine tasting, etiquette, how to play cards, how to mingle with upper-class toffs. He had been . . . fatherly.

Ethan remembered the day Jenkyn had taken him to a Savile Row tailor, where a referral from a well-established client was required before one could become a customer.

"Always have your waistcoats made with four pockets," Jenkyn had told him, seeming amused by Ethan's wonder and excitement at putting on tailored clothes for the first time. "This upper side pocket is for railway tickets and a latch key. The other side is for loose sovereigns. The lower pockets are for a timepiece, a handkerchief, and banknotes. Remember, a gentleman never keeps paper money in the same pocket as coins."

That memory, and countless others, kindled a sense of gratitude that even eight tons of missing dynamite couldn't entirely destroy. Ethan held on to the feeling deliberately, letting it soften him.

He heard Jenkyn's dry voice. "Aren't you going to ask what I've done with the explosives?"

Ethan lifted his head and gazed at him steadily, smiling slightly. "No, sir."

Seeming reassured, Jenkyn settled more deeply in his chair. "Good lad," he murmured. Ethan hated the momentary glow the words gave him. "We see the world the same way, you and I," the older man continued. "Most people can't bring themselves to face the ugly reality that some lives must be sacrificed for the greater good."

That sounded like the explosives would be used for another terrorism plot, something similar to what had been planned for the Guildhall. "What if some of the victims turn out to be Englishmen?" Ethan asked.

"Don't be obtuse, my boy. Our own people *have* to be targeted—the more prominent, the better. If the Guildhall plot had succeeded, it would have shocked and angered the entire nation. Public opinion would have turned against the Irish radicals who dared to attack innocent British citizens, and it would have ended any question of Ireland's independence."

"But Irish radicals weren't responsible," Ethan said slowly. "We were."

"I would call it a joint enterprise." Jenkyn tapped the ash from his cigar into a crystal tray. "I assure you, there's no shortage of Irish political insurgents who are more than willing to resort to violence. And if we don't continue to assist their efforts, some lunatic bill on Home Rule may eventually become law." As he drew in another mouthful of smoke, the end of the cigar glowed like a malevolent red eye. "Anyone who thinks the Irish are capable of governing themselves is as mad as a bedbug. They're a brutish race that respects no law."

"They would respect the law more if it didn't fall so hard on them," Ethan couldn't resist saying. "The Irish are taxed higher than the English, in return for only half the justice. Duty is hard when there's no back of fairness to it."

Jenkyn blew out a stream of smoke. "You're right, of course," he said after a moment. "Even the strongest opponents of Home Rule can't claim that Ireland has been ruled justly. However, Irish independence isn't the answer. The damage it would do to the Empire is incalculable. Our only concern is what's best for England's interests."

"You know I live for queen and country," Ethan said flippantly.

Undeceived, Jenkyn studied him closely. "Does it weigh on your conscience that innocent lives will be lost as a result of our efforts?"

Ethan gave him a sardonic glance. "I have no more use for a conscience than I do for neckties. I may have to wear one in public, but I don't bother with one in private."

Jenkyn chuckled. "This week I want you to help Gamble with some security arrangements. It's for a charity event at the Home Secretary's private residence. A number of MPs and cabinet ministers will attend. With all the recent political unrest, one can't be too careful."

Ethan's pulse quickened. More than anywhere else in the world, the London house occupied by Lord Tatham, the Home Secretary, was the place he most wanted access. But he frowned at the mention of William Gamble, a fellow secret-service agent who would have been perfectly willing to shoot him on command. Jenkyn often liked to play them against each other, like a pair of bull terriers bred for the pit.

"Security isn't Gamble's strong suit," Ethan said. "I'd rather make the arrangements by myself."

"I've already put him in charge. Follow the procedures he lays out, to the letter. I want you to focus on the exterior of the house, and provide Gamble with an analysis of any landscape features or structures that might pose a risk."

Ethan sent him a mutinous glance but didn't argue.

"You will both attend the event," Jenkyn continued, "and of course, you'll keep your eyes and ears open. Gamble will pose as an under-butler."

"And me?" Ethan asked warily.

"You'll be a speculative builder from Durham."

That placated Ethan slightly. He might enjoy lording it over Gamble a bit at the event. However, Jenkyn's next remarks extinguished the flicker of satisfaction. "As an enterprising young man about town, you would likely be escorting an eligible lady to the soirée. It would make your guise more believable. Perhaps we should find someone to accompany you. An attractive and accomplished woman, but not one so highborn as to be beyond your reach."

There was no specific threat in the words, but they caused a swooping plummet of his stomach. Without even thinking, he began to regulate his breathing in the way the guru in India had taught him. *Let each breath flow smoothly . . . four counts in, four counts out.*

"I don't know any ladies," he said calmly.

"Is that so?" he heard Jenkyn ask, affecting mild surprise. "I was under the impression that lately you've been keeping company with quite an interesting lady. Dr. Garrett Gibson."

Now Ethan's stomach no longer felt like it was swooping. It felt like it had crashed through a window and was plummeting in a shower of broken glass. Any time Jenkyn was sufficiently aware of a fellow human being to mention his or her name, their life span became statistically shorter.

Somewhere within the iced-over machinery of his brain, he registered that Jenkyn was speaking again.

"Never stub the end of a good cigar, Ransom, it doesn't deserve a violent death. Let it burn out with dignity. You haven't answered my question."

Ethan looking down at the collapsed foot of his cigar, which he hadn't even been aware of crushing into the ashtray. As the flood of ruined smoke bit inside his nostrils, he asked tonelessly, "What question?"

"Obviously I would like you to tell me about your relationship with Dr. Gibson."

Ethan's face felt stiff, as if it had been covered in plaster and left to dry. He needed to produce a smile, something that looked genuine, and he searched frantically through the chaos of his thoughts until the phrase "scrotal chafing" came to mind. That was enough to help him crack a grin. Relaxing back in his chair, he lifted his gaze to Jenkyn's, and saw a hint of surprise at his self-possession. *Good.*

"There's no relationship," Ethan said easily. "Who told you there was?"

The older man ignored the question. "You've been following Dr. Gibson to the Clerkenwell area. You accompanied her to a special evening market and visited her home afterward. What would you call that?"

"I was trifling with her." It required the full force of Ethan's will to remain calm as he realized he'd been shadowed, almost certainly by another agent. Probably Gamble, the disloyal prick.

"Dr. Gibson is not the kind of woman one trifles with," Jenkyn said. "She's unique. The only female in the entire British medical profession—what does it take to achieve that? Superior powers of mind, a cool disposition, and courage equal to any man's. If that weren't enough, she's reportedly quite pleasing to the eye. A beauty, even. Regarded as a saint in some circles, a she-demon in others. You must be fascinated by her."

"She's a curiosity, is all."

"Oh come," Jenkyn said with amused chiding, "she's a good deal more than that. Even Dr. Gibson's sharpest detractors won't deny that she's extraordinary."

Ethan shook his head. "She has a high way with her. Hard as flint."

"I'm not displeased by your interest in her, my boy. Quite the opposite."

"You've always said women are a distraction."

"So they are. However, I've never asked you to live like a monk. A man's natural passions are meant to be exercised in moderation. Prolonged celibacy makes the constitution irritable."

"I'm not irritable," Ethan snapped. "And I'm no more interested in Dr. Gibson than I am in staring at a bucket of dirt."

Jenkyn appeared to suppress a smile. "Thou doth protest too much." Seeing Ethan's lack of comprehension, he asked, "Haven't you read the copy of *Hamlet* I gave to you?"

"I didn't finish it," Ethan muttered.

The older man was obviously displeased. "Why not?"

"Hamlet spends all his time talking. He never *does* anything. It's a revenge play with no revenge."

"How do you know, if you haven't finished it?"

Ethan shrugged. "I don't care how it ends."

"The play is about a man who's forced to face the reality of human depravity. He lives in a fallen world, in which 'right' and 'wrong' is whatever he decides. 'There is nothing either good or bad, but thinking makes it so.' I assumed you would have had enough imagination to put yourself in Hamlet's place."

"If I were in his place," Ethan said sullenly, "I'd do more than stand around making speeches."

Jenkyn regarded him with a touch of fond paternal exasperation. Something in that interested, caring look pierced down to the place in Ethan's heart that had always yearned for a father. And it hurt.

"The play is a mirror held up to a man's soul," Jenkyn said. "Read the rest of it, and tell me about the reflection you see."

The last thing Ethan wanted to see was the reflection of his own soul. God help him, it might look far too similar to the man sitting across from him.

But there was his mother's influence. More and more often of late, Ethan had found himself thinking about her shame at the sins her circumstances had obliged her to commit, and her hopes that he would grow up to be a good man. She'd turned to religion near the end of her life, and had worried constantly about salvation, not only her own, but also her son's. She had died of cholera not long after Ethan had joined K division.

One of Ethan's last memories of his mother was how she'd wept with pride upon first seeing him in the blue uniform. She'd thought it would be the saving of him.

Oh, how she would have hated Sir Jasper Jenkyn.

"As for Dr. Gibson," Jenkyn continued, "my compliments on your taste. A woman with a brain will keep you interested out of bed as well as in it."

If Jenkyn thought Ethan cared for Garrett, he would use her as a pawn to manipulate him. She might be threatened or harmed. She might simply disappear one day, as if into thin air, never to be seen again unless Ethan did whatever unspeakable thing Jenkyn wanted of him.

"I prefer a woman who's easy for the taking, and easy to discard," Ethan said curtly. "Unlike Dr. Gibson."

"Not at all," came Jenkyn's softly chilling reply. "As you and I are both aware, Ransom . . . anyone can be discarded."

LEAVING WHITEHALL ON foot, Ethan headed north and cut across to the Victoria Embankment, a road and river walk along the Thames. The new roadway along the granite-faced embankment had been expected to ease the crush of daytime traffic along Charing Cross, Fleet Street, and the Strand, but it seemed to have made no appreciable difference. At night, however, the embankment was comparatively quiet. Occasional puffs of smoke or steam rising through the iron ventilation grids reminded pedestrians of the subterranean world beneath their feet: tunnels, telegraph wires, underground railways, and pipes for gas and water.

Wandering near a coal and forage wharf, Ethan reached a maze of alleys crowded with excavating equipment and temporary contractors' workshops. He slipped behind a massive stone-channeling machine and waited.

In less than two minutes, a dark figure entered the alley.

As Ethan had expected, it was Gamble. The lean, wolfish face and sharp brow were distinctive even in the shadows. Like Ethan, he was tall but not so towering that he would stand out in a crowd. With his big arms and bulldog chest, he carried most of his power in his upper torso.

There were many things to admire about William Gamble, but very little to like. He was physically adept and aggressive, able to tolerate brutal punishment and keep coming back for more. His tenacity had driven him to train harder than any of Jenkyn's men. He never complained or made excuses, never exaggerated or boasted. Those were all qualities Ethan respected.

But Gamble had been born into a coal-mining family in Newcastle, and the desperate poverty of his childhood had engendered a ferocity that had burned out any softer qualities. He had come to revere Jenkyn with an intensity that verged on zealotry. There was no sentiment in him, no trace of empathy, which Ethan had once judged as a strength but had turned out to be a weakness. Gamble tended to miss the fiddly little clues and signals that people unconsciously gave away in conversation. As a result, he didn't always ask the right questions, and often misinterpreted the answers.

Keeping still, Ethan watched Gamble come farther into the space between the sheds. He waited until Gamble's back was turned, and sprang from behind, fast as a striking cobra. Hooking the bend of his arm around the thick neck, Ethan jerked the man back against his chest. Ignoring Gamble's violent writhing, he gripped his own left bicep and fitted his hand against the back of the man's head to increase the pressure of the choke. The combination of pain and oxygen deprivation worked in a matter of seconds.

Gamble submitted, going still.

In a quietly vicious tone, Ethan asked near his ear, "How long have you been reporting on me to Jenkyn?"

"Weeks," Gamble gasped, clutching at the arm around his throat. "You made it easy . . . sodding idiot . . ."

"An idiot who's about to crush your larynx." Ethan slowly tightened his arm against the trachea. "You've put an innocent woman at risk. If anything happens to her, I'll beat the marrow out of you and hang you up like salted pork."

Straining to breathe, Gamble didn't reply.

For a moment, the urge to finish him off was nearly overpowering. It would be so easy to constrict his grip a few degrees more, and prolong the hold until the bastard was properly throttled.

Uttering a low curse, Ethan released him with an abrupt shove.

Wheezing, Gamble pivoted to face him. "If anything happens to her," he retorted hoarsely, "it will be *your* fault. Did you think Jenkyn wouldn't find out? Someone else would have told him if I hadn't."

"You're daft as a rock if you think Jenkyn will like you better for turning into a snitch." Seeing Gamble's defensive posture, his muscles tensed to fend off an attack, Ethan said sardonically, "If I were going to kill you, I'd have done it already."

"You should have."

"I'm not the enemy," Ethan said in exasperation.

"Why in God's name are you wasting time and effort fighting me?"

"Eliminate a rival without mercy," Gamble quoted, "or one day he'll try to replace you."

Ethan snorted, unimpressed. "Parroting Jenkyn makes you sound like more of a lackwit than you already are."

"As long as I've known Jenkyn, he's never been wrong about anything. Before we left for India, he predicted that someday one of us would kill the other. I told him I would be the last man standing."

Ethan smiled without humor. "He said the same thing to me. I told him to kiss my arse. Jenkyn's a manipulative bastard. Why should you and I turn into a pair of dancing monkeys every time he winds up the barrel organ?"

"Because *that's the job.*"

Ethan shook his head slowly. "No, Gamble," he said, his voice pure acid. "Because we each want to be his favorite. He chose us because he knew we would do anything, no matter how vile, to win his approval. But I've had enough of it. 'Tis not a job, but a deal with the devil. I'm not a well-read man, but I have the impression those never turn out well."

IT HAD BEEN a dreadful week. Garrett had gone through each day in a mechanical fashion, feeling bleak and empty. Food had no flavor. Flowers had no scent. Her eyes were itchy and sore from lack of sleep. She couldn't pay attention to anyone or anything. It seemed the rest of her life would be an infinity of monotonous days.

The lowest moment had occurred on Tuesday evening, when Garrett had gone on her usual visit to the Clerkenwell workhouse, and afterward had dared to blow a short, hopeful little summons on her silver whistle.

There had been no response.

Even if Ethan were somewhere nearby, keeping an eye on her . . . he wasn't going to come to her.

The realization that she would probably never see him again had plunged her into a sullen void.

Her father hadn't understood the reason for her low spirits, but he had assured her that everyone had a fit of the doldrums sooner or later. The best cure, he'd said, was to spend time with cheerful people.

"Is there a second choice?" Garrett had asked dully. "Because at the moment, the only thing I'd like to do with cheerful people is push them into the path of an oncoming carriage."

However, the following morning, Garrett was finally able to feel something other than gloom. It was during an appointment with one of the clinic's new patients, a watchmaker's wife named Mrs. Notley, who had given birth eight months earlier and feared she might be with child again. After examining her, Garrett gave her the welcome news that she was *not* expecting. "None of the various evidences of pregnancy are there," she told Mrs. Notley. "Although your worry is understandable, it's not uncommon for a woman's monthly courses to be irregular while her infant is still nursing."

Mrs. Notley was overcome with relief. "Praise God," she exclaimed, dabbing at her eyes with a handkerchief. "My husband and I didn't know what we were going to do. We have four little ones already, and can't afford another so soon. We live in constant dread of when the next baby might come."

"What method of prevention do you use?"

The woman blushed and looked uncomfortable at Garrett's frankness. "We count the days after my monthly turn."

"Does your husband practice withdrawal?"

"Oh, *no*, doctor. Our pastor says it's a sin for a man to do that outside his wife's body."

"Have you considered contraception such as douches or sponges?" Garrett asked.

Mrs. Notley looked aghast. "That's against Nature."

A wave of impatience swept over Garrett, but she managed to keep her expression pleasant. "Nature must occasionally be prevented from having its way, or we should have no inventions such as running water or lace-up shoes. As modern women, we need not produce more offspring than we can adequately feed, clothe, and raise to be satisfactory adults. Let me tell you about some safe options that will reduce the chances of unwanted pregnancy."

"No, thank you."

Garrett's brows drew together. "May I ask why not?"

"Our pastor says a large family is a blessing, and we mustn't refuse gifts from God."

On any other day, in any other mood, Garrett might have tried to coax her into viewing the issue from a different perspective. Instead, she found herself saying curtly, "I suggest you tell your pastor that it's none of his business how many children you have, unless he offers to help pay for them. One rather doubts the Good Lord wishes for you and your entire family to end up in the poorhouse."

Surprised and offended, Mrs. Notley stood from her chair, still clutching the tear-dampened hand-kerchief. "I should have expected blasphemy from a female doctor," she snapped, and stormed out of the consultation room.

Garrett lowered her forehead to her desk, stewing in frustration and guilt. "Suffering savior," she muttered.

Before five minutes had passed, Dr. Havelock came to stand at the doorway. Before he even spoke, Garrett saw from his expression that he'd heard about what had happened.

"I shouldn't have to remind you that our patients are not mechanical creatures," he said matter-of-factly. "They come to us with physical *and* spiritual concerns. You have an obligation to treat their opinions—and feelings—with courtesy."

"Why is Mrs. Notley's pastor dispensing medical advice?" Garrett asked defensively. "He should stick to his line of work, and leave me to mine. I don't go to his church to deliver sermons, do I?"

"A fact for which his congregation is profoundly grateful," Havelock assured her.

Garrett dropped her gaze and rubbed her face wearily. "My own mother died in childbirth because she didn't receive adequate medical attention. I would like my female patients to know how to protect and care for themselves. At the very least, they should understand how their own reproductive systems work."

Havelock's gravelly voice softened. "As you're well

aware, girls are taught from early childhood that any interest in the workings of their own bodies is shameful. A young woman is praised and admired for her ignorance of sexual matters until her wedding night, when she's finally introduced to intimacy with pain and confusion. Some of my female patients are so reluctant to discuss their own anatomy that they have to point to an area on a doll to tell me where it hurts. I can scarcely imagine how difficult it must be for a woman to take responsibility for her physical health when she's always been told she hasn't the moral or legal right to do so. What I do know is that it is neither up to you, nor me, to judge her. When you speak to a patient like Mrs. Notley, keep in mind that women receive more than enough condescension and arrogance from male doctors—they don't need it from you as well."

Humbled and contrite, Garrett mumbled, "I'll write her a letter of apology."

"That would be appropriate." There was a long pause. "You've been ill-tempered all week. Whatever your personal problems are, they have no place at work. Go on holiday if necessary."

Go on holiday? Where in heaven's name did he think she would go? What was there for her to do?

Havelock regarded her dourly. "In light of your current disposition, I hesitate to mention it . . . but I would like you to accompany me to a soiree at the Home Secretary's private residence, at the behest of a colleague I've known for many years. Dr. George Salter."

"No, thank you." Garrett lowered her forehead to the desk again.

"*Dr. George Salter,*" Havelock repeated. "The name has no significance to you?"

"Not really," came her muffled voice.

"He was recently appointed as the chief medical officer of the Privy Council. Having learned of the report you're writing on workhouse conditions, Salter asked me to bring you to the soiree."

"I would rather set myself on fire."

"Good God, woman, Salter is an advisor to the queen! He helps to shape public health legislation and administration for the *entire British Empire*. He would like to include a female perspective on these issues, especially as they pertain to women and children. There's no woman more qualified than you to provide him with informed opinions and recommendations. It's the opportunity of a lifetime."

Garrett knew she should be excited. But the thought of dressing up to attend a formal event and mingle with a crowd of political people filled her with gloom. She raised her head to look at him dully. "I'd rather not meet him on some frivolous occasion. Why can't I visit his office instead? One can't exactly project an air of gravitas while prancing through a polka."

Havelock's bushy white brows rushed downward. "You have more than enough gravitas. Try for charm instead."

"One of the reasons I entered the medical profession is so I would never have to be charming."

"A goal you've achieved with great success," Havelock informed her sourly. "However, I insist that you come with me to the soiree, and try to be amiable."

"Is Mrs. Havelock coming with us?"

"No, she's away visiting her sister in Norwich." He pulled a handkerchief from his pocket and extended it to her.

"I don't need that," Garrett said irritably.

"Yes, you do."

"I'm not weeping."

"No. But you have pencil shavings on your forehead." Although Havelock's face was expressionless, he couldn't quite keep the hint of satisfaction from his tone.

Chapter 10

No fairy godmother could have been more efficient than Lady Helen Winterborne, who had thrown herself enthusiastically into the project of making Garrett ready for the soiree. She had enlisted the store's chief dressmaker, Mrs. Allenby, to alter a new dress she hadn't yet worn, and refused to allow Garrett to pay for it. "You've done so much for me and my family," Helen had insisted. "Don't deprive me of the enjoyment of doing something for you in return. I intend to outfit you in a dress that does you justice."

Now, on the evening of the event, Garrett sat at the vanity in Helen's spacious dressing room. Helen had asked her own lady's maid to arrange Garrett's hair.

Unlike many lady's maids who affected gallic names and accents to please their employers, Pauline was actually French. She was an attractive woman of middling height—broomstick thin, with the keen, world-weary eyes of someone who had, at an earlier time in her life, endured hard experience. As Garrett conversed with her in French, Pauline relayed that as a girl she had been a Parisian seamstress, and had nearly starved to death while working eighteen-hour days sewing slop-shirts. A small bequest from a deceased cousin had enabled her to move to London and find work as a housemaid, and eventually become trained for the position of lady's maid.

To Pauline, the preparations for an evening out were a serious undertaking. After scrutinizing Garrett thoroughly, she picked up a pair of tweezers, used two fingers to stretch the skin of Garrett's brow, and began to pluck.

Garrett flinched at each little sting of uprooted hair. "Is this necessary?"

"*Oui.*" Pauline continued to pluck.

"Aren't they thin enough already?"

"They're caterpillars," Pauline replied, wielding the tweezers mercilessly.

Helen intervened in a soothing tone. "Pauline is only removing a few stray hairs, Garrett. She does the same for me."

Regarding Helen's sleek, fine brows, the tips ending in precise points, Garrett subsided uneasily. When the unruly brows had been deemed sufficiently tamed, Pauline used a soft-bristled brush to dust a fine veil of pearl powder over her face, giving it a satiny, even finish.

Garrett frowned as she watched Pauline set a pair of curling tongs over a spirit lamp in a wrought-iron base. "What are you planning to do with those? I can't wear my hair in curls. I'm a doctor."

Ignoring her, Pauline divided her hair into pinned-up sections, brushed out a long lock, and folded a curling paper around it. A waft of steam rose as she skillfully wrapped the hair around the tongs. Garrett held deathly still, fearing any sudden movement might result in scorch marks on her forehead. After approximately ten seconds, Pauline slid out the tongs and removed the paper.

Garrett blanched as she beheld the long corkscrew-shaped curl. "Dear God. You're going to make me look like Marie Antoinette."

"I think I'll ring for some wine," Helen said brightly, and hurried to the bellpull.

Pauline proceeded to turn every lock of hair on Garrett's head into a bouncy spiral, while Helen distracted her with conversation. As the clock struck eight, Helen's little half-sister Carys came into the room. The six-year-old was dressed in a ruffled white nightgown, her fine blond hair twirled around strips of calico that had been tied into little bundles on her head.

Reaching out with careful fingers to touch one of the long curls, Carys asked, "Are you going to a ball?"

"A soiree, actually."

"What is that?"

"A formal evening with music and refreshments."

Carys moved to sit on her older sister's knee. "Helen," she asked earnestly, "do Prince Charmings go to soirees?"

Sliding her arms around the child, Helen cuddled her close. "Sometimes they do, darling. Why do you ask?"

"Because Dr. Gibson hasn't caught a husband yet."

Garrett laughed. "Carys, I would rather catch a cold than a husband. I have no wish to marry anyone."

Carys gave her a wise glance. "You will when you're older."

Helen buried a smile amid the little rag-curl bundles on the child's head.

Pauline turned Garrett's chair to face away from the vanity mirror, and began to pin her hair up section by section. She used a fine-toothed comb to tease and texture the roots of each curl before twisting and pinning it into place. "*C'est finie*," she finally pronounced, and handed Garrett a hand mirror so she could view both the front and back.

To Garrett's pleased surprise, the coiffure was lovely. The front had been left in gentle waves, with a few loose tendrils at the hairline. The rest had been formed into a soft coronet of loops and curls at the top of her head, leaving her neck and ears exposed. As a finishing touch, Pauline had inserted a few hairpins tipped with clear glass beads that glittered among the upswept locks.

"Not Marie Antoinette?" Pauline asked, looking smug.

"No, indeed," Garrett said with an abashed grin. "*Merci*, Pauline. You've done a magnificent job. *Tu es artiste.*"

With great care, the lady's maid helped Garrett into an elegant dress of pale blue-green silk with a transparent shimmering overlay. The gown needed little ornamentation other than a "fraise" trim, a thin froth of ruffle at the neckline. The skirts were drawn back to reveal the shape of her waist and hips, with the excess folds and draperies flowing gracefully to the floor. It concerned Garrett that the bodice was cut so low, although both Helen and Pauline assured her that it was by no means improper. The sleeves were little more than gauzy puffs through which her shoulders and arms could easily be seen. Carefully lifting the hem of the skirts, she stepped into heeled evening slippers covered in blue silk and sewn with glittering crystal beads.

Garrett went to the full-length looking glass, and her eyes widened as she beheld this new version of herself. How odd it felt to be dressed in something light, glimmering, and luxurious, the skin of her throat and chest and arms exposed. Was she making a mistake, going out like this?

"Do I look foolish?" she asked uncertainly. "Is this unseemly?"

"My goodness, no," Helen said earnestly. "I've never seen you look so beautiful. You're . . . prose that's turned into poetry. Why would you worry about appearing foolish?"

"When I'm dressed like this, people will say I don't look like a doctor." Garrett paused before continuing wryly. "On the other hand, they already say that, even when I'm wearing a surgeon's cap and gown."

Carys, who was playing with the left-over glass beads on the vanity table, volunteered innocently, "You've always looked like a doctor to me."

Helen smiled at her little sister. "Did you know, Carys, that Dr. Gibson is the only lady doctor in England?"

Carys shook her head, regarding Garrett with round-eyed interest. "Why aren't there others?"

Garrett smiled. "Many people believe women aren't suited to work in the medical profession."

"But women can be nurses," Carys said with a child's clear-eyed logic. "Why can't they be doctors?"

"They are many female doctors, as a matter of fact, in countries such as America and France. Unfortu-

nately, women aren't allowed to earn a medical degree
here. Yet."

"But that's not fair."

Garrett smiled down into the girl's upturned face.
"There will always be people who say your dreams
are impossible. But they can't stop you, unless you
agree with them."

AFTER ARRIVING AT the Winterborne residence, Dr.
Havelock looked her over with approval, pronounced
her "quite presentable," and collected her in his private
carriage. Their destination was the Home Secretary's
private residence on Grafton Street, at the northern
end of Albemarle. Many of the neighborhood's grand
homes were inhabited by government officials who insisted it was essential for them to live as men of high
social position at taxpayers' expense. "The drawing-
room work," it was claimed, "is but a part of the office
work," and therefore lavish social entertainments such
as this were ultimately for the public benefit. Perhaps
that was true, Garrett thought, but it had all the appearance of indulging in the sweets of high office.

They were welcomed into the opulently decorated
house, its rooms filled with fine art and massive swags
of flowers, the walls covered in silk or hand-painted
paper. It immediately became apparent that at least four
hundred guests had been invited to an event that could
only have comfortably accommodated half that number. The crush of bodies made the atmosphere stifling
and hot, causing ladies to perspire in their silks and
satins, and gentlemen to stew in their black evening
coats. Servants moved through the gauntlet of shoul-

ders and elbows with trays of iced champagne and chilled sherbet.

The Home Secretary's wife, Lady Tatham, insisted on taking Garrett under her wing. The silver-haired, heavily bejeweled woman steered her expertly through the crowd, introducing her to a large number of guests in rapid succession. Eventually they reached a group of a half dozen dignified older gentlemen, all looking serious and vaguely perturbed, as if they were standing around a well into which someone had just tumbled.

"Dr. Salter," Lady Tatham exclaimed, and a gray-whiskered gentleman turned toward them. He was a short man of sturdy build, his face kind and jowly beneath a neatly trimmed beard.

"This fetching creature," Lady Tatham told him, "is Dr. Garrett Gibson."

Salter hesitated as if uncertain how to greet Garrett, then seemed to come to a decision. Reaching out, he shook her hand firmly in a man-to-man fashion. A gesture of equals.

Garrett adored him instantly.

"One of Lister's protégées, eh?" Salter remarked, his eyes twinkling from behind a pair of octagonal spectacles. "I read an account in the *Lancet* about the surgery you performed last month. A double ligature of the subclavian artery—the first time it's been done successfully. Your skill is to be commended, Doctor."

"I was fortunate in being able to use the new ligatures Sir Joseph is developing," Garrett replied modestly. "It allowed us to minimize the risk of sepsis and hemorrhage."

"I've read about this material," Salter said. "Made of catgut, is it?"

"Yes, sir."

"How is it to work with?"

As they continued to discuss the latest surgical advancements, Garrett felt very comfortable in Dr. Salter's presence. He was affable and open-minded, not at all the kind of man who would treat her with condescension. In fact, he reminded her more than a little of her old mentor, Sir Joseph. Now she was sorry for having been so grumpy when Dr. Havelock had insisted she attend the soiree. She would have to admit to him that he'd been right, and she'd been wrong.

"If I may," Salter eventually said, "I would like to prevail on you from time to time, to have your opinions concerning matters of public health."

"I would be delighted to help in any way I can," Garrett assured him.

"Excellent."

Lady Tatham broke in then, laying a glittering gem-weighted hand on Garrett's arm. "I'm afraid I must steal Dr. Gibson away, Dr. Salter. She is much in demand, and guests are clamoring to make her acquaintance."

"I can't blame them a bit," Salter said gallantly, and bowed to Garrett. "I look forward to our next meeting at my office in Whitehall, Doctor."

Reluctantly Garrett allowed herself to be drawn away by Lady Tatham. She would have loved to prolong the conversation with Dr. Salter, and was annoyed by Lady Tatham's insistence on pulling her away. One might have assumed from the woman's claim about "clamoring guests" that people had been forming a queue to meet her, which was certainly not the case.

Lady Tatham guided her purposefully toward a

looming gold-framed pier glass filling the wall space between two windows. "There is a gentleman you simply *must* meet," she said brightly. "A close associate and personal friend of my husband's. It would be impossible to overstate his importance in matters of national security. And he is a frightfully clever man—my poor brain can scarcely follow him."

They approached a fair-haired man standing at the pier glass. His form was thin and elongated, as if he were a figure from a work of French Medieval art. There was something striking about him, something repugnant and yet compelling, although Garrett couldn't identify what it was. She only knew that something twisted sickly inside her as she met his gaze. His eyes, unblinking and copper-colored like an adder's, were set deeply in the narrow framework of his face.

"Sir Jasper Jenkyn," Lady Tatham said, "this is Dr. Gibson."

Jenkyn bowed, his gaze taking in every subtle variation of her expression.

Garrett was grateful to feel a sense of cold, steady purpose descend over her, as it always did just before a particularly difficult surgical procedure, or in an emergency. But underneath the surface, her thoughts raced. This was the man who posed such danger to Ethan Ransom. The one Ethan thought might have him killed. Why had Lady Tatham made a point of introducing them? Had Jenkyn somehow found out that Garrett was acquainted with Ethan? And if so, what did he want with her?

"Sir Jasper is one of the men in my husband's inner sanctum," Lady Tatham said lightly. "I confess,

I'm never quite certain how to describe his occupation other than to say he is Lord Tatham's 'officially unofficial' advisor."

Jenkyn chuckled briefly. He didn't smile naturally—the muscles of his face seemed poorly designed for it. "That description is as accurate as any other, my lady."

How about "treasonous bastard"? Garrett thought. But she kept her expression perfectly bland as she said demurely, "A pleasure, sir."

"I've been eager to make your acquaintance, Dr. Gibson. What an exceptional creature you are. The only woman admitted to the honors of this soiree on her own merit, rather than as some gentleman's accessory."

"Accessory?" Garrett repeated, her brows lifting. "I hardly think the ladies present deserve to be described that way."

"It is the role most women choose for themselves."

"Only for lack of opportunity."

Lady Tatham giggled nervously and tapped Jenkyn's arm lightly with her fan in girlish rebuke. "Sir Jasper likes to tease," she told Garrett.

Jenkyn made Garrett's skin crawl. There was a quality about him, a malignant vitality that people would interpret as magnetism instead of corruption.

"Perhaps you're in need of an accessory, Dr. Gibson," he said. "Shall we find some virile young trophy for you to flaunt on your arm?"

"I already have an escort."

"Yes, the estimable Dr. Havelock. I see him over there at the side of the room. Would you like me to take you to him?"

Garrett hesitated. She didn't want to spend another second in Jenkyn's company, but neither did she want to take his arm. Unfortunately, according to etiquette, a woman was not allowed to walk across the room unescorted at a formal event.

"I would be obliged," she said reluctantly.

Jenkyn looked over her shoulder. "Ah, but wait— we're being approached by an acquaintance of mine, who appears most intent on meeting you. Allow me to make an introduction."

"I would rather not."

Lady Tatham leaned to whisper close to Garrett's ear, making her shiver irritably. "Oh, but you *must* meet this young man, my dear. He may lack family connections, but he is an unattached gentleman of means. A speculative builder from Durham. And he's exceptionally fine-looking. A blue-eyed stunner, as one of my friends put it."

A strange feeling came over Garrett. Her gaze lifted to the massive pier glass, which was filled with a blur of color dabs, like a painting by Monet. She glimpsed herself in the vast mosaic of reflections . . . the shimmering blue-green dress, her pale face beneath upswept hair. A dark form was moving through the crowd toward her with a controlled and lethal grace she'd seen before in only one man.

Alarmed by the violent pulse that had begun to lash in her wrists and throat, Garrett closed her eyes briefly. Somehow she knew who the blue-eyed stunner would turn out to be, she was *sure* of it, and while her brain warned that something was very wrong, her senses were running wild with anticipation.

She could feel a tide of color rising to the surface

of her skin, a bloom of exhilaration and desire. There was nothing she could do to suppress it. The room was an oven. She was being braised alive. To make matters worse, her corset had been cinched a half-inch tighter than usual to accommodate Helen's slender measurements, and while it hadn't been a problem up until now, she suddenly couldn't take in enough air.

Someone came up behind her, a large form pausing amid the crush of bodies until there was sufficient room to move to her side. All her skin changed, gooseflesh rising despite the sweltering heat.

Garrett was filled with ice and fire, nearly ill with excitement as she turned to confront an unfamiliar version of Ethan Ransom, all steely masculine perfection in formal black and white, every inch of him polished and impeccably groomed.

"What are you doing here?" he asked quietly, in the English accent that seemed jarring now that she was familiar with his real one.

Confused and uncertain—they were supposed to be strangers, weren't they?—Garrett asked faintly, "H-have we met?"

Something in his stone-cold face softened. "Sir Jasper knows we're acquainted. He assigned me to help with the security arrangements for tonight, but neglected to mention you would be here. And for some reason your name was left off the guest list." He leveled a hard glance at Jenkyn.

"I asked Lord and Lady Tatham to make certain Dr. Gibson would attend," Jenkyn explained in a silken tone. "I thought it would enliven the evening— particularly for you, Ransom. I do so like to see young people enjoying themselves."

Ethan's jaw set. "Apparently it slipped your mind that I have a job to do."

Jenkyn smiled. "I felt quite certain of your ability to do more than one thing at a time." He glanced from Ethan's hard face to Garrett's flushed one. "Perhaps you might take Dr. Gibson to the refreshment room for champagne. She seems rather overcome by my little surprise."

Ethan held the older man's gaze for a long moment, while tension laced through the air like metallic thread. Garrett inched closer to him uneasily, realizing he was fighting for self-control. Lady Tatham's fatuous smile began to dissolve. Even Jenkyn seemed subtly relieved when Ethan turned to Garrett.

She took his arm, her fingertips curling into the sleek, expensive fabric of his dress coat.

"A delight to have made your acquaintance, Dr. Gibson," she heard Jenkyn say. "As I expected, you are a woman of sharp wit." After a sliver of a pause, he added, "And even sharper tongue."

Had Garrett not been so dumbfounded at finding herself in Ethan Ransom's presence, she might have thought of some withering retort. Instead she responded with a distracted nod and allowed Ethan to lead her away.

There was little opportunity to speak as they moved through a crowd as tightly packed as olives in a jar. Not that it mattered: Garrett doubted she could have managed to put more than three or four sensible words together. She couldn't believe she was with him. Her gaze went to the neat shape of his ear. She wanted to kiss it. She wanted to press her mouth to the place where his close-shaven beard started, and move down to his throat where she could feel him breathing. But he seemed so unyielding, so unreachable in his iced-over wrath, that she wasn't at all certain he would reciprocate.

Silently Ethan led her through the circuit of rooms and out to a stairwell landing with a cluster of potted palms near one corner. The palms had been arranged to partially conceal a small, plain door that must have led to the service area of the house.

With effort, Garrett managed to speak. "Is that the man you referred to as your mentor? Why did he want me to be here tonight?"

"It's a warning for me," Ethan said flatly, not looking at her.

"A warning about what?"

The question seemed to fracture Ethan's self-assured façade. "He knows that where you're concerned, I . . . have . . . a preference." Guiding her past the palms, he opened the service door and took her to the landing of a servants' stairwell. The abrupt cessation of noise was an unspeakable relief. It was cool and dimly lit in the stairwell, the dank staleness relieved by a slight breeze filtering in through outside air vents.

"Preference," Garrett repeated cautiously. "What does that mean? You prefer me to what?"

As they stopped in a corner, Ethan's head and broad shoulders were silhouetted in the faint glow of a sconce on the opposite wall. She began to tremble as he stood over her, big and dark, his nearness awakening a pulse of high music in her.

"I prefer you to everything," he said gruffly, and bent to take her mouth with his.

Chapter 11

As ETHAN KISSED HER roughly, Garrett melted against him, a moan catching in her throat. Too much pleasure, too much feeling, and yet she wanted more. She couldn't seem to draw it in fast enough. His body was solid and heavy, raw power wrapped in civilized formal attire. Her hands slid inside his black evening coat, following the lean contours of his waist up to the muscled vault of his ribs and chest. Ethan tensed and shivered at her touch, and angled his head to fit their mouths more tightly together. Still not enough. She had to feel more of him, all of him. Daring to reach down to his hips, she pulled him closer, and gasped at the feel of his aroused form against hers.

Ethan broke the kiss with a muted growl, the heat of his breath collecting in her ear as he bit gently at her earlobe. Embers caught low inside her and spread heat to every tender place in her body. She was light-headed, weak—every heartbeat riding on a hard-coursing breath.

Ethan's head lifted abruptly. One of his fingers came to rest gently against her lips.

Garrett was silent, trying to hear over the roar in her ears.

Footsteps, and echoes of footsteps, rose from the depths of the stairwell. She heard the rattle of glass and porcelain, the grunts of effort as a servant carried a heavy-laden tray up from the kitchen.

Garrett's heart clattered to a halt as she realized she was about to be caught in a scandalous embrace in a servants' stairwell. But Ethan nudged her farther into the corner and blocked her with his much larger form. She leaned into the concealment of his chest, her fingers clamping on the edges of his coat lapel.

The footsteps came nearer, then halted.

"Don't mind us," Ethan said over his shoulder, sounding relaxed. "We won't tarry long."

"Yes, sir." The footman walked past them.

Ethan waited until the servant had left the stairwell before he murmured against Garrett's hair, his breath stirring the pinned-up curls. "You're more beautiful every time I see you. You shouldn't be here."

"I didn't—"

"I know. It's Jenkyn's doing."

She tilted her head back to look up at him, her face tense with worry, not for herself but for him. "How did he find out we were acquainted?"

"One of his men followed me and saw us at the night market. From now on, Jenkyn will try to use you to manipulate me. He fancies himself a chess master, and all the rest of us pawns. He knows I'd do anything to protect you."

Garrett blinked at that. "Should we pretend to have a falling-out?"

Ethan shook his head. "He'd see through that."

"Then what's to be done?"

"You can start by leaving the soiree. Tell Lady Tatham you have the vapors, and I'll find a carriage for you."

Garrett stepped back from him and gave him an indignant glance. "The 'vapors' is a term for a hysterical fit. Do you know what it would do to my career if people thought I might succumb to vapors in the middle of a medical procedure? Besides, now that Sir Jasper knows about our mutual attachment, I wouldn't be any safer at home than I am here."

Ethan looked at her alertly. "Mutual?"

"Why else would I be lurking with you in a servants' stairwell?" she asked dryly. "Of course it's mutual, although I haven't your pretty way of putting things—"

She would have continued, but his mouth had fastened on hers. His fingers cradled her jaw and cheek as he drew up pleasure from some depthless well inside her. Blindly she clung to his neck and lifted on her toes to make the kiss deeper, stronger.

His chest expanded with a violent breath or two, and then he fumbled to clasp her arms and hold her back. "You have to leave, Garrett," he said unsteadily.

She tried to gather her wits. "Why can't I stay?"

"I have something important to do."

"What is it?"

Unaccustomed to taking anyone into his confidence, Ethan hesitated before replying. "I have to obtain something. Without being noticed by anyone."

"Including Jenkyn?"

"Especially him."

"I'll help you," Garrett said readily.

"I don't need help. I need you to be far away from here."

"I can't leave. It would look odd, and I have my own reputation to consider. Besides, my presence provides an excuse to slip away and steal whatever it is you're after. Take me with you, and Sir Jasper will assume we've gone somewhere to . . . well, to do what we're doing right now."

Ethan's face might have been carved from granite. But his touch was gentle as he stroked her cheek with the backs of his knuckles. "Have you ever heard the expression 'catching a wolf by the ears'?"

"No."

"It means you're in trouble whether you hold on or let go."

Garrett nuzzled her cheek against his hand. "If you're the wolf, then I'll hold on."

Recognizing the impossibility of sending her away, Ethan uttered a quiet curse and pulled her so close that her heels were suspended from the floor. His mouth found her neck, and did something between a kiss and a bite, very gentle but with the edges of his teeth. The flat of his tongue stroked her, and she gasped at the corresponding throb down between her thighs.

"Tonight I'm Edward Randolph," she heard him say quietly. "A builder from Durham."

It took Garrett a moment to understand. Gamely she entered into the pretense. "Why have you come all the way from Durham, Mr. Randolph?"

"To persuade a few members of Parliament to vote against a bill on building regulations. And while I'm in town, I'm taking in the sights of London."

"What do you most want to see? The Tower? The British Museum?"

His head lifted. "I'm looking at it," he said, his gaze holding hers for a few searing seconds before he took her into the refreshments room.

Chapter 12

RELENTLESS NOISES SLURRIED THE air: conversation; laughter; the creaking of the floor underfoot; the clinks of silver, porcelain, and glass; the rattling of trays, the snapping of fans. Guests surrounded the long tables in the effort to obtain lemonade or ices. As a footman entered the room bearing a tray of desserts, Ethan reached out to snatch one before the servant reached his destination. The movement was so deft and quick that the footman hadn't even noticed it.

Drawing Garrett to a corner where a tall feather palm occupied a terra-cotta pot, Ethan handed the glass dish to her. It contained a frosty mound of lemon ice, with a tiny mother-of-pearl demitasse spoon tucked at the side.

Garrett received it gratefully and took a bite of the tart, icy fluff. It melted on her tongue instantly, luscious thin coldness sliding down her throat.

A sense of unreality drifted over her as she stared up into Ethan Ransom's face. The severe perfection of his appearance was slightly unnerving.

After taking another bite of lemon ice, she asked hesitantly, "How have you been since we last met?"

"Well enough," Ethan said, although his expression conveyed he hadn't been well at all.

"I tried to imagine what you were doing, but I have no idea what your typical day is like."

He seemed vaguely amused by that. "I don't have typical days."

Garrett tilted her head as she looked up at him. "Would you mind if you did? That is, would you dislike keeping to a regular schedule?"

"It would help if the job were interesting."

"What would you do, if you could choose anything?"

"Something in law enforcement, probably." His gaze swept the room, his expression inscrutable. "I have a hobby I wouldn't mind spending more time on."

"Oh?"

"I design locks," he said.

Garrett regarded him uncertainly. "Are you speaking as Mr. Randolph?"

His lips twitched as he looked down at her. "No, I've meddled with locks since I was a boy."

"No wonder you were so critical of my front door," Garrett said, fighting the temptation to reach up and touch the dimple in his cheek. "Thank you for the improvements you made . . . the lock and hinges . . . and the lion's-head knocker. I like it very much."

Ethan's voice was soft. "Did you like the violets?"

She hesitated before shaking her head.

"No?" he asked, more softly still. "Why not?"

"They reminded me that I might never see you again."

"After tonight, you probably won't."

"You say that every time we meet. However, you keep popping up like a jack-in-the-box, which has made me increasingly skeptical." Garrett paused before adding in an abashed tone, "And hopeful."

His gaze caressed her face. "Garrett Gibson . . . as long as I'm on this earth, I'll want to be wherever you are."

She couldn't help smiling ruefully. "You're the only one who does. I've been in a foul mood for the past two weeks. I've offended nearly everyone I know, and frightened off one or two of my patients."

His voice was dark velvet. "You needed me there to sweeten your temper."

Garrett couldn't bring herself to look at him as she admitted huskily, "Yes."

They were both silent then, suffused in the awareness of each other's presence, nerve endings collecting invisible signals as if their bodies were communicating by semaphore. Garrett made herself take the last bite of lemon ice, little more than a spoonful of slush, but her throat was so tight with pleasure she could hardly swallow.

Gently Ethan took the bowl from her and gave it to a passing servant. He escorted Garrett back to the drawing room, where they joined a circle of a half dozen ladies and gentlemen. Ethan turned out to be accomplished at drawing-room etiquette, at ease with the courtesies expected of a gentleman introducing himself. It hardly escaped Garrett's notice that he drew every female gaze in the vicinity. Ladies fluttered and preened in his presence, one even brazenly fanning her bosom in the attempt to draw his notice. Although Garrett tried to muster some sophisticated amusement, the feeling was soon crushed flat by annoyance.

The small talk was interrupted as the Home Secretary, Lord Tatham, appeared at one of the drawing-room doorways. He announced that the ladies and gentlemen were now invited into the double salon for some musical entertainment. The mass of humid, suffocated bodies began to move as a herd. Ethan held back with Garrett, letting people push past them.

"There'll be nothing left but the worst seats in the back rows," Garrett warned, "if there are any left at all."

"Exactly."

She realized Ethan intended to steal whatever it was he'd come for while the guests were being entertained.

A familiar gravelly voice intruded on her thoughts. "I seem to have been replaced as your escort, Dr. Gibson." It was Dr. Havelock, who appeared to be in a jovial mood. "However, since you're in the company of Mr. Ravenel, I will relinquish my role with good grace."

Garrett blinked in surprise, having never known the keen-minded Havelock to make such a mistake before. She glanced quickly at Ethan's expressionless face, and back to the older man. "Dr. Havelock, this is Mr. Randolph of Durham."

Perplexed, Dr. Havelock looked more closely at Ethan. "I beg your pardon, sir. I could have sworn you were a Ravenel." He turned to Garrett. "He favors the earl's younger brother, does he not?"

"I couldn't say," Garrett replied, "since I haven't yet been introduced to Mr. Ravenel, although Lady Helen has promised it will happen someday."

"Mr. Ravenel came to the clinic," Dr. Havelock remarked, "to visit Lady Pandora after her surgery. Were you not introduced to him then?"

"Regretfully, no."

Dr. Havelock shrugged, and smiled at Ethan. "Randolph, is it? A pleasure." They exchanged a firm handshake. "In case you weren't aware, my good fellow, you are in the company of one of the most skilled and accomplished women in England. In fact, I would say Dr. Gibson has a male brain in a woman's body."

Garrett grinned wryly at his last comment, which she knew had been intended as a compliment. "Thank you, Doctor."

"Despite my short acquaintance with Dr. Gibson," Ethan said, "her brain seems entirely female to me." The remark caused Garrett to stiffen slightly, as she expected a mocking comment to follow. Something about how a woman's mind was changeable, or shallow, the usual clichés. But as Ethan continued, there was no hint of teasing in his tone. "Keen, subtle, and quick, with an intellect strengthened by compassion—yes, she has a woman's mind."

Thrown off guard, Garrett stared at him with a touch of wonder.

In that brief, private moment, Ethan looked as if he really did prefer her to everything else in the world. As if he saw all of her, the good and the bad, and wouldn't change a thing about her.

As if from a distance, she heard Havelock's voice. "Your new friend has a silver tongue, Dr. Gibson."

"Indeed, he does," Garrett said, managing to tear her gaze from Ethan's. "Would you mind if I continue to keep company with Mr. Randolph?"

"Not at all," Havelock assured her. "That spares me from having to listen to the musicale, when I would much rather indulge in a cigar with friends in the smoking room."

"A cigar?" Garrett repeated, pretending to be shocked. "After all the times I've heard you refer to tobacco as a 'poisonous luxury?' Not long ago you told me you hadn't smoked a single cigar since your wedding."

"Few men can defeat a willpower as strong as mine," Havelock said. "But by Jove, I've done it."

After Dr. Havelock had left them, Garrett studied Ethan closely. "He was right about something—you do have the look of the Ravenels. Especially your eyes. I can't think how I missed that before. What an odd coincidence."

Ethan didn't reply to that, only frowned as he asked, "Why does Lady Helen want to introduce you to Weston Ravenel?"

"She seems to think we would enjoy each other's company, but I haven't had the time to meet him yet."

"Good. Don't go near the bastard."

"Why? What's he done?"

"He's a Ravenel. That's reason enough."

Garrett's brows lifted. "You bear ill will toward the family?"

"Aye."

"Even Lady Helen? She's the gentlest, sweetest-natured woman in the world. No reasonable person could dislike her."

"'Tis none of them in particular I hate," Ethan said in a low tone, "but all of them in general. And if you ever take up with Ravenel, I'll have to throttle him with my bare hands."

For a moment Garrett was too taken aback to respond. She stared at him with cool disapproval. "I see. Beneath that smartly tailored evening suit, there's nothing but a jealous brute with no ability to control his primitive urges. Is that it?"

Ethan regarded her without expression, but after a moment she saw a glint of humor in his eyes. Bending his head over hers, he murmured, "It's probably best for both of us, *acushla*, if you never find out what's beneath my evening suit."

Garrett had never been the kind of woman who blushed easily, if at all, but she found herself turning as red as a beetroot. Looking away from him, she tried to bring the rampant color under control.

"How can you hate an entire family?" she asked. "They can't *all* have done something to you."

"'Tis not important."

Obviously that wasn't true. But Helen hadn't mentioned a word about any conflict between the Ravenels and Ethan Ransom. What in the world could have made him so hostile? She decided to take the matter up with him in the future.

They lingered in the refreshments room until most of the crowd had departed for the double salon, and they drifted out with the last few stragglers. Lady Tatham's voice could be heard in the distance, announcing the first of the entertainers. The serene piano notes of Chopin's Polonaise in E-flat Major rippled into the hallway like the cool, soothing water of a brook. Instead of heading toward the music, however, Ethan took Garrett along a hallway to the other end of the house, and down a set of private stairs.

"Where are we going?" Garrett asked.

"Tatham's private study."

They proceeded to the ground-floor level, crossed the entrance hall, and went along a quiet hallway.

They reached a door near the end, and Ethan tried the handle. It refused to budge.

Lowering to his haunches, Ethan examined the lock.

"Can you open it?" Garrett asked in a whisper.

"A pin-and-tumbler lock?" he asked, as if the answer should have been obvious. He fished a pair of slender metal tools from an inside coat pocket. Meticulously he inserted an instrument with a crook at the end into the bottom of the keyhole, and used the other pick to work the pins inside, lifting them one by one. *Click. Click. Click.* In no time at all the barrel turned, and the door opened.

After guiding Garrett into the dark room, Ethan took a tiny steel match case from his pocket and deftly lit a batwing lamp that extended from the wall. A short, wide sheet of flame filled the glass bowl shade, spilling a white glow through the room.

Garrett turned to view her surroundings, and started at the sight of an Irish setter sitting calmly by the hearth before she realized the canine had been stuffed by a taxidermist. The study was bursting with an abundance of decorative objects: peacock feathers sprouting from a crane-necked vase, bronzes, figurines, and ornamental boxes. Most of the walls were covered by towering black walnut cabinetry with drawers and shelves, some of them with locks built into the front. What little wall space remained was filled with paintings of dogs and hunting scenes, as well as small artifacts and oddments displayed behind glass-fronted frames. Beyond the swags of velvet drawn back from the windowpanes, embellished iron bars and scrollwork formed a protective cage around each casing.

Ethan had gone behind the desk and was running his fingers lightly over a section of wall paneling set at dado height.

"What are you looking for?" Garrett asked in a hushed voice.

"Account ledgers." He pressed a length of framed molding and released a hidden catch. The paneling swung open, revealing the front of a rather astonishing object, a massive steel sphere affixed to an iron pedestal.

Garrett came up behind him. "What is that?"

"A cannonball safe."

"Why isn't it shaped like a rectangle?"

"More secure this way. You can't blow the door off: there's no place to insert explosives. No bolts, rivets, or screws to pull out, and no joints to force wedges into." Lowering to his haunches, Ethan examined a curious brass dial with numbers and notches at the edge. It had been attached to the center of the faceplate.

"A keyless lock," he murmured, before Garrett could ask. He reached into his coat and pulled out a brass disk. A brief shake and the instrument extended into a narrow cone. It was a collapsible telescopic ear horn, the kind many of Garrett's elderly patients used. She was mystified as he hooked the wire earpiece over his ear and bent to listen intently as he rotated the brass dial.

"I need to find the sequence that will open the lock," Ethan said. "The clicks of an inner drive wheel will tell me how many numbers make up the combination." Returning his attention to the task, he rotated the dial and kept the ear horn pressed to the door. "Three numbers," he said eventually. "Now for the hard part—figuring out what they are."

"Is there some way I could help?"

"No, it's—" he began, and stopped as a thought occurred to him. "Do you know how to plot markers on a line chart?"

"I should hope so," Garrett said, lowering to a crouch beside him. "I could hardly maintain my patients' records properly otherwise. Would you prefer the markers connected or left scatterplot?"

"Connected," Ethan said. He shook his head slightly as he glanced at her, the hint of a dimple appearing. Reaching into his pockets, he pulled out a small notebook, the pages printed with a faintly inked grid. He handed the book to her. "Starting position numbers are on the horizontal axis. Contact point numbers are on the vertical axis. As I test numbers on the dial, I'll tell you which ones to map out."

"I had no idea safecrackers used coordinate paper," Garrett said, taking a tiny pencil from him.

"They don't. Yet. At the moment, I'm probably the only man in England who can get past this lock. It's a mechanical device with its own set of rules. Even the craftsmen who make it can't do it."

"Who taught you, then?"

Ethan hesitated before replying. "I'll explain later." He bent to his task, setting the ear horn back against the safe. As he gently manipulated the dial, listened for clicks, and murmured sets of numbers to Garrett, she plotted them out efficiently. In no more than ten minutes, they were finished. She handed back the book and pencil. Ethan studied the pair of jagged lines on the chart, and drew crosses at the points where they converged. "Thirty-seven . . . two . . . sixteen."

"What order do they go in?"

"That's a matter of trial and error." He dialed the numbers from largest to smallest, with no result. Next, he tried from smallest to largest. As if by magic, a smooth mechanical sound reverberated from the innards of the safe.

"How very satisfying," Garrett exclaimed triumphantly.

Although Ethan was trying to maintain his concentration, it seemed he couldn't hold back a grin. "You have the makings of a fine criminal mind, Doctor." He rose to his feet and wrenched the top handle of the safe downward. A circular door, at least seven inches thick, soundlessly pivoted open to reveal the interior.

Somewhat anticlimactically, the contents consisted of a simple stack of files and ledgers. But Ethan's breath had quickened, and a notch of concentration had appeared between his thick brows. Garrett could tell that his thoughts were in a ferment of activity as he pulled out the stack and set it on the desk. Searching through the materials, he found a volume he wanted, and spread it flat. He began to thumb rapidly through the pages, his gaze taking in dozens of entries at a time.

"I expect we'll be discovered soon," he said without looking up. "Go to the door and watch through the crack. Tell me when someone approaches."

His voice was dispassionate, his actions swift but measured as he sorted through the stack.

Garrett's insides tightened with unease. She went to

the closed door and discovered there was just enough of a space between the edge and the jamb for her to squint through. With a touch of amazement, she realized Ethan was so attuned to detail, so aware of everything in his periphery, that he noticed such things as a quarter-inch-wide crack in a door.

Two or three minutes passed while Ethan rifled through the account book. He pulled a folding knife from his coat and flicked it open. The blade flashed as he severed a few pages neatly from the bound spine.

"Are you nearly finished?" Garrett asked in a hushed voice.

He responded with the briefest of nods, his expression impassive. She wondered at his excessive calmness, when anxiety percolated all through her.

As she returned her attention to the hallway, she saw a flicker of movement, and her stomach flip-flopped. "Someone's coming," she whispered. Hearing no response, she looked back over her shoulder, and saw Ethan gathering the files and ledgers back into a stack. "Someone—"

"I heard."

Garrett looked through the crack again. The distant figure had enlarged rapidly—the man had reached the door—she started and took several steps backward as the knob rattled.

Casting a wild glance at Ethan, Garrett saw that he had set the stack of materials back into the safe and was fiddling with the lock.

A key was inserted into the door.

Garrett's heart performed acrobatic feats, seeming to launch skyward as if it had been shot from a cannon, descending with gathering velocity, then cata-

pulting again. What in God's name should she do?
How should she react? In the midst of her panic, she
heard Ethan's quiet voice.

"Don't move."

She obeyed, frozen and struggling in every muscle.

With a swiftness that defied the laws of physics,
Ethan closed the safe and pushed the paneling back
over it. He tucked a handful of folded pages neatly
inside his coat. Just as the key twisted in the lock, he
vaulted sideways over the desk with stunning ease, the
fingertips of one hand touching the surface lightly as
he passed over it.

Garrett turned toward him blindly as he landed
with catlike grace. In the next moment, she felt his
arms close around her. A panicked sound escaped her,
and he smothered it with his mouth.

Her head was pushed back from the hard, hungry
pressure of his kiss, but he gripped the back of her
neck with a supportive hand. The tip of his tongue
flicked between her lips like the touch of flame, and
she couldn't help opening for him. He gathered her
more firmly into his embrace, the kiss intensifying
until her bones turned molten and she felt faint. All
she wanted was to relax into darkness and sensation.

Ethan's hand stroked her face as he eased his mouth
slowly from hers and guided her head to his shoulder. The sheltering tenderness of his touch contrasted
sharply with the soft menace of his tone as he spoke
to the man who had entered the study. "What do you
want, Gamble?"

Chapter 13

"THIS ROOM IS OFF-LIMITS," came an accusing, rough-sawn voice. "What are you doing in here?"

"Isn't it obvious?" Ethan asked dryly.

"I'm going to report this to Jenkyn."

Tucked securely against Ethan's chest, Garrett risked a quick glance at the intruder, who was dressed in the evening livery of a butler, or under-butler, but certainly didn't behave like one. He had the same air of alert physicality as Ethan, although his build was more wiry and spare. His hair was black and cut tight to the skull, emphasizing the aggressive angle of his brow. The skin of his face was youthful, unlined, a few pockmarks pitting the cheeks and chin. An unusually thick neck pressed the front notch of his standing collar slightly open. As Garrett found herself staring into eyes as hard and flat as a pair of stove plates, she thought he looked like the kind of man she would have crossed the street to avoid.

Feeling her stiffen, Ethan toyed with the soft hairs at her nape. His touch soothed her, communicating a wordless message of reassurance.

"Of all the rooms you could have chosen," Gamble asked, "why Tatham's office?"

"I thought I'd help him out by doing some filing," Ethan said sarcastically.

"You're supposed to be helping with security."

"So are you."

The air was charged with conflict. Garrett stirred uneasily within the covert of Ethan's hard arms. Earlier he'd warned her that she was holding a wolf by the ears. Well, at the moment, she felt as if she were in the company of a pair of wolves, both bristling with aggression.

Gamble looked at Garrett as if he were lining up rifle sights. "I've been watching you." At first she thought he was referring to the soiree. But then he continued, "Going wherever you please, any time of day or night. Doing a man's work, when you should be at home with a mending basket. You'd do more good for the world that way than trying to become a man."

"I have no desire to become a man," Garrett said coolly. "That would be backsliding." Feeling the iron tension in Ethan's arm at her waist, she clamped her fingers on the hard muscle, silently willing him not to react to the other man's baiting.

Her assessing gaze returned to Gamble's notched standing collar, where one side was pushed outward a few millimeters more than the other. A hint of swelling was just visible at the top edge. "How long have you had that lump on your throat?" she asked.

Gamble's eyes widened in surprise.

When it became evident that he wasn't going to answer, Garrett said, "The location on your thyroid gland would indicate the presence of a goiter. If so, it can be remedied quite easily with iodine drops."

Gamble regarded her with raw animosity. "Bugger off."

Ethan gave a faint growl and started for him, but Garrett spun around and set both her palms on his chest. "*No*, Mr. Ransom," she murmured. "Not the best idea." Especially not when his coat pocket was filled with information stolen from the Home Secretary's private safe.

Gradually the wall of muscle relaxed beneath her hands. "If he leaves the lump untreated," Ethan asked hopefully, "how long before he chokes on it?"

"Get out," Gamble snapped, "or you'll choke on my fist down your gullet."

AFTER THEY LEFT the private study, Ethan escorted Garrett down the hallway and pulled her into the space beneath the grand staircase. They stood in the shadows, where the unmoving air was cool and slightly stale. Ethan filled his gaze with her, so feminine and fine, with glimmers dancing across her dress and little crystal things sparkling in her hair.

Despite her outward delicacy, there was something remarkably sturdy about her, an unyielding toughness he admired more than she would have believed. The life she'd chosen had come with the never-ending obligation to demonstrate what a woman was and was not, and what a woman could be. People would allow her no room for mistakes or ordinary human frailty. God knew she endured it all far better than Ethan would have.

Thinking of the way she'd put Gamble in his place, he said a touch sheepishly, "The lump on Gamble's throat . . . I may have been responsible for that."

"How?"

"The other night, when I found out he'd been following me and reporting to Jenkyn, I caught him in an alley and put a stranglehold on him."

Garrett made a few little clicking sounds of disapproval that she secretly enjoyed. "More violence."

"He put you at risk," Ethan protested, "and betrayed me in the bargain."

"His actions needn't have turned you into a brute. There are choices other than retaliation."

Although Ethan could have made an excellent argument in favor of brutish retaliation, he hung his head in a show of penitence and covertly assessed her reaction.

"Nevertheless," Garrett said, "you didn't cause the lump on Mr. Gamble's throat. It's almost certainly a goiter." She leaned into the hallway to make certain no one was approaching, and turned back to him. "Did you leave any evidence behind in the study?"

"No. But they'll realize the safe was breached when they try to open it. I scrambled the combination to protect the account ledgers."

Garrett moved closer to him. "What about the information you took?" she whispered.

The stolen pages inside his coat seemed to be burning their way through to his skin. Just as Nash Prescott had told him, the ledgers contained information beyond price. The secrets in his possession could end or save lives. At least a dozen people would have been willing to shoot him on the spot if they knew what he'd just done.

"I found proof that Jenkyn, Tatham, and others in the Home Office have been conspiring with political radicals to commit bomb attacks against British citizens."

"What are you going to do now?"

Ethan had told her far too much already, and involved her to an extent that appalled him. But if he moved quickly to deliver the information into the right hands, it would prevent her from becoming a target. "I'll bring the pages to Scotland Yard," he said. "The commissioner will leap at the chance to be rid of Jenkyn. Tomorrow, hell will break loose at Whitehall."

One of her hands came lightly to his coat lapel. "If all goes as it should, will you and I be free to—"

"No," Ethan interrupted gently. "I told you before, I'm not for the likes of you." Seeing her bewildered expression, he floundered for a way to make her understand his limitations, the things she would want that he couldn't give. He would never be civilized enough for her. "Garrett . . . I've never had the kind of life with dinner bells and mantel clocks and tea tables. I roam half the night and sleep half the next day. I live in a rented flat on Half Moon Street with an empty pantry and a bare wooden floor. The only decoration is a picture of a circus monkey wearing a top hat and riding a bicycle. It was left by the man who lived there last. I'm too used to being alone. I've seen some of the worst things people can do to each other, and I carry it with me all the time. I don't trust anyone. The things in my head . . . God help me if you knew."

Garrett was silent for a long moment, her gaze thoughtful. "I've also seen some of the worst things people can do to each other," she eventually said. "I daresay there's little left in this world that would shock me. I'm aware of what kind of life you've led, and I would hardly try to turn you into a tame man about the house."

"I'm too set in my ways."

"At your age?" Her brows lifted.

Ethan was simultaneously amused and offended by the way she spoke to him, as if he were some cocksure lad who considered himself more worldly-wise than his experience merited. "I'm nine and twenty," he said.

"There," she said, as if that had proved something. "You can't be such a hardened case as all that."

"Age has nothing to do with it." The conversation was a thin veneer over the real discussion taking place between them. Ethan felt his insides tighten with yearning and dread as he let himself think of what she might ask of him, what he might promise in a moment of insanity. "Garrett," he said brusquely, "I'll never fit into a conventional life."

A curious smile edged her lips. "Do you think my life is conventional?"

"Compared to mine."

She seemed to look inside him, taking his measure. Ethan stood there helplessly, more bound by those green eyes than by forty fathoms of ship's chain. He was filled with regret for all the moments he would never have with her. God, his desire for her was intolerable. But there was an inescapable reckoning laid up for men like him.

"Then I'm to have nothing of you?" she asked. "A few pressed violets in a book and a new front-door lock—that's all I'll have to remember you by?"

"What would you like?" he asked readily. "Name it. I'll steal one of the crown jewels for you."

Garrett's eyes softened, and she reached up to stroke his cheek. "I'd rather have the monkey picture."

Ethan looked at her in bewilderment, thinking he hadn't heard right.

"I would like you to bring it to me after you've taken care of your other business," she said. "Please."

"When?"

"Tonight."

Ethan was thunderstruck. She looked so innocent, as if she weren't proposing something that went against every social and moral principle. "*Acushla,*" he managed to say, "I can't spend the night with you. That right belongs to the man you'll marry."

Garrett leveled that direct, disarming stare at him. "My body is my own, to be shared or withheld as I choose." Standing on her toes, she pressed a soft kiss to his lips. Her slim hands framed the sides of his face, her thumbs on his taut jaw. "Show me what you can do," she whispered. "I think I might like to try a few of those one hundred and twenty positions."

Ethan was almost too aroused to stand upright. His head lowered until his forehead rested against hers. That was the only place he could touch her—if he let his hands take hold of her, he would lose control entirely.

His voice was scratchy. "They're not for virgins."

"Then show me how you make love to a virgin."

"Damn you, Garrett," he muttered. There were things about her he didn't want to know: the curve of her naked back, the secret scents and textures of her skin. The intimate colors of her. The rush of her breath against his neck as he entered her, the quickening pleasure-rhythms of their joined bodies. Knowing such things would turn the pain of leaving her into agony. It would turn living without her into something worse than death.

On the other hand, chances were he'd end up in a weighted sack in the Thames before the week was out.

Garrett stared up at him, her eyes bright with challenge. "My bedroom is on the second floor, to the right of the stairs. I'll keep a lamp burning." Her lips curved slightly. "I would leave the front door unlocked . . . but since it's you, there's no need."

Chapter 14

ETHAN WENT DIRECTLY FROM the soiree to the upper-class Belgravia address belonging to Fred Felbrigg, the commissioner of the Metropolitan Police. Taking the stolen evidence to Felbrigg was a logical choice, since he had both the authority and incentive to bring the Home Office conspirators to justice.

When Tatham's and Jenkyn's crimes were brought to light, a great deal of unpleasantness would ensue: arrests, resignations, select committees, hearings, and trials. But if anyone could be trusted to do the right thing, it was Felbrigg, a devoutly religious man who prized order and routine. On top of that, the police commissioner despised Jenkyn. It was no secret at Scotland Yard that Felbrigg was appalled by the spymaster's unauthorized position at the Home Office, and the unsavory intelligence-gathering methods of his handpicked agents.

Disgruntled at having to leave his bed in the middle of the night, Felbrigg came down to his study with a dressing robe thrown over his nightclothes. With his ginger whiskers, short, spindly build, and the flaccid nightcap with a tasseled end dangling over the back of his head, he looked like an elf. An irate elf.

"What's this?" he asked, scowling down at the pages Ethan had set on the desk of his study.

"Proof of an operational link between the Home Office and the Guildhall bombers," Ethan said quietly.

As Felbrigg had sat there in shocked silence, Ethan proceeded to tell him about the Home Secretary's safe and the records of secret government funds diverted to known hostiles and radicals.

"Here's an entry concerning the missing shipment of explosives from Le Havre," Ethan said, nudging one of the pages closer. "The dynamite has been supplied to a group of London-based Fenian activists. They were also given cash money, and an order for admission to the visitors' gallery at the House of Commons."

Pulling off his nightcap, Felbrigg blotted his perspiring face with it. "Why would they want to visit Commons?"

"It's possible they were reconnoitering." At the commissioner's blank look, Ethan added in a matter-of-fact tone, "For a potential attack on Westminster." It was no wonder, he thought privately, that Jenkyn kept outmaneuvering this man over and over again. To call him a plodder wouldn't have been entirely fair, but neither would it have been inaccurate.

Felbrigg bent his head over the pages, reading slowly.

Something nagged at Ethan as he watched the commissioner pore over the evidence. He was certain Felbrigg would never look the other way if he had any inkling that Jenkyn was conspiring to kill the innocent citizens he'd sworn to protect. Felbrigg hated Jenkyn. He'd suffered more than his share of slights and insults from the man. Felbrigg had every reason, personal and professional, to use this information against him.

Still, Ethan's instincts were jangling unpleasantly. Felbrigg was sweating, tense, nervous, and while that could easily be attributed to having been taken by surprise, his reaction didn't feel right. Ethan had expected some clear signs of outrage and perhaps a hint of triumph at being given the instrument of his enemy's downfall. But Felbrigg's white-faced quietness unnerved the hell out of him.

The move had been made, however. There was no way to take it back. *Something* had been set in motion, and whatever it was, the only choice now was to keep to the shadows until Felbrigg had taken action.

"Where will you be tomorrow?" Felbrigg asked.

"Out and about."

"How will we be able to communicate with you?"

"You have enough evidence for investigations and subpoenas," Ethan said, watching him closely. "I'll communicate with you when it's necessary."

"The account ledgers are still in Lord Tatham's safe?"

"Still there," Ethan said, neglecting to mention that he'd changed the combination. He kept his eyes on Felbrigg, who found it difficult to hold a shared gaze for more than one or two seconds.

What aren't you telling me, you bastard?

"This matter will be handled properly and swiftly," Felbrigg said.

"I knew it would be. You're known as a man of honor. You swore before a justice at Westminster to execute the duties of your office 'faithfully, impartially, and honestly.'"

"And so I have," Felbrigg retorted, visibly annoyed. "Now that you've ruined my night's rest, Ransom,

I'll bid you good night, while I deal with the damned mess you've set before me."

Which made Ethan feel slightly better.

He returned to his flat and changed into a workingman's clothes: cotton trousers, an open jacket, a workshirt, and short leather boots. Taking a moment to wander through the spare rooms, he wondered for the first time why he'd lived like a recluse for so long. Bare walls, hard furniture, when he could afford a fine home. But he'd chosen this place. His job required anonymity, isolation, with Jenkyn as the hub of his existence. He'd chosen that, too, for reasons he didn't understand and didn't want to examine.

Stopping in front of the monkey engraving, Ethan stared at it closely. What would Garrett make of it? It was an illustration for an advertisement, with the product name cropped off. A grinning top-hatted monkey, pedaling circles in front of onlookers who kept their distance. Its eyes were melancholy—or maniacal—Ethan couldn't quite decide. Was there a ringmaster just out of view, who'd dressed him up and set him to his task? Was the monkey allowed to stop when he was tired?

Why had Garrett asked him to bring this damned picture to her? She thought it would reveal something about him—which it didn't, by God. He resolved she would never set eyes on the thing—he'd be bloody embarrassed to show it to her. Why had he left it on the wall? Why had he even mentioned it to her?

It would be better for both of them if he disappeared tonight for good. He could go to the other side of the world, change his name, become someone else. God knew it would increase his life expectancy. Garrett would achieve even greater renown, perhaps build a hospital, teach, inspire. She might marry and have children.

But for Ethan, she would live as a dream in the shadows of his memory. Certain words would always make him think of her. So would the sound of a police whistle. And the smell of violets, and the sight of green eyes, and a sky full of fireworks, and the taste of lemon ice.

He started to reach for the picture, swore quietly, and jerked his hand back.

If he went to her . . . God . . . the possibilities filled him with fearful wonder. And hope—a deadly emotion for a man of his profession.

What was one night worth? What would it cost each of them?

GARRETT CAME TO the drowsy awareness of tender warmth brushing her face, like sun-warmed petals falling onto her skin. A soft breath rushed hotly over her cheek. *Ethan.* She smiled and stirred, experiencing the delight of waking in another's presence for the first time. He smelled like night air and mist. With a sleepy murmur, she nudged upward into the velvet caresses, catching at a firm, sweet mouth. Beneath the covers, her bare toes curled.

"I didn't hear you," she whispered. She was a light sleeper, and her floor creaked—how had he reached her so quietly?

Ethan was leaning over her, his hand smoothing her hair. She had gathered the long, curling locks into a single bunch at the back of her neck and tied them with a ribbon. His heavy lashes lowered as he glanced down her body, clad in a simple white nightgown with little pleats at the bodice. Gently he settled his hand over her chest, the tip of his middle finger touching the hollow above her clavicle, where her heartbeat thrummed visibly. His gaze returned to her face.

"Garrett . . . doing this will make everything worse."

Pressing her mouth beneath his jaw, she drew in the delicious scent of him, and rubbed a kiss into the texture of shaven beard. "Take off your clothes," she whispered.

She felt his swallow ripple beneath her lips. He took an unsettled breath and stood.

While Garrett sat up in the small bed to watch, Ethan undressed without haste. One by one, the garments were tossed into a careless heap.

He had the most beautiful form Garrett had ever seen, long-limbed and sleek, his shoulders and chest broad, his flesh toughened and polished to a hard sheen from years of brutal exertion. The light from a frosted glass lampshade caught multiple curves of muscle as he moved, silvered crescents gleaming over the powerful surface of his body. She had already known he was well-endowed, but that wasn't the same as actually *seeing* him like this. Oh, he was something. Handsome all over. A potent male in his prime, completely comfortable in his nakedness.

Whereas she, who was hardly ever disconcerted by nudity, felt nervous, embarrassed, shaky with desire.

Before returning to the bed, Ethan's gaze swept over the personal objects on Garrett's dresser and vanity table: a mother-of-pearl brush-and-comb set, an embroidered lamp mat she'd made in school, the hairpin box with a crocheted cover—a long-ago gift from Miss Primrose—and a little porcelain jar of almond-oil salve. He paused to look more closely at the small framed object on the wall, a pair of tiny knitted baby's mittens, each with a ribbon-work flower on the back.

"My mother made them for me," Garrett said, a bit sheepishly. "Perhaps it's silly to keep them on the wall, but I have very little to remember her by. She was clever with her hands."

Ethan came to sit on the bed. He took her hands and lifted them to his lips, kissing her fingers and palms. "That's where you came by it, then."

Garrett leaned forward to press her cheek against the thick layers of his hair. "Did you bring the picture?" she asked.

"I set it by the door."

Resting her chin briefly on his shoulder, she saw a wrapped rectangular parcel leaning against the wall. "May I see it?"

"Later," Ethan said. "God knows what you'll make of it. The monkey looks homicidal."

"I'm sure he has good reason," she said, pulling back to look at him. "Bicycle seats can cause chafing and perineal numbness."

For some reason, Ethan seemed to find the comment more amusing than it warranted. Laughter glimmered in his eyes, and the dimple appeared in his cheek. Garrett was unable to resist touching the tempting little hollow with her fingertip. She leaned forward to press her lips against it.

"Every time I see this, I want to kiss it," she told him.

"Kiss what?"

"Your dimple."

Ethan looked genuinely perplexed. "I don't have a dimple."

"Yes, you do. It shows when you smile. Has no one ever mentioned it?"

"No."

"Haven't you seen it in the mirror?"

The outside corners of his eyes crinkled. "I don't usually smile at the mirror." His hand curled around the back of her neck, and he possessed her mouth with warm, hungering pressure. She opened to the silky intrusion of his tongue, the exquisite taste of him making her head swim. He eased her back onto the bed, kissing her lazily, filling her senses with slow fire. Gentle hands moved over the nightgown, learning the shape of her body through the thin muslin.

Tentatively she touched the light mat of hair on his chest, the curls soft and crisp against her fingertips. She reached around him, and her eyes flew open as she felt how deeply developed and distinct the muscles of his back were. "Good heavens."

Ethan lifted his head and gave her a questioning look.

"Your trapezius and deltoids are *remarkable*," she said dreamily, her hands wandering over him. "And your latissimus dorsi are so perfectly defined."

A low laugh broke from him as he unfastened her nightgown. "You'll embarrass me with all these flowery compliments."

His weight settled partially over her, his thigh nudging hers apart, and she felt his lips on her chest, skimming softly over newly revealed skin. Her breathing deepened, her pulse rushing, while his hands wandered everywhere, tugging at her nightgown, slipping under it. Soon she was naked, with all the textures of him, roughness, smoothness, hardness, silk, covering her gently. He was utterly in control, guiding her into a realm where he was the master and she was the novice.

His strong hands moved over her slim body with gossamer-light strokes. "I've dreamed of this for so long," he whispered. "The first time we met, part of my brain said, 'I want that one.'"

Garrett smiled against the furry surface of his chest. She nuzzled against the neat, dark circle of a male nipple and touched her tongue to it. "Why didn't you pursue me, then?"

"I knew you were too fine for me."

"No," she protested softly. "I'm not a highborn lady, I'm a commoner."

"There's nothing common about you." Ethan began to play with her long hair, sifting his fingers through it, lifting a lock to brush the ends against his lips and cheeks. "Do you want to know why I gave you violets? They're beautiful and small, but tough enough to grow in the cracks of city pavement. More than once, I've been in some dark place and seen them clustered near a broken stoop, or at the base of a brick wall, bright as jewels. Even without sunlight or good soil, they show up to do a flower's job."

He bent to press his lips against the gilded curve of her breast, as if he could taste the light on her skin. "There was no need to leave a lamp burning in your room," he whispered. "I could find you anywhere, in daylight or darkness." Slowly he kissed and licked a trail of heat between her breasts, leaving faint traces of wetness that cooled in the wake of his breath. He delved into her navel and blew gently into the small hollow . . . and paused as an unexpected scent caught his attention. "Lemon," he murmured, hunting for the source of the fragrance.

"It's . . . a sponge," Garrett said cautiously, a wash of color spreading over her throat and face. One of the ways to guard against pregnancy was to insert a piece of soft sponge dampened with lemon juice. "It . . . it goes inside . . ."

"Yes, I know," Ethan murmured, nuzzling lower on her stomach.

"You do?"

A smile curved against her skin. "I'm no fledgling lad."

Gently his hand parted her thighs, his fingertips sliding down the insides to her knees, and back up again. Down . . . up . . . the stroking was hypnotic, undulating, as if she were being teased by delicate tentacles. His mouth ventured along the crease of her leg and groin, an electrifying hint of bristle rasping across the tenderness as he nudged deeper, lower. Slowly his fingers slid into the protective curls that covered her sex, kneading and stroking, his thumbs parting the soft furrow. He pushed his tongue in and upward, separating the folds with a long, sinuous lick.

Garrett stiffened and gasped, pushing at his head.

Ethan propped himself on his elbows, a gleam of tenderly mocking amusement in his eyes. "Have I shocked you, love?"

Garrett found it hard to think. Her entire body was throbbing. "A little," she said unsteadily. "It is my first time."

"But you sounded so adventurous earlier, with all

your talk of positions." His fingers began to toy with her indecently, sifting among the feathery curls.

Desire seemed to radiate from her—she was surprised not to see wisps of steam rising from her skin. "I . . . I expected we'd start in a more civilized way, and work up to more adventurous things later."

One corner of his mouth quirked lazily. "You didn't invite me to your bed expecting a civilized lover." His thumb stroked into the tender slit of her sex and circled through a slick of wetness. A shiver of pleasure centered in the depths of her body.

He shot her a glance of concentrated blue heat across the blushing surface of her skin, seeming to read her thoughts as if they'd been emblazoned in the air. "You wanted to find out how much I could make you feel. You wanted to know what it was like to lose yourself in passion, and find yourself safe in my arms afterward. Now I'm here, and I'm going to love you with everything I have in me."

His fingers gently parted her, teasing their way among silky pleats and petals. Mesmerized, she watched his head lowering, the powerful shoulders flexing. He began to feast on her slowly, and it felt so good she thought she might faint. His tongue coaxed and tormented, darting and swirling. Her flesh became wetter, silkier, the inner lips turning full and hot, intimate muscles clamping helplessly on emptiness. He searched the intricate secrets of her sex, growling softly in satisfaction at the private taste of her. *Please please please* she wanted to beg, but the only sound she could make was a quiet whimper. The desire he aroused left no room for dignity.

Nothing could have drawn her attention away from

him and what he was doing to her. An entire marching band could have come blaring through the room, and she wouldn't have noticed. She had become a purely physical being, writhing mindlessly until Ethan's arms slid beneath her thighs and curled around them, holding her snug and still. His attention centered on the peak of her clitoris, drawing it out, flicking delicately. Desperately she reached down to grip his upper arms, the bulges of muscle so hard that her fingertips couldn't make the slightest dent.

His tongue began a new rhythm, crossing over the sensitive bud in fluid, steady stroking, like fingers turning the pages of a book. Intense feeling coursed through every part of her, making her hips jerk helplessly in his cradling grip. The agile tongue never faltered, urging her into a dizzying rise of sensation. She arched at the summit, her breath stopping, her heart laboring too hard to distinguish the spaces between the beats. Pleasure came in a series of hard shudders . . . again . . . again . . . until what tension remained broke into finespun shivers. His mouth soothed her for a measureless interval, easing her into peacefulness, until she was as limp as an empty glove. Eventually he moved up beside her and gathered her in his arms. She made a frazzled little sound against his shoulder, drawing a chuckle from him.

"You liked that," he said with masculine satisfaction.

Garrett nodded dreamily.

Gently Ethan reached down to bring her hips against his as they lay sideways. "You'll need to stay relaxed," he whispered, "to take me inside."

She felt his shaft against her belly, heavy and stiff,

searing hot. The evidence of his desire excited her, reawakening the need to be possessed . . . filled . . . taken. She slid her arm around his shoulder and tried to roll to her back with him, but he kept them on their sides, and drew her top leg over his hip. Leaning over her, he kissed the side of her neck and closed his teeth lightly against a sensitive place. His hand slid over her body, fondling and stroking. She was pressed against the solid strength of him, her breasts teased by the silky-coarse hairs on his chest.

He reached between them, adjusting the angle of his erect length, rubbing the broad, hard head of it against the vulnerable cove between her thighs. She tensed in readiness. But he didn't push, only maintained a gentle, constant pressure, a heated presence there at the entrance of her body. His mouth teased and sucked at hers, invading playfully. Cupping her breast with his hand, he rotated his palm gently over the stiff tip before taking it between his fingers.

She couldn't help squirming at the wickedly experienced caresses, the undulation of her hips working against the head of his shaft. The opening of her body smarted and stretched. The intrusion felt impossibly wide. Daunted, she tried to hold still, but his beguiling hand slid down, fingers dancing over the folds of her sex, spreading and teasing her. Hunger knotted deep in her belly, and she was overcome by the impulse to press herself into those erotic, tickling caresses. He was mercifully slow, letting her accept him at her own pace—oh, those fingers felt so good—

"Breathe," he whispered.

She gasped, stretched, ached, quivered on his shaft. He helped her with gentle pushes, inching gradually in a slow, patient possession. Leisurely minutes passed while his wet fingertips stroked, kneaded, and circled until, unbelievably, the pleasure crested again. This time, she was filled so tightly that her muscles could barely clench around him.

When the last ripples of release had faded, he changed their position, lifting her easily, sitting up and letting her slide down until she was in his lap with her legs wrapped around his waist. His hands cupped beneath her bottom, carefully controlling the depth of his penetration to keep from hurting her.

Bewildered, she sat with her arms around his neck.

His eyes were dark and slightly glazed as they stared into hers. "Being inside you like this . . . I wouldn't have thought I could feel so much without dying of it."

She leaned her forehead against his, their breaths mingling in unsteady surges. "Tell me what to do."

"Don't move. Stay like this. Feel how much I want you." He panted and trembled, his deeply muscled thighs flexing beneath her. The small motion sent a rain of sparks across her vision. He adjusted the angle of her hips until she felt him pressing against something deep and sensitive inside her, nudging in a steady rhythm.

She brought her lips to his, and he rewarded her with a rough, ardent kiss. Devouring her soft moans, he kept up the ceaseless rocking of his hips while her insides quivered over the stiff length of him. His body was so powerful, beneath her, all around her—he could crush her so easily—but his hold was careful and cradling, as if she were something exquisite he was afraid of breaking.

Lowering her mouth to his shoulder, she savored the taste of salt and maleness. He was very deep now—her body had relaxed enough to take more—she rode the upward nudging of his hips, and everything was soreness and delight and wonder. The heavy muscles of his back twitched with pleasure as her fingers scored lightly over the surface, leaving invisible markings of ownership.

His breath stopped as release caught up to him at last, the rhythm breaking. Blindly he nuzzled at her throat and made a quiet sound like a lost, wild creature. She curled her arms around his head, rubbing her mouth into the satiny locks of his hair, while her body contained the shocks of his release, the liquid heat, the slow, unfolding relief.

They lay in a tangle, drowsing and caressing, as the night gradually thinned into a sharp white dawn. At the first hint of approaching daybreak, Ethan stretched and sat up, lowering his feet to the floor.

Garrett rose to her knees and hugged him from behind, her breasts flattening against his back. *Don't leave,* she longed to beg, but instead said quietly, "Come to me as soon as you're able."

Ethan was silent for a long moment. "I'll try, *acushla.*"

"If things don't go as they should . . . if you should have to go away somewhere . . . promise you'll take me with you."

Ethan turned to face her then. "Love . . ." He shook his head slightly. "I wouldn't do that to you. Your family and friends, your patients, your practice . . . everything is here. It would ruin your life to leave all that."

"It would ruin my life not to have you." As soon as the words left her lips, Garrett realized it was the truth. "I could be a doctor anywhere. I have a little nest egg set aside. Once we settle somewhere, I'll be able to earn enough to provide for us until you find a suitable occupation. We'll manage. I'm afraid we would have to take my father with us, but—"

"Garrett." A rapid succession of emotions crossed Ethan's face, an odd smile twisting his lips. Taking her head in his hands, he imprinted a brief, hard kiss on her mouth. "You wouldn't have to support me. I have enough to . . . well, it doesn't matter. It won't come to that." He pulled her head against his chest and rocked her slightly, crushing a kiss against her hair. "I'll come to you if I'm able. I swear it."

Closing her eyes in relief, Garrett slid her arms around him.

THE NEXT EVENING, Ethan walked along the footway of Blackfriars Bridge, a structure that was cinched across the lowest banks of the Thames like a buckled luggage strap. Five wrought-iron spans set on enormous red-granite river piers supported the bridge's steep gradient. No matter which direction vehicles or pedestrians came from, it was a long dead pull to get to the other side.

Although the light was fading, the air was still thick with the growls and hisses of factories, the commotion of dockyards, and the bone-jarring clamor of a nearby railway bridge.

Ethan passed a series of pulpit-shaped niches filled by sleeping vagrants covered with tattered newspapers. None of them stirred or made a sound as he walked by.

Finding a place to stand at the railing, he proceeded to eat the dinner he'd bought at a fish shop on the Southwark side. For a penny, a customer could have a meal as fine as any wealthy toff in London: a fillet of fresh haddock or cod dredged in bread crumbs and fried over a coal fire in an iron cauldron of boiling fat. When the inside was firm and white, and the outside crust a sizzling deep brown, the fillet was wrapped in parchment along with a hot lemon wedge and a few sprigs of parsley fried into salted green crisps.

Leaning against the curved railing, Ethan ate slowly and considered his situation. He had kept moving throughout the day, wandering inconspicuously among crossing-sweeps and dustmen, sandwich men wearing billboards front and back, shoeblacks, horse-holders, piemen, and pickpockets. He was weary to the bone, but he felt safer out in the streets than trapped in the confines of his flat.

Crumbling the bit of parchment into a ball, Ethan dropped it over the bridge railing and watched it descend more than forty feet until it hit the smeary black water. Despite ongoing efforts—stricter legislation, new sewer lines and pumping stations—to reduce the foul substances released into the Thames, the water's oxygen levels were too low to support fish or marine mammals.

The little ball vanished slowly beneath the opaque surface.

Ethan's gaze lifted to the dome of St. Paul's, the tallest structure in London. Beyond it, a ragged veil of clouds glowed with milky luminescence, flashes of pink and orange piercing through a few places like veins pulsing with light.

He thought of Garrett, as he always did during quiet moments. At this time of day, she was usually at home. Not far from here, slightly less than three miles. Some part of his brain was always calculating her probable location, the distance between them. The thought of her soothed and pleasured him, made him aware of his humanity as nothing else could.

A thunderous sound heralded a train crossing along the railway between Blackfriars and Southwark bridges. Although Ethan was well accustomed to railway noise, he flinched at the violent rattling of metal plate girders, ironwork rail supports, and rolling stock couplings. Continuous earsplitting puffs of steam were punctuated regularly by the combustive roar of the firebox. Turning from the water, Ethan began to resume his walk along the footpath.

He was stunned by a tremendous wallop to his chest, as if someone had struck him with a cudgel. He was thrown backward onto his arse, the breath knocked out of him. Wheezing and choking, he worked to pull air back into his lungs. A strange buzzing feeling circled through his insides.

It took all his strength to rise to his feet. His limbs weren't working properly, muscles quivering and bunching in response to the confused signals of his brain. The buzzing turned into something searing and terrible, hotter than fire. It didn't seem possible that human flesh could harbor so much pain. Unable to identify the cause, Ethan looked down at himself in bewilderment. A flooding dark stain spread over the front of his shirt.

He'd been shot.

His numb gaze lifted to behold William Gamble walking toward him, a short-gripped bulldog revolver in hand.

The deafening roar of the train went on and on, while Ethan backed up to the bridge railing and leaned against it to keep from collapsing.

"Counting on Felbrigg's honor, were you?" Gamble asked when the noise had faded. "He's a bureaucrat at heart. He'll always defer to the next man up the chain. Tatham and Jenkyn convinced him their plans were all for the greater good."

Ethan stared at him dumbly. *Christ Jesus.* The commissioner of police was going to allow scores of innocent people, including women and children, to be maimed and murdered . . . all for the sake of political advantage.

". . . robbing Tatham's safe on my watch, you bastard," Gamble was saying irritably. "The only reason Jenkyn hasn't put a bullet in my head is because he was the one who made a hash of it by inviting Dr. Gibson to the soiree in the first place." He approached Ethan slowly. "I didn't want to finish you off like this. I wanted it to be a fair fight."

"'Twas fair enough," Ethan managed to say. "Should've . . . seen you coming." There was a salty liquid rattle in his throat. He coughed and saw blood spatter on the ground. As he leaned over, he glanced through the stone balustrades at the expanse of dark water below. Lifting himself up, he braced heavily against the railing.

There was no way to win. No path to survival.

"You should have," Gamble agreed. "But you've

been distracted for weeks, thinking of nothing but that green-eyed bitch. She's brought you to this."

Garrett.

She wouldn't know he'd been thinking of her at the last moment. She would never know what she'd meant to him. It would make dying so much easier if only he'd told her. But she would do well without him, just as she had before. She was a strong, resilient woman, a force of nature.

He only worried that no one would bring her flowers.

How strange that as his life was spinning down to its end, there was no anger or fear, only soul-scorching love. He was dissolving in it. There was nothing left but the way she'd made him feel.

"Was she worth it?" Gamble jeered.

Gripping the railing behind him, Ethan smiled faintly. "Aye."

In the next moment, he tipped back and let the momentum bring his legs up, his body rolling into a backward flip before heading into the water feet first. During the dizzying plummet, he was vaguely aware of more shots being fired. Holding his breath, he braced for the impact.

The world exploded into foul, freezing blackness, like hell after all the fire and brimstone had been extinguished. Liquid death. He struggled feebly, unable to see or breathe. Finally he had reached the level of damage his body could not endure.

He was pulled downward into a cold, insistent silence where there was no time, no light, no self. He vanished beneath the great river and the city of millions and its inscrutable sky, his body nothing but mites and motes of fleeting mortality. The throbs of his failing heart echoed the rhythm of one name . . . *Garrett . . . Garrett.* She was somewhere. Not far. He clung to that thought as he was pulled by the ancient current to his fate.

Chapter 15

"ELIZA," GARRETT SAID WEARILY, rubbing her eyes, "just because my father wants something doesn't mean you have to give it to him."

The cookmaid faced her defensively as they stood in the kitchen, where the heavy, ripe sweetness of mincemeat pie hung thickly in the air. "I gave 'im the thinnest sliver, no wider than your finger—look, I'll show the pie to ye—"

"I don't want to see the pie. I want you to follow the weekly menu I gave you."

"'E can't abide eatin' like an invalid."

"He *is* an invalid."

After working long hours at the clinic, Garrett had returned home to discover that Eliza had taken it upon herself to make one of her father's favorite dishes, an enormous mincemeat pie that was too heavy and rich for his sensitive digestive system. It was also frightfully expensive, made with six pounds of currants and raisins, three pounds of apples, three pounds of suet, two pounds of sugar, two pounds of beef, a pint each of wine and brandy, and a variety of spices, all loaded into a flour crust and baked into a dark, sticky mass.

There was no sound from her father's room upstairs—Eliza had already carried a slice up to him, and he was undoubtedly gorging on it as fast as possible. "In an hour or two, he'll be complaining of stomach pains," Garrett said. "Mincemeat pie is made with everything that's bad for him, from suet to sugar."

Half defiant, half apologetic, Eliza retorted, "Mr. Gibson used to eat it every Sunday. Now 'e's never allowed a single bite. What pleasures 'as he got left? No wife, no sweets, can't 'ardly walk, eyes too poor for readin' . . . just sits in his room and counts the days until 'is next game of draw poker. I say let 'im have a midge o' joy now and then."

An impatient reply hovered on Garrett's lips, but she bit it back as she considered Eliza's words.

The cookmaid had a point. Stanley Gibson, once a vigorous and active man—a constable with a London beat—now spent most of his days in a quiet room. A cheerful, comfortable room, but even so, there must be times when it felt like a prison. What harm would it do to allow him a little indulgence now and then? In Garrett's concern over doing everything she could to preserve what remained of his physical health, she mustn't deny him the small enjoyments that made life tolerable.

"You're right," she said reluctantly.

Eliza's mouth sagged open. "I am?"

"I agree that everyone deserves a midge of joy now and then."

"It's right fair-minded of ye to say so, Doctor."

"However, if this particular 'midge' keeps him up half the night with a bellyache, you're going to help me with him."

The cookmaid's lax mouth stretched into a satisfied grin. "Yes, Doctor."

After going upstairs to visit her father, who had looked vastly pleased with himself and stoutly insisted the mincemeat pie would cause him no troubles whatsoever, Garrett went down to the front receiving room. She sat at the escritoire desk and sorted through correspondence, and picked at the slice of mincemeat pie Eliza had brought her. She could only manage a bite or two. She'd never been fond of sweet-and-savory dishes, and she'd certainly never shared her father's fondness for this one. In her opinion, mincemeat pie was a jumble of ingredients that had never been meant to unite in one crust. It was a heavy, overpowering dish, entirely resistant to digestive enzymes.

Even before the pie, her stomach had felt unsettled. She had worried all day, knowing that by now Ethan had taken the incriminating information to Scotland Yard. The machinery of justice had been set in motion, and both Lord Tatham and Sir Jasper would surely be on the defensive, trying to save their own necks. She reassured herself with the thought that Ethan was familiar with every inch of London, and he was as sharp and surefooted as any man alive. He could take care of himself.

In a few days, when the conspirators were safely behind bars, Ethan would call on her. It cheered Garrett to think about him at her doorstep, big and handsome, perhaps a bit nervous as she invited him inside. They would discuss the future . . . their future . . . and she would convince him that despite his concerns, they would be happier together than apart. And if Ethan couldn't bring himself to propose to her, Garrett would simply have to do it herself.

How did one go about proposing marriage?

In the novels, a couple emerged after a moonlight stroll with the engagement as a *fait accompli*, leaving the reader to imagine the scene. Garrett had heard that the suitor went down on one knee, which she certainly wasn't going to do for anyone unless she were helping to load him onto an ambulance stretcher.

Since lilting romantic phrases were hardly Garrett's forte, it really would be better if Ethan were the one to propose. He would say something lovely and poetic in that beguiling Irish accent. Yes, she would find a way to make him do it.

Was she really considering marriage to a man she knew so little? Had another woman been in this situation, Garrett would have advised her to wait and find out more about the prospective husband. There were more ways for it to all go wrong than there were ways for it to go right.

But I've had to wait for so many things in my life, she thought. She'd spent years studying and working while other young women were being courted. Becoming a doctor had been her dream and her calling. She had never trusted that in the future she would find a stable and loving partner who would take care of her. She hadn't wanted to depend on someone out of necessity.

Garrett had no regrets: This was the life she had wanted. At the same time . . . she was tired of being cautious and responsible. She yearned to fling herself headlong into the experience of being loved, desired, possessing, and possessed. And Ethan Ransom was the only man who'd ever made her want to take the risk of true intimacy, not only physically, but also emotionally. It would be safe to allow him inside her most private thoughts and feelings—he would never mock or hurt her, or take more than he gave. At the same time, he would be a demanding lover who wouldn't let her hide or withhold anything, and that was as frightening as it was exciting.

A sharp rapping of the lion's-head knocker jarred Garrett from her reflections. It was well past calling or delivery hours. Before five seconds had passed, another burst of percussion resounded through the air.

Eliza sped to the entranceway, exclaiming beneath her breath about people knocking fit to wake the dead. "Evenin'," Garrett heard the cookmaid say. "What business are you about?"

A muffled conversation ensued.

Unable to make out what was being said, Garrett frowned and half turned in her chair to look at the sitting-room doorway.

Eliza came into view, holding a folded card. She frowned and chewed at her lips before saying, "It's one of Lord Trenear's footmen, Doctor. He bid me to give you this while he waits."

Garrett extended her hand for the note. Breaking the wax seal, she saw a few lines written in a hasty forward slant, the *t*'s crossed to the right of the stems, the dot of one of the *i*'s missing. It was from Kathleen, Lady Trenear, the earl's wife.

Dr. Gibson,
   If you are able, I beg you to come to
Ravenel House with all possible haste. There
has been an accident involving a guest. As
the matter is sensitive, I ask your discretion

in keeping this matter entirely private. Thank you, my friend.

—K

Garrett stood up so abruptly that her chair nearly toppled backward. "Someone's been injured," she said. "I'm off to Ravenel House. Make certain the surgical kit is in my bag, and fetch my coat and hat."

Eliza, bless her, wasted no time with questions, and scampered off. She had helped Garrett on many occasions when speed was of the essence in seeing to a patient.

Although Garrett was Lady Helen's doctor as well as Pandora's, the rest of the Ravenels usually relied on the services of a trusted family physician. Why hadn't they sent for him? Was he unavailable, or had they decided Garrett was better equipped to deal with the situation?

The footman, a tall, fair-haired fellow, obeyed instantly as she gestured for him to follow her to the surgery.

"Who's been injured?" Garrett asked briskly.

"Afraid I don't know, miss . . . er, ma'am. Doctor. A stranger."

"Male or female?"

"Male."

"What happened to him?" At his hesitation, Garrett said impatiently, "I must know the nature of the injury so I can bring the right supplies."

"It was an accident with a firearm."

"Right," she said briskly, snatching up a wire basket filled with odds and ends, and dumped it out on the floor. Hurrying to a supply shelf, she began selecting bottles and putting them in the basket. Chloroform, ether, carbolic acid, iodoform, collodion, bismuth solution, cotton lint, gauze, rolled bandages, glycerin, catgut ligatures, isopropyl alcohol, metallic salts . . .

"Carry this," she said, shoving the basket at the footman. "And this." She hefted a large jug of sterilized water and gave it to him. He curved his free arm around it, staggering slightly. "Come," she said, striding to the entranceway, where Eliza was waiting with her hat and walking coat.

"I don't know how long I'll be away," Garrett said to the cookmaid, tugging on the coat. "If my father complains about his stomach, give him a dose of the digestive tonic in his bedroom cabinet."

"Yes, Doctor." Eliza handed her the heavy leather doctor's bag and cane.

The footman hurried to the front door and struggled to open it with both arms full, until Eliza darted forward to do it for him.

Garrett stopped at the threshold as she saw the plain black carriage with no identifiable insignias or designs. Glancing at the footman suspiciously, she asked, "Why is it unmarked? The Ravenel carriage has the family crest lacquered on the side."

"It was Lord Trenear's decision. It's a private matter, he told me."

Garrett didn't move. "What are the names of the family dogs?"

The footman looked slightly affronted. "Napoleon and Josephine. Little black spaniels."

"Tell me one of Lady Pandora's words."

Pandora, one of the twins, often used made-up

words such as *frustraging* or *flopulous*, when the ordinary ones didn't suit her. Despite her attempts to curb the habit, they still slipped out from time to time.

The footman thought for a moment. "Lambnesia?" he ventured, as if hoping that would satisfy her. "She said it when Lady Trenear misplaced her basket of wool knitting yarn."

That sounded like Pandora. Garrett gave him a decisive nod. "Let's proceed."

The drive from King's Cross to Ravenel House, on South Audley, was approximately three and a half miles, but it felt like three hundred. Garrett simmered with impatience as she held her doctor's bag on her lap and kept a hand on the basket of rattling, sloshing bottles beside her. She was eager to do whatever she could for the Ravenels, who had always been gracious and kind, and had never put on airs despite their elevated social status.

The current earl, Devon, Lord Trenear, was a distant Ravenel cousin who had inherited the title unexpectedly after the last two earls had died in quick succession. Although Devon was a young man with no experience at running a large estate and managing its attendant financial obligations, he had shouldered the burden admirably. He had also taken responsibility for the three Ravenel sisters, Helen, Pandora, and Cassandra, all unmarried at the time, when he could have easily thrown them to the wolves.

At last the stately Jacobean house came into view, its squared-off shape ornamented with lavish scrolls, pilasters, arches, and parapets. For all its great size, the residence was welcoming and warm, comfortably mellowed with age. As soon as the carriage stopped, one footman was there to open the door while another reached in to assist Garrett.

"Take this," Garrett said without preamble, handing the basket of supplies to him. "Be careful—most of these chemicals are caustic and highly flammable."

The footman shot her a glance of suppressed alarm and gripped the basket carefully.

Garrett alighted from the carriage by herself and strode across the flagstone tiles to the front steps of the house, almost running in her haste.

Two women waited for her at the threshold: the plump silver-haired housekeeper, Mrs. Abbot, and Lady Cassandra, a fair-haired young woman with blue eyes and the kind of face that belonged on a cameo. Behind them, the grand entrance hall bustled with a sense of controlled panic, housemaids and footmen running back and forth with cans of water, and what appeared to be dirty toweling and linens.

Garrett's nose twitched as she caught an ambient scent in the air, a taint of some kind of organic matter mixed with caustic chemicals . . . whatever its source, the smell was rank and rotten.

The housekeeper helped Garrett remove her hat and coat.

"Dr. Gibson," Cassandra said, her pretty features drawn and anxious. "Thank goodness you arrived so quickly."

"Tell me what happened."

"I'm not altogether sure. A man was brought here earlier by the river police, only they asked us not to tell anyone about it. He was thrown into the river, and they said when they pulled him out, they thought he was dead, but then he started coughing and groaning. They brought him here because he was carrying one of Cousin West's calling cards in his wallet, and they didn't know where else to take him."

"Poor fellow," Garrett said quietly. Even a healthy man who'd been exposed to the toxic waters of the Thames would become seriously ill from it. "Where is he now?"

"They carried him into the double library," Mrs. Abbot said, gesturing toward a nearby hallway. "It's a dreadful mess in there. Lord and Lady Trenear have been trying to wash the filth from him and make him more comfortable." She shook her head and fretted, "The carpets . . . the furniture . . . no doubt all ruined."

"Why would an earl and countess personally tend to a stranger?" Garrett asked, puzzled.

A new voice joined the conversation as a man approached them from the hallway. "He's not a stranger." His voice was deep and easy, the accent refined.

As Garrett turned to face him, a shock of excitement and confusion stopped her breath. *Ethan.* Blue, blue eyes . . . the dark hair . . . the big, athletic frame . . . but it was not him. A leaden weight of disappointment settled over her, followed by a chill of premonition.

"I'm West Ravenel." The man glanced beyond her to Cassandra. "Darling," he murmured, "let me have a few moments with the doctor." The girl left at once, accompanied by the housekeeper. Turning back to Garrett, Ravenel said quietly, "The wounded man is an acquaintance of yours. You're here because he asked for you."

Cold barbs of fear lodged in Garrett's chest. The

few bites of mincemeat she'd had earlier seemed to rise in her esophagus. Swallowing against the nausea, she forced herself to ask, "Is it Mr. Ransom?"

"Yes."

More sharp spikes were driven into her chest, pinning her pounding heart in place. She felt her face contorting, spasming.

Ravenel spoke with measured slowness, trying to give her time to absorb the information. "There's a bullet in his chest. He's lost a great deal of blood. The wound doesn't seem to be bleeding now, but his condition is very bad. He goes in and out of consciousness. We sent for you not out of any hope that you could heal him, but because he wanted to see you one last time."

Garrett tried to think above a flood of sick horror. She wanted to scream, weep, collapse. But as she thought of the men who were responsible for harming him, a bolt of fury engulfed her, searing through the smothering despair. *How dare they do this to him?* The burst of rage steadied her and gave her strength. Her fist tightened around the handles of her leather bag.

"Show me to him," she heard herself say in a level voice. "I'll fix him."

Chapter 16

"I DON'T THINK YOU UNDERSTAND the severity of his condition," Ravenel said as he led the way to the double library. "He's hanging by a thread."

"I understand his condition quite well," Garrett said, proceeding along the hallway with heel-digging strides. "Any perforating wound of the chest is life-threatening. Furthermore, the Thames is contaminated with bacteria, nitrates, and poisonous chemicals. One can hardly do enough to disinfect him."

"But you think there's a chance of saving him?" he asked skeptically.

"I *will* save him," Garrett gave an impatient shake of her head as she heard the quaver in her voice.

They entered the library, two spacious joined rooms lined with acres of mahogany bookshelves. The interior was arranged with a few pieces of stately, heavy furniture, including a massive table running along the center and a long, low settee. An expanse of sodden Persian carpeting was heaped with toweling and cans of water. A foul scent competed with the acrid freshness of carbolic soap, commonly used for horses and difficult household cleaning.

The small, slim form of Kathleen, Lady Trenear, and the far more substantial one of her husband,

Devon, were bent over a still form laid out on the settee.

Garrett's heartbeat was so rough that the lights in the room seemed to pulse in front of her eyes. "Good evening," she said, trying to sound composed, without success.

Both of them turned toward her.

Kathleen, a red-haired woman with delicate, almost feline beauty, regarded her with concern. "Dr. Gibson," she murmured.

"Countess," she said distractedly, and gave a cursory nod to the tall, dark-haired earl. "Lord Trenear." Her gaze went to Ethan.

If not for the continuous trembling that shook Ethan's long frame, she would have assumed he was already dead. His complexion was waxen, his lips blue-tinged, his eyes closed and sunken. They had covered his body with a quilt but had left his shoulders and one arm bare. His hand lay palm upward with the fingers slightly curled, the nails lavender-gray.

Setting down her doctor's bag, Garrett knelt on a folded towel beside the settee and reached for his wrist to check his pulse. It was nearly too weak to detect. His veins were colorless and flattened. *Oh God*. He'd lost too much blood. Anything she did was going to kill him.

Ethan jerked a little at her touch. The thick lashes lifted to reveal a flash of unearthly blue. His disoriented gaze settled on her, focusing with effort. A faint smile ghosted across his lips. "Garrett. My time's . . . run short."

"Nonsense," she said firmly. "I'll have you back to rights quite soon."

She began to pull back the quilt, but his big, cold hand slid over hers, stopping her. "I'm dying, love," she heard him whisper.

The words shook Garrett by the spine, as nothing ever had before. She was distantly amazed that she could manage a coherent reply. "I'll thank you to leave the diagnosing to me."

His fingers wrapped around hers. The feel of them was unfamiliar, devoid of their natural heat and strength. "Garrett . . ."

She used her free hand to ease the quilt down until the bullet wound was visible. It was a surprisingly neat, small circle. Given the elasticity of skin, the bullet was undoubtedly larger than the hole's diameter.

Ethan's gaze fixed on hers as he spoke with effort. "The first moment I saw you, I knew you were my share of the world. I've always loved you. If I could choose my fate, I'd never be parted from you. *Acushla . . .* pulse of my heart, breath of my soul . . . there's nothing on this earth more fair and fine than you. Your shadow on the ground is sunlight to me."

He fell silent, his eyes closing. Tremors racked his body. Pain drew his eyebrows together as if he were concentrating very hard on something.

Clumsily Garrett drew away from him to rummage in her bag, yanking out a stethoscope. Her heart was dashing itself to pieces. She wanted to throw herself on him and howl in despair. *I'm not strong enough for this,* she thought. *I can't bear it. God, please don't let this happen . . . please . . .*

But as she looked down at Ethan's ashen face, a mantle of calm determination settled over the blaze of anguish. She would *not* lose him.

Carefully she set the stethoscope at various points on his chest, from just above his collarbone down to the bottom of his rib cage. Although his breathing was far too rapid and shallow, his lungs didn't appear to have been damaged. Clinging to that one small bit of good news, she reached into her supplies, found her hypodermic needle case, and prepared a syringe of morphine.

"Ethan," she asked quietly, "can you tell me what kind of gun it was? Did you see how far away the shooter was standing?"

His eyes slitted open, staring at her without comprehension.

Devon, Lord Trenear, answered from behind her. "From the powder burns, it appears he was shot at point-blank range. There's no exit wound. I would guess it was a large-caliber round shot at low velocity."

She hoped he was right: the inward track of a heavy bullet through the flesh would be wider, which would make probing and removal easier.

"He said it was one of Jenkyn's men," Trenear continued. "A professional assassin would use one of the more modern bullets, with a conical shape instead of round. If so, it would be partially encased in a shell of copper or steel."

"Thank you, my lord." A pointed tip made it likely the bullet had pursued a direct course instead of bouncing and ricocheting inside him. And if the projectile was covered by a hard casing, the lead wouldn't have fragmented.

Trenear gave her an astute glance, understanding that she was going to operate on Ethan right there, in a last-minute effort to save his life. His eyes were dark blue rimmed with black . . . *Ethan's eyes*. Was she going mad? No, she wouldn't think about anything except the work that awaited her.

"What do you need?" Kathleen asked, coming to stand beside her. "We have three large cans of boiled water, and more in the process of heating. We've been using it to wash him with carbolic soap."

"Excellent," Garrett said. "The footman has carried in a basket of surgical chemicals. If you would, my lady, please find the one labeled sodium hypochlorite, and pour the entire contents into one of the cans of water. Use that to disinfect every inch of the library table, and cover the surface with clean linen sheets. We'll need as many lamps in here as you're able to provide." She turned to Devon. "My lord, can you send someone to fetch Dr. Havelock?"

"I'll fetch him myself."

"Thank you. Also, make certain he brings the Roussel transfuser. He won't want to, but don't let him come without it." Continuing to kneel beside the settee, Garrett swabbed Ethan's upper arm with antiseptic solution. Tilting the morphine syringe upward, she expertly forced the air from the small glass chamber until a clear drop appeared at the tip of the hollow needle.

Ethan stirred and blinked, seeming to regain his sensibilities. "Garrett," he said carefully, as if he knew her but wasn't quite sure of the name. His gaze flickered to the hypodermic needle in her hand. "Don't need that."

"You'll be glad of it when I start probing for the bullet."

His chest rose and fell with an agitated breath.

"Don't even think about opening me up like . . . a tin of boiled ham."

"You're going to receive proper medical treatment," she informed him.

"If I made it through surgery, the fever would kill me."

"You will make it through surgery, and you will definitely have fever. A nasty one. After being doused in that filthy river, you're teeming with inflammatory microbes. Fortunately, I've brought a variety of antiseptic solutions. Before long I'll have you as clean as a bobbin."

"For God's sake, woman—*ahh, damn it,* what is that?"

"Morphine," she said, depressing the plunger slowly to release the medicine into the thick muscle of his upper arm.

Ethan subsided, realizing there would be no stopping her. "You haven't one romantic bone in your body," he muttered.

That sounded so much like his usual self that Garrett almost smiled. "I reassembled an entire disarticulated skeleton in medical school. There's no such thing as a romantic bone."

He turned his face away from her.

Garrett was wrenched with love and agonized concern. She felt her lips tremble, and she clamped them shut. She knew Ethan understood how close to death he was, and had resigned himself to what he thought was inevitable. He wanted to spend the last few minutes of his life lucid and aware, in the arms of the woman he loved.

But instead of caressing him, her hands would be plying surgical instruments. Instead of gazing at him adoringly, she would be examining inner contusions and lacerations.

No, her way was not romantic.

She wouldn't be the woman he loved, however, if she didn't use all her skills in an effort to save him.

Setting aside the hypodermic syringe, Garrett looked down at the perfect shape of his ear. She bent to rub her lips softly against the lobe. "Éatán," she whispered, "listen to me. This is what I do. I'll bring you through this and take care of you. I'll be with you every minute. Trust me."

His cheek nudged back toward her. She saw that he didn't believe her. All the light in his eyes had vanished save a last glint or two, like the ember of a candlewick that had just been snuffed.

"Tell me you love me," he whispered.

Panicked words fluttered and darted inside her . . . *I love you I need you Oh God please stay with me* . . . but she had the terrifying premonition that saying it would allow him to let go. As if she would be giving him permission to pass away peacefully instead of fighting for his life.

"Later," she said gently. "When you wake up after the surgery, I'll tell you."

BY THE TIME Dr. Havelock had arrived, Ethan had been transferred to the massive oak library table. It had taken the combined efforts of West Ravenel and three footmen to move him as carefully as possible, in the fear of dislodging possible bone shards or lead fragments, or causing other damage. Ethan had slipped into a delirium, only letting out an occasional groan or wordless exclamation.

With Kathleen's help, Garrett had wiped Ethan's form from head to toe with disinfectant solution and shaved around the gunshot wound in preparation for surgery. They had draped a towel across his hips for modesty, and covered him with clean cotton blankets afterward. A blue-white pallor gave his flesh the illusion of cool marble perfection, sculpted and polished to a silky sheen.

It was somehow worse to see a man of such robust health reduced to this condition. The morphine had taken what effect it would, but Ethan was still in obvious pain, and Garrett didn't dare give him any more with his blood pressure so low.

Garrett had never been so relieved as she was when Dr. Havelock arrived. His capable presence made her feel that together, they would pull Ethan through. Havelock's distinctive shock of snow-white hair had been brushed back hastily, his cheeks and chin glinting with the day's growth of silver beard. He examined Ethan with quiet efficiency, responding to the wounded man's incoherent murmurs with a few soothing words.

When Havelock had finished his evaluation, Garrett went with him to the far end of the library for a private conference.

"He's on the verge of circulatory collapse," Havelock said quietly, his expression grave. "In fact, I've never seen a patient with a capacity to endure such severe hemorrhage. The bullet penetrated the left pectoral muscle. I wouldn't be surprised if an artery has been completely severed."

"That's what I thought—but if so, it should have been immediately fatal. Why has the bleeding stopped? If it were leaking into the chest cavity, his lung function would be impaired, but it isn't."

"It's possible the artery has constricted and retracted within its sheath, thereby sealing itself temporarily."

"If it turns out to be the axillary artery, would there be enough blood supply left for the arm if I tie it off?"

"Yes, there would be sufficient collateral circulation. But I wouldn't advise it."

"What would you advise, then?"

Havelock regarded her for a long moment, his gaze kind in a way she didn't like. "Make the poor fellow as comfortable as you can, and let him die in peace."

The words were a slap in the face. "*What?*" Garrett asked dazedly. "No, I'm going to save him."

"You can't. Based on everything you've taught me about antiseptic medicine, this man is so contaminated, within and without, there's no hope. Subjecting him to unnecessary surgery is folly and selfishness. If we did manage to delay his death for a day or so, he would go through unspeakable agony. His entire body would become riddled with sepsis until all his organs failed. I won't have that on my conscience, and I don't want it on yours."

"Let me worry about my own conscience. Just help me, Havelock. I can't do this by myself."

"Operating when the medical facts don't warrant it— when it will only cause the patient needless suffering— that is malpractice by any standard."

"I don't care," Garrett said recklessly.

"You'll care very much if this destroys your career. You know there are many who would leap at the chance to revoke your medical license. The first female physician in England, driven out of the profession because of scandal and misconduct . . . what would that do to the women who dream of following in your footsteps? What about the patients you'll never be able to help in the future?"

"If I do nothing for this man, I'll never be of any use to anyone," Garrett burst out, trembling from the force of her emotions. "It would haunt me forever. I couldn't live with the thought that there was a chance to save him but I didn't take it. You don't know him. If our positions were reversed, he would do anything for me. I have to fight for him. *I have to.*"

The older man stared at her as if he didn't recognize her. "You're not thinking clearly."

"I'm thinking more clearly than I ever have in my life."

"This is the man you met at Lord Tatham's house last evening."

Garrett flushed but held his gaze as she admitted, "He and I were already acquainted. He's my . . . he's . . . important to me."

"I see." Havelock was silent then, stroking his white whiskers, while precious seconds of Ethan's life ticked away.

"Did you bring the transfuser?" Garrett burst out, impatient to decide on a course of action.

Havelock looked grim. "I've attempted blood transfusion on seven different occasions, and every case but one ended in shock, pain, and stroke or heart failure. No one has yet discovered why some blood is compatible and some isn't. You haven't seen what happens when the procedure fails. I have. Never again will I knowingly inflict such agony on a patient."

"Did you bring it?" she persisted.

"I did," he grated. "God help you and that poor wretch if you try to use it. Be honest, Dr. Gibson: Are you acting on behalf of your patient, or yourself?"

"Both of us! I'm doing it for both of us."

She saw from his expression that it was the wrong answer.

"I can't help you to do something against your own interests as well as his," Havelock said. "This is madness, Garrett."

He never used her first name.

As she stood there in stricken silence, he gave her a look that was somehow both pleading and stern, before departing the library.

"You're leaving?" she asked in bewilderment.

He continued past the threshold without replying.

Garrett felt hollow and numb. Dr. William Havelock—her partner, advisor, supporter, and confidant, a man with the unfailing ability to discern right from wrong even in the most complex situations—had just walked out on her. He would take no part in what she was doing. Not because he was wrong, but because *she* was. He was sticking to his principles, whereas she . . .

She had no principles when it came to Ethan Ransom. She only loved him.

Shaken, despairing, she blinked against a burning wet blur. She was choking on her own breath.

Damn it, *damn it,* now she was crying.

Someone was standing at the doorway. It was West

Ravenel, leaning a broad shoulder against the jamb, his gaze level and appraising. His blue eyes were startling against the sun-browned richness of his complexion.

Garrett lowered her head, swallowing repeatedly against the needling pain in her throat. She had no defenses left. He must have contempt for her, or pity, and either way, one word from him would destroy her.

"Go on and take a crack at it," she heard Ravenel say casually. "I'll help you."

Her head bobbed upward. She stared at him, dumbfounded. It took her a moment to realize he was offering to assist with the surgery. After clearing her throat twice, the clenched muscles loosened enough for her to speak. "Do you have any medical training?"

"Not a bit. But I'll do whatever you tell me."

"Do you have any problems with the sight of blood?"

"Lord, no, I'm a farmer. I'm around blood all the time, both animal and human."

Garrett regarded him dubiously, blotting her cheeks with the edge of her sleeve. "There's that much blood involved in farming?"

Ravenel grinned. "I didn't say I was any good at it." The flash of his smile was so oddly like Ethan's that Garrett felt a sharp pang in her chest. Tugging a handkerchief from inside his coat, he came forward to give it to her.

Mortified for him to have seen her crying, Garrett wiped her cheeks and eyes, and blew her nose. "How much did you hear?"

"Most of it. Sound carries all through this library."

"Do you think Havelock was right?"

"About which part?"

"That I should make Mr. Ransom comfortable during his last few minutes on earth instead of torturing him with surgery?"

"No, you've already managed to ruin a moving deathbed scene. I couldn't wait to hear what came after 'your shadow on the ground is sunlight to me,' but then you started giving orders like a drill sergeant. You might as well operate on Ransom: we won't get any more good lines out of him tonight."

Garrett stared at him with a bewildered frown. The man either didn't know or didn't care how inappropriate it was to joke in these circumstances. She suspected it was the latter. On the other hand, she found his cool insouciance rather reassuring. She sensed he could be a bit of a bastard when it suited him, not at all the kind who would fall apart under pressure, and at the moment, that was exactly what she needed.

"All right," she said. "Go to the kitchen and wash the upper half of your body with carbolic soap and hot water. Make certain to scrub beneath your fingernails." She looked down at his hands, which were elegantly long-fingered and scrupulously clean. The nails were pared nearly down to the quick, with only the thinnest possible white crescents showing.

"What should I wear?" Ravenel asked.

"A bleached linen or cotton shirt. Don't touch *anything* afterward—especially not tables or doorknobs— and come back here directly."

He gave her a short nod and strode away with a confident stride. His voice could be heard in the hallway. "Mrs. Abbot, I'm going to the kitchen to wash. You'll want to warn the housemaids to shield their eyes from the sight of my manly torso."

Kathleen, Lady Trenear, came to Garrett. "Whose

housemaids would he be referring to?" she asked dryly. "Ours will be crowding into the scullery to obtain the best possible view."

"Is he reliable?" Garrett asked.

"Solid as a rock. West manages the estate farms and leaseholds, and is experienced at everything from spring lambing to tending sick livestock. He can handle anything, no matter how revolting. And I'm usually like that also, but . . ." Kathleen paused and looked chagrined. "I'm with child again, and I'm queasy most of the time."

Garrett looked at the countess with concern, seeing that she was clammy and ashen, and visibly unsteady. The foul smell of polluted water must have made her wretched. "It's not good for you to be exposed to this contamination," she said. "You must bathe at once, and lie down in a well-ventilated room. Also, have your cook make tea with fresh gingerroot. That will help to settle your stomach."

"I will." Kathleen smiled at her. "You'll have West and the servants to help you. My husband will be making arrangements for Mr. Ransom to be spirited away from London as soon as possible. He must be taken to a safe place until he's well again."

"I fear you may have rather too much faith in my abilities," Garrett said grimly.

"After the surgery you performed on Pandora? . . . there's no doubt in any of our minds that you have miracles up your sleeves."

"Thank you." To Garrett's annoyance, her eyes began to water again.

Kathleen's small hands came to hers and gripped them warmly. "Do your best, and let fate take its course. You can't blame yourself for the outcome if you know you did everything you could."

Garrett managed a wobbly smile. "Forgive me, my lady . . . but you don't know much about doctors."

"ARTERY FORCEPS," GARRETT said, pointing in turn to the gleaming sterilized instruments on a linen-covered tray. "Torsion forceps. Wound forceps. Suture forceps. Amputating knife. Double-edged amputating knife. Catlin knife. Resection knife. Middle pointed scalpel, curved scalpel, straight and curved scissors—"

"You'll have to tell me as we go along. My mind went blank after 'amputating knife.'"

West Ravenel stood beside Garrett at the library table, where Ethan's unconscious form was draped in clean white sheets and a cotton blanket. Garrett had administered chloroform by careful drops into a cylindrical inhaler filled with sterilized lint, while Ravenel had held a nose-and-mouth piece attached to a length of silk-covered tubing over Ethan's face.

Carefully Garrett folded back the sheets to expose the sinewed, powerfully honed shape of his torso down to his navel.

"What a specimen," she heard Ravenel say flippantly. "He has muscles in places I didn't know there were muscles."

"Mr. Ravenel," Garrett said, picking up a large irrigator syringe, "please keep your remarks to a minimum." Carefully she flushed out the wound with a chloride of zinc solution, and set the syringe aside. "Hand me the Nélaton probe—the one tipped with unglazed porcelain."

After inserting the probe, she discovered the bullet's path was a straight track, running at a slight upward slant toward the outer border of the first rib. The probe's tip tapped against something hard. Garrett withdrew the probe, and regarded the blue mark on the end.

"What is that?" Ravenel asked.

"The porcelain turns blue where it comes into contact with lead."

The bullet had ended up in an area rich with major veins, arteries, and nerves, all protected by an abundance of tough, unyielding muscle.

Garrett had been taught in medical school never to operate on a family relation or someone with whom she had an emotional attachment. A surgeon needed objectivity. But as she looked at Ethan's still face, she realized she was about to begin one of the most difficult procedures of her career on a man she'd fallen in love with. *God help me,* she thought, not as blasphemy but as prayer.

"I need the scalpel with the curved edge," she said.

Ravenel gingerly handed the instrument to her. As she prepared to make an incision just beneath the clavicle bone, she heard him ask, "Do I have to watch this part?"

"I would prefer that you hand me the correct instrument when I ask for it," she said crisply, "which would require keeping your eyes open."

"Just asking," he said. "They're open."

She cut down carefully, dividing fibrous tissue and fascia, and clamped the edges of the incision.

The bullet was lodged in the axillary artery, along with what appeared to be a bit of woven fabric from a shirt or waistcoat. As Havelock had suspected, the ends of the severed artery had contracted and sealed inside its sheath. The other side was blocked by the lead slug.

"He should have bled to death within minutes," she murmured. "But the bullet has temporarily occluded the artery. That, along with coagulum, is acting as a plug." Still staring intently at the wound, she asked, "Can you thread a needle?"

"Yes."

"Good, use a pair of forceps to remove a catgut ligature from that bottle, and use it to thread the thinnest needle on the tray." She positioned Ethan's arm farther upward to form a right angle with his chest.

As Ravenel saw where she was preparing to make a second incision, he asked, "Why are you going to cut near his armpit when the wound is on his chest?"

"I need to tie off the distal end of the artery first. Please let me concentrate."

"Sorry. I'm used to operations on farm animals. If he were a plague-ridden cow, I would understand exactly what was happening."

"Mr. Ravenel, if you don't stop talking, I will chloroform you and do this by myself."

He shut his mouth obligingly.

For the next several minutes, Garrett performed the delicate work of ligating the artery in two places, taking care not to damage the network of nerves and veins in the axillary region. She removed the bullet and the bit of cloth, debrided damaged tissue, and irrigated the wound to flush out debris and bacteria. At her direction, Ravenel used a curette to freshen the exposed incisions with antiseptic solution. She installed rubber drainage tubes, painstakingly stitched them in place with carbolized silk, and dressed the wounds with boracic gauze.

"Are we finished?" Ravenel asked.

Garrett was too occupied with evaluating Ethan's condition to reply immediately.

His knees and feet had acquired a mottled appearance, and his countenance was deathly white. His pulse had fallen to forty beats per minute.

He was sinking.

"Not yet," she said, trying to think herself into calmness. Her insides were roiling. "I need . . . we need someone else. One person to donate blood, and the other to assist me. The . . . the Roussel apparatus . . . where is it? . . ."

"You're talking about a blood transfusion?" Ravenel asked. "Does that usually work?"

She didn't look at him as she replied flatly, "At least half the cases die within an hour."

Lord Trenear's quiet voice came from the corner of the room. "I have the apparatus right here."

Garrett hadn't realized he'd been watching the operation—she'd been too intent on her work to notice his arrival.

Coming forward, Trenear set a gleaming rosewood case on the library table. "What can I do?" he asked.

"Open the case but don't touch anything inside it. I need one of you to donate the blood, and the other to help with the transfuser."

"Take my blood," the earl said readily.

"No," Ravenel said, "I insist on being the donor. If he lives, it will annoy him far more." He smiled slightly as his gaze met Garrett's. Something about his presence was so relaxed and steady that it smoothed the edges of her panic.

"Very well." She took a measured breath. "Lord Trenear, please wash your hands in the basin on the other side of the table, and douse them with carbolic solution. Mr. Ravenel, remove your shirt and sit on the table so that your left arm is positioned next to Mr. Ransom's right one."

The transfuser was already sterilized. It was a strange-looking device, a collection of delicate unvulcanized rubber tubes sprouting from a rigid cupping glass, like a mechanical sea creature. One tube was connected to a water aspirator, another to a tiny junction tap and a cannula with a needle, and another to a balloon pump regulator.

The unwieldy mass shook a little in Garrett's hands as she lifted it carefully from the case. Although she had assisted in a transfusion once, the operating surgeon had used a far simpler and more old-fashioned apparatus.

If only Havelock had stayed, damn him, and given her some advice about how this contraption worked.

As Garrett looked up from the transfuser, she blinked at the sight of a shirtless West Ravenel hoisting himself easily onto the table. Despite his earlier crack about Ethan's athletic form, he was certainly no physical lightweight himself. He had the hard, rippling musculature of a man accustomed to lifting and carrying heavy weight. But what had surprised Garrett was the discovery that his torso was tanned the same shade of golden brown as his face. All over.

What kind of gentleman went outside in the sun for that long with no shirt?

Ravenel's lips quirked as he saw her expression. A twinkle of arrogant amusement appeared in his eyes. "Farmwork," he said in a matter-of-fact tone. "And I do some quarrying."

"Half naked?" Garrett asked tartly, setting the transfuser on an expanse of clean linen.

"I've been loading rock into horse carts," he said. "Which suits my intellectual capacity perfectly. But it's too hot for a shirt."

Although Garrett didn't smile, she appreciated the touch of humor, which helped to stave off an attack of nerves. One mistake—an air bubble in the vein— would finish Ethan off in short order.

The earl came to her. "What now?" he asked.

She handed him a sterilized glass vessel. "Fill this with boiled water."

While the earl attended to the task, Garrett listened to Ravenel's heart with the stethoscope and checked his pulse. He had the heart of an ox, the rhythm strong and regular. She filled the water aspirator of the transfuser and tied a length of surgical bandage firmly around the thick muscle of his upper arm. "Make a fist, please." His brawny forearm flexed. "A perfect median basilic," she said, swabbing the inside of his arm with isopropyl alcohol. "I could find it without even tying a band around your arm."

"I would preen and bask in your admiration of my vein," Ravenel said, "if I didn't see that three-inch needle attached to one of those tubes."

"I'll be as gentle as possible," she said, "but I'm afraid it will be uncomfortable."

"Compared to a bullet in the chest, I suppose one can't complain without sounding like a milksop."

His older brother told him kindly, "We all know you're a milksop. Go ahead and complain."

"You may wish to look away, Mr. Ravenel," Garrett murmured, "and keep making a fist."

"Call me West."

"I don't know you well enough for that."

"You're draining the life essence from my median basilic," he pointed out. "I'm on a first-name basis with women who've done far less to me than that. *Son of a bitch!*" The profanity burst out as he felt Garrett ease the hollow curved needle into his vein. He frowned down at the sight of his blood running along the rubber tube into the aspirator. "How much of this is he going to need?"

"Probably no more than ten ounces. We'll replenish his vessels just enough to restore his pulse to its normal rate and volume." Garrett tied a band around Ethan's lax upper arm and hunted for a vein. None were visible. "Lord Trenear, if you would help me by applying pressure to his arm here, and here . . ." The earl clamped his fingers on the places she had indicated.

Nothing. No vein.

No pulse.

Ethan's last breath escaped in a sigh.

He was gone.

"*No, you don't,*" Garrett said fiercely, swabbing his arm and picking up a scalpel. "You're bloody well *not* going to do this to me, you sow-buggering bastard!" Deftly pinching a fold of cool skin, she made a quick incision to expose a depleted vein. "Hand me the director," she said through gritted teeth. As Trenear hesitated over the tray of instruments, she snapped, "The pointy one." Immediately he picked it up and handed it over to her.

Within seconds, Garrett had lifted the vein with the director, made a transverse cut with a scalpel, and inserted a cannula. While Lord Trenear held the cannula in place, she connected it with the transfuser and used the pumps and aspirator to withdraw every dram of air in the line and flush it with sterile water. Although she'd never used this kind of transfuser before, her hands somehow knew what to do, guided by a part of her brain that was thinking ten times faster than usual. A twist of a silver stopcock, and blood began to flow into the vein.

The two men were now connected by a hermetically sealed channel.

Garrett exerted pressure on the balloon pump to release the blood into Ethan's arm at a slow pace, to keep from overwhelming the heart. Her lips moved in a ceaseless incantation: *come back come back come back . . .*

After one minute had passed, a miraculous change came over the lifeless form. His pulse resumed. His color rose rapidly. His chest lifted once, twice, and he began to breathe in deep, fitful gasps. Another minute, and he was perspiring and twitching.

Garrett let out a sigh of relief that sounded embarrassingly like a whimper. Feeling her eyes brim, she covered them with one hand and fought for self-control. A few profane words escaped her lips as a tear slid down to her chin.

"You curse so beautifully," she heard Ravenel say dryly. "Few women can do it with such natural ease."

"I learned at the Sorbonne," Garrett said with her hand still over her eyes. "You should hear me curse in French."

"I'd rather not, or I might fall in love with you. By the way, does Ransom have enough blood now? Because I'm starting to feel a bit light-headed."

AFTER GARRETT HAD cleaned her instruments and the transfuser equipment, she checked Ethan's vital signs for the tenth time. Pulse, one hundred. Temperature, ninety-nine. Respirations, thirty. He was sweating profusely, and stirring uneasily as the effects of anesthesia slowly faded.

Leaving him in the care of Mrs. Abbot, Garrett unsteadily made her way to a corner of the library and sat on a small carved stepladder. Bending forward, she rested her head on her knees. She was distantly aware that she was shaking as if from a seizure. She couldn't think what to do about it, only crouched there and quivered until her teeth rattled.

Someone was beside her, lowering to his haunches. A large, warm hand settled high on her back. A sideways glance revealed that it was West Ravenel. There were no glib comments, only a calm, friendly quietness that soothed her. His touch reminded her a little of the way Ethan would sometimes stroke or gently grip the nape of her neck. She began to relax, the tremors fading. He stayed like that, the pressure of his hand light and comforting, until she let out a shuddering sigh and sat up.

Ravenel's hand slid away. Wordlessly he gave her a glass filled with a small portion of whiskey, or brandy—something alcoholic—and she took it gratefully. Her teeth clattered against the edge of the glass as she took a swallow. The smooth amber fire helped to drain a few last shudders of nervous tension.

"It's been almost an hour," Ravenel said. "The transfusion was successful, wasn't it?"

Garrett drank again. "He won't die from the damage done by the bullet," she said dully, her fingers clutched around the glass. "He'll die from what was allowed inside by the bullet track. Viruses, bacteria, lethal microbes, chemical contaminants. I'd rather have immersed him in poison than that river. The Thames would turn up Neptune himself within five minutes."

"I wouldn't say death is a foregone conclusion," Ravenel said. "He comes from tough stock. A long line of vicious bastards. As he's already proven, he can survive things other men wouldn't."

"You're acquainted with his family?" she asked.

"He hasn't told you, then. The Ravenels are his family. His father was the old earl. If Ransom hadn't been born a bastard, he would be Lord Trenear right now, instead of my brother."

Chapter 17

WEST SMILED SLIGHTLY AS Garrett Gibson stared at him with dazed green eyes. "That explains the resemblance," she said after a long moment.

How very small she seemed, tucked in the corner of the library with her knees drawn up. For the past hour and a half, she had been a commanding figure, strung tight with energy, her gaze stern and steely. She had worked in millimeters, doing tiny, crucial things to veins and cellular tissue with astonishing precision. Although West knew nothing about surgery, he'd understood that he was witnessing someone perform with rare skill.

Now, in her exhaustion, the brilliant surgeon resembled an anxious schoolgirl who had taken a wrong turn on the way home.

West liked her a great deal. In fact, he was rather sorry now that he'd kept shrugging off Helen's efforts to introduce them. He'd envisioned the female doctor as a severe matron, probably hostile toward men, and Helen's assurances that Dr. Gibson was quite pretty hadn't been at all convincing. Helen, with her completely unjustified affection for humanity, loved to overestimate people.

But Garrett Gibson was more than pretty. She was

riveting. An intelligent, accomplished woman with an elusive quality . . . a suggestion of hidden tenderness . . . that intrigued him.

The evening had been one surprise after another, starting with Ethan Ransom being carried in half dead by a pair of terrified river police who clearly wanted nothing to do with the affair. Having stopped their patrol boat beneath Blackfriars Bridge for a forbidden drink of whiskey from a flask, the officers could hear the murder in progress above them. After the assassin had left the bridge, they'd managed to haul the wounded man aboard and searched his pockets, and had found nothing to identify him other than West's calling card. But they'd heard enough to realize that reporting the matter would result in more trouble than they cared to deal with.

"Who did this?" West had asked Ransom as he lay in a filthy, crumpled heap on the settee.

"One of Jenkyn's men," Ransom had gasped, fighting to stay conscious, his eyes unfocused.

"Jenkyn ordered it?"

"Yes. Don't trust police. Felbrigg. When they find me . . ."

"They won't find you."

"They'll come."

Let them try, West had thought, livid as he saw what had been done to his kinsman.

Kathleen had bent over the dying man, using a soft white cloth to wipe some of the grime from his face. Ransom lost consciousness for several seconds, and reawakened with a groan. "May I send for someone?" she had asked gently, and he'd responded with a string of nearly unintelligible words that she'd somehow managed to make sense of. She had turned to West with a perplexed and sorrowing look. "He wants Dr. Gibson."

"Gibson's in King's Cross, isn't she? We can fetch our family physician far more quickly."

"He doesn't want her as a doctor," Kathleen had said softly. "He wants the woman he loves."

It had struck West as a highly improbable pairing, the doctor and the government agent. But after seeing them together, he realized their connection didn't have to be understood by anyone except the two of them.

Rising to his feet and looking down at Garrett's strained face, West saw that she'd nearly reached the breaking point. She stared back at him vacantly, too drained and overwhelmed to ask a single question.

"Doctor," he said gently, "I've just spoken to my brother, who's arranged for us to take Ransom to Hampshire. We're leaving in a few hours."

"He can't be moved."

"He's not safe here. No one else is, either. There's no choice."

Garrett snapped back to attention, her gaze sharpening. "All the jolting could kill him. It's out of the question."

"I swear to you he'll be conveyed quickly and carefully."

"On rough country roads?" she asked scornfully.

"We're transporting him by private train carriage. We'll reach the family estate by dawn. It's quiet and secluded there. He'll be able to heal in privacy."

West could hardly wait to return to Eversby Priory. He was beginning to hate London and its hard-hearted chaos of streets, buildings, vehicles, and trains, filth, smoke, glitter, and grandeur. Oh, he missed the city from time to time, but after a few days he was always eager to get back to Hampshire.

The Ravenels' ancient manor house was positioned on a hill from which anyone who approached could be seen for miles. The estate's tens of thousands of acres had belonged to the family since the days of William the Conqueror. It seemed appropriate that Ethan Ransom, who—although illegitimate—was in the family's direct line of descent, should be guarded from his enemies in the home of his ancestors. He and Garrett Gibson would be safe there. West would make sure of it.

Garrett was shaking her head. "I can't leave my father . . . he's old and ill . . ."

"We'll take him with us. Now, tell me what Ransom will need for the journey."

West was fairly certain that in ordinary circumstances, Garrett would have argued over the plan. But she looked at him dumbly, seeming paralyzed.

"If you don't wish to come with us," he said after a moment, "I'll hire a nurse for Ransom. That might be for the best, actually. You can remain in London and maintain appearances, while—"

"We'll need an ambulance cart from the clinic to convey him from here to the station," Garrett interrupted with a scowl, "as well as from the Hampshire station to your home. We'll have to take it with us."

"An entire cart?" West asked, wondering how they could fit that onto the train carriage. "Can't we make do with a stretcher and a good mattress?"

"The cart's framework is fitted with special elastic

springs to absorb jolts. Otherwise, the artery ligations won't hold, and he'll hemorrhage. We'll also need portable water tanks, an ice box, hand lanterns, pails, basins, linens, toweling—"

"Write it all down," West said hastily.

"We'll also have to take my cookmaid with us, to look after my father."

"Whatever you need."

Her green eyes narrowed. "Why are you doing this? Mr. Ransom doesn't like the Ravenels. The very name makes him hostile."

"That's because Edmund, the old earl, treated both Ransom and his mother quite badly." West rolled up his loose shirtsleeve and began to pick at the strip of adhesive plaster Garrett had affixed over the puncture left by the hollow needle. It had stopped bleeding by now, and the bandage was beginning to itch. "I'm willing to help Ransom because in the past, he was kind to Helen and Pandora. Also because, whether he likes it or not, he's a Ravenel, and there are damned few of us left. My brother and I were orphaned when we were young, and deep down I've always harbored idiotic fantasies of large family dinners and children and dogs running through the house."

"I doubt Mr. Ransom would want any part of that."

"Perhaps not. But we men aren't quite as simplistic as we appear. A bullet in the chest could inspire a man to reconsider his opinions."

GARRETT WAS ONLY vaguely aware of the whirlwind of preparations taking place around her. She stayed with Ethan in the Ravenels' formerly elegant library, now a wreckage of sodden, soiled upholstery and stained carpeting. The situation now appeared to be beyond her control. Lord Trenear and West Ravenel were making decisions without her, and she was too weary to try and insert herself into the process.

Ethan gradually awakened from the surgery in great pain, disoriented, and wretchedly ill from the effects of anesthesia and the toxic aftereffects of the Thames. He barely seemed to recognize Garrett, and answered questions only in monosyllables. She did what she could to ease his misery, giving him another injection of morphine, bathing his face with cool water, and sliding a small pillow beneath his head. Sitting at the table, she lowered her head to her folded arms. For a moment, she shut her eyes and felt herself sinking into sleep.

"Doctor," came Kathleen's gentle voice.

Garrett jerked her head up, trying to collect herself. "How are you feeling, my lady?"

"Much better, thank you. We've sent two of the servants to help your cookmaid pack for herself and your father. Lord Trenear and I have a proposition we would like you to consider."

"Yes?"

"We had already planned to leave town for the summer. But before retreating to Eversby Priory, we had accepted an invitation to spend a fortnight in Sussex with Pandora's in-laws, the Duke and Duchess of Kingston. They have a lovely seaside manor with a private sandy cove, and ample room for guests. I think it would do your father some good to come with us, and perhaps take some seawater baths and do a bit of sunning. That way, you'll only have to concern yourself with nursing Mr. Ransom back to health, instead of having your attention divided."

"My lady, I could never impose on you that way, not to mention the Duke and Duchess—"

"After the way you saved Pandora's life, they would be delighted to welcome your father. He would be treated like royalty."

Rubbing her sore eyes, Garrett said distractedly, "He's my responsibility. I don't think—"

"There's also the matter of his safety," Kathleen pointed out gently. "If any trouble should arise over Mr. Ransom's presence at Eversby Priory, I'm sure you would prefer your father to be kept out of harm's way."

"Perhaps you're right. I'll have to ask my father what he would prefer. However, I doubt he'll like the idea of staying with strangers."

"Your cookmaid would accompany him, of course." Kathleen regarded her with a warm, concerned gaze. "I'll bring him to you as soon as he arrives, and you can discuss it."

"He'll want to go with me," Garrett said. "I'm all he has."

But, when Stanley Gibson arrived at Ravenel House and the choice before him was laid out, his reaction wasn't exactly what Garrett had expected.

"A holiday at the seashore with a duke?" her father exclaimed, looking befuddled. "Me, a man who's never sea-bathed in his life? A constable, hobnobbing with upper-class toffs, eating dinner off gold dishes and drinking fancy French wine?"

"I understand, Papa," Garrett said. "You don't have to—"

"By Jove, I'll accept!" he exclaimed heartily. "If the duke wants my company, he shall have it. I suppose it will do him good to spend time with a man like me, learn a thing or two about my years on the beat."

"Papa," Garrett began in muted alarm, "I don't think the duke specifically requested—"

"All settled, then," Eliza broke in hastily. "Wouldn't do to disappoint a duke, would it? You and I will have to brace up and go to Sussex, Mr. Gibson, to humor His Grace—'Do what ye can for other people,' Mum always says. Come now, the housekeeper has a room for you to rest in 'til we leave for our train in the morning."

Before Garrett could utter a word of protest, the pair had bustled out of the library.

WITH A SPEED and efficiency that was nothing short of miraculous, the Ravenels had acquired every item on Garrett's list before dawn. Ethan was carefully strapped into a stretcher, which was carried out by a pair of footmen and the earl himself, to the waiting ambulance cart behind the mews. The sky was unrelieved black, the only light coming from streetlamps that cast crooked shadows across the pavement.

Sitting beside Ethan in the covered cart, Garrett could see very little of their route or direction. West had told her that they were going to a private railway station just south of London, where they would board a special train without being observed, and bypass the usual permissions and restrictions. Extra precautions had been taken for guarding crossings and securing facing points, which would be timed to allow the train to run without stoppages.

A single horse pulled the ambulance cart at a mea-sured pace. Despite the vehicle's shock-absorbing springs, Ethan was jostled and jarred until stifled groans escaped him. Unable to imagine what hell he was enduring, Garrett held his hand, not letting go even when his grip turned bone-crushingly tight.

The cart slowed as they came to a place so dark and quiet that it seemed as if they had entered some remote forest. Peeking beneath the hem of the cart's canvas covering, Garrett saw towering gates covered with ivy, and ghostly sculptures of angels, and solemn figures of men, women, and children with their arms crossed in resignation upon their breasts. Graveyard sculptures. A stab of horror went through her, and she crawled to the front of the cart to where West Ravenel was sitting with the driver.

"Where the devil are you taking us, Mr. Ravenel?"

He glanced at her over his shoulder, his brows raised. "I told you before—a private railway station."

"It looks like a cemetery."

"It's a cemetery station," he admitted. "With a ded-icated line that runs funeral trains out to the burial grounds. It also happens to connect to the main lines and branches of the London Ironstone Railroad, owned by our mutual friend Tom Severin."

"You told Mr. Severin about all this? Dear God. Can we trust him?"

West grimaced slightly. "One never wants to be in the position of having to trust Severin," he admitted. "But he's the only one who could obtain clearances for a special train so quickly."

They approached a massive brick and stone build-ing housing a railway platform. A ponderous stone sign adorned the top of the carriage entrance: *Silent Gardens.* Just below it, the shape of an open book emblazoned with words had been carved in the stone. *Ad Meliora.* "Toward better things," Garrett translated beneath her breath.

West looked back at her in surprise. "You've studied Latin?"

She sent him a sardonic glance. "I'm a doctor."

A quick, apologetic grin crossed his face. "Of course."

The ambulance cart came to a halt at the platform, where the Ravenel carriage and two other vehicles were already parked. The instant the brake was applied, footmen and a pair of porters rushed forward to begin the process of removing the stretcher from the vehicle.

"Be careful," Garrett said sharply.

"I'll manage them," West told her, "while you board the train carriage."

"If they bump or jar him—"

"Yes, I understand. Let me handle it."

Frowning, Garrett descended from the cart and took in her surroundings. A reverse-painted glass sign beside the door listed the contents of each floor: mortuary rooms, crypts, storerooms, and third-class waiting rooms on the basement level; chapel, robing rooms, and second-class waiting rooms on the main level; and offices and first-class waiting rooms on the upper levels.

A second sign instructed mourners as to which funeral carriages on the train were designated for first-class coffins, and which ones were for second and third class.

Staring more closely at the sign, Garrett gave a bemused shake of her head at the discovery that corpses on the train were divided into social classes just as living passengers were. To a doctor, however, there were no class divisions between one unclothed body and another, whether living or dead. Every man, rich or poor, was alike in his natural state.

An amused male voice with a Welsh accent broke into her thoughts. "Aye, even a corpse must know its place."

Garrett turned quickly. "Mr. Winterborne!" she exclaimed. "No one told me to expect you. I'm so sorry to have troubled you."

Her employer smiled down at her. Little reflected lights from nearby gas lamps gleamed in his dark eyes. "No trouble, Doctor. This is close to the time I rise every morning. I wanted to make sure the train carriage was stocked and ready for you."

Her eyes widened. "It's your train carriage?"

"The passenger carriage is mine, but the locomotive and extra rolling stock belong to Tom Severin."

"Sir, I'm indebted to you more than I can say—"

"Not at all. Lady Helen and I consider you one of the family. Helen sends her love, by the way." Winterborne hesitated, his gaze chasing restlessly around the platform before returning to hers. "I was told about Havelock's refusal to assist in the surgery. For what it's worth, his decision doesn't sit well with me."

"Please don't blame him."

"You don't?"

Garrett shook her head. "'Faithful are the wounds of a friend,'" she quoted with a grim smile. "A true friend will tell you when he thinks you're making a mistake."

"A true friend will be making the mistake with you," Winterborne said dryly. "As it happens, I don't agree that you did anything wrong. Had I been in your place, I would have made the same choice."

"You would?"

"If there were any chance of saving someone I loved, I'd take it and be damned to anyone who stood in my way." Looking her over, Winterborne said frankly, "You're at the length of your tether. There are two staterooms in the train carriage—try to steal a few minutes of rest before you reach Hampshire." He reached into his coat and withdrew a weighty leather envelope. "Take this."

Cautiously Garrett peeked inside the pouch, which was stuffed with hundred-pound notes. It was more cash money than she'd ever held in her life. "Mr. Winterborne, I couldn't possibly—"

"Money doesn't solve every problem," he said, "but it never hurts. Send for me if there's anything you need. When Ransom's condition improves, let me know."

"Yes, sir. Thank you."

As Winterborne escorted her onto the train, they passed a crew of shopmen busily removing the wheels of the ambulance cart to make its transport easier. The stretcher had already been conveyed onto the railway carriage, which was a virtual palace on wheels. It had two staterooms, each with its own connected toilet room equipped with hot and cold running water, an observation room, and a parlor with movable velvet-covered chairs and reading lamps.

Winterborne's carpenters had devised a suspension of the stretcher on cross supports attached to the wall with heavy metal spring hooks. Garrett winced briefly as she saw that the hooks had been bolted directly into the carriage's beautiful quartered English oak woodwork. However, the arrangement would work well to minimize shocks and jolts once the train started moving.

After the stretcher was settled into its makeshift berth, Garrett pushed a chair to the place beside it. She laid her palm tenderly across Ethan's forehead, which was dry and hot to the touch, and took up his wrist to check his pulse. He was flushed and restless, his breath fitful.

Coming to stand at the other side of the wounded man, Winterborne regarded him with a deep frown of concern. "He's always seemed indestructible," he said quietly. "He's made powerful enemies. I don't like it that you're in the cross wires with him."

"He didn't like it, either. He tried to keep a distance between us."

Winterborne looked sardonic. "Not hard enough, it seems."

Garrett smiled faintly. "I made it difficult for him. I can be stubborn at times."

"I've noticed." But Winterborne's gaze was kind.

Staring down at Ethan's face, Garrett said, "He expected from the beginning that it would come to this. He thought there was no other possible path for his life to take."

"Perhaps you should prove him wrong," she heard Winterborne murmur.

"I will," she said. "If I have the chance, I will."

Chapter 18

$\mathcal{A}$S THE TRAIN HEADED southwest to Hampshire, the subdued grays and blues of London gave way to a palette exploding with brilliant color. A pink-and-orange sunrise melted to reveal a pristine blue sky. To the eyes of a lifelong city dweller, Hampshire looked like a storybook land, with winding streams, ancient old-grown forests, and green pastures divided by endless miles of hedgerows.

Ethan had fallen into an uneasy sleep, lulled by the constant subtle rocking of the train's motion. Garrett had to restrain herself from reaching over to fuss with him constantly, like a finicky artist working on a clay sculpture. She turned her attention to West Ravenel, who was sitting by a window and watching the passing scenery with keen interest.

"How did you find out about Mr. Ransom?" Garrett asked.

West's gaze was warm and audacious, far different from Ethan's secretive and penetrating one. He seemed to be at ease with himself and the world, a rare gift at a time when men of his class were faced with economic and social upheaval that threatened the loss of their traditions.

"About his connection to the family?" West asked

easily, and continued without requiring an answer. "Recently I learned about a secret bequest of land that had been made to him in the old earl's will. A longtime family servant confirmed that Ransom was Edmund's by-blow with an Irish girl, who was likely a prostitute." His mouth twisted. "Since Edmund wouldn't provide for the girl or her babe, she eventually married a Clerkenwell prison guard. I've no doubt it was a hard life. The fact that Edmund could leave both the child and the mother to the wolves, and live with that on his conscience, should tell you something about what kind of man he was."

"Perhaps he doubted the child's paternity?"

"No, Edmund confided to his valet that the child was his. And Ransom bears the obvious stamp of his sire." West paused and shook his head. "My God, I never expected to be bringing Ransom to Hampshire. When I met him in London a few weeks ago, he couldn't have been more hostile. He wants nothing to do with any of us."

"He was devoted to his mother," Garrett said. "It's possible he feels that forming an attachment to the Ravenels would be disloyal to her memory."

West considered that with a frown. "Whatever the old earl did to Ransom and his mother, I'm sorry for it. But Ransom should know that the abuse was hardly limited to him. Edmund's children were his favorite victims. Ask any of his daughters—they'll tell you that living with him was no picnic-party."

A jolt from the train caused Ethan to groan in his drugged sleep. Garrett smoothed his hair, normally so satiny, now rough and stiff like a dog's coat.

"We'll be there soon," West said. "I can't wait.

I nearly left London a few days ago, pining for the place."

"What did you miss about it?"

"I've missed every turnip, every hay bale, every chicken in the poultry yard, and bee in the box-hives."

"You sound like a born farmer," Garrett said, amused. "But you're blue-blooded."

"Am I?" West glanced at her then, the tiny fan-lines at the outer corners of his eyes deepening. "Although I tried not to look, it seemed quite red to me." Stretching out his long legs comfortably, he laced his fingers together over his midriff. "My brother and I are descended from a far-flung branch of the Ravenels. No one ever expected us to darken the doorstep of Eversby Priory, much less for Devon to inherit the title and all that came with it."

"How did it fall to you to manage the land and tenant farms?"

"Someone had to. Devon was better suited to handle a snarl of legal and financial matters. At that point, my impression of farming was that one was obliged to arrange hay in picturesque stacks. It turned out to be slightly more complicated than that."

"What do you like about farming?"

West considered the question, while the train puffed and clambered resolutely up the incline of a broad hill covered with golden-flowered furze. "I like clearing a new field and hearing the roots crack and watching stumps being pulled under the plow blades. I like knowing that after I sow three bushels of wheat on an acre, the proper mixture of sun, rain, and manure will yield sixty-four bushels. After having lived in London for so long, I'd reached a point where I needed something to make sense." His gaze turned absent and dreamy. "I like living in the seasons. I love the summer storms that come in from the sea, and the smell of good soil and mown hay. I love big breakfasts with new-laid eggs boiled until the yolks are set but still a bit soft, and hot buttered muffins spread with comb honey, and rashers of fried bacon and slabs of Hampshire ham, and bowls of ripe blackberries just picked from the hedgerows—"

"Please," Garrett said thickly, beginning to feel nauseous from the train's oscillation. "Don't talk about food."

West smiled. "After some rest, and a day or two of fresh air, you'll find your appetite."

Instead of stopping at the public station in the market town of Alton, the special train proceeded to a private railway halt located on the east side of the vast Eversby Priory estate.

The halt consisted of a single platform covered by a wooden-and-iron scrollwork canopy. The two-story signal box had been constructed of brick and wood, with multipaned glass windows and a green tiled roof. Having been built to service a nearby hematite quarry on Ravenel land, the private station included a number of small buildings and freight facilities. There were also wagons for quarrying, tramways that led to and from the quarry site, steam drills, pumps, and boring equipment.

A mild early-morning breeze swept inside the train carriage as West opened the door. "It will take a few minutes for the ambulance cart to be unloaded and reassembled," he said. After a pause, he added apologetically, "You'll probably want to give him something extra for pain during the last part of the journey. Not all the roads are paved."

Garrett's brows rushed down. "Are you _trying_ to kill him?" she demanded in a scathing whisper.

"Obviously not, or I would have left him in London."

After West left the railway carriage, Garrett went to Ethan, who had begun to stir. His eye sockets appeared bruised and sunken, and his lips were dry as chalk.

She held a flexible rubber tube to his lips, and he sucked in a few sips of ice water.

Ethan's lids cracked open, and his unfocused gaze found her. "Still here," he said in a hoarse whisper, not appearing entirely happy about the fact.

"You're going to be better soon. All you have to do now is sleep, and heal."

Ethan looked as though he were puzzling over some foreign language, trying to interpret it. There was a brittleness about him, as if spirit and flesh were coming unstitched from each other. He trembled with fever chills despite the dry-baked heat of his skin. _Traumatic inflammation,_ the clinical part of her brain noted. Wound-fever. Despite the abundant use of antiseptic fluids, infection had set in. The rigors would soon be accompanied by a rapid elevation of temperature.

She coaxed him to take another sip of water.

"I'm in a bad takin'," Ethan whispered after he'd swallowed. "Need something."

God only knew what it had cost him to complain.

"I'll give you morphine," she said, and swiftly prepared another syringe.

By the time the injection took effect, the ambulance

cart had been reassembled and hitched to a broad-backed, placid-tempered dray. The ride to Eversby Priory manor seemed interminable as the cart's India-rubber wheels rolled gingerly over the rough terrain.

Eventually they approached a massive Jacobean house on a broad hill. The brick-and-stone residence was dressed with parapets, arches, and long rows of diamond-paned windows. Rows of elaborate chimney stacks gave the flat roof the appearance of a birthday cake covered with candles.

The ambulance cart stopped at the entrance. Four footmen and an elderly butler emerged from the oak double doors. Without preamble, Garrett explained how to detach the stretcher and unload it from the cart. She was annoyed when West interrupted her instructions.

"They're footmen, Doctor. Carrying things is nine-tenths of their job."

"He is not a *thing*, he's my . . . my patient."

"They're not going to drop your patient," West said, escorting her past the front threshold. "Now, Dr. Gibson, this pleasant-looking lady with the gaze of a brigadier general is our housekeeper, Mrs. Church. And all those capable young women are housemaids—we'll introduce them later. For now, all you need to know is that we have two Marthas, so that's the name to call out if you want something."

The housekeeper curtsied hastily to Garrett before directing the footmen to carry the stretcher bearing the wounded man upstairs. Her matronly form bounded up the stairs with unexpected agility. As Garrett followed, she had only a cursory look at her surroundings, but it was enough to allay any concerns about the manor's condition. Despite its venerable age, the house appeared scrupulously clean and well-ventilated, the air scented with beeswax and rosin soap. The soft white paint on the walls and ceilings showed no trace of mold or damp. Garrett had been in hospital wards that had been maintained in far worse condition.

Ethan was carried into a small but tidy room. A screen had been fitted into the open window space to filter out insects and dust and allow cooling breezes to flow into the room.

"Did they know in advance of our arrival?" Garrett asked, noticing that the gleaming wood floor had been divested of rugs and the bed covered in white linen, as appropriate for a sickroom.

"Telegram," West said succinctly, helping the footmen set the stretcher on the floor near the foot of the bed. On his count, they lifted Ethan with great care, keeping him supported at a horizontal angle. Once he was settled, West turned to Garrett, rubbing the pinched muscles at the back of his neck. "You haven't slept at all. Let Mrs. Church watch over him for a few hours while you take a nap."

"I'll consider it," Garrett said, although she planned to do no such thing. The room was clean by ordinary standards, but it was far from a sterile environment. "Thank you, Mr. Ravenel. I'll take charge now." She ushered him from the room and closed the door.

Mrs. Church helped Garrett to draw away the sheets and blanket that had covered Ethan during the journey, and replace them with fresh ones. He was dressed in a thin cotton nightshirt donated by Lord Trenear. Later Garrett would change him into one of the garments obtained from the clinic, a patient night-shirt made to open in either the front or the back.

Ethan awakened just long enough to give her a bleary glance, his eyes vivid blue black in his fevered complexion. He was shivering from head to toe.

Garrett weighted him with another blanket and gently touched his bristled cheek. She'd never seen him a day past a shave. More by force of habit than necessity, her fingers slid to his bare wrist to find his pulse. His hand moved, twisting until his long fingers curled around hers. He blinked once, twice, and sank into slumber.

"Poor, handsome lad," the housekeeper exclaimed softly. "How was he injured, Doctor?"

"Gunshot wound," Garrett said, slowly disentangling her fingers from his.

Mrs. Church shook her head. "The Ravenel temper," she said darkly. "It's been the end of more than one promising young man in his prime."

Startled, Garrett shot her a questioning glance.

"I know a Ravenel when I see one," the housekeeper said. "Those high cheekbones and the long nose, and the way the hairline grows in that slight peak." Staring down at Ethan thoughtfully, she continued, "The old master Edmund's indiscretions were hardly a secret. I'd guess this is a natural child of his. Probably not the only one."

"It's not for me to confirm," Garrett murmured, tucking the covers more closely around Ethan's still form. She felt protective of him, defensive on his behalf. Not only had he been made physically helpless, but also one of his deepest secrets was now being discussed over his sickbed. "However, his injury is not the result of an unruly temperament. He was attacked after risking his own life to protect a great number of innocent people."

Mrs. Church regarded Ethan for a long, wondering moment. "A good, brave man, then. The world needs more like him."

"It certainly does," Garrett agreed, although she knew Ethan would have mocked such pronouncements about his heroic nature.

"What is his prognosis?"

Garrett gestured for the housekeeper to come away from the bedside and stand with her at the window. "The wound is contaminated," she said, "and it's poisoning his blood. His fever will rise until he reaches a crisis. We'll have to keep him very clean, to help his system rid itself of infection, and keep the wound from suppurating. Otherwise—" She stopped, her heart twisting. Turning to the window, she stared out at neatly tended garden walks curving beside stone walls covered with flowering vines. In the distance, a row of glasshouses glittered in the morning light. This was a world away from London, so ordered and serene that it seemed nothing bad could happen here.

The housekeeper was waiting patiently for her to resume.

Garrett gave a short nod toward a nearby table, decorated with a small vase of fresh flowers, a miniature framed painting, and an assortment of books and periodicals. "I'll need that table cleared. Also, please send up a stack of clean bleached toweling, and a can of hot water that's been kept at a hard boil for at least thirty minutes. And have the footmen carry up all the supplies and equipment from the ambulance cart as quickly as possible. After that, no one except you is to come into this room unless it's by my leave. No one is to touch him without first scrubbing his or her hands with carbolic soap. The walls must be washed with a bichloride solution, and the floor sprinkled with disinfecting powder."

"Will McDougall's powder suffice? We use it in the stables."

"Yes, that's perfect."

Mrs. Church gathered up the flower vase and the reading materials from the table. "I'll see that it's all done in a jiff."

Garrett liked the housekeeper immensely, perceiving that she would be an invaluable help in the days to come. Perhaps it was the mixing of liking and weariness that loosened her tongue, but she found herself saying, "You immediately noticed his likeness to the Ravenels, whereas Lady Helen and Pandora have never remarked on it. Nor did I put two and two together."

Mrs. Church paused at the threshold and smiled. "I've been in service since I was a girl of fifteen, Doctor. It's a servant's job to notice details. We learn the family's habits and preferences. We read their faces to anticipate what they'll need before they think to ask. I daresay I pay more attention to the Ravenels than they pay to each other."

After the door had closed, Garrett reached for Ethan's hand once more. It was strong and elegantly shaped, the knuckles and fingertips slightly roughened. His skin radiated heat, like stones baking under the sun. The fever was coming on fast.

Inside his veins and connective tissue, microscopic processes were taking place, unseen battles raging among cells, bacteria, chemicals. *So much of it is out of my control,* she thought helplessly.

Very lightly she set down his hand and laid her palm on his chest, over the blanket, measuring the quick, shallow motions of his breathing.

Her feelings for him seemed to unfurl in all directions.

Tentatively she let herself think about what he'd said to her before the surgery, the words he'd thought would be his last. She couldn't fathom what it was about her, a practical woman with a scientific mind, that had inspired such passion.

But as she stood there with her hand on him, she found herself uttering words unlike anything she'd ever said or thought in her entire sensible life.

"This is mine." Her fingers spread wider over his heart, collecting precious heartbeats as if they were scattered pearls. "You're mine, you belong to me now."

Chapter 19

By the next day, Ethan's temperature had gone up to one hundred and three degrees, and the day after that, it reached one hundred and five. He had fallen into delirium, his fevered mind prowling through memories and blood-haunted nightmares that left him weak and agitated. He spoke gibberish, tossing and turning, and not even a dose of the strongest opiate could ease him. At times he would sweat profusely, burning up from the heat, but soon afterward would shake with bone-jarring chills.

Garrett left the sickroom for only a few minutes at a time to see to her own needs. She slept in a chair beside Ethan's bed, dozing with her chin on her chest, waking instantly at the slightest noise or movement. She trusted only Mrs. Church to help her change the sheets and bathe Ethan's body with cool antiseptic-soaked cloths. When his temperature skyrocketed, they packed him in waterproof bags of ice wrapped in linen. Garrett drained and cleaned his wound frequently, and bullied him into taking sips of water and purifying tonic. His injuries appeared to be healing, but even so, toward the third evening he seemed to retreat to a place where she couldn't reach or soothe him.

"I've nine devils in my skull," he muttered, struggling to rise from the bed. "Cast 'em out, don't let me—"

"Hush," Garrett said, trying to apply an iced cloth to his forehead, but he twisted away with a desperate sound. She was terrified that all his violent movement would start a hemorrhage. "Ethan, lie still. *Please*." As she tried to press him down against the pillow, he shoved her in his delirium, and she staggered and fell backward.

But instead of careening to the floor, she found herself neatly caught from behind, a solid arm closing around her.

It was West Ravenel, his clothes scented of outside air and forest greenery and an earthy whiff of horses that Garrett ordinarily wouldn't have liked, but at the moment seemed agreeably masculine and bracing. After steadying her, he went to the sweating, thrashing figure on the bed. "Ransom," he said in a firm tone, instead of a quiet sickroom murmur. "No devils here. They're gone. Lie back and rest, there's a good fellow." He put his hand on Ethan's forehead. "Hot as hellfire. Your head must be splitting. Mine always is during a fever." Reaching for a waterproof ice bag that had been dislodged from Ethan's chest, he carefully set it against the top of his skull.

To Garrett's amazement, Ethan subsided and began to breathe more deeply.

"Did you wash your hands?" she asked West.

"Yes. But believe me, any bacteria I may have brought in are no match for his." His frowning gaze remained on Ethan, whose features were pallid and sharp. "How high is the fever?"

"One hundred and five," Garrett said dully. "He's in the worst of it now."

West's attention moved to her. "When did you last eat?"

"I had bread and tea an hour or two ago."

"Twelve hours ago, according to Mrs. Church. And I'm told you haven't slept for three damned days."

"I have slept," Garrett said curtly.

"I meant the kind in which one applies the body to a horizontal surface. It's not sleeping if it's in a chair. You're about to collapse."

"I'm perfectly able to assess my own condition."

"You can hardly focus your eyes. You've worked yourself into a state of exhaustion, when there's a bevy of female servants who've been waiting impatiently for a chance to soothe Ransom's fevered brow. If we don't let the head housemaid at least give him a sponge bath, she'll hand in her notice soon."

"A *sponge*?" Garrett asked in weary outrage. "Do you know what kind of harmful bacteria a sponge contains? There are at least—"

"Please. I already know far too much about bacteria." West watched with exasperation as she headed toward the bedside chair. "Doctor, I'm begging you— with no lascivious intent whatsoever—go to bed. Just for an hour. I'll look after him."

"What nursing experience do you have?"

He hesitated. "Does a sheep with pasture bloat count?"

Garrett resumed her seat at the bedside. "I'll be perfectly alert after a cup of strong tea," she said stubbornly. "I can't leave him now. He's at the crisis."

"You're having your own crisis. You're just too run-down to realize it." An abbreviated sigh escaped him. "Fine, then. I'll ring for tea."

After summoning the housekeeper and conducting a brief murmured conversation at the door, West went to the bed. "How does the wound look?" he asked, curling an arm loosely around one of the corner posts. "Is it healing?"

"It appears to be," Garrett said, "but there could be secondary sources of infection nearly anywhere in his body."

"Are there any signs of that?"

"Not yet." She sat in a state of nervous depletion, staring fixedly at the figure on the bed.

The tea was brought. Mumbling her thanks, she took the cup in her hands, not bothering with the saucer. She drank it all without tasting it.

"What are you using to dress the wound?" West asked, looking over the collection of bottles on the table.

"Glycerin and disinfecting drops, and a layer of oiled muslin."

"And you're keeping him packed with ice."

"Yes, and trying to make him take a sip of water at least once every hour. But he won't . . ." Garrett paused as a *swoosh* went through her head. She closed her eyes—a mistake—the entire room seemed to tilt.

"What is it?" she heard West ask. His voice seemed to come from very far away.

"Dizzy," she mumbled. "Need more tea, or . . ." Her lashes fluttered upward, and she had to fight to keep her eyes open. West was in front of her, easing the china cup from her lax fingers before it could drop.

His assessing gaze ran over her, and it was then that she realized what he'd done.

"What was in my tea?" she asked in a panic, trying to rise from her chair. "What did you put in it?" The room revolved. She felt his arms close around her.

"Nothing but a pinch of valerian," West said calmly. "Which wouldn't have had nearly this much of an effect if you weren't ready to drop from exhaustion."

"I'm going to kill you," she cried.

"Yes, but to do that you'll have to have a nice little rest first, won't you?"

Garrett tried to strike him with her fist, but he ducked easily beneath her flailing arm, and picked her up as her knees buckled.

"Let go! I have to take care of him—he needs me—"

"I can manage the basics of nursing him while you sleep."

"No, you can't," Garrett said weakly, and was horrified to hear a sob breaking from her throat. "Your patients all have four legs. H-he only has two."

"Which means he'll be half the trouble," West said reasonably.

Garrett writhed with helpless rage. Ethan was on his deathbed, and this man was making light of the situation. He contained her struggles with maddening ease.

As West carried her along the hallway, Garrett desperately tried to stop crying. Her eyes were on fire. Her head throbbed and ached, and it had become so heavy that she had to rest it on his shoulder.

"There, now," she heard him murmur. "It's only for a few hours. When you awaken, you'll have any revenge you want."

"Going to dissect you," she sobbed, "into a million pieces—"

"Yes," West soothed, "just think about which instrument you'll start with. Perhaps that two-sided scalpel with the funny handle." He brought her into a pretty bedroom with flowered paper on the walls. "Martha," he called. "Both of you. Come see to Dr. Gibson."

No MYSTIC'S VISION of hell, with sulphurous chasms and human forms charred to ember, could have been worse than the place where Ethan was trapped. Demons with steel claws leaped at him in the darkness. He thrashed to escape, but every movement drove the claws deeper into his flesh. They dragged him to pits of fire and roasted him over white-hot coals, cackling with laughter as he cursed them.

Sometimes he was aware that he was bedridden, while a calm-faced angel tended his tortured body in ways that unleashed fresh shocks of pain. He almost preferred the demons. His wracked mind couldn't summon her name, but he knew who she was. She insisted on tethering him to the earth with those slim, inexorable hands. He wanted to tell her he'd slipped too far, there was no coming back. But her will was stronger than his weakness.

A tide of fire rose from the floor, blossoming with blue heat. He whimpered and gasped, climbing to escape it, pulling himself up from the deep well of curling flame. There was a circle of light above him, a man reaching down. Seeing his father's muscular arms and knotted hands, Ethan reached upward frantically.

"Da," he whispered. "Fire—pull me out—don't let it take me—"

"You're out. I have you." A powerful grip enclosed his hand.

"Don't let go, Da."

"I won't. Lie still now." His father pulled him up and laid him back, and stroked something cold over his face and neck. "Easy. The worst is over." So much kinder than he'd ever been in life, the mean edges of his temper weathered down to patient strength.

Ethan relaxed and shivered slightly as blessed coolness was distilled all through him, and the stroking cloth paused. Groping for his father's wrist, Ethan blindly urged the big hand back to his face. The soothing movements resumed, and Ethan's tired mind threaded its way into quietness.

He awakened to the steady light of morning on his eyelids, while someone tugged at his bandage, peeling it away like the skin of a fruit. Burning liquid was applied to his shoulder in steady, measured drips. During the process, a man was talking. Not to him, but *at* him, in a light, aimless flow that required no response.

It was bloody annoying.

". . . I've never had this much to do with another man's body before. For that matter, I don't think I've had quite this much to do with a woman's body. I may have to become a monk after this."

The man was winding a bandage neatly over his chest and around his back, leaning close to lift him slightly with each pass.

". . . as heavy as a Hampshire hog . . . more muscle than other breeds, which is why they weigh more than they look. Take my word for it, you'd be a prize-winning baconer. I mean that as a compliment, by the way."

With an antagonized grunt, Ethan shoved at the man, breaking his hold and sending him staggering back. After a swift glance at his surroundings, Ethan half rolled toward the table near the bedside and grabbed a metal utensil. Ignoring the vicious stabbing ache of his shoulder, he stayed on his side and glared at the man by the bed.

It was West Ravenel, who regarded him with a slightly tilted head. "Feeling better today, are we?" he asked in a tone of artificial cheer.

"Where am I?" Ethan asked hoarsely.

"Our hallowed ancestral domain, Eversby Priory." West glanced at the bandage on Ethan's chest, which had begun to unravel. He reached for the loose end. "Let me finish wrapping that, or—"

"Touch me again," Ethan growled, "and I'll kill you with this."

West drew his hand back instantly, his gaze falling to the utensil in Ethan's grip. "That's a spoon."

"*I know.*"

The corner of West's mouth twitched, but he retreated a step or two.

"Where is Garrett?" Ethan demanded.

"After performing surgery, traveling to Hampshire and staying up for thirty-six hours to look after you, she was obliged to rest a bit. Your fever broke during the night, which will undoubtedly be welcome news when she awakens. In the meantime, I've been taking care of you." West paused. "So far, I preferred it when you were unconscious."

Ethan felt a flush of humiliation creeping over him as he realized this man had cared for him during his delirious ravings. Oh God . . . the dream about his father . . . the moments of paternal tenderness he'd always craved from the man who'd raised him. And the handholding—had he imagined that, or—

"Relax," West said calmly, although his eyes twinkled with amusement. "We're family."

It was the first time he'd directly addressed Ethan's connection to the Ravenels. Ethan glanced at him warily, refusing to reply.

"In fact," West continued, "now that my blood is running through your veins, we're practically brothers."

Ethan shook his head, perplexed.

"Transfusion," West explained. "You received ten ounces of Ravenel 'forty-nine . . . a fairly decent vintage, it seems, since it brought you back to life when your heart stopped after surgery." He grinned at Ethan's expression. "Cheer up, you might develop a sense of humor now."

But Ethan's intent stare wasn't one of dismay or resentment . . . he was amazed. All he knew about transfusion was that damned few people survived it. And West Ravenel, the cavalier ass, had willingly gone through a remarkable amount of trouble, risk, and discomfort for his sake. Not only in donating his own blood, but also in taking Ethan to Eversby Priory and looking after him, in full awareness of the dangers of doing so.

As Ethan looked into the blue eyes so like his own, he saw that West expected an ill-tempered, ungracious remark. "Thank you," he said simply.

West blinked in surprise and looked at Ethan more

closely as if to assure himself of his sincerity. "You're welcome," he said, just as simply. After an awkward but not unfriendly silence, he continued, "If you like, I'll try to make you presentable before Dr. Gibson sees you. Before you refuse, you should know that your beard is like steel-brush wire, and you smell like an Angora goat—and I know whereof I speak. If you'd prefer someone other than me to spruce you up, I suppose I could sterilize my valet. Although I'm not certain he'd hold still for it."

GARRETT AWAKENED BENEATH a weight of numbness. Even before her mind was conscious, her body had perceived the awaiting catastrophe.

A full, sun-infused morning pushed insistently through the shuttered windows, spilling through the edges and between the slats. Dully Garrett stared up at the white nothingness of the plaster ceiling.

By now, the natural process of Ethan's fever had proceeded to its logical end.

The pupils would be dilated and unresponsive to light. The body temperature would have dropped to that of the surrounding environment. She could hold the shell of him in her arms, but his spirit was somewhere she couldn't reach.

She would never forgive West Ravenel for depriving her of the last few minutes of Ethan's life.

Moving like an old woman, she eased out of bed. Every muscle and joint was sore. Every inch of her skin hurt. She went into the connecting toilet room to make use of the facilities and wash her face, taking her time. There was no need to rush.

An unfamiliar dressing robe made of green flowered fabric had been laid out for her on a chair, with a pair of slippers on the floor. She had a vague memory of two housemaids helping her change into a night-gown and taking down her hair. Her clothes were no-where in sight, and there wasn't so much as a hairpin on the dresser. She wrapped the robe around her front and tied the drawstring at her waist. The slippers were too small for her feet.

She padded barefoot from the room, toward the chasm of grief that awaited. She would keep walking over the edge, into an endless fall. Ethan had blazed through her life and disappeared before she'd even fully come to comprehend all there was to mourn.

Sunlight pierced the windows and shot across the floors. The sounds of servants going about their daily tasks made her flinch. Now she understood why peo-ple shrouded the house in times of grief: any kind of stimulation was jarring.

Her footsteps slowed as she heard the sounds of conversation coming from the sickroom. West Rav-enel, with his usual irreverence, was chatting casually with someone in a dead man's room.

But before rage could assert itself, Garrett reached the doorway and saw a figure sitting upright on the bed. Her body went as taut as umbrella wire. One of her hands fumbled at the door frame to secure her balance.

Ethan.

The air exploded into sparks that showered into her eyes and filled her lungs. For a moment she couldn't see, couldn't breathe. Her blood rushed with wild fear and joy. Was it real? She couldn't trust her own senses. Blindly she turned in West's direction. She had to blink and blink before she could see him, and even then he was a watery blur. Her voice came out in a croak. "His fever broke and *you didn't wake me*?"

"What would be the point? You needed sleep, and I knew he'd be no less alive in the morning."

"You'll be a damned sight less than alive by the time I'm through with you!" she cried.

West lifted his brows, looking smug. "Am I going to begin every day of your visit being showered by death threats from the two of you?"

"It seems likely," Ethan said from the bed.

There was the sound of his voice, familiar and wry and lucid. Trembling, Garrett brought herself to face him, terrified he might disappear.

Ethan was sitting up, propped on pillows, clean-shaven and washed. He looked unreasonably normal, considering how close to death he'd been a few hours earlier. His gaze moved over her, taking in her un-bound hair, the velvet dressing robe, the tight knots of her bare toes peeking from beneath the hem. His blue eyes, the farthest edge of sky, the darkest ocean depths, were filled with warmth, concern, tenderness . . . all for her . . . only for her.

She made her way to him as if she were wading through hip-deep water. Her legs would barely support her. When she reached him, he grasped her arm and gently tugged her closer until she was perched on the edge of the mattress. "*Acushla*." His hand came up to cradle the side of her face, his thumb caressing the crest of her cheek. "Are you all right?"

"Am *I* . . ." Amazed that his first question was about her, Garrett felt herself begin to crumple like a ball of fragile paper.

Slowly Ethan drew her across his body, guiding her head against his good shoulder. To her self-disgust, she had broken into tears of utter relief, when she would have liked so much to muster a semblance of dignity. It didn't help that Ethan had closed an arm around her and had begun to smooth her loose hair and murmur softly near her ear. "Aye, you're in for a hard time of it now, love. You wanted me, and now you'll have me." The comfort left her as weak and exposed as a newborn thing.

"You're holding me too close," she said when she was able, trying to pull away from him. "I'll cause a s-secondary hemorrhage—"

His arm tightened. "I'll decide when you're too close." A gently exploring hand moved over her back. She melted against him while he crooned softly and cuddled her. Soothering.

"I feel superfluous now," West announced from the doorway. "I suppose it's time for my exit. But first, Doctor, you'll probably want to know that the patient's wound was dressed and the bandage changed this morning. Still no signs of suppuration. We gave him some barley water, which he refused, and then we tried toast water, which led to increasingly violent demands for actual toast, until we finally had to humor him. He also made us give him tea to wash it down with. I hope that won't cause any problems."

"Has he harmed you in any way?" Garrett asked in a muffled voice.

"No," West replied, "but he threatened me with a spoon."

"I was asking Ethan."

A faint smile curved Ethan's lips as he looked down

at her, his fingers twining gently in her hair. "I've no complaints, save for the barley water." He looked over her head at the man in the doorway. Although his tone wasn't what anyone would have called affectionate, it contained a note of cautious friendliness. "Thank you, Ravenel. I'm sorry for the way I behaved when we met before."

West shrugged casually. "There's family for you: 'more kin than kind.'"

The quote snared Ethan's attention, the motion of his breathing pausing beneath Garrett's head. "That's from *Hamlet*, isn't it? Do you have a copy of it here?"

"There's a complete set of Shakespeare's plays in the library," West said, "including *Hamlet*. Why are you interested?"

"Jenkyn told me to read it. He said it was a mirror to a man's soul."

"God. No wonder I hate it."

Garrett drew back to look at Ethan. He was pale and exhausted, the lines of his face set in a way that she knew meant he was in pain. "The only thing you're going to do for the next week is lie still and rest," she told him. "Reading *Hamlet* is too much excitement for you."

"Excitement?" West repeated with a snort. "It's a play about procrastination."

"It's a play about misogyny," Garrett said. "Regardless, I'm giving Mr. Ransom an injection of morphine now, so he can sleep."

"'Good night, sweet prince,'" West said cheerfully, and left the room.

Ethan closed his hand over the shape of Garrett's

thigh through the folds of her robe and nightgown, preventing her from leaving the bed. "No morphine just yet," he said. "I've been out of my head for days."

He was pale and exhausted, his cheekbones standing out in sharp relief, his eyes shocking blue. He was beautiful. Alive and breathing, and hers. The familiar private energy was coursing between them again, the invisible connection she had never felt with anyone else.

"Ravenel told me some of what happened," Ethan said, "but I want to hear the whole of it from you."

"If he made me out to be an evil-tempered shrew," she said, "I'm not sure I would disagree."

"He said you were as valiant and wise as Athena. He has a high regard for you."

"Does he?" That surprised Garrett. "I've never doubted myself more than I have these past few days. Nor been so afraid." She stared at him anxiously. "After you heal from the surgery, you may be left with slightly less strength and range of motion on that side. You'll still be more fit than the average man. But it may take months before you stop feeling stabs of pain when you lift your arm. I know you're not accustomed to any kind of vulnerability. If you should end up in a fight, and someone strikes the site of the wound—"

"I'll be careful." With a wry twist of his mouth, Ethan added, "The devil knows I won't be seeking out any fights."

"We'll have to stay here until you're stronger. You can't go anywhere for at least a month."

"I can't wait that long," he said quietly.

They both fell silent, aware of all they had yet to

discuss, but agreeing tacitly that it could be set aside until later.

Tentatively Garrett slipped her hand into the front opening of Ethan's nightshirt to make certain the bandage was secure. He covered her hand with his, trapping it against his warm, lightly furred chest. The silky-coarse hair, to which she'd given no notice during his fever, now felt acutely intimate as it brushed her knuckles, awakening a flurry of butterfly-tickles in her stomach. His free hand cupped the back of her head and drew her toward him.

Mindful of his condition, Garrett kept the kiss careful and light. His lips were dry, hot, but not from fever . . . it was the clean, healthy male warmth she remembered so well. She couldn't help opening to the softly urgent pressure, detecting the hint of sugared tea and the beguiling taste of *him* . . . oh God, she'd never thought to have it again. His mouth slanted more firmly over hers, dark erotic pleasure wrapping around her senses like velvet. She tried to end the kiss, but his arms wouldn't loosen, and she didn't dare risk hurting him by pushing at his chest. One minute swooned into another, while his lips caught at hers with soft, seductive bites.

Flustered, Garrett twisted her mouth away long enough to gasp, "For heaven's sake, you were near death a matter of hours ago."

His lashes half lowered as he stared at the base of her throat, where a frenetic pulse beat. A leisurely fingertip investigated the slight hollow and stroked tenderly. "I'm on a bed with you. I'd have to be dead not to rouse to that."

Garrett darted a quick glance at the partially opened doorway, mindful that a passing servant might see them. "Raising your blood pressure could literally kill you. For the sake of your health, any and all sexual expenditures are forbidden."

Chapter 20

IT TOOK ETHAN APPROXIMATELY a fortnight to seduce her.

Garrett had written out a precise schedule for his recovery. On the first day, he would be allowed to sit up in bed, propped on pillows. On the fourth or fifth day, he could leave the bed and sit in a chair for an hour, once in the morning and once in the afternoon. It would take a month, she informed him, before he could walk about the house unassisted.

The two of them were, for the most part, left to their own devices, as West was occupied with problems that had gone unaddressed during his stay in London. He was busy with tenants and their land improvements, as well as supervising the use of some newly purchased machinery for haymaking. Usually he left the house at sunrise and didn't return until dinner.

In the absence of Garrett's usual responsibilities, there was more leisure time to fill than she could remember having even in childhood. She spent nearly every minute with Ethan, who was recovering at an astonishing rate. His wound was healing and closing without any trace of infection, and his appetite had returned in full measure. The delicate invalid offerings sent up from the kitchen—beef tea, blancmange, jellies, and puddings—had been roundly rejected in favor of regular food.

Ethan slept a great deal at first, especially since the opiates Garrett administered for pain made him drowsy and relaxed. During the hours he was awake, she sat by his bedside reading *Hamlet* aloud, as well as the most recent editions of the *Times* and the *Police Gazette*. Garrett found herself bustling about in a state of barely contained joy, doing small things for him, straightening the covers, monitoring everything he ate and drank, measuring out tonic in neat little cups. Sometimes she sat at the bedside just to watch him sleep. She couldn't help it—after having nearly lost him, she took intense satisfaction in having him safely in bed, clean and comfortable and well-nourished.

Ethan must have found her attentions smothering— any man would have—but he never said a word. Often she caught him watching her with a faint smile as she busied herself with little tasks—reorganizing her supplies, rolling freshly sterilized bandages, misting carbolic spray around the room. He seemed to understand how much she relished—needed—the feeling of having everything under control.

During the second week, however, Ethan became so restless from confinement that Garrett reluctantly allowed him to leave the bed and sit outside on a small second-floor terrace overlooking the vast estate gardens. With his shirt removed and his wound lightly covered with gauze, he lounged like a tiger, dozing and stretching in the sun. Garrett was amused to notice a few of the housemaids gathering at an upstairs parlor window that afforded a view of the private terrace, until Mrs. Church came to shoo them away. One could hardly blame them for wanting a glimpse of the half-dressed Ethan, with his dark good looks and superb physical build.

As one lazy sun-washed day followed another, Garrett was forced to accommodate the relaxed pace at Eversby Priory. There was no other choice. Time moved at a different pace here, where the manor's thick walls had once housed no less than a dozen monks, and the fireplaces in the common rooms were large enough to stand in. The clamor of locomotives on railway tracks, omnipresent in London, was rarely heard. Instead there was the sound of chiffchaffs and warblers in the hedgerows, the chiseling of woodpeckers in the nearby forest, and the whickers of farm horses. Distant bursts of hammering and sawing could be heard as carpenters and craftsmen worked on the south façade of the house, but that was a far cry from the tumult of London's public construction works.

There were two daily mealtimes at Eversby Priory: a hearty breakfast and a hedonistic dinner. In between, an artful miscellany of leftovers was arranged in a sideboard buffet. There was no end of cream, butter, and cheese made from summer grass milk. Juicy, tender bacon and smoked ham were served at nearly every meal, either on their own or chopped into salads and savory dishes. There were always abundant vegetables from the kitchen garden, and ripe fruit from the orchards. Accustomed as Garrett was to the quick and Spartan fare at home, she had to force herself to eat slowly and linger at the table. In the absence of any schedule or responsibilities, there was no need to rush.

While Ethan slept in the afternoons, Garrett fell into the habit of taking a daily walk through the estate's formal gardens. The summer-flowering beds had been beautifully maintained but intentionally left just a bit disheveled, lending offhand charm to the otherwise disciplined design.

There was something about being in a garden that made thinking easier. Not just regular thinking, but the kind that went a few layers down. *This*, she mused on her walk one day, was why Havelock had advised her to go on holiday.

As she passed a bronze fountain of frolicking cherubs, and a bed of chrysanthemums with curled and tangled white blossoms, she recalled something else Havelock had said on that occasion: *"Our existence, even our intellect, hangs upon love—without it, we would be no more than stock and stones."*

Now she had done both things he'd advised: gone on holiday—although it certainly hadn't started that way—and found someone to love.

How extraordinary this all was. She had spent most of her life running from the guilt of having caused her mother's death, never slowing enough to notice or care what she might be missing. This was the one thing she'd never bargained for. Love had appeared mysteriously, taking root like wild violets growing in the cracks of city pavement.

Havelock would probably caution her that she hadn't known Ethan long enough to be sure of him, or of her own feelings. Most people would say it had happened too fast. But there were a few things about Ethan Ransom that Garrett was absolutely certain of. She knew he accepted her flaws as readily as she did his: they could do that for each other when they couldn't do it for themselves. And she knew he loved her without condition. They had each arrived at a crossroads in life, and this was their chance to go in some new direction together, if they were brave enough to take it.

On the way back to the house, Garrett took a detour on a winding path that led to the estate's kitchen gardens and poultry house. Instead of the standard shed with an attached wire pen, the Eversby Priory chickens lived in a poultry *palace*. The central brick-and-painted-wood structure was topped with a slate roof and openwork parapets, and fronted by a colonnade of white pillars. Two wings curved outward from the main building, encompassing a paved court and a small pond for the birds' use.

Garrett walked around to the back of the building, where the wire exercise pens had been planted with fruit-bearing trees. At one of the corner posts, an elderly gardener was standing and talking, while a younger man sat on his haunches to mend a fencing panel.

The younger of the two was big-framed and very fit, his hands deft as he spliced broken wires together with a pair of pliers. Even before Garrett saw the face beneath the battered hat, she knew it was West Ravenel from the deep resonance of his voice.

"God help me, I don't know what the damned things need," he was saying ruefully. "Try taking them out of the cold frame and putting them back into the glasshouse."

The gardener's response was muffled and fretful.

"*Orchids.*" West made the word sound like a profanity. "Just do what you can. I'll shoulder the blame."

The older man nodded and shambled away.

Noticing Garrett's approach, West rose to his feet and made a motion of touching his hat brim respectfully, pliers still in hand. Dressed in work trousers and a rumpled shirt with the sleeves rolled up over his forearms, he appeared far more like a salt-of-the-earth farmer than a pedigreed gentleman. "Good afternoon, Doctor."

Garrett smiled at him. Despite West's high-handed act of dosing her tea with valerian, she grudgingly acknowledged that he'd been well-intentioned. Now that Ethan was recovering so well, she had decided to forgive him. "Good afternoon, Mr. Ravenel. Please don't let me interrupt your task, I just wanted to have a look at the poultry house. It's quite spectacular."

West ducked his head to blot his perspiring face on his upper shirtsleeve. "When we first took up residence at Eversby Priory, the poultry house was in far better condition than the manor. The order of precedence around here clearly favors hen over human."

"May I ask what the pavilions are for?"

"Laying nests."

"How many—" Garrett began, but was startled into silence by a fury of sound and motion: a pair of large geese were rushing at her with wings outspread, hissing and honking and making earsplitting whistling sounds. Even though the aggressive birds were on one side of the fencing and she was on the other, instinct caused her to jump back.

Quickly West interposed his body between Garrett and the irate creatures, gripping her arms lightly to assure himself of her balance. "Sorry," he said, his blue eyes alive with amusement. He turned to the geese, warning, "Back off, you two, or I'll use you both for mattress stuffing." After he guided Garrett a bit farther away from the fence, the geese quieted but continued to glare at her. "Please forgive the ill-mannered beggars," West said. "They're hostile to any stranger who isn't a chicken."

Garrett straightened her straw sunbonnet, which was little more than a flattened circle with a small knot of ribbons and flowers at the side. "Ahh, I see. Guard geese."

"Precisely. Geese are territorial, and they have keen eyesight. Whenever a predator comes near, they raise the alarm."

She chuckled. "I'll vouch for their effectiveness." As she meandered along the enclosure fencing, taking care to keep her distance from the suspicious geese, she said, "I couldn't help overhearing your conversation with the gardener. I hope you're not having difficulty with Helen's orchids?"

One of the estate's four glasshouses had once housed an extensive collection of bromeliads, cared for by Helen. Most of the exotic plants had been transported to London, where Winterborne had built a glass rooftop conservatory for Helen in their home. Some of the orchids, however, had been left behind at Eversby Priory.

"Naturally we're having difficulty with them," West said. "Orchid keeping is nothing but a desperate effort to delay the inevitable outcome of dry sticks in pots. I told Helen not to leave the damned things behind, but she wouldn't listen."

"Surely Helen won't scold," Garrett said, amused. "I've never heard her say a cross word to anyone."

"No, she'll merely look a little disappointed, in that way she has. It won't bother me personally, but one hates to see the entire gardening staff weep." He leaned down to pick up a hammer from the carpenter's tool basket next to the fence post. "I assume you'll check on Ransom when you return to the house?"

"No, he's been sleeping in the afternoons while I walk."

"Not lately, he hasn't."

She shot him a questioning glance.

"Three days ago," West said, "Ransom asked for a complete set of floor plans and outside elevations for the entire house, including an accounting of the alterations and remodeling we've done so far. And the ground plans. When I quite reasonably asked why, he looked annoyed and said he would tell me if I needed to know something." He paused. "Yesterday he interrogated one of the housemaids about the servants' quarters and common rooms, and the location of the gun room."

"He's supposed to be resting!" Garrett said in outrage. "He's still at risk for secondary hemorrhage."

"I was actually more concerned about what he wants with the gun room."

Garrett sighed shortly. "I'll try to find out."

"Don't make me out to be the tattletale," West warned, "or I'll deny it with a show of great indignation. I don't want Ransom angry with me."

"He's in his sickbed," Garrett said over her shoulder. "What could he do to you?"

"The man has been trained to murder people with common household items," he called after her, and she had to bite back a grin as she walked away.

AFTER RETURNING FROM her walk, Garrett changed into a light, lemon-colored gown, purloined from Kathleen's clothes closet. Mrs. Church had brought a collection of such garments to her, after having seen the two sensible broadcloth dresses Eliza had packed.

"You'll stew in those dark, heavy things," the housekeeper had told her frankly. "Broadcloth is a misery in the Hampshire summer. Her ladyship would insist that you borrow a few dresses of hers to wear." Garrett had accepted them gratefully, and had instantly come to love the airy, easy creations of silk and printed muslin.

She went to Ethan's room and tapped on the door before entering. As she had expected, he was lounging on the bed with a sheaf of huge quarto-sized pages covered with intricate diagrams and specifications.

"You're supposed to be resting," she said.

One of the pages lowered. Ethan's mouth curved as he saw her. "I'm on the bed," he pointed out.

"As my father would say, that's splitting straws with a hatchet."

Garrett entered the room and closed the door. Her heart skipped a beat at the sight of him, relaxed and lazy and masculine, with that chocolatey-dark hair falling over his forehead. He was barefoot, and clad in a shirt and pair of trousers borrowed from West. Two leather braces crossed over his back and came down over his front to fasten at his waistband: a necessity, since the trousers hung a bit loose at the waist and wouldn't stay up otherwise.

He was drinking a glass of cold tea brewed with healing herbs—honeysuckle, milk thistle. As his gaze swept over her, bright filaments of awareness awakened all through her body, and she felt an absurd pang of shyness. "You're as pretty as a daffodil in that dress," he said. "Come closer and let me see it."

The yellow dress, consisting of thin layers of silk tissue, was an afternoon "at-home" gown, fastening with only a few buttons and loops. It had been cleverly designed to give the appearance of a corset worn underneath, allowing the wearer to go without stays. Her hair was arranged in a softer style than usual, by a housemaid who aspired to be a lady's maid and had asked to practice on her. The maid had curled it into loose waves, pulled it back loosely in front with a silk ribbon, and pinned it in a French twist in the back.

As Garrett came to the bedside, Ethan reached out to catch a fold of the yellow silk in his fingers. "How was your walk, *acushla*?"

"Very pleasant," she said. "I went to see the poultry house on the way back."

"Near the kitchen garden."

"Yes." She glanced at the plans with a quizzical smile. "Why are you studying the estate's layout?"

He took his time about replying, making a project of gathering the scattered pages. "Assessing weak spots."

"You're worried that someone might try to break into the house?"

He hitched one shoulder in an evasive half-shrug.

"'Tis a miracle they haven't been robbed blind by now. No one ever seems to lock the doors."

"It's because of all the repair work," Garrett said. "There are so many contractors and craftsmen coming and going, it's easier to leave things open for the time being. Mr. Ravenel told me they've had to pull up floors to install modern plumbing, and replace entire walls that were rotting from bad drainage. In fact, the entire east wing has been closed until they can restore it at some future date."

"It would be better to raze the whole house to the ground and build a new one. Why try to resurrect an oversized old rubbish heap?"

Garrett's lips quirked at his description of the elegant and historic estate. "Ancestral pride?" she suggested.

Ethan snorted. "From what I know of the Ravenel ancestors, they have little reason for pride."

Garrett sat on the edge of the mattress with one leg folded beneath her. "They're your ancestors too," she pointed out. "And it's a renowned family name."

"That means nothing to me," Ethan said irritably. "I have no right to the Ravenel name, and no desire to claim kinship with any of them."

Garrett strove for a neutral tone, but she couldn't quite keep the concern out of her voice. "You have three half sisters. Surely you'll want to become acquainted with them."

"Why would I? What would that get me?"

"A family?"

Ethan's eyes narrowed. "You'd like a connection to them, would you? You should have let Lady Helen introduce you to West Ravenel. By now you'd be a member of the family in full."

Taken aback by how quickly his mood had changed, Garrett replied calmly. "Good heavens, how cross you sound. I don't want Mr. Ravenel, I want *you*. It doesn't matter to me what your name is, or what connections you have. If it makes you unhappy to associate with the Ravenels, we won't. Your feelings matter to me more than anything else."

Ethan gave her an arrested stare, the chill vanishing rapidly from his eyes, and he reached for her with a quiet groan, pulling her close.

Mindful of the bandage beneath his shirt, Garrett protested, "Please—be careful of your wound—"

But the muscles in his arms kept tightening until she was forced to lean on his sturdy chest. His fingers wove into her hair, disheveling the loosely pinned locks, and he nuzzled his face against her head. They stayed like that, breathing together.

At length, Ethan said, "How could I ever say Angus Ransom wasn't my father? He took my mother to wife and raised me as his own, and never let on to me that I was another man's bastard. A decent man, he was, for all that he went on the drink more than he should, and was too fond of giving me the back of his hand. He kept me fed and taught me to work, and more to the back of all that, he saw to it that I learned to read and cipher. There were things I hated about him. But I loved the man."

"Then you must honor his memory," Garrett said, touched by his loyalty. "Do what you feel is right. Just remember that it's not fair to blame Mr. Ravenel and Lord Trenear for past events they had nothing to do with. They've done nothing but try to help you. Mr. Ravenel went so far as to give you his own blood." She made her voice very soft as she added, "That deserves some gratitude, doesn't it?"

"Aye," Ethan said gruffly, and fell silent, his fingers moving lightly in her hair. "About the transfusion . . ." he said eventually. "Does it alter a man . . . change his nature in some way . . . if he's given someone else's blood?"

Garrett lifted her head and regarded him with a faint, reassuring smile. "That question is still being debated among scientists. But no, I don't believe so. Although blood is a vital fluid, it has nothing to do with a person's characteristics, any more than the heart has to do with one's emotions." Reaching up with her hand, she softly tapped her forefinger against his temple. "Everything you are, all you think and feel, is in here."

Ethan looked baffled. "What do you mean about the heart?"

"It's a hollow muscle."

"It's more than that." He sounded vaguely outraged, like a boy who'd just been told there was no Father Christmas.

"Symbolically, yes. But emotions don't actually come from there."

"They do," Ethan insisted. Taking her hand, he brought it down to his chest and pressed her palm flat against the strong beat. "The love I have for you—I *feel* it, right here. My heart beats faster for you all on its own. It aches when we're apart. Nothing tells it to do that."

If Garrett had any defenses left, they fell away in that moment like scaffolding from around her heart.

Rather than debate physiology or explain the brain's influence on muscular action, she raised herself over his chest to kiss him tenderly.

She had intended the contact to be brief, but Ethan responded passionately, sealing their mouths together. He continued to press her hand against his chest, and she thought of the first night they had arrived at Eversby Priory, when she had stood by his bed and collected his heartbeats in her palm.

He consumed her, taking deeper, rougher tastes, sucking and gnawing as if he were pulling sweetness from a honeycomb. It went on for fevered minutes, kisses of soft velvet and slow fire, until she became aware that the big masculine body beneath hers was primed for an activity he wasn't nearly ready for yet. As she felt the stiff ridge of his arousal through the layers of their clothes, her brain clamored a warning through the erotic haze. She tried to roll off him, but his hands clamped on her hips to keep her in place.

Turning her mouth from his, she gasped, "Let me down—I'll hurt you—"

"You're as light as a petal."

Trying a different avenue of escape, Garrett wriggled downward, but the movement sent a deep, hot throb of sensation through her. She stopped, her pelvis frozen against his, all her nerves and muscles tensed at the verge of release. Quivering, all she could think of was how much she wanted to grind against that hard shaft in tight circles.

She glanced at Ethan, whose eyes were lit with wicked amusement. Her face flamed as she realized he knew exactly what she was feeling.

One of his hands slid over her bottom, cupping firmly. His hips nudged upward, making her gasp. "Let me help you, *agra*," he whispered.

"You can help me by resting, and not re-opening your wound from too much exertion."

He nuzzled at her throat, and had the audacity to say, "I still have one hundred and eighteen positions left to show you."

Garrett pushed his hands away and rolled off him carefully. Her hair tumbled from its pins as she sat up. "Not unless you want to expire in the attempt."

"Sit right here," he invited, patting his lap. "We'll do something easy and slow."

"It's not just the physical effort I'm worried about, it's your blood pressure. You had arterial surgery two weeks ago, Ethan. You must stay calm and quiet until it heals completely."

"It already has. I'm almost back to normal."

Garrett gave him an exasperated glance as she tried to twist up her hair and pin it. "Unless you've found a way to defy the laws of biological science, you most certainly have *not* healed completely."

"I've healed enough for this."

"As your doctor, I disagree."

"I'll prove it to you." Watching for her reaction, he slid his hand downward to the bulging front of his trousers, and began to rub slowly.

Garrett's eyes widened. "You're not really going to—Good God. *Stop that*, this instant—" She grabbed his wrist, tugging his hand away from his groin. To her annoyance, he was chuckling richly.

Flustered and annoyed, she muttered, "Oh, go on then, and stimulate yourself into an aneurism."

Ethan grinned. "Stay and watch," he said, shocking her further. Hooking an arm around her waist, he took her down with him, and grunted in discomfort as they both fell heavily to their sides. "*Ah*. Damn it."

"It serves you right," Garrett exclaimed, while he continued to chuckle.

"Don't scold," he coaxed, nestling her back into him. "Stay here and lie with me." His smiling lips played tenderly behind her ear and along her neck. "Stay in my arms where you belong, *cushla macree*." He ran his hand over her body, fondling lightly here and there. "I've a matter to take up with you, by the way." He rubbed his lips against the edge of her ear. "You haven't kept your promise."

Perplexed, Garrett turned her face in his direction. "What promise?"

His mouth brushed her cheek as he spoke. "The night of the surgery. The last thing I asked for was a few words from you. But you wouldn't say them."

"Oh." Color rushed beneath the tender pressure of his lips. "I was afraid to," she confessed huskily. "I thought you might live longer if I made you wait."

"I'm still waiting."

"I didn't mean to—I'm sorry, I've been so—but I do. Of course I do." Carefully Garrett turned within the warm haven of his arms and lay facing him. She cleared her throat before saying in a slightly clenched voice, "I love you."

At the very same moment, Ethan had begun to ask, "Do you mean you—"

They both fell silent. How thoroughly awkward. With a defeated groan, Garrett turned onto her back and closed her eyes, too embarrassed to look at him.

The first time she'd ever said it to a man, and she'd made a hash of it.

"I love you," she repeated. But didn't sound at all the same as when he'd said it. She wanted to add something to make it more eloquent, but she couldn't think of what. "You had such a lovely way of putting it," she grumbled, "even when you were half conscious. I wish I could say something poetic, because I feel . . . I feel . . . but you were right, I don't have a romantic bone in my body."

"Sweet love . . . look at me."

She opened her eyes to find Ethan staring down at her in a way that made her feel sun-dazzled.

"You don't have to be poetic," he said. "You've held my life in your hands. When I was near death, you were the anchor to my soul." His fingertips slid from her temple and down over her flushed cheek, stroking tenderly. "I never dared to dream of hearing those three words from you. They're beautiful when you say them."

Garrett smiled reluctantly. "I love you," she said again, and this time it felt easier and more natural.

His lips strayed over the tip of her nose, her cheeks, her chin, before wandering back for another dizzying kiss. "Let me pleasure you. After all the care you've taken of me, let me do at least that much for you."

The idea quivered through her. But she shook her head and said, "I didn't go to the trouble of saving your life merely for you to toss it away in a moment of self-indulgence."

"I only want to play," Ethan coaxed, unloosening the fastenings of her bodice.

"It's a dangerous game—"

"What's this?" His fingers curled around a long pink silk cord and tugged, gently unearthing a small object from beneath her chemise. It was the little silver whistle he'd given her. Closing his hand around the bright metal, still warm from her skin, he sent her a questioning look.

Turning pink, Garrett confessed sheepishly, "It's a sort of . . . talisman. Whenever you're not with me, I pretend I can use it to send for you, and you'll magically appear."

"Whenever you want me, love, I'll always come running."

"You didn't the last time I tried it. When I'd finished my rounds at the workhouse, I stood on the front steps and blew this whistle with no results whatsoever."

"I was there." Ethan stroked the hollow of her throat with the rounded end of the whistle. "You just couldn't see me."

"Truly?"

He nodded, setting aside the gleaming little tube. "You were wearing the dark green dress with the black trim. Your shoulders were drooping, and I knew you were tired. I thought of all the women in London who were safe and cozy in their homes, while you were standing out in the dark, after spending your evening taking care of people who couldn't afford a penny for your services. You're the best woman I've ever known . . . and the most beautiful . . ."

He tugged her chemise down and drew the spread fingertips of one hand over her exposed chest, the side of his smallest finger brushing a tender pink bud as if by accident. Her throat closed on a whimper. Using his fingertips, he rolled and stroked the sensitive peak, then moved to her other breast, gently clamping the nipple between his thumb and forefinger.

"It's too soon for this," Garrett said anxiously, and managed to turn onto her side, facing away from him.

Ethan reached out and tucked her back into the exciting weight and hardness of his body. She felt the curve of his smile at the nape of her neck, as if her perfectly rational concerns were unwarranted. "*Acushla*, you've had your say for the past two weeks, and I've abided by your rules—"

"You've fought my rules every step of the way," she protested.

"I've been drinking that evil tonic you keep giving me," he pointed out.

"You've been pouring it into a potted fern whenever you think I'm not looking."

"It tastes worse than the Thames," he said flatly. "The fern thought so too, which is why it turned brown and died."

A laugh bubbled up before she could stop it, but her breath caught as one of his muscular legs came between hers and urged her thighs apart. His hand slid under her skirts and into the open seam of her drawers, until he found the bare skin above the top of her stocking garter. The massaging stroke of his thumb, high inside her thigh, made her weak with excitement.

"You want me," Ethan said with satisfaction as he felt her tremble.

"You're impossible," she moaned. "You're the *worst* patient I've ever had."

His husky laugh tickled her neck. "No," he whispered, "I'm the best. Let me show you how good I am."

Breathing raggedly, Garrett started to wriggle away from him, then checked the movement.

That made him laugh again. "That's right, don't struggle. You might hurt me."

"Ethan," she said, trying to sound stern, "this is too much exertion for you."

"I'll pull away if I feel myself starting up in a passion." He untied her garters and pulled down her drawers, murmuring in her ear all the while, telling her how sweet she was to the touch, how he longed to kiss and love every part of her. His hand slid between her parted thighs, stroking the folds of her sex open, teasing and teasing until her skin was sweat-misted and hot and all her muscles were clenching. Gently his fingertip found the entrance to her body and wriggled into silkiness, wetness, pulsing warmth.

They both groaned softly.

Garrett tried desperately not to move as his finger eased farther into the wet, grasping depths, pushing in deep, sliding out slowly and back in again. "Éatán," she begged, "let's wait until you've healed properly. Please. *Please*. Seven more days, that's all."

A breath of laughter rushed across her bare shoulder as he worked at the front of his trousers. "Not seven more seconds."

Garrett squirmed as she felt the pressure of a smooth, broad shape at the tender breach of her sex. She couldn't hold back a moan. The rim of her entrance contracted, tiny muscles grasping for the blunt silken pressure.

"You're trying to pull me in," came his dark whisper. "I can feel it. Your body knows where I belong."

She felt a liquid nudge, her flesh tightening then yielding at the helpless sensation of being opened and penetrated. He entered an inch or two. Agitation quickened her blood as she lay there cradled and surrounded, with that hot, teasing presence just inside her.

Garrett had no idea how many minutes passed while they lay together, motionless except for the rhythms of their breathing. Her body stretched . . . a slight relaxation . . . and there was another slight easing inward. In the dreamlike stillness, she began to feel fuller and fuller . . . he was gradually moving deeper, occupying her in such slow increments that she couldn't perceive whether the impetus was coming from him or herself. Some of it had to be her own doing: the maddening craving had made it impossible to stay absolutely still. Her hips kept spasming with the urge to push down on that tantalizing hardness.

Every sensation was magnified in the silence. She was acutely aware of the air against her bare legs, the coolness of the linen sheets and knitted cotton bedding beneath her. The hairiness of Ethan's arm across her, the resinous spice of shaving soap, the faint, salty traces of intimacy.

Her eyes closed as she felt the throb of his shaft far up inside her. He was buried to the hilt now, filling her so thickly that she could feel every twitch and pulse of him. They were both outwardly still, while deep inside her flesh was shaping around him, eagerly caressing his hard length, enticing him to stay. She clamped against the swollen invasion, and pleasure washed down to her toes and up to the top of her skull, and the stiff length inside her throbbed and jerked in response, and that made her inner muscles clench again. Over and over again, their joined flesh squeezing, swelling, throbbing, the deep and secret movements as uncontrollable as her heartbeat. Exquisite heat suffused her until she couldn't stand it any longer.

His name broke from her lips in a dry sob. *"Éatán."*

His hand slid down over her front to the place where she clasped him, and he massaged her sex tenderly, steadily. She arched, her hips locking tight to his, and she convulsed and shuddered within his cradling embrace, the release surging out of control, draining her until she collapsed in his arms like a handful of wilted meadow flowers.

ETHAN FELT HER tremble as she realized he was still erect. He ran a soothing hand over her hip and thigh, wishing she were fully naked. She was exquisite, so slim and finely made, her flesh tender and yet filled with tensile strength. They reclined together amid swaths of yellow silk, with her legs and chest bared. He loved the colors of her, pink and mauve and ivory, all washed in light. The glistening tumble of her hair held the colors of autumn: chestnut, maple, russet, umber. He could see her toes curling and relaxing . . . clean, pink little toes, the nails gleaming and filed.

Her flesh was snug and lively in the aftermath of her climax, gripping repeatedly to keep hold of him. It was bliss to be inside the hollows and heat and vibrant life of her. She would bend to no man's will—not even his—but she would yield to him out of trust and desire. Only him. Carefully he pulled up her top leg and hooked it back over his, spreading her wider. She made a feeble protest, something about overexerting himself, and he hushed her and kissed behind her ear.

"Trust me," he whispered. "I'll thrive none the worse for loving you, I promise. Now, let me have a little more of you."

Now that she was relaxed and accustomed to him, he was able to slide farther inside. She gasped in surprise and caught at his wrist. Concerned that he might be hurting her, he withdrew slightly, but her hips promptly followed the movement, taking him deep again.

A grin crossed his lips. "Hot little wench," he said near her ear. "You'll have your fill of me, if that's what you want." Closing his hand on her hip, he began to move her languidly on his hard, wet shaft, controlling the rhythm, keeping it slow and steady. Her breathing hastened, and she melted against him, letting him guide her easily. Every awareness converged as he went deeper and deeper into the mysterious soft depths of her, and there was no world but her, no breath, no language, no sun, no stars, nothing that didn't begin and end with her.

He felt her pleasure take flight again, the slender body arched and taut in the steep ascent, the unfolding rapture. He was with her, inside her, caressing her with every part of himself. The culmination, as it approached, was severe and blinding, searing through him with unimaginable force. He withdrew and slid his shaft against the sweet groove of her firm pale buttocks, and let himself be immolated in the scorching white fire, feeling purified by it, lust and love and pleasure mingling until there was nothing but ecstasy within and without. He felt her quiver at the hot spill of his release against the small of her back. Gently he rolled her to her stomach, and used her discarded drawers to wipe away the residue.

Gathering her back in his arms, he let out a long, shivering sigh of contentment, a chuckle stirring in his chest. He moved to catch the lobe of her ear with his teeth, and touched it with his tongue. "If that didn't kill me," he couldn't resist murmuring, "nothing will."

Chapter 21

THE NEXT DAY, AFTER Garrett left for her afternoon walk, Ethan ventured downstairs to the first floor by himself. He knew what she would have said about his excursion, and she would have been right, but it was necessary. He was a sitting duck at Eversby Priory, and by extension so were Garrett, West Ravenel, and every other member of the household. He damned well couldn't make an accurate assessment of the situation from his bedroom.

From his visits to the upstairs terrace, and a few brief meanderings around the second floor, Ethan had a good sense of his limitations. Overall, he was still weak and prone to tiring easily. He hadn't yet recovered his strength, balance, or mobility. For a man accustomed to functioning at the highest level of physical fitness, it was infuriating to have trouble walking down a flight of stairs. The bullet wound and the surrounding tissue still ached, and there were stabs and zings of pain when he moved his arm or shoulder in certain ways. Garrett had decided it was better not to immobilize the limb, to keep it from weakening and turning stiff.

Ethan gripped the balustrade to keep himself steady as he made his painstaking way down the grand staircase. When he was at the halfway point, a footman passing through the entrance hall below caught sight of him and stopped abruptly.

"Sir?" The footman, a young, big-shouldered fellow with the soft brown eyes of a puppy dog, stared up at him with unease. "Is there . . . do you . . . may I help?"

"No," Ethan replied pleasantly, "I'm stretching my legs a bit, that's all."

"Yes, sir. But the stairs . . ." The footman began to ascend the staircase hesitantly, as if fearing Ethan would topple right in front of him.

Ethan didn't know how much the servants had been told about who he was, or about the specifics of his condition, but clearly this footman knew he shouldn't be going anywhere on his own.

Which was irritating.

It also reminded him of how precarious his situation was. All it would take was a whispered confidence between one of these servants and someone in the nearby village, or a casual comment from a deliveryman or workman, to start rumors spreading.

"All servants talk," Jenkyn had once told him. *"They notice every deviation from the household's normal pattern, and they draw conclusions. They know what secrets the master and his wife are keeping from each other. They know where the valuables are, how money has been spent, and who's been fucking whom. Never believe a servant who claims not to know something. They know everything."*

"If I may, Mr. Smith," the footman said, continuing up toward him, "I'll accompany you the rest of the way."

Mr. Smith? That was the alias they'd come up with?

"Holy hell," Ethan said under his breath. Out loud, he murmured. "No, there's no need." Perceiving there was no way the footman was going to leave him alone, he added dryly, "But suit yourself."

The footman came to his step and descended at the same pace, ready to spring into action should Ethan require assistance. As if he were a small child or old man.

"What's your name?" Ethan asked.

"Peter, sir."

"Peter, what's the belowstairs talk about my presence at the estate?"

The footman hesitated. "We were told that you're a friend of Mr. Ravenel's, and you were involved in a shooting accident. We're to keep it private, as we do all our guests' business."

"And that's all? No rumors or speculation?"

Another, longer hesitation. "There are rumors," Peter said quietly.

"Tell me what's being said." They reached the bottom of the stairs.

"I . . ." The footman dropped his gaze and fidgeted uncomfortably. "I shouldn't, sir. But if I may show you something . . ."

Intrigued, Ethan went with him down a long hallway that opened into a narrow rectangular gallery. The walls were covered from floor to ceiling with framed paintings. The footman led him slowly past a row of portraits, all of Ravenel ancestors in the dress of their time. Some of them were as large as life, in heavy gold frames up to seven feet high.

They stopped in front of a stunning full-length

painting of a dark-haired, blue-eyed man in a commanding posture. Strikingly, he was dressed in a full-length blue brocade robe with a gold rope belt. Power and arrogance radiated from the canvas. There was a disconcerting hint of sensuality in the long-fingered hand braced on a lean hip, and in the coolly appraising, secretive stare. And there was something cruel about the mouth.

Riveted and repelled, Ethan instinctively backed away from the portrait. He saw the likeness to himself, and his soul revolted. Managing to drag his gaze away, he focused on the worn Persian rug.

"That's Master Edmund," he heard the footman say. "I came to Eversby Priory after his lordship had passed on, so I never met him. But some of the older servants saw you when you were brought in and . . . they knew. They knew exactly who you were. They were very moved, sir, and said we must all do our best for you. Because you're the last living man in the true bloodline, you see."

At Ethan's silence, the footman continued helpfully, "Your blood goes all the way back to Branoc Ravenel, who was one of Charlemagne's twelve paladins. He was a great warrior, the first Ravenel. Even if he was French."

Ethan's mouth twitched, despite his inner turmoil. "Thank you, Peter. I'd like to be alone for a few minutes."

"Yes, sir."

After the footman had left, Ethan went to set his back against the opposite wall. He leveled a brooding stare at the portrait, his thoughts in a welter.

Why had Edmund chosen to be portrayed for posterity in such unconventional attire? It seemed like a gesture of disdain, as if he couldn't be bothered to dress for his own portrait. The robe was thickly embroidered and luxurious, something a Renaissance prince might have worn. It conveyed the rather spectacular self-assurance of a man who didn't doubt his own superiority, no matter what he wore.

Memories jolted loose as Ethan stared at the resplendent figure in the portrait. "Ah, Mam," he whispered unsteadily. "You shouldn't have had a damned thing to do with him."

How could his mother have thought any good would come of it? She must have been awestruck. Intoxicated by the idea of being desired by a man of high position. And some corner of her heart had always been kept for him, this man who had treated her like an object to be used and discarded.

Ethan closed his eyes. They turned hot and liquid beneath his lids.

A casual masculine voice broke the silence.

"Up and about, I see. I'm glad they managed to find clothes to fit you."

Ethan froze, horrified to be caught in a vulnerable moment by West Ravenel. He darted a blurred glance at him and forced his mind to focus on the conversation. Something about clothes. West's butler and valet had brought an assortment of garments in varying sizes from his closet and trunks for him to make use of. Some of the clothes had been costly, with perfect tailoring and buttons made of gold or ornamental stones such as agate or jasper, but they had been too roomy for Ethan to wear.

"Aye, they did," Ethan muttered. "Thank you."

Swiftly he dragged a coat sleeve across his eyes and found himself saying the first thing that came to mind. "You used to be fat."

West seemed amused rather than offended. "I prefer 'pleasingly plump.' I was a London rake, and for your information, all true rakes are fat. We spend all our time indoors, drinking and eating. Our only exercise consists of bedding a willing wench. Or two." He gave a nostalgic sigh. "God. There are times when I miss those days. Fortunately I can take a train to London when the need arises."

"There are no women in Hampshire?" Ethan asked.

West gave him a speaking glance. "You're suggesting I bed the innocent daughter of a local squire? Or a wholesome milkmaid? I need a woman with *skills*, Ransom." He wandered to a space next to Ethan and braced his back on the wall in an identical posture. As his gaze followed Ethan's to the towering portrait, he looked sardonic. "That painting captures him perfectly. A member of the Upper Crust, lording it over the crustless."

"Did you know him well?"

"No, I saw the earl only a handful of times at large family events. Weddings and funerals and such. We were the poor relations, and our presence didn't exactly improve a gathering. My father was a violent sod, and my mother was a coquette who, as they say, 'had a tile loose.' As for my brother and I, we were a pair of sullen tots who went around trying to pick fights with our cousins. The earl couldn't stand either of us. He caught me by the ear on one occasion, and told me I was a bad, wicked lad, and someday he would see to it that I was placed as a cabin boy on a trading vessel bound for China, which would undoubtedly be captured by pirates."

"What did you say?"

"I told him I hoped he would do it as soon as possible, because pirates would do a much better job of raising me than my parents."

Ethan felt a grin cross his face, when he would have sworn nothing could have made him smile, standing in front of that blasted portrait.

"My father thrashed me within an inch of my life afterward," West said, "but it was worth it." He paused reflectively. "That was the last memory I have of him. He died not long after that, brawling over a woman. Dear old Papa was never one to let rational conversation get in the way of his fists."

It hadn't occurred to Ethan that West and Devon Ravenel had led anything other than a sheltered and pampered existence. The revelation gave him an unexpected feeling of empathy and kinship. He couldn't help liking West, who was irreverent as hell, at ease with himself and the world, while still retaining the subtle flintiness of a man with few illusions. This was someone he could understand and talk to.

"Did you ever meet the earl?" West asked, wandering slowly along the row of portraits.

"Once." Ethan had never told a living soul about it. But in the quiet out-of-time atmosphere of the portrait gallery, he found himself sharing the memory that had haunted him for years. "When my mother was younger, the earl kept her for a time. She was a shopgirl when they met, and a beauty. She lived in a set of rooms he paid for. The arrangement lasted until she found out she was with child. The earl didn't want her after that, so he gave her some money and a reference for a job that fell through. Her family had cast her off, and she had nowhere to turn. She knew if she gave her baby to the orphanage, she could take a factory job, but she decided to keep me instead. Angus Ransom, who was a prison guard at Clerkenwell, offered to marry her and raise me as his own.

"But times grew hard," Ethan continued. "There came a day we couldn't pay the butcher's bill and had no fuel for the hearth. Mam took it upon herself to go to the earl for help. She thought it wasn't too much to ask of him, to spare a few coins for his own child. But it wasn't the earl's way to give something for nothing. Mam had kept her looks, and he still fancied her for a tumble. After that, she would slip off to meet him when we needed money for food or coal."

"Shame on him," West said softly.

"I was still a young boy," Ethan said, "when Mam took me for an outing one day in a hansom cab. She said we were going to visit a gentleman friend of hers, who wanted to meet me. We went to a house like nothing I'd ever imagined, fine and quiet, with polished floors, and gold columns on the sides of the doorways. The earl came downstairs, wearing a velvet dressing robe, similar to that one." Ethan gave a brief nod in the direction of the painting. "After asking me a few questions—did I go to school, which Bible story was my favorite—he patted me on the head, and said I seemed a bright boy for all that I had the accent of an Irish tinker. He pulled a little sack of sweets from the pocket of his robe and gave them to me. Barley-sugar sticks, they were. Mam bade me sit in the parlor while she went upstairs to talk with the earl. I don't know how long I waited there, eating barley sweets. When Mam came down, she appeared the same as when we'd arrived, not a hair out of place. But there was something humbled in the look of her. I was old enough to understand they'd done something wrong, that he'd done something to her. I left the little bag of sweets beneath the chair, but it took weeks for the taste of barley sugar to fade from my mouth.

"On the way home, Mam told me the man was very important, a highborn gentleman, and he was my real father, not Angus Ransom. I could tell she took pride in it. In her mind I'd gained something, now that I knew I was the son of a great man. An aristocrat. She didn't understand I'd just lost the only father I'd ever known. I could hardly look at Angus for months afterward, now that I knew I wasn't his. 'Til the day he died, I always wondered how many times he glanced at me and saw another man's bastard."

Ravenel was silent for a while, looking angry and resigned. "I'm sorry," he eventually said.

"'Twas none of your doing."

"I'm still sorry. For centuries, the Ravenels have turned out one generation of cruel, irresponsible arses after another." West shoved his hands in his pockets and glanced over the rows of stern, haughty faces from the past. "Yes, I'm referring to you," he said to the crowd of portraits. "The sins of your fathers rained down on you like poison, and you passed it down to your children, and then they did the same. There wasn't a decent man in the lot of you." He turned to Ethan. "Soon after Devon's son was born, he came to me and said, 'Someone has to absorb all the poison that's been passed down through generations, and keep it away from the ones who come after us. It has to stop with me. God help me, I'm going to protect my child from my own worst instincts. I'm going to block every violent, selfish impulse that was instilled in me. It won't be easy. But I'll be damned if I turn out a son who's exactly like the father I hated.'"

Ethan stared at him, struck by the wisdom and resolve in those words. He realized these distant Ravenel cousins were far more than a pair of carefree toffs who'd had the luck to come into an unexpected inheritance. They were trying like hell to save an estate, and even more, to save a family. For that, they had his respect.

"Your brother may be the first earl who's ever been worthy of the title," Ethan said.

"He didn't start out that way," West replied, and laughed. When the brief flare of amusement faded, he said, "I understand why you want nothing to do with the Ravenels. Edmund was an unfeeling monster, and on top of that, no one likes to admit they're the product of six centuries of inbreeding. But everyone needs someone to turn to, and we are your family. You should get to know us. If it helps, I'm the worst of the lot—the rest are all much better than me."

Ethan approached him and extended a hand. "You'll do well enough for me," he said gruffly. West grinned at him.

When they shook hands, it felt like a promise had been made. A commitment.

"Now," Ethan said, "where do you keep the guns?"

Ravenel's brows shot upward. "Ransom, if you don't mind, I prefer easing into a new topic with a transitional phrase or two."

"Usually I do," Ethan said. "But I tire easily, and this is my nap time."

"May I ask why we're arming ourselves instead of napping?"

"Because we were nearly murdered two weeks ago, and we're fairly certain someone will come to finish the job."

West turned serious, his gaze sharpening. "If I'd been through what you have, Ransom, the devil knows I'd be jumpy too. But no one's going to come here looking for you. Everyone thinks you're dead."

"Not without a body," Ethan said. "Unless they find one, they'll never stop looking for me."

"Why would they even suspect you're here? They won't connect you to the Ravenels. The river police who brought you to Ravenel House were too terrified to say a word to anyone."

"At the time, they probably were. But either of them could have mentioned it to a friend or sweetheart, or bend the elbow a time too many at the local tavern and say something to the barkeep. Eventually they'll be taken in for questioning because they were on patrol that night. They won't hold out for long under interrogation. Furthermore, any of the servants at Ravenel House may let something slip. A housemaid could say something to the fruit seller at the market."

West looked skeptical. "Do you really think a few careless words in a tavern, or a bit of gossip from a housemaid to a market seller, would make its way to Jenkyn's ears?"

The question was reasonable, but it almost stunned Ethan. He realized he'd lived for too damned long in Jenkyn's complex and secretive world—he'd forgotten that most people had no idea what was really taking place around them.

"Long before Jenkyn recruited me," Ethan said, "he started constructing a network of informants and spies all over the United Kingdom. Ordinary people in ordinary towns. Coachmen, innkeepers, sellers, prostitutes, domestic servants, factory workers, university students . . . all part of an intelligence-gathering apparatus. They're paid stipends with secret grant money Jenkyn receives from the Home Office. The Prime Minister knows about it, but says he prefers to remain unaware of the details. Jenkyn has made a science of gathering and analyzing information. He has at least eight active officers who've been specially trained to carry out any task he assigns. They're outside the law. They have no fear. They have no scruples. They have little to no regard for human life, including their own."

"And you're one of them," West said quietly.

"I was. Now I'm a target. By now, someone in the village knows that a pair of strangers have been staying at Eversby Priory."

"My servants wouldn't say a word to anyone."

"You have carpenters, painters, and workmen coming and going. They have eyes and ears."

"Very well. Let's assume you're right, and Jenkyn will send someone after you. I can close this house as tight as tuppence."

"There's not one lock in this entire house they couldn't pick in less than a minute, including the front door. And your servants don't seem to bother with locks in the first place."

"They will if I tell them to."

"That would be a start." Ethan paused. "I'll have

recovered enough to leave for London in a week. But until then, we have to take security measures in case Jenkyn's men find me here."

"I'll show you to the gun closet."

"There's a gun *room* in the floor plans. On this level of the house."

"We turned that into an office room with a connecting lavatory. Now we keep the firearms in a gun closet off the servants' hall, under charge of the butler."

Ethan gave him a narrow-eyed glance.

West looked irritable. "Does it look like we can afford to host long, expensive shooting parties? We sold off the hounds. Our gamekeeper is a fossil. We let him have a few birds only to give him something to do. The animals on this estate are used for food, work, and profit, not entertainment. And before I take you belowstairs to see the gun closet, you should be prepared for the fact that most of the guns are old and rusted. Hardly anyone here except me even knows how to use one."

"Are you a good shot?"

"Middling. I'm an excellent shot if the targets hold still, but they so rarely do."

As Ethan considered the situation, he fought against a wave of exhaustion. "Forget about the gun closet, then. We'll do what we can to shore up our defenses. Tell the servants to start locking the damn doors at night, including their own doors when they're asleep. And we'll need bolts installed in every attic and basement opening, cellar and jib door, luggage hoist, coal lift . . . every means of internal communication. Also, pull down the scaffolding and platforms on the south side of the house."

"*What?* No, I can't do that."

"The scaffolding provides outside access to any window or balcony on that entire façade."

"Yes, Ransom, that's the point. I have stonemasons restoring ornamental openwork." Faced with Ethan's unyielding expression, West groaned. "Do you know how many days the stonemasons took to build that scaffolding? Do you have any idea of what they're going to do to me if I tell them to pull it all down and put it back up a week later? You won't have to worry about assassins from London. My workmen will happily string us both up in short order."

A terrible weariness had begun to invade Ethan's muscles, and he felt a pressing need for sleep. *Damn it.* "I'd spare you all of this by leaving now, if I were able," he muttered, passing a hand over his forehead.

"No," West said instantly, his tone changing. "Pay no attention to my complaining. God knows no one else does. You belong here." He ran an evaluating glance over Ethan. "You look ready to drop. I'll accompany you upstairs."

"I don't need help."

"If you think I'm going to risk having anything happen to you, and then face Dr. Gibson's wrath, you're mad. I'd rather take on a baker's dozen of assassins."

Ethan nodded and headed out of the gallery. "They won't send more than three men," he said. "They'll come in the wee hours of the morning, while it's still dark and the household is sleeping soundly."

"Eversby Priory has over two hundred rooms. They won't know the layout."

"Yes, they will. The floor plans and specifications

can be retrieved from the offices of any architect, contractor, or surveyor who's had anything to do with the rebuilding of this place."

West heaved a sigh, conceding the point. "Don't forget my London banker," he said glumly. "He asked for copies when we were arranging for loans."

Apologetically, Ethan said, "They won't want to cause unnecessary casualties. All they'll want is to find me. I'll surrender myself before I let anyone here get hurt."

"Damned if you will," West retorted. "The Ravenel family motto is 'Loyalty binds us.' I'll blow the head off of any bastard who threatens one of my kinsmen."

Chapter 22

"IS THIS HOW THEY did it at Miss Primrose's?" Ethan asked, standing back as a pair of footmen—supervised by the elderly butler, Sims—ceremoniously laid tablecloths on the ground beneath a shade tree. They proceeded to set out china plates, silver flatware, and crystal goblets.

Garrett shook her head, watching with a bemused smile as ice buckets filled with bottles of lemonade, ginger beer, and claret were arranged beside the dishes. "Our picnics were bread, jam, and a slice of cheese, carried in a tin pail."

It had been her idea to have lunch with Ethan on the estate grounds, within the shelter of a high garden wall. She had told Ethan about the picnics she and her classmates used to enjoy at school, and he said he'd never been on one. Garrett had asked the housekeeper if she could borrow a basket to carry out some items from the daily sideboard buffet. Instead, the cook had provided what she called "a proper picnic" in a pair of massive wicker and leather hampers.

After Sims and the footmen had departed, Ethan sat with his back against the tree trunk and watched as Garrett unearthed a feast from the hampers. There were boiled eggs, plump olives, stalks of crisp green

celery, jars of pickled carrots and cucumbers, sandwiches wrapped in paraffin paper, cold fried oyster-
patties and wafer crackers, jars of finely chopped
salads, a weighty round of white cheese, muslin-lined
baskets filled with finger cakes and pastry biscuits, a
steamed cabinet pudding left in its fluted stoneware
mold, and a wide-mouthed glass bottle filled with
stewed fruit.

As they ate a leisurely meal beneath the dense green
beech canopy, Garrett was pleased to see Ethan relaxing. For the past five days, he had been more active
than she would have preferred, going through every
nook and cranny of Eversby Priory with West. As with
most ancient manor houses, many modifications and
additions had been made over the centuries, resulting
in quirks, oddly shaped spaces, and offset stairs and
windows.

Despite Garrett's concerns that he would set back
his recovery, Ethan had painstakingly made his way to
each level of the house to assess it with his own eyes.
New bolts and locks had been installed, and the outside scaffolding had been removed. Doors were now
routinely locked every night, and so were the ground
and basement windows. The household staff had been
instructed to raise an alarm if they heard suspicious
noises at night, but under no circumstances should
they confront a housebreaker on their own.

Although Ethan had continued to heal and improve at an impressive rate, it would take weeks or
even months for him to reach the level of health he'd
enjoyed before his injury. It exasperated him to be
constrained by his physical limitations, having been

accustomed to inexhaustible reserves of energy and strength.

It had been almost three weeks since Ethan had been shot. In ordinary circumstances, Garrett would have insisted that he wait twice that amount of time before leaving the estate. However, this situation was far from ordinary. Whether or not she approved, Ethan had told her, he had to leave for London the day after tomorrow. He couldn't continue to remain at Eversby Priory and put the household at risk. Nor could he stand by and do nothing after Jenkyn had diverted eight tons of stolen explosives to a terrorist group that could conceivably blow up the House of Commons.

Reaching out to the luxuriant undergrowth of wintergreen shrubs beneath the stand of beeches, Ethan plucked a sharp minty leaf. He lay back on the cloth and nibbled on the bit of green, staring up at the canopy of sky and leaves overhead. The beeches were gnarled and graceful, their branches tangling as if they were holding hands. All that could be heard were rustling leaves and the trill of a wood warbler. The air was fresh with the loamy scent of rich earth. Rustling leaves and the occasional trill of a wood warbler were the only sounds they could hear.

"I've never been in a place so peaceful, outside of a church," Ethan said.

"It's a world away from London. All the clashing fire bells and the roar of railways and construction . . . and the air filthy with smoke and dust . . . and all those tall buildings blocking out the sun . . ."

"Aye," Ethan said. "I miss it too."

They both chuckled.

"I miss my patients, and the clinic," Garrett confessed. "Now that you're too healthy for me to fuss over, I must have something to do."

"You could begin writing a memoir," he suggested.

Unable to resist the temptation he presented, Garrett bent over until their noses nearly touched. "My life," she told him, "hasn't been nearly sensational enough for my memoir to be interesting."

"You're in hiding with a fugitive," he pointed out.

Her lips quirked. "That means you're the one with an interesting life, not me."

Ethan traced the edge of her low-necked gown with his fingertips, and hooked his forefinger into the soft valley between her breasts. "We'll return to London soon, and I'll provide all the excitement you want." His lips brushed hers with teasing dry warmth, and she let him draw her down, increasing the pressure until the kiss was strong and damp and savoring. Her senses were filled with him, the sweet taste of his mouth, the vital feel of his body as he pulled her full length against him.

In the past week, Ethan had made love to her twice more, managing to overcome her concerns with the perfect mixture of reassurance and temptation. The man was a silver-tongued devil. He spent long minutes whispering, kissing, caressing her, until every subtle movement sent delight humming through deep-secreted chords in her body.

Trying to keep her mind on the conversation, Garrett turned her mouth from his long enough to ask, "What are you planning to do when we return? Go to the Lord Chancellor? The Attorney-General?"

"I'm not sure who to trust," Ethan said ruefully. "I

think it's best to put them all on the hook by making the information public."

Propping up on her elbow, Garrett looked down into his face with a slight frown. "But you gave the evidence to Commissioner Felbrigg. Will we have to break into Lord Tatham's safe again?"

"I kept a few extra pages," he said. "Just in case."

Her eyes widened. "Where did you put them?"

A lazy smile curved Ethan's lips. He was a handsome sight, his skin gold-dusted in the light, his eyes dark and vivid blue. "Can't you guess?"

"Somewhere in your flat?"

"I gave them to you."

"To me? How . . . *Oh*." Garrett laughed. "You wrapped them with the monkey picture."

"I pasted an envelope to the back of it," he said. "It contains the pages, and a copy of my will."

Although Garrett had been about to ask more about the evidence, she was distracted by that last part. "You have a will?" she asked skeptically.

He nodded. "I named you as the sole beneficiary."

Surprised and touched, Garrett said, "That's very kind of you. But shouldn't you leave your possessions to a relation?"

"My mother was cast off by her family. I'd never give them a farthing. And anyone on the Ransom side would put it to ill use. No, it's all for you. When the time comes—hopefully none too soon—you'll be well taken care of. My lawyers will help you through the patent rights transfers, not only here but abroad. Everything will be put in your name, and—"

"What in heaven's name are you talking about?" Garrett asked in bewilderment. "Patents for what?"

"For lock designs." He began to toy with the trimmings on her dress, tracing the seams with his forefinger. "I have about three dozen. Most of them are insignificant and don't turn a farthing in profit. But a few—"

"I call that impressive," Garrett exclaimed, beaming with pride. "How many talents you possess. You're going to be a great success someday—in some profession other than spying, I mean."

"Thank you," Ethan said, enjoying her praise. "But there's more to tell you. You see—"

"Yes, tell me everything. When did it start?"

"It was while I was still apprenticing for the Clerkenwell locksmith. I'd worked out a way to make the standard cell locks pick-proof, by adding a stop-plate to the bolt. The prison governors—and the locksmith— had me draw the plans and write out the specifications, and then they took out a patent on the invention. They made a pretty penny on it." With a cynical twist of his mouth, Ethan added, "They cut me out of the profits, since I was only a boy."

"Scoundrels," Garrett said indignantly.

"Aye," came his rueful agreement. "But the experience put me in the learning of patent applications. In the years after that, whenever I came up with an improvement on an existing lock design, or a new prototype, I registered a patent under the name of an anonymous holding company." He paused. "A handful of them still earn royalties."

"How wonderful." Her brain began to calculate possibilities. "If we add those to what I earn, someday we might be able to sell my house in King's Cross and buy a larger one."

For some reason, the statement seemed to disconcert Ethan.

Garrett's face flamed as she realized the assumption she'd made. "Forgive me," she said hastily, "I didn't mean to imply—there's no obligation—"

"Hush," Ethan interrupted firmly, and pulled her head down to his. After quieting her with a long, searching kiss, he drew back and smiled at her. "You jumped to the wrong conclusion, love. Let me explain."

"You don't have to—"

His forefinger touched her lips in a brief caress. "I receive annual income from selling usage rights and privileges to manufacturers. Sometimes I take shares of a company in lieu of cash. I have stock and securities in more businesses than I could name offhand. I run everything through holding companies to remain anonymous. I employ three solicitors full-time just to handle patent infringements, and I have two others on general retainer."

Slowly it dawned on Garrett that this so called hobby of his was far more lucrative than she'd assumed. "But you said your patents were insignificant."

"I said most of them are. But a handful turned out to be not so insignificant. A few years ago, I came up with the idea for a permutation lock."

"What is that?"

"It's an assortment of active and passive tumblers arranged around a central spindle, all enclosed in a ring that adjusts them—" Ethan paused as he saw her puzzled expression. "The kind of lock with a dial instead of a key."

"Like the one on the cannonball safe?"

His eyes crinkled slightly at the corners. "Like that one."

Perhaps it was the proximity of his warm body, or the gently wandering hand on her leg and hip, but Garrett's dumbfounded brain was slow to work through the implications of what he'd just revealed. "Was that *your* design?" she managed to ask. "Is *that* how you knew how to open it?"

"Aye." Ethan continued slowly, giving her time to digest the information. "Those locks are used by banks, shipping and railway companies, dockyards, warehouses, military outposts, government buildings . . . everywhere."

Her eyes turned huge. "Ethan," she began, and paused, unable to think of a civilized way to phrase it. "Are you rich?"

He nodded gravely.

"Regular-rich," she asked, "or vulgar-rich?"

Leaning closer, he whispered near her ear, "Swiney-rich."

Garrett gave a bemused laugh, then shook her head in confusion. "But then why would you work for Sir Jasper? It makes no sense."

The question brought a troubled look to Ethan's face. "By the time the patent royalties started coming in, I'd already been recruited by Jenkyn. I didn't want to stop. He was a fatherly figure. His approval . . . his interest . . . meant a great deal to me."

"I'm sorry," she said softly, her heart wrenching as she realized how painful Jenkyn's vicious betrayal must have been for him, and perhaps would always be.

Ethan gave a short laugh. "I've never had much luck in the way of fathers."

"Does Sir Jasper know about your patents?"

"I don't think so. I've always been careful to cover my tracks."

"Is that why you lived in an empty flat? To keep anyone from suspecting you had another income?"

"Partly. It's also never mattered what kind of bed I sleep in, or what kind of chair I sit on."

"But it does matter." It concerned and puzzled Garrett that he would deny himself an ordinary life of comfort. "It should matter."

Their gazes met for a long moment. "It does now," Ethan said in a low voice.

Filled with tenderness and worry, Garrett laid her hand against his lean cheek. "You haven't been kind to yourself. You must deal more gently with yourself."

He nuzzled into her palm. "I have you to be kind to me. I have you to deal with me in any manner you wish."

"I'd like to domesticate you just a little," she said, holding her thumb and forefinger a half-inch apart. "But not so much that you would feel like a lap dog."

"I wouldn't mind." Amusement glinted in his eyes. "It all depends on the lap." He pressed her to the white cloth on the ground. His lips touched her collarbone and followed it to the base of her throat.

A glittering mosaic of sun, blue sky, and green leaves filled her vision as he browsed over her slowly, drawing in the scent and taste of her, feeling the shape of her limbs through her thin dress. "Someone might see," she protested, squirming as she felt his tongue swirl in the hollow of her clavicle.

"We're behind a pair of hampers the size of river barges."

"But if one of the footmen should come back—"

"They know better than that." He unfastened her bodice and inched it down until the tips of her breasts were revealed. His thumbs grazed the soft buds in circles, bringing them to aching tightness, making them ready for his mouth.

Garrett closed her eyes against the dappling of light from the branches far overhead. By now her body had become so attuned to the sensitive skill of his touch that it took only the slightest overture for her nerves to light with anticipation. His lips closed over her breast, tugging at the swollen pinkness, the tip of his tongue flirting and stroking. Lightly his hands moved over and beneath her clothing, unfastening, gently pulling, until the thin layers of fabric offered no defense.

There were times when desire made her restless, wanting to clamber all over him. But there were other times, such as now, when a strange hot lassitude weighted her limbs, and she could only lie beneath him passively, her heart pounding, her muscles twitching and laboring for the pleasure he offered. He murmured in between kisses, telling her how beautiful she was, how he loved the softness and strength of her. His thumb and forefinger closed over each satiny inner lip of her sex in turn, fondling delicately. A moan broke from her lips, and she lifted to him, her hips catching a helpless arch.

"Patience," he murmured, a smile curling against her skin. "You'll have your pleasure when I'm ready to give it."

But as his thumb slid to the inflamed little crest of her clitoris, gently stroking and cosseting, a deep pulse of ecstasy went all through her. She quivered hard, sensation running through her with the resonance of a bell tone. Ethan gave a subtle growl of delight and kissed her throat. He scolded her softly, pretending displeasure at her lack of control, her wetness, and while he was admonishing her, he slipped two fingers deeply inside and teased her into more delicious spasms.

She was too dazed to summon words, only clutched her arms around his neck and spread her legs wide, wanting him so badly that nothing else mattered.

A whisk of laughter fanned her ear. Ethan whispered that she was lovely and shameless and naughty, and there was only one thing to be done with her. Her skirts were pulled up high, and he mounted her, the masculine weight of him lowering between her thighs. He entered her with infinite care, filling her not as an act of possession but of worship, using himself to caress her inside and out. His kisses tasted of spearmint and his skin was fragrant with salt and sun, the wonderful smell of summer. His eyes were ardent, the color of a hot blue midnight, his face flushed as he thrust slowly within her.

God, the way he moved . . . sinuous and natural, like the flickering of a flame or the rippling of water. Undulating, surging. One of the long strokes angled just the right way, rubbing exquisitely inside her, while his groin nudged the tingling center of her sex, and she whimpered in response. He did it again, and again, while his mouth fastened over hers in a deep, drugging kiss. She felt her body clinging to him, reshaping itself for him. She felt him in every part of herself, in her blood and bones, in the primal earthly rhythm of pushing and pulling, opening and closing, rising and falling.

Half mad with desire, she tugged her mouth away from his. "Finish inside me," she begged. "Don't pull back at the last moment, I want all of you, I want—"

Ethan hushed her with his mouth, kissing her strongly. "*Acushla*," he said with a low, uneven laugh, "for a woman who doesn't like to be spontaneous, you have your moments." He pressed his shaven cheek hard against hers. "When we're back safe in London, I'll give you anything you want."

"I want a life with you." Years with him. A fireside of children with him.

"My life is yours," he said huskily. "You own every minute I have left. You know that . . . don't you? . . ."

"Yes. Yes." Sensation flooded her and swept away every thought, every awareness except the two of them, summer-heated and bound in love, merging and fusing until it seemed as if they were sharing one body, one soul.

Chapter 23

𝒥N THE THREE WEEKS since she had arrived at Eversby Priory, Garrett had discovered that, contrary to popular opinion, one did *not* sleep more deeply in the peace and quiet of the countryside. Without the familiar lulling mixture of city sounds, she was surrounded by silence so comprehensive that even the hopeful chirp of a cricket or the croak of a lonely toad, would bring her sitting bolt upright in bed.

Since she couldn't resort to medicinal remedies to induce sleep, she had tried reading, with mixed results. A book that was too interesting only made her even more awake, but if it was too dull, it couldn't hold her attention long enough to help her relax. After searching through the extensive library on the ground floor, she had finally found Livy's *History of Rome* condensed into five volumes, which suited her perfectly. So far, she had finished the first volume, ending with the first Punic War and the destruction of Carthage.

Her rest was especially difficult tonight. She tossed and turned in the broken hours past midnight, never descending into a full sleep. Her brain refused to stop milling, grappling with the knowledge that they would return to London the day after tomorrow. For a brief, longing moment she considered going to Ethan's room for reassurance and comfort. However, she knew exactly where *that* would lead, and he needed rest far more than she did.

Wishing she had thought to bring volume two of the *History of Rome* upstairs with her, Garrett debated whether it was worth going down to the library in the middle of the night. After plumping her pillow, she lay back in her rumpled bed and tried to concentrate on something monotonous. Sheep marching single file through a gate. Drops of water falling from a rain cloud. She recited the alphabet forward and backward. She went through the multiplication table.

Finally, she gave an exasperated sigh and went to squint at the mantel clock. It was four in the morning, too late and yet too early, the hour of dairy farmers and coal miners and insomniacs and the *History of Rome, Volume II*.

Yawning, she donned a dressing robe and a thin pair of shoes, and carried the oil lamp by its finger handles as she left the room.

The common areas of the house were dimly lit by tiny pilot lights in the hallway gas lamps. In the entrance hall, the grand staircase was illuminated by the very faint glow of a pair of bronze cherub lamps affixed to the newel posts below, and the pilot lights of the chandelier. If the house's main gas supply line were completely shut off each night, it would entail too much risk and work to relight all the lamps every morning.

The house was still and quiet, pleasantly cool and fragrant with rosin and furniture oils. After passing through the entrance hall, she walked along a shadowy hallway and approached the library. But just before she crossed the threshold, she heard a sound that gave her pause.

A series of distant but raucous cries was coming from somewhere, from . . . outside?

Garrett went down a small passage that led toward the back of the house, and entered a cleaning room used by the valets and footmen to polish shoes and boots, and clean and brush coats. After setting the glass lamp on a small cabinet, she unlocked and cracked open a window, and listened intently.

The sound came from beyond the kitchen gardens. It was the aggressive honking of the geese in the poultry yard. They were raising a veritable war council. *They've probably seen an owl,* Garrett thought. But her heart had begun to beat unevenly, as if with a drunkard's gait. She had a momentary feeling of weightlessness, as if the floor had dropped out from her feet. As she bent to the lamp, she had to work for enough air to blow out the flame.

Her nerves were crawling. Stinging. The "creevles," she'd once heard it called, by a patient who said his nerve disorder made him want to jump out of his skin.

The geese were quieting now. Whatever had antagonized them had moved on.

Garrett's fingers trembled as she eased the window shut and relocked it.

She heard small noises near the back of the house. A rattle, a metallic clack. The thin squeak of a hinge. The creak of a floorboard.

Someone had entered the house through the kitchen.

Panic made her insides collapse. Her hand fluttered

to her throat, searching until she found the silk cord that led down to her silver whistle. It would produce a sound that would travel at least four city blocks. If she blew a few shrills in the entrance hall, it would alert the entire household.

Her fingers curled around the slender silver tube. She left the room and stole along the short passageway to the hallway, pausing at the corner. Seeing no sign of intruders in either direction, she ran full-bore toward the entrance hall.

A dark shape intersected her path, and a blow came out of nowhere, catching her temple and sending her crashing to the floor. Disoriented, she lay in a heap. A bright ache blossomed in her head. Her jaw was clamped in hard fingers as someone pushed a wad of cloth in her mouth. Garrett tried to turn her face away, but there was no escaping the viselike grip. Another length of cloth was cinched over her mouth and tied behind her head in a cleave gag.

The man crouching over her was very large, his movements swift and efficient. He was in exceptional physical condition, but his face was heavyset and too broad, as if his features were gradually being absorbed over time. The eyes were ugly and shrewd. The small mouth appeared further diminished by a thick black mustache, so meticulously trimmed and waxed that it was obviously a source of pride to its owner. Although Garrett couldn't see a knife, he used something to sever the silk cord from her neck, and coiled it a half dozen times around her wrists. After wrapping the cord crossways to cinch the loops tight, he finished with a knot opposite her thumbs.

The man jerked her to her feet. Casually he dropped

the silver whistle to the wooden floor and crushed it beneath his booted heel.

Garrett's eyes and nose stung as she saw the flattened, split piece of metal, ruined beyond repair.

A pair of shoes entered her field of vision. She looked up and saw William Gamble. Reflexively she reared backward with such force that she would have fallen had the large man not reached out to steady her. For a terrible instant, she felt her gorge rise, a rude churning behind her ribs, and she was afraid she might be sick.

Gamble surveyed her without expression, and reached out to push back a few loose tendrils of her hair, regarding the abrasion on her temple and cheek. "No more marks on her, Beacom. Jenkyn won't like it."

"What's it to him if I rough up a housemaid?"

"She's no housemaid, idiot. She's Ransom's woman."

Beacom stared at her with new interest. "The female sawbones?"

"Jenkyn said to bring her back to London if we found her."

"A pretty piece," Beacom commented, running his hand along the curve of her back. "She's mine to play with until we get there."

"Why don't you take care of business first?" Gamble asked shortly.

"It's as good as done." Beacom held up his right hand, which was fitted with a contraption resembling a set of brass knuckles. It was made of jointed iron, with sharpened knobs protruding from the top. He used his thumb to pull back a tiny hook on the side, and pressed a button that caused a talon-like blade to snap out.

Garrett's eyes widened in horror. The mechanism was like the spring lancets used for bloodletting.

Beacom grinned at her expression. "With this one little blade," he told her, "I can drain a man as empty as weekday church."

Gamble rolled his eyes. "You could do it just as easily with a small folding knife."

"Toss off," Beacom told him good-humoredly, and loped to the grand staircase, effortlessly ascending the steps two at a time as he headed to Ethan's room.

A muffled scream tore from Garrett's throat. She ran after him, only to feel Gamble's arms latch around her from behind. She used all her weight to plant her feet hard on the ground, just as Ethan had taught her. The maneuver pulled Gamble a degree off balance. Garrett sidestepped and used her bound hands to strike backward at his crotch.

Unfortunately her aim was off, turning what would have been an incapacitating blow to the groin into a glancing swat. But it hurt Gamble enough to make his arms loosen. Twisting away, Garrett raced up the stairs, making as much noise as the gag would allow.

Gamble caught up to her as she reached the next floor, and gave her a hard shake. "Stow it," he growled, "or I'll break your neck right here, no matter what Jenkyn wants."

Garrett went still, panting, as she heard noises in different parts of the house—a crash of what sounded like glass and furniture, and a heavy thud. Good God, how many men had Jenkyn sent?

Flicking a contemptuous glance at her, Gamble said, "You should have let Ransom die from the bullet wound. Would've been a damn sight more merciful than what Beacom's doing to him." He gave her a slight push. "Show me to his room."

A few burning tears runneled down to Garrett's chin as Gamble pushed and prodded her along the hallway. She reminded herself that Ethan was a light sleeper. It was possible he'd awakened in time to defend himself, or hide somewhere. Soon the servants would realize the house had been invaded, and they would come down from the third floor. If Ethan could manage to stay alive until then . . .

The door to his bedroom was wide open. The interior was faintly illuminated by the pilot lights from the hallway lamps, and a weak spill of moonlight from the window.

Garrett let out a muffled cry as she saw that Ethan was in his bed, facing away from the doorway. He lay on his side, making quiet sounds as if he were in pain, or lost in a nightmare. What was wrong with him? Was he ill? Was he pretending to be incapacitated?

Gamble steered her into the room with his hand at the back of her neck.

She felt a hard pressure against her skull, and heard the ratcheting click of a pistol hammer.

"Beacom," Gamble said quietly. He moved to glance back at the hallway, while keeping the gun to Garrett's head. "Beacom?"

No answer.

Gamble switched his attention to the man on the bed. "How many times do I have to keep killing you, Ransom?" he asked dryly.

Ethan made an incoherent sound.

"I have Dr. Gibson with me," Gamble taunted. "Jenkyn wants me to bring her to him. Too bad. His interrogations never end well for women, do they?"

On the periphery of Garrett's vision, a shadow

lengthened slowly on the floor, like a spill of warm tar. Someone was approaching from behind. She resisted the temptation to look directly at the shadow, instead keeping her attention on Ethan's still form.

"Should I put a bullet in her head instead?" Gamble asked. "As a kindness to an old friend? I'm sure you'd rather have her shot than tortured." The muzzle of the revolver lifted from Garrett's head. "Should I start with you, Ransom? If I do, you'll never know what happens to her. Maybe you should beg me to shoot her first." He pointed the gun at the figure on the bed. "Go on," he said. "Let me hear it."

As soon as Gamble took aim at Ethan, Garrett burst into action, using her right elbow to deliver a sharp blow to his throat.

The explosive jab took Gamble by surprise. Although she hadn't managed to hit him squarely, it caught enough of his goiter to make him wheeze and clutch his neck with his free hand. He staggered back, barely managing to retain the revolver.

Although Garrett's wrists were bound, she leapt toward his gun arm, grabbing desperately for his wrist. But before she could reach him, she slammed against a big, dark shape that had come between them. It was like hitting a stone wall.

Shaken and stunned, she stumbled backward and tried to make sense of what was happening. The room was filled with violent motion, as if a storm had found its way inside. Two men were fighting in front of her, using fists, elbows, knees, feet.

Reaching up to the tightly cinched gag, Garrett managed to tug it from her mouth. She spat out the sodden cloth and worked her dry, rough tongue against the sides of her cheeks. Without warning, the pistol came skidding across the floor, its trajectory so close that she was able to stop it with her foot. She fumbled to snatch up the weapon and hurried to Ethan's bedside.

Croaking out his name, she tugged back the covers . . . and froze.

The man in the bed was Beacom. He was battered and only semiconscious, his body immobilized with a collection of trouser braces and surgical bandages.

Utterly bewildered, Garrett turned back to the brawling figures near the doorway. One of them had collapsed to the floor. The other had straddled him and was pummeling him unmercifully, intent on murder. He was dressed only in trousers, his upper half bare. She recognized the shape of his head, the breadth of his shoulders.

"*Ethan,*" she cried, running forward. Every movement he made strained arterial ligations and threatened to tear newly healed tissue. Every blow he delivered could start a fatal hemorrhage. "*Stop! That's enough.*" Ethan didn't respond, lost in blind, brutal rage. "*Please stop—*" Her voice broke with an anguished sob.

Someone rushed into the room. It was West, followed closely by two male servants in nightshirts and breeches. One of them carried a lamp that threw a steady yellow glow into the room.

Taking in the situation with one glance, West dove for Ethan and hauled him off Gamble. "Ransom," he said, restraining him with considerable difficulty. Ethan resisted, snorting like a maddened bull. "*Ransom*, he's down. It's done. Easy, now. Calm yourself. We have enough homicidal madmen in the house as it is."

He felt Ethan begin to relax. "There, that's it. Good fellow." He glanced at the servants accumulating in the hallway. "It's dark as Hades in here. Someone light the damned hall sconces and bring more lamps. And find something to tie up that bastard on the floor."

The servants hastened to obey.

"Garrett," Ethan muttered, shoving free of West's grasp. "Garrett—"

"Over there," West said. "She's in shock, and she's holding a cocked pistol, which is making me nervous."

"I'm not in shock," Garrett said tartly, although she was shaking with full-body tremors. "Furthermore, my finger's not on the trigger."

Ethan came to her swiftly. After easing the gun from her hand and pushing the hammer spur back to a resting position, he set it on the nearby hearth mantel. He reached for a pair of wick trimming scissors and cut the cord around her wrists. He made a low animal sound as he saw the pressure marks left on her skin.

"I'm all right," she said hastily. "They'll fade in a few minutes."

Hunting over her as if the past few minutes had been transcribed on her body, Ethan found the sore, throbbing abrasion on her temple and upper cheek. He grew very, very calm, his eyes darkening in a way that chilled her blood. Gently he angled her face for a better view. "Which one of them did this?" he asked in a mild tone that didn't deceive her in the least.

She gave him a wobbly smile. "You don't really expect me to tell you."

Scowling, Ethan looked over her head at West. "We need to search the house."

"The footmen are going through it room by room

as we speak." West stood over the prone form of William Gamble. "Ransom, I'm afraid your friends won't be allowed to visit if they can't learn to play nicely. We caught a third intruder, by the way."

"Where is he?"

"In my room, trussed like a pigeon for roasting."

Ethan blinked in surprise. "You fought him?"

"I did."

"Single-handedly?"

West gave him a sardonic glance. "Yes, Ransom. He may be a trained assassin, but he made the mistake of waking a Ravenel from a sound sleep." He gestured to the doorway. "Why don't you take Dr. Gibson to her room while I see to this mess? I'll have our guests lodged in the icehouse until you decide what's to be done with them."

ALTHOUGH GARRETT HAD always prided herself on her steady nerves during an emergency, she couldn't control the tremors that ran through her. If she weren't so worried about Ethan's condition, she might have been amused by the way they walked to her room like a crotchety old couple, both of them stiff and wincing.

She went directly to her doctor's bag on the table and rummaged for her stethoscope. "I need to examine you," she said through chattering teeth, fumbling with her supplies. Her fingers weren't working properly. "Secondary hemorrhage occurs most commonly between the second and fourth weeks after a gunshot injury, although that's usually in cases when the wound hasn't closed properly, and yours is—"

"Garrett." Ethan took hold of her from behind, and compelled her to face him. "I'm fine."

"I'll be the judge of that. Heaven knows what damage you may have done to yourself."

"You can examine the altogether of me, head to toe, later on. But right now I'm going to hold you."

"I don't need that," she said, twisting to reach her doctor's bag.

"*I* need it." Ignoring her protests, Ethan pulled her to the bed and sat with her on his lap, drawing her in securely.

She was held against the broad, hairy surface of his chest, his heartbeat steady beneath her ear. The scent of him, raw sweat and maleness, was comforting and familiar. He smoothed her hair and murmured endearments, his arms enfolding her in a warm, safe haven. She felt herself relaxing deeply. Her teeth stopped chattering.

How could he be so gentle with her, right after he'd dispatched two assailants with unnerving skill and ease? On some level, violence came just as naturally to him as it did to the brutal men who'd come here in search of him. She didn't think she would ever be comfortable with that side of him. But he had proven that he was capable of empathy and selflessness. He was true to his own code of honor. And he loved her. That was more than enough to work with.

"When I heard a sound from downstairs," Ethan murmured, "the first thing I did was go to your room. I saw you were missing."

"I went to the library for a book," Garrett said, and told him about hearing the geese, and being seized by Mr. Beacom. "He broke my whistle," she finished, pressing her face to his smooth shoulder, her lashes turning wet. "He dropped it to the floor and stepped on it."

Ethan cradled her more closely, his lips gently brushing the crest of her cheek. "I'll give you another one, little love." He ran a tender hand over her back, the warmth of his palm settling at the center of her spine. "And then I'll settle the score with Beacom."

Garrett stirred uneasily against him. "You've already thrashed him quite soundly."

"That's not enough." Ethan angled her head to have another look at the abrasion on her temple. "He's the one who hit you, isn't he? For that I'll beat him into a bloody puddle on the ground. All except for the head. I'm going to take the head and use the skull for—"

"I don't want you to do that," she said, mildly alarmed by his quiet savagery. "Revenge isn't going to help anything."

"It will help me."

"No, it won't." She guided his face to hers. "Promise you won't go near any of those men."

He didn't answer, his mouth set in sullen lines.

"Besides," Garrett added, "there isn't time. We have to leave for London right away, before Sir Jasper discovers what's happened."

Ethan spoke in a deliberately neutral tone. "'Tis best if I go to London on my own, while you stay here."

Garrett's head jerked up, and she looked at him with a mixture of surprise and outrage. "Why would you say that? How can you even *think* of leaving without me?"

"When I saw Gamble holding a gun to your

head . . ." Ethan gave her a haunted glance. "I've never been afraid of anything in my life until tonight. It would break me to lose you. I'd have to be put down like a lame horse. Let me handle what I must while knowing you're safe, and then I'll come back for you."

"And leave me to agonize every minute that you're gone?" Garrett asked, shaping her hand to his taut cheek. "I'm no helpless damsel to be kept waiting in a tower, Ethan. Nor do I want to be worshipped like some marble goddess on a pedestal. I want to be loved as an equal partner who belongs at your side. And you need me there."

Ethan's gaze sank inside her, down to places in her heart that were reserved only for him. A long moment passed before he looked away, cursed, and scrubbed his fingers through his short, disheveled hair. As she waited for him to come to a decision, Garrett nuzzled her face against the warm column of his throat.

"All right," he said reluctantly. "We'll go together."

She drew back and smiled at him.

"You won't always have your way," Ethan warned, seeming none too pleased by the situation.

"I know."

"And I *will* keep you on a pedestal . . . if only a small one."

"Why is that?" she asked, toying with the soft curls on his chest.

"First . . . you are a goddess to me, and that will never change. Second . . ." He curved his fingers over the back of her head, and brought her mouth close to his. ". . . I'm too tall for you to reach the good parts of me, otherwise."

Garrett's soft breath of laughter fanned against his

lips. "My dear love," she whispered, "*all* of you is the good parts."

BY DAYBREAK, THEY were ready to depart for the railway station in the nearby market town of Alton. Although West had offered to accompany them to London, it had been agreed that he would be of more use staying at Eversby Priory with Jenkyn's three agents in his custody. They were being kept in the root cellar under the close supervision of the Ravenel servants, who were collectively outraged that anyone would dare force their way into the manor.

"If any of them give you trouble," Ethan said to West as the three of them walked out to the front drive where the family carriage awaited, "use this." He handed him the Bull Dog pocket revolver. "It's a double-action model. You only need to cock the hammer once, and it will fire a round with every pull of the trigger."

West regarded the gun dubiously. "If any of those louts give me trouble, I have a shed full of farming implements to use on them. You'll need this if you're planning to confront Jenkyn."

"We'll be armed with something far more powerful than bullets," Garrett told him.

West looked at Ethan with mock alarm. "You're taking the spoon?"

Reluctant amusement tugged at the corner of Ethan's lips. "No. Dr. Gibson means we'll be armed with words."

"Words," West repeated doubtfully, pocketing the revolver. "I've always been skeptical when people say 'The pen is mightier than the sword.' It's only true if the pen is glued to the handle of a German steel cutlass."

"The words will be printed in a newspaper," Garrett said. "We're going to the *Times* office."

"Oh. That's fine, then. The *Times* is mightier than the pen, the sword, and Her Majesty's entire Royal Army." West offered his hand to help Garrett into the carriage, and she ascended to the movable step. Pausing to look back at West, who was now at eye level, she smiled with such warmth that Ethan felt a sting of jealousy. He had to remind himself that West had been a friend and ally to Garrett during one of the most difficult times of her life.

"You may not be the most highly trained surgical assistant I've ever had," she told West, her eyes twinkling, "but you are my favorite." She leaned forward to kiss his cheek.

After Garrett had gone into the carriage, West grinned at Ethan's expression. "There's no need to glare daggers at me," he said. "As delightful as Dr. Gibson is, she doesn't have the makings of a farmwife."

Ethan's brows lifted. "Are you thinking about taking a wife?"

West shrugged. "The nights can be long and quiet in the country," he admitted. "If I found a woman who was an interesting companion and attractive enough to bed . . . yes, I'd consider marrying her." He paused. "Better yet if she were educated. A sense of humor would be icing on the cake. Red hair isn't a requirement, but I do have a fatal weakness for it." West's mouth twisted with a self-mocking grin. "Of course, she'd have to be willing to overlook the fact that I was an undisciplined and obnoxious swill-tub until about three years ago." A nearly imperceptible look of bitterness flashed across his face before he masked it.

"Who is she?" Ethan asked softly.

"No one. An imaginary woman." Averting his gaze, West used the toe of his boot to flick a loose pebble to the side of the drive. "Who happens to despise me," he muttered.

Ethan regarded him with sympathetic amusement. "You might be able to change her opinion."

"Only if I could travel back in time and beat my former self to a pulp." West shook his head as if to clear his thoughts, and gave Ethan an assessing glance. "You don't look well enough to travel," he said bluntly. "You're pushing yourself too hard."

"I don't have the luxury of time," Ethan said. Lifting a hand to rub and pinch the sore muscles at the back of his neck, he admitted, "Besides, I'd rather confront Jenkyn as soon as possible. The longer I wait, the more difficult it will be."

"Are you afraid of him?" West asked quietly. "Any one would be."

Ethan smiled without humor. "Not physically. But . . . I learned more from him than I ever did from my father. There are things about him I admire, even now. He understands my strengths and weaknesses, and his brain is as sharp as a winter's night. I'm not exactly sure what I'm afraid of . . . he could say a few words that might kill something inside me . . . ruin everything, somehow." Glancing back at the house, Ethan rubbed absently at the healed-over place on his chest. "I went to have another look at Edmund's portrait at daybreak," he continued absently. "The way the light came through the windows, all gray and silver, made it seem as if the figure in the painting were floating in front of me. It reminded me of that scene in *Hamlet* . . ."

West understood instantly. "When the ghost of his father appears to him, dressed in full body armor?"

"Aye, that one. The ghost commands Hamlet to murder his uncle, out of revenge. Without even offering proof of guilt. What kind of a father would tell his son to do that?"

"Mine would have loved to order me to kill someone," West said. "But since I was only five years old, I'm sure my assassination skills were disappointing."

"Why would Hamlet obey a father who commands him to do something evil? Why doesn't he ignore the ghost and leave the vengeance to God, and choose his own destiny?"

"Probably because if he did, the play would be shortened by about two and a half hours," West said. "Which, to my mind, would be a vast improvement." He regarded Ethan speculatively. "I think Sir Jasper was right—the play is a mirror to the soul. But I suspect you've drawn different conclusions than he intended. No man is entitled to your blind obedience, no matter what he's done for you. Furthermore, you don't have to be your father's son, especially if your father happens to be an amoral arse who's hatching plots to kill people."

Garrett stuck her head out of the carriage window. "We must leave soon," she called out, "or we'll miss our train."

West gave her a chastising glance. "We're having an important psychological discussion, Doctor."

She drummed her fingertips on the window frame. "Psychological discussions usually lead to dithering, and we don't have time for that."

Ethan felt a slow grin spreading across his face as Garrett retreated back into the carriage. "She's right," he said. "I'll have to act now and think later."

"Spoken like a true Ravenel."

Ethan pulled a slip of paper from his pocket and gave it to West. "As soon as the telegraph office opens, will you have this wired?"

West looked over the message.

POST OFFICE TELEGRAM

SIR JASPER JENKYN
43 PORTLAND PLACE LONDON

OPEN ORDER PURCHASE HAS BEEN COMPLETED. RETURNING WITH SURPLUS MERCHANDISE REQUIRING IMMEDIATE DELIVERY. PARCEL WILL BE CONVEYED TO YOUR RESIDENCE LATE THIS EVENING.

—W.GAMBLE

"I'll take it to the telegraph office myself," West said, and reached out to shake his hand. "Good luck, Ransom. Take good care of our little parcel. Wire me if you need anything else."

"That goes for you as well," Ethan replied. "After all, I still owe you for the pint of blood."

"Bugger that, you owe me for all the scaffolding I had to pull down."

They exchanged grins. The grip of their hands felt

warm and solid. Safe. This must be a brotherly feeling, Ethan thought, this sense of camaraderie and connection, this unspoken understanding that they would always take the other's side.

"One last bit of advice," West said, finishing the handshake with a hearty squeeze. "The next time someone shoots at you . . . try ducking."

Chapter 24

AFTER MIDNIGHT, ETHAN AND Garrett arrived at Portland Place in a carriage provided by Rhys Winterborne. They were accompanied by a pair of well-trained and competent private guards who were responsible for the security of his warehouses.

The sophisticated terrace houses of Portland Place glowed in the illumination of streetlamps. Jenkyn's terrace was one of the largest in the enclave, with a double-fronted entrance and attached corner houses flanking it on either side. Bypassing the stately portico in front, the carriage went to the narrow street and mews behind, and stopped at the back entrance intended for servants and deliverymen.

"If we don't come out in fifteen minutes," Ethan murmured to the warehouse guards, "proceed as planned."

They both nodded in agreement and checked their pocket watches.

Ethan helped Garrett from the carriage and regarded her with a mixture of concern and pride. She was exhausted, just as he was, but she had endured the long, tense, tedious day without a single word of complaint.

They had retrieved the pages of evidence from Garrett's home, and proceeded to Printing House Square, the London court inhabited by the leading journals of the city. The ground had fairly trembled from the basement engines running a multitude of presses. Soon after they had entered the *Times* building, they were led to the chief editor's office, known as the "lion's den." It was there they had spent eight hours in the company of the managing and night editors and an editorial writer, while Ethan provided facts, names, dates, and detailed accounts of criminal conspiracies originating from Jenkyn and his cabal of officials in the Home Office.

Throughout the process, Garrett had been patient and stoic. Ethan had never known any woman who could match her for stamina. Even after foregoing sleep and proper meals, she was clearheaded and ready to face whatever would come.

"Are you sure you won't wait out here for me?" Ethan asked hopefully. "I'll be back in fifteen minutes."

"Every time you've asked that," Garrett said with exquisite patience, "I've said no. Why do you keep doing it?"

"I thought it might wear down your resistance."

"No, it's making me more stubborn."

"I'll have to remember that in the future," Ethan said dryly, adjusting the brim of his hat lower over his eyes. He had visited the terrace only three times in his entire acquaintance with Jenkyn. With any luck, the servants wouldn't look closely enough to recognize him.

"Here," Garrett said, reached up with a white handkerchief. She tucked it into the front of his collar, creating a bulge similar to Gamble's goiter. Her green eyes met his, and she caressed his cheek with gentle fingers. "It will be all right," she whispered.

With a mixture of astonishment and annoyance, Ethan realized he was visibly nervous. His body felt like a collection of separate mechanisms, none of them quite synchronized with the others. He took a measured breath, released it slowly, and turned Garrett to face away from him. Carefully he grasped her wrist and twisted her arm behind her back to make it appear as if he were forcing her to accompany him.

"Should I curse and struggle as we go through the house, until you subdue me?" Garrett suggested, warming to the role.

Ethan had to grin at her enthusiasm. "No, *acushla*, there's no need to take it that far." Pressing a gentle kiss behind her ear, he murmured, "But I'll subdue you later, if you like." Feeling the little shiver that ran through her, he smiled and rubbed his thumb into the soft hollow of her palm.

In the next moment, he made his expression inscrutable and knocked on the door.

They were shown inside by a tall and wiry butler, with thick Prussian brows and hair that was brindled in shades of steel and white. Ethan kept his face low. "Tell Jenkyn I have the delivery he wanted," he said hoarsely.

"Yes, Mr. Gamble. He's been expecting you." The butler didn't spare one glance for Garrett as he led them through the house. The interior had been designed with an abundance of curved forms: oval niches, circular ceiling recesses and apses, and sinuous hallways. Ethan found the serpentine layout disconcerting, preferring the neatness of right angles and corners and edges.

They crossed a circular anteroom to a private suite. The butler showed them into a gentleman's room lined with rich dark paper, gold trim and millwork, with thick crimson carpeting underfoot. Heads of exotic animals had been mounted on the wall: a lioness, a cheetah, a white wolf, and other carnivora. A fire had been lit in the heart, flames springing and writhing as they consumed crackling splits of oak. The air was as hot as blood.

The butler departed, closing the door behind him.

Ethan's heart thumped uncomfortably as he saw Jenkyn sitting by the fireplace, a sheaf of papers in hand.

"Gamble," Jenkyn said without looking up from the pages. "Bring your guest over here, and deliver your report."

Ethan caressed Garrett's wrist surreptitiously before releasing it. "The job didn't go exactly as planned," he replied curtly, tugging the handkerchief out of his collar.

Jenkyn's head jerked up. He fixed Ethan with an unblinking gaze, his eyes dilated to black surrounded by bleach-white.

Something vicious and ugly stirred inside Ethan as they stared at each other. For a few appalling seconds, he felt suspended in some mad place between murder and weeping. The place where he'd been shot seemed to throb. He fought the temptation to cover it with a protective hand.

Jenkyn was the first to speak. "Gamble was so certain he'd be the last man standing."

"I didn't kill Gamble," Ethan said flatly.

That seemed to surprise Jenkyn nearly as much as

the sight of Ethan having returned from the dead. Remaining in his chair, the spymaster withdrew a cigar from a stand on a nearby table. "I wish you had," he said. "Gamble's of no use to me if he hasn't managed to dispatch you after two attempts." His tone was cold, but there was a visible tremor in his fingers as he lit the cigar.

Ethan realized that neither of them were entirely in control. Garrett, by contrast, was self-possessed and almost relaxed, wandering slowly around the room to investigate shelves and cabinetry and paintings. Since she was a mere woman, Jenkyn paid little attention to her, keeping his focus on Ethan.

"What is the nature of your connection to the Ravenels?" Jenkyn asked. "Why did they decide to harbor you?"

So he didn't know. Ethan was inwardly amazed to discover there were some secrets beyond Jenkyn's reach. "It doesn't matter," he said.

"Never tell me that," Jenkyn snapped, reverting to their usual dynamic. "If I ask a question, it matters."

"I beg your pardon," Ethan said softly. "I meant to say 'none of your business.'"

An incredulous look came over Jenkyn's face.

"While I was recuperating," Ethan continued, "I had a chance to finish reading *Hamlet*. You wanted me to tell you what reflection I saw in it. That's why I'm here." He paused as he saw the flicker of interest in the older man's gaze. The astonishing realization came to him that Jenkyn did care about him in some undefinable way, and yet he'd tried to have him killed regardless. "You said in a fallen world, Hamlet realized there's no good or bad, no right or wrong . . .

everything is just a matter of opinion. Facts and rules are useless. Truth isn't important." Ethan hesitated. "There's a kind of freedom in that, isn't there? It lets you do or say whatever you want to achieve your goals."

"Yes," Jenkyn said, the reflected firelight dancing in his copper eyes as he gazed steadily at Ethan. His face had softened. "That's what I hoped you would understand."

"But it's not freedom for everyone," Ethan said. "It's only freedom for you. It means you can sacrifice anyone for your benefit. You can justify killing innocent people, even children, by saying it's for the greater good. I can't do that. I believe in facts, and the rule of law. I believe something a wise woman told me not long ago: every life is worth saving."

The light seemed to die out of Jenkyn's eyes. He reached for a match and heated the clipped end of the cigar binding, taking refuge in the ritual. "You're a naïve fool," he said bitterly. "You have no idea what I would have done for you. The power you could have had. I would have brought you along with me, and taught you to see the world as it really is. But you'd rather betray me, after all I've given you. After I *created* you. Like any simpleminded peasant, you'd rather cling to your illusions."

"Morals," Ethan corrected gently. "A man of high position should know the difference. You shouldn't be in government, Jenkyn. No man who changes his morals as easily as he does his clothes should have power over other people's lives." A sense of peace and lightness came over him, as if he'd been untethered, cut loose from a burden he'd carried for years.

He glanced at Garrett, who appeared to be browsing over objects arranged on the mantelpiece, and he felt a surge of intense tenderness mingled with desire. All he wanted was to take her away from here, and find a bed somewhere, anywhere. Not in passion . . . at least, not yet . . . He longed just to hold her safe in his arms, and sleep.

Ethan pulled a pocket watch from his waistcoat and consulted the time. One-thirty in the morning. "The presses have started by now," he said casually. "One of the editors at the *Times* told me they can churn out twenty thousand copies of the paper per hour. That means they'll have at least sixty, perhaps seventy thousand copies ready for the morning edition. I hope they don't misspell your name. I wrote it out carefully for them, just to make sure."

Slowly Jenkyn set the cigar on a crystal dish, staring at him with emerging fury.

"I almost forgot to mention the meeting I had with them today," Ethan said. "I was full of interesting information, and they seemed very eager to hear it."

"*You're bluffing,*" Jenkyn said, his face darkening with rage.

"We'll find out soon, won't we?" Ethan began to tuck the pocket watch back into the waistcoat, and nearly dropped it as he was startled by the sound of something whipping through the air, a sickening impact of blunt force on flesh, the crack of bone, a scream of pain.

Ethan's entire body tensed in preparation for action, but he stopped in response to Garrett's staying gesture. She stood beside Jenkyn with a fireplace poker in hand, while the older man was doubled over in his chair, gripping his forearm and crying out in agony.

"My aim was at least three inches off," Garrett said, regarding the iron in her hand with a perturbed frown. "Probably because it's heavier than my cane."

"What did you do that for?" Ethan asked, bewildered.

She picked up an object from the small table and showed it to him. "This was fitted into the cigar stand. He took it out when he lit the cigar."

As Ethan came to take the gun from her, Garrett said, "Sir Jasper seems to believe he created you, and therefore has the right to destroy you." She regarded the groaning man in the chair with cool green eyes and said crisply, "Wrong on both counts."

The butler and a footman burst into the room, followed immediately by the two warehouse guards. As the room erupted with questions and shouts, Garrett stood back to let Ethan handle it. "After we're finished here, darling," she asked, just loudly enough for him to hear over the commotion, "could we possibly find a place where someone *doesn't* want to shoot you?"

Chapter 25

In THE TUMULTUOUS DAYS that followed, Garrett found many reasons for joy. Her father returned from his holiday at the Duke of Kingston's seaside estate, and the healthful regimen of sun, fresh air, and sea bathing had done wonders for his health. He had put on a bit of weight, and he was rosy-cheeked and in high spirits. According to Eliza, who was also refreshed and glowing, the Duke and Duchess, and everyone in the Challon family, had spoiled, indulged, and made much of Stanley Gibson.

"They laughed at all of 'is jokes," Eliza had reported, "even the old one about the parrot."

Garrett had winced and covered her eyes with her hands. "He told his parrot joke?"

"Three times. And they all liked it just as much the third time as the first!"

"They didn't like it," Garrett had moaned, looking at her through the screen of her fingers. "They were just being remarkably kind."

"And the duke played draw poker with Mr. Gibson twice," Eliza had continued. "You'd faint if I told you how much he won."

"The duke?" Garrett had asked weakly, while visions of debtor's prison had flashed before her eyes.

"No, your father! It turns out, the duke is the *worst* draw poker player in the world. Mr. Gibson gave him a fleecing, both times. Your father would have beggared the poor man if we'd stayed longer." Eliza had paused to regard her with bemusement. "Doctor, why is your head on the table?"

"Just resting it," Garrett had said in a small voice. The Duke of Kingston, one of the most powerful and influential men in England, owned a gaming club and had run it himself in his younger years. He was *not* the worst draw poker player in the world, and had almost certainly used the game as a pretext to funnel money into her father's empty pockets.

Her discomfort over having imposed on the Challon family's generosity was quickly forgotten in the joy of returning to the clinic and having patients to see again. Her first day back began with a bit of much needed fence-mending with Dr. Havelock, who approached her with a hesitancy that wasn't at all like him.

"Can you forgive me?" was the first thing he had asked.

Garrett had given him a radiant smile. "There's nothing to forgive," she said simply, and caught him thoroughly off guard with a spontaneous embrace.

"This is most unprofessional," he grumbled, but he hadn't pulled away.

"I will always want your honesty," Garrett had said, pressing her cheek to his shoulder. "I knew at the time you were trying to do what was right for me. I didn't agree with your position, but I certainly understood it. And you weren't wrong. It's just that I had some unexpected luck, as well as a patient who was as tough as whit leather."

"It was a mistake for me to underestimate your skill." Havelock had given her a rare, fond glance as she pulled back. "I won't do so again. And yes, your young man is an uncommonly durable fellow." His snowy brows had lifted as he had asked with a touch of waggish anticipation, "Will he be stopping by the clinic to pay a call? I'd like to ask him a question or two about his intentions toward you."

Garrett had laughed. "I'm sure he will when he's able. However, he's already warned me that he will be much occupied for the next few days."

"Yes," Havelock had said, sobering, "These are tumultuous times, with scandal and upheaval in both the Home Office *and* the Metropolitan Force. And your Mr. Ransom seems to be a key figure in all of it. He's gained renown in a remarkably short period of time. I fear his days of wandering through London unrecognized are over."

"I suppose you're right," Garrett had murmured, rather stunned by the notion. Ethan was so accustomed to absolute privacy and freedom— now he was coping with his altered circumstances.

She had no opportunity to ask him, however. During the next two weeks, Ethan didn't come to see her even once. A note arrived almost daily, consisting of a few hasty sentences scrawled on a correspondence card. Sometimes the note was accompanied by a fresh flower posy or a basket of violets. Garrett was obliged to hunt through newspaper reports to track his daily whereabouts. The *Times* had shocked the nation with a series of articles concerning the illegal private detective force that had been operating out of the Home Office. Ethan was constantly on the move as his participation was required in multiple investigations and confidential meetings.

It was bad enough for Jenkyn to have been implicated in unauthorized intelligence gathering. But when it was reported that he had been cooking up entrapment plots and conspiring with violent radicals and known criminals—all to destroy the prospect of Home Rule for the Irish—it caused a public furor. Jenkyn and his secret operation was disbanded, and most of his active officers had been placed under arrest.

Soon the missing shipment of explosives from Le Havre was recovered, and its disappearance was conclusively linked to special agents employed by the Home Office. The resignation of Lord Tatham, the Home Secretary, soon followed. Both houses of Parliament appointed investigating committees and scheduled hearings to learn the extent of the corruption in the Home Office.

Heads were rolling. Fred Felbrigg was forced to resign and submit to investigation for alleged illegal actions and procedures. Meanwhile, the Metropolitan Police fell into disarray. It was recognized that a significant reorganization of the entire force was required, although no one seemed to have any good ideas on how to proceed.

All that mattered to Garrett was Ethan's welfare. He'd been plunged into a whirlwind of activity ever since he had returned from Hampshire, when he should have been resting. Had it interfered with the healing process? Was he eating properly? Garrett had no choice but to bury herself in her work and wait patiently.

On the fourteenth day, after Garrett had seen her

last patient of the day, she stood at the counter in her surgery and made notes, when there came an unexpected knock at the surgery door.

"Doctor," came Eliza's voice through the paneling. "There's one more patient for you to see."

Garrett frowned, setting down her pen. "I didn't schedule anyone."

After a pause, Eliza said, "It's an emergency."

"What kind of emergency?"

Silence.

Garrett's nerves went hot and cold, and her pulse began to rampage. She forced herself to walk to the door, when every impulse screamed for her to sprint. With great care, she turned the handle of the door and opened it.

There was Ethan, bigger than life, leaning a shoulder against the doorjamb and smiling down at her. A rush of elation made her dizzy. He was even more handsome than she remembered, more breathtaking, more *everything*.

"Garrett," he said softly, as if her name were a word for a dozen different lovely things, and she had to stiffen her knees to keep from melting right in front of him.

Two weeks, and not even one short visit, she reminded herself sternly.

"I don't have time for another patient," she told him, her brows rushing down.

"'Tis a serious affliction I have," he said somberly.

"Oh?"

"The old tiblin bone is actin' up again."

She had to gnaw furiously on the insides of her cheeks and clear her throat to keep from laughing.

"I'm afraid you'll have to take care of that yourself," she managed to say.

"It needs professional attention."

Folding her arms across her chest, she regarded him with narrowed eyes. "I've waited and worried for two weeks, and then you appear without a word of warning, wanting me to—"

"No, no, *acushla*," Ethan said softly, his blue eyes drinking her in. "All I want is to be near you. I've missed you so, darlin'. I'm fair ravished in love for you." One of his big hands gripped the side of the door frame. "Let me in," he whispered.

Yearning caught inside her like fire to tinder. She opened the door more widely, and stepped back on ramshackle legs.

Ethan crossed the threshold, closed the door with his foot, and pinned her against the paneling. Before she could draw breath, his mouth closed over hers, and he kissed her with the craving of years and dark, aching dreams. She moaned softly, arching against him, lost in the feel of his strength all around her. He cupped the side of her face in his hand, stroking her gently.

"I've wanted you every minute," he whispered, brushing his lips over hers in satiny touches. He drew back to stare down at her with a smile glowing in his eyes. "But I've been helping to disassemble the Metropolitan Police, fix the broken parts, and put it all back together again. And testifying before two committees, and discussing new job prospects . . ." He bent to kiss an exposed part of her throat, his mouth hot and searching.

"I suppose those are good excuses," Garrett said

grudgingly, and sought his lips again. After another deep, exquisite kiss, she opened her eyes and asked hazily, "What job prospects?"

He touched his nose to hers. "They want to appoint me as assistant commissioner. I would organize a new investigation department with different sections, and the supervisor of each section would report directly to me."

Garrett looked up at him in wonder.

"I would also have my own handpicked force of twelve detectives, to train and supervise as I see fit." He paused and laughed unsteadily. "I don't know if I'll be any damned good at it. They only offered it to me because half of Felbrigg's supervisors have resigned, and the rest are in jail."

"You'll be exceptional at it," Garrett said. "The question is, do you want to?"

"I do," he confessed with a slightly crooked grin, the dimple she adored appearing in his cheek. "I'd have to keep to more regular hours. And the offer comes with a fine house in Eaton Square and a direct telegraph line to Scotland Yard. After some negotiation, I made them throw in a phaeton and pair of matched horses for my wife."

"For your wife," Garrett repeated, her stomach filling with butterflies.

Ethan nodded, reaching into his pocket. "I'm not going to do this the conventional way," he warned, and she laughed breathlessly.

"That's perfect, then."

He pressed something smooth and metallic into the palm of her hand. She looked down and saw a whistle cast in silver, strung on a glinting, glimmering silver chain. Noticing there was something engraved on it, she looked more closely.

Whenever you want me

"Garrett Gibson," she heard him say, "you've a rare skill at healing—I'm living proof of that. But if you don't marry me, you'll have my broken heart to mend. Either way, I'm afraid you're stuck with me, as I love you too much to be without you. Will you be my wife?"

Garrett looked up at him through bright, blurred eyes, too overwhelmed with joy to summon a single word.

She soon made the discovery that it was hard to blow a whistle when you were smiling.

But she managed it anyway.

Author's Note

Dear Friends,

Although all my books are a labor of love, this one is especially close to my heart because it was inspired by a magnificent real-life woman, Dr. Elizabeth Garrett Anderson. Against great opposition, she earned a medical degree at the Sorbonne in 1870. In 1873, she managed to become the first licensed female physician in Britain. The British Medical Association promptly changed its rules afterward to prevent any other women from joining for the next twenty years. Dr. Anderson went on to co-found the first hospital staffed by women and became the first dean of a British medical school. She was also active in the women's suffrage movement and became the first female mayor and magistrate in England, serving in the splendid town of Aldeburgh.

The Thames was so contaminated by sewage and industrial chemicals in Victorian times that tens of thousands of London residents were killed by cholera. In 1878, a pleasure steamship called the *Princess Alice* collided with another boat and sank. Over six hundred passengers died, with many of the deaths blamed, not on drowning, but asphyxiation. According to an account of the time, the Thames water was "hissing like soda water with baneful gasses." In modern times, the Thames has been transformed into the cleanest major river that runs through a major city in the world and is teeming with fish and wildlife.

Although the conspiracy plot in *Hello Stranger* is, of course, fictional, there really was a secret and unauthorized team of agents, supervised by Edward George Jenkinson. He ran clandestine operations from the Home Office, often competing with Scotland Yard. Jenkinson was dismissed in 1887 and his force was replaced by the official "Special Irish Branch."

As someone who gets a little weak-kneed at the sight of blood, it wasn't always easy to research various aspects of Garrett's work, but it was always fascinating. The history of blood transfusions was especially interesting. Early recorded attempts at transfusion used sheep or cows' blood, transfused into human patients. The experiments didn't go well, to put it mildly, and the practice was banned for about 150 years. Scientists and doctors began working on the problem again in the 1800s, with varying results. Then in 1901, Dr. Karl Landsteiner of Austria discovered the three human blood groups—A B, and O—and found that you couldn't mix blood from incompatible individuals. Until then, successful blood transfusions depended on whether you were lucky enough to receiving blood from a compatible donor.

Thank you, as always, for your encouragement and kindness—you make my job a joy!

—*Lisa*

Garrett's Refreshing Lemon Ice

 $\mathcal{S}$ OME PEOPLE ARE SURPRISED to learn that ices, sorbets, and ice creams were served at afternoon teas or soirees in the Victoria era. Ices were actually popularized in England back in the mid-1700s by French and Italian confectioners who had settled in London. A wonderful variety of flavors was available, such as elderflower, pineapple, apricot, rosewater, pistachio, and even brown bread ice! Here is a simple and easy recipe for Dr. Garrett Gibson's favorite: lemon ice.

Ingredients

6 lemons (or $^1/_2$ cup lemon juice)
1 orange (or $^1/_4$ cup orange juice)
2 cups water
2 cups sugar

Directions

1. Zest one of the lemons (only the yellow part of the rind, the white is bitter).
2. Squeeze the juice out of the orange and lemons.
3. Mix water and sugar, and simmer until sugar is completely dissolved.

4. Add lemon zest, lemon juice, and orange juice.
5. Pour into a metal pan (loaf pan worked well for us).
6. Place in freezer and stir it with a fork every half hour, for about three hours, or until lemon ice has a heavy, slushy texture that you can scoop out.

Note: If you don't care about historical accuracy, replace one of the cups of sugar with Karo syrup—it makes the texture of the ice much smoother.

$\mathcal{P}$HOEBE HAD NEVER MET West Ravenel, but she knew one thing for certain: He was a mean, rotten bully. She had known it since the age of eight, when her best friend, Henry, started writing to her from boarding school.

West Ravenel had been a frequent subject of Henry's letters. He was a big, sarcastic, hardened case of a boy, but his constant misbehavior had been overlooked, as it was in nearly any boarding school of the time. It was seen as inevitable that older boys would dominate and browbeat younger boys, and anyone who dared tell tales would be severely punished.

Dear Phoebe,

I thought it would be fun to go to bording school with other boys, but it's not. There's a boy named West who always takes my breakfast roll and he's already the size of an elefant.

Dear Phoebe,

Yesterday it was my job to change the candklestiks. West Ravenel sneaked trick candles into my basket and last night one of them went off like a rocket and singed

Mr. Farthing's brows. I got my hand caned for it. Mr. Farthing should have known I wouldn't have done something so obvyus. West isn't a bit sorry. He said he can't help it if the teacher is an idyut.

Dear Phoebe,
I drew this picture of West Ravenel for you, so if you ever see him, you'll know to run away. I'm bad at drawing, which is why he looks like a pirate clown. He also acts like one.

For four years, West Ravenel had annoyed and plagued poor Henry, Lord Clare, a small and slight boy with a delicate constitution. Eventually Henry's family had withdrawn him from school and brought him back to live in Heron's Point, not far from where Phoebe's family resided. The mild, healthful climate of the coastal resort town, and its famed seawater bathing, had helped to restore Henry's health and good spirits. To Phoebe's delight, Henry had visited her home often, and had even studied with her brothers and their tutor. His intelligence, wit, and endearing eccentricities had made him a favorite with the Challon family.

There had never been a specific moment when Phoebe's childhood affection for Henry had turned into something new. It had happened gradually, twining all through her like delicate silver vines, blossoming into a jeweled garden, until one day she looked at him and felt a thrill of love.

She had needed a husband who could also be a friend, and Henry was her best friend in the world. He understood everything about her, just as she did him. They were a perfect match.

Phoebe had been the first one to broach the subject of marriage. However, she'd been stunned and hurt when Henry had gently tried to dissuade her.

"You know I can't be with you forever," he'd said, wrapping his thin arms around her, twirling his fingers in the loose curls of her red hair. "Someday I'll fall too ill to be a proper husband or father. To be of any use at all. That wouldn't be fair to you or the children. Or even to me."

"Why are you so resigned?" Phoebe had demanded, frightened by his quiet, fatalistic acceptance of his mysterious ailment. "We'll find new doctors. We'll find out whatever it is that's making you ill, and we'll find a cure. Why are you giving up the fight before it's even started?"

"Phoebe," he'd said softly, "the fight started long ago. I've been tired for most of my life. No matter how much I rest, I scarcely have enough stamina to last through the day."

"I have stamina for both of us." Phoebe had rested her head on his shoulder, trembling with the force of her emotions. "I love you, Henry. Let me take care of you. Let me be with you for however long we'll have together."

"You deserve more."

"Do you love me, Henry?"

His large, soft brown eyes had glistened. "As much as any man has ever loved a woman."

"Then what more is there?"

They had married, the two of them a pair of giggling virgins discovering the mysteries of love with affectionate awkwardness. Their first child, Justin, was a dark-haired and robustly healthy boy who was now four years old.

Henry had gone into his final decline a year ago, just before the birth of their second son, Stephen.

In the months of grief and despair that had followed, Phoebe had gone back to live with her family, finding a measure of solace in the loving home of her childhood. But now that the initial year of mourning had passed, it was time to start a new life as a young mother of two boys. A life without Henry. How strange that seemed. She would have to move back to the Clare estate in Essex—which Justin would inherit when he came of age—and she would try to raise her sons the way their beloved father would have wished.

But first, she had to attend her brother Gabriel's wedding.

Knots of dread tightened in Phoebe's stomach as the carriage rolled toward the ancient estate of Eversby Priory. This was the first event she had attended since Henry's death. Even knowing she would be among friends and relations, she was nervous. But there was another reason she was so thoroughly unsettled.

The bride's last name was Ravenel.

Gabriel was betrothed to a lovely and unique girl, Lady Pandora Ravenel, who seemed to adore him every bit as much as he did her. It was easy to like Pandora, who was outspoken and funny and imaginative. In fact, Phoebe had found herself liking the other Ravenels she'd met when they'd come to visit her family's seaside home. There was Pandora and her twin sister, Cassandra, and their distant cousin, Devon Ravenel, who had inherited the earldom recently. His wife, Kathleen, was friendly and charming. Had the family stopped there, all would have been well.

But Fate had turned out to have a malicious sense of humor: Pandora's distant cousin, Devon's younger brother, was none other than West Ravenel.

Phoebe was finally going to have to meet the man who'd made Henry's years at school so wretched. There was no way for her to avoid it.

West lived on the estate, no doubt puttering about, pretending to be busy while sponging off his older brother's inheritance. Recalling Henry's descriptions of the big, lazy sloth, Phoebe envisioned West drinking and laying abed until noon, leering at the housemaids as they cleaned up after him.

It didn't seem fair that someone as good and kind as Henry should have been given so few years, when a cretin like West Ravenel would probably live to be a hundred.

"Mama, why do you look cross?" her son Justin asked innocently from the opposite carriage seat. The elderly nanny beside him had leaned back to doze in the corner.

Phoebe cleared her expression instantly. "I'm not cross, darling."

"Your brows were pointed down, and your lips were pinched up like a trout," he said. "You only do that when you're cross, or when Stephen's diaper is smelloquent."

Phoebe smiled, recognizing one of Pandora's made-up words. Looking down at the baby in her lap, who had been lulled by the repetitive motion of the carriage, she murmured, "The baby is quite dry, and I'm not at all out of humor. I'm . . . well, you know I haven't kept company with people for a long time. I feel a bit shy about jumping back into the swim of things."

"When Grandfather taught me how to swim in cold water," Justin volunteered, "he said not to jump in all at once. He said go in up to your waist first, so your body knows what's coming. This will be practice for you, Mama."

Considering her son's point, Phoebe regarded him with fond pride. "I'll try to go in gradually," she said. "What a wise boy you are. You do a good job of listening to people."

"I don't listen to *all* people," Justin told her in a matter-of-fact tone. "Only to the ones I like."

Kneeling up on the carriage seat, the child stared at the ancient Jacobean mansion in the near distance. Once the fortified home of a dozen monks, the huge, highly ornamented structure bristled with rows of slender chimneys. It was earthbound, stocky, but it reached for the sky at the same time.

"It's big," Justin said in awe. "The roof is big, the trees are big, the gardens are big, the hedges are big . . . what if I get lost?" He didn't sound worried, however, only intrigued.

"Stay where you are and shout until I find you," Phoebe said. "But there'll be no need for concern, darling. When I'm not with you, you'll have Nanny . . . she won't let you stray far."

Justin's skeptical gaze went to the dozing elderly nanny, and his lips curled in an impish grin as he looked back at Phoebe.

The caravan of fine carriages progressed along the drive, conveying the entourage of Challons and their servants, as well as a mountain of leather-bound bags and trunks. The estate grounds, like the surrounding farmland, were beautifully maintained, with deep, mature hedges, and old stone walls covered with climbing roses and soft, fluttery bursts of purple wisteria. Jessamine and honeysuckle perfumed the air as the carriages came to a slow halt in front of the portico.

Nanny awoke from her light snooze with a start and began to gather little odds and ends into her carpet bag. She took Stephen from Phoebe, who followed Justin as he bounded out.

"Justin . . ." Phoebe said uneasily, watching him dart through the mass of servants and family members like a hummingbird, chirping little hellos. She saw the familiar figures of Devon and Kathleen Ravenel—Lord and Lady Trenear—welcoming the arriving guests. There were her parents, and her younger sister Seraphina, and Pandora and Cassandra, and a dozen people she didn't recognize. Everyone was laughing and talking, animated by the excitement of the wedding. A shrinking feeling came over Phoebe at the thought of meeting strangers and making conversation. Sparkling repartee wasn't even a possibility. If only she were still dressed in protective mourning, with a veil concealing her face.

In the periphery of her vision, she saw Justin trotting up the front steps, unaccompanied. Aware of Nanny starting forward, Phoebe touched her arm lightly. "I'll run after him," she murmured.

"Yes, milady."

Phoebe was actually glad Justin had wandered inside the house—it gave her an excuse to avoid the gauntlet of guests being received.

The entrance hall was busy, but it was still calmer

and quieter than outside. A man directed the tumult of activity, giving curt instructions to passing servants. His hair, a shade of brown so dark it could easily have been mistaken for black, gleamed like liquid as the light moved over it. The man listened closely to an issue the housekeeper was explaining about the arrangements of bedrooms. Simultaneously he tossed a key to an approaching under-butler, who caught it with a raised hand and dashed off on some errand.

The stranger radiated a sort of contained vigor that Phoebe found striking. He didn't have the relaxed, languid manner of a gentleman. He was well-dressed in simple, expertly tailored clothes, not livery. Perhaps he was an estate manager? But his complexion was the glowing golden-brown of someone who labored in the sun. How curious.

Justin had ventured to the side of the grand staircase to investigate the elaborate wood carving.

Phoebe went to him quickly. "Justin, you mustn't wander off without telling me or Nanny," she whispered.

"Look, Mama."

Her gaze followed the direction of his small forefinger. She saw a carving of a little nest of mice, a playful and unexpected touch, especially considering the grandeur of the staircase.

Phoebe smiled. "I like that."

"Me too."

As Justin crouched to stare at the carving more closely, a glass marble dropped out of his pocket and hit the inlaid parquet floor. Dismayed, Phoebe and Justin watched the little glass sphere roll away rapidly.

But its momentum was brought to an abrupt halt

as the dark-haired man pinned it with the tip of his shoe in an impressive display of timing. Finishing his conversation, the man bent to pick up the marble. As the housekeeper bustled away, the man turned his attention to Phoebe and Justin.

His eyes were shockingly blue in that sun-tanned face, the brief smile a dazzling flash of white. He was *very* handsome, his features strong and even, with faint, pale whisks of laugh lines radiating from the outer corners of his eyes. He seemed like someone who would be irreverent and amusing, but there was also something shrewd about him, something a bit flinty. As if he'd had his share of experience in the world and had few illusions left. Somehow that made him even more attractive.

He approached without haste, moving with athletic ease. It was only when he stopped next to them that Phoebe realized how very tall he was, his shoulders broad and sturdy. Her lungs contracted, forcing her to take an extra breath.

The strangest feeling came over her, something that reminded her a little of the early days of her marriage to Henry . . . that shaky, embarrassing, inexplicable desire to press her body intimately against someone else's. Until now, she'd never felt it for anyone but Henry, and never anything like this fire-and-ice jolt of awareness.

Feeling guilty and confused, Phoebe backed away a step, pulling Justin with her.

But Justin resisted, evidently feeling it had fallen to him to begin the introductions. "I'm Justin, Lord Clare," he announced. "This is my Mama. Papa isn't here with us because he died."

Phoebe felt a brilliant pink flush, never flattering on a redhead, race from her scalp down to her toes.

The man wasn't a bit flustered, only sank to his haunches to bring his face level with Justin's. His voice was gentle and low, and made Phoebe feel as if she were stretching across a deep feather mattress.

"I lost my father when I wasn't much older than you," he said to Justin.

"Oh, I didn't *lose* mine," came Justin's earnest reply. "I know where he is. Heaven."

The stranger smiled, his eyes warm. "A pleasure to meet you, Justin." The two shook hands gravely. He held the marble up to the light, viewing the tiny porcelain figure of a sheep embedded into the clear glass marble. "This is a fine piece," he remarked, and handed it to Justin. "Do you ever play Ring Taw, Lord Clare?"

"Oh, yes."

"Double castle?

Justin shook his head. "I don't know that one."

"We'll play a game or two during your stay here, if your Mama doesn't object."

Phoebe was mortified by her inability to reply. Her heartbeat was stampeding out of control.

"Mama isn't used to talking to grown-ups," Justin said. "She likes children better."

"I'm very childlike," the man said promptly. "Ask anyone around here."

Phoebe found herself smiling up at him as he stood to face her. "You're the estate manager?" she asked.

"Most of the time." His rueful grin weakened her knees. "But there's no job at this estate, scullery maid included, that I haven't tried at least once, to gain at least some small understanding of it."

A strange, terrible suspicion flickered through Phoebe's mind.

"How long have you been employed here?" she asked cautiously.

"Since my brother inherited it." The blue-eyed stranger bowed before continuing. "West Ravenel . . . at your service."

**For the story of Mr. West Ravenel
and Phoebe, Lady Clare,
keep an eye out for**

Devil's Daughter